PRAISE FOR
CHRISTOPHER GOLDEN

"Christopher Golden is one of the most hardworking, smartest, and talented writers of his generation, and his books are so good and so involving that they really ought to sell in huge numbers. Everything he writes glows with imagination."
—Peter Straub

"A new book by Chris Golden means only one thing: the reader is in for a treat. His books are rich with texture and character, always inventive, and totally addictive."
—Charles de Lint,
author of *Someplace to Be Flying*

Praise for *BALTIMORE*
by Christopher Golden and Mike Mignola

"The lush, labyrinthine *Baltimore* evokes the best from two of our most gifted artists. Christopher Golden and Mike Mignola have created a book that will be enjoyed and admired for decades to come." —Peter Straub

"With *Baltimore*, Mike Mignola and Christopher Golden lay siege to the reader's imagination with a grim battalion of gothic images and a thunderous barrage of narrative artillery. This is not a novel: it's a war machine. Surrender immediately."
—Joe Hill, author of *Heart-Shaped Box*

"*Baltimore* is an old-time rootin' tootin' sense of wonder story dragged through a modern blender, then slow baked in hell. I loved it. It's a velvet bullet—speedy and rich in sensation. Go, boys, go."
—Joe R. Lansdale, author of *Lost Echoes*

THE BORDERKIND

"This fast-paced dark fantasy adventure should appeal to fans of Neil Gaiman, Charles de Lint, and Robert Holdstock."
—*Publishers Weekly*

"Even more exciting than the first installment, *The Borderkind* builds on and expands the rich universe Golden established in the previous book. Readers will wait impatiently for the third installment." —*Booklist*

"*The Borderkind* is noticeably darker than *The Myth Hunters*, mainly because a lot of the wide-eyed wonder that the characters experienced in the first book has been tainted by how cruel this world of myths can be, but also because there is a lot more at stake.... I can see this series ... leaving a lasting mark on everyone who picks it up." —DreadCentral.com

"The latest novel by Bram Stoker Award-winning Golden excels in darkness and mystery, bringing a touch of horror to an urban fantasy that will appeal to fans of Charles de Lint and Tanya Huff." —*Library Journal*

"Superior dark fantasy by a master of horror ... Christopher Golden proves himself to be a master of his craft.... Lyric, fluid and mesmerizing ... It's tough to find anything negative about *The Borderkind*. The dialogue is robust, the characters well drawn, the prose clear ... so distinctive and unique that it is well worth reading." —SciFi.com

"Golden truly outdid himself with this latest addition to the Veil series.... A flawless middle chapter to a one-of-a-kind epic fantasy that is sure to live on throughout the ages. I give *The Borderkind* by Christopher Golden my highest recommendation for anyone who wants to lose themselves in a grand sweeping epic fantasy that can unflinchingly stand up against the finest of the genre." —Horrorworld.com

THE MYTH HUNTERS

"Stoker winner Golden launches a promising new dark fantasy series with this chiller.... Fast pacing, superior characterization and sound folklore yield a winner." —*Publishers Weekly*

"Vivid action and snappy dialogue... A fun and creepy adventure story." —*Kirkus Reviews*

"The colorful, vividly imagined world and unresolved major plotline of Golden's thrilling yarn make a sequel a sure thing."
—*Booklist*

"A chillingly suspenseful tale of nightmares and childhood legends come to life." —*Library Journal*

"A fast-paced and highly original book." —*Dallas Morning News*

"The most innovative and spellbinding novel I have read this year... a dark masterpiece. Original and creative, Golden's tale integrates characters from fairy tales, urban folklore, and world mythology.... This, people, is Golden at his best. My rating? I give it a 5. Drop whatever you're doing immediately and buy this book!!!" —Horror-Web.com

"One of those novels that started off good and got even better as it went along... a fantasy that didn't feel like it was merely reusing all of the existing clichés in the same old tired manner that has been done myriad times before... a true classic."
—*Green Man Review*

"A throat-gripping monster adventure... What's really great about Golden is that he manages to straddle nicely between... the world of page-turning surreal adventure and the world of page-turning mainstream adventure. Golden manages to snag the most appealing aspects of both worlds and combine them in his novels, to make the best parts of each seem new when juxtaposed within his work. Thus, his novels seem consistently exciting and surprising." —*Agony Column*

"Christopher Golden brings intrigue to old-fashioned horror by complementing the unknown with the eerily familiar. This is not the typical horror story of things that go bump in the night, but rather the horrific potential in those things most familiar to us—the potential to lose them. Horror readers will enjoy this novel both for its old standards done well, and for the novelty of its exploration of the horror in mind and memory."
—*Alternate Reality WebZine*

"Golden does the remarkable in this book, creating a loving young couple and then putting them through the singular hell of alienation, disaffection and rediscovery. *The Twilight Zone* often used the motif of our loved ones being used as a mask for something alien and terrible; Golden employs this to brilliant effect, finding the things that are most unsettling, most disturbing...a subtle, atmospheric work....Recommended."
—SFRevu.com

"Pathos is one of the hardest emotions to sustain in a novel of the supernatural, yet Christopher Golden manages it very well in *Wildwood Road*. This is a story bathed in wan November moonlight, a little lost girl by the side of the road, the fey touch of a Ray Bradbury in the haunting....What I found most rewarding about his style was that he develops his story through his characters....Subtle is the storytelling of this author."
—cosmik.com

"Modern contemporary horror, fused in a counterpoint with the classic horror elements that will always thrill and unnerve us. A truly great, fast-paced read that hits all the buttons and gate-crashes the reader's composure with wild abandon. Just brilliant." —*SF Crowsnest*

"Golden latches onto a very intimate situation that's thoroughly understandable, and makes the fear all the more chilling because of it....The novel's internal logic is, perhaps, its greatest strength....Golden is becoming more assured in his plotting and pacing...and it has only made him a more effective, readable author."—*Fangoria*

"I'm going to go out on a crazy limb and say that, in my humble opinion, Christopher Golden is the newest horror/supernatural master.... *Wildwood Road*, like every other Christopher Golden novel I've read, will knock your socks off with its brilliant dialogue, truthful characters, and its plot—which always leads you exactly where you would never think you were headed. It's a good read and I promise you, I didn't feel too comfortable turning off the lights at night when I was reading this one—a true sign of a new horror classic!"—G-Pop.net

THE BOYS ARE BACK IN TOWN
One of Booklist's Top Ten SF/Fantasy

"Christopher Golden collides the ordinary and the supernatural with wonderfully unsettling results. *The Boys Are Back in Town* is a wicked little thriller. Rod Serling would have loved it."
—Max Allan Collins, author of *Road to Perdition*

"Well-crafted... a nostalgic, unsentimental portrait of adolescence [with a] suspenseful plot and strong atmosphere."
—*Publishers Weekly*

"Christopher Golden is the master of the slow creep—the kind of story that sneaks out of the everyday so quietly that you don't realize anything is really amiss until the world seems to shift and the ground gets all spongy underfoot.... Golden has a wonderfully smooth prose style [and] the payoff is immense. And intense... An eerie, fascinating tale."
—Charles de Lint, *F&SF*

"Golden's exploration into high school and high school reunions is anything but sentimental... a page-turner... a careening joyride into the vicious nature of high school friendships."
—*Baltimore Sun*

"Harkens back to classic Stephen King...Golden weaves a greatly suspenseful tale involving witchcraft and a destructive lust for power and revenge....Once you begin reading this one, you won't want to put it down." —*Dark Realms*

"Incredibly different...Very few novels are able to convey a sense of dread and horror while at the same time making you think about yourself and your own life....Compassionate and terrifying." —creature-corner.com

"Breathtaking...couldn't put it down!...The style and story are so perfectly matched that you don't even think about it, it flows like a well-directed episode of *The Twilight Zone*." —Horror-Web.com

"Spellbinding." —*Boston* magazine

"Captivated me from the first page and did not let go until the last. Mr. Golden is so talented that the reader believes anything and everything is possible....Chilling. I loved it." —*Rendezvous*

"Christopher Golden continues to stake his claim as a modern master of horror with *The Boys Are Back in Town*...a rip-roaring story reminiscent of early Stephen King." —*Romantic Times*

"Golden takes a truly creepy fantastic premise and delivers in spades; this gripping story is not to be missed." —*Booklist*

"Rod Serling territory...Golden takes another step toward becoming a major player in horror fiction." —*San Francisco Chronicle*

"*The Boys Are Back in Town* is a winner. It is a smart, thoughtful, and delightfully unpredictable novel that does not disappoint. For fans of the fantastic, these Boys should be near the top of the to-be-read list." —*Surreal* magazine

ALSO BY CHRISTOPHER GOLDEN

THE BORDERKIND: BOOK TWO OF THE VEIL

THE MYTH HUNTERS: BOOK ONE OF THE VEIL

WILDWOOD ROAD

THE BOYS ARE BACK IN TOWN

THE FERRYMAN

STRAIGHT ON 'TIL MORNING

STRANGEWOOD

THE SHADOW SAGA

OF SAINTS AND SHADOWS

ANGEL SOULS AND DEVIL HEARTS

OF MASQUES AND MARTYRS

THE GATHERING DARK

WITH MIKE MIGNOLA:

BALTIMORE, OR, THE STEADFAST TIN SOLDIER AND THE VAMPIRE

THE LOST ONES

BOOK THREE OF THE VEIL

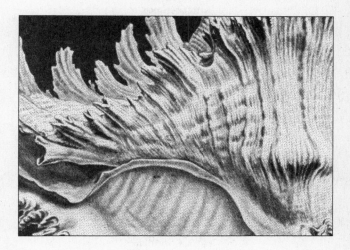

CHRISTOPHER GOLDEN

BANTAM BOOKS

THE LOST ONES
A Bantam Book / April 2008

Published by Bantam Dell
A Division of Random House, Inc.
New York, New York

Book design by Lynn Newmark

Bantam Books, the rooster colophon, Spectra, and the portrayal of a boxed "S" are
registered trademarks of Random House, Inc.

Library of Congress Cataloging-in-Publication Data

Golden, Christopher.
The lost ones / Christopher Golden.
p.   cm. — (The Veil ; bk. 3)
ISBN 978-0-553-38328-7 (trade pbk.)
I. Title.

PS3557.O35927L67 2008
813'.54—dc22
2007027924

Printed in the United States of America
Published simultaneously in Canada

www.bantamdell.com

BVG 10 9 8 7 6 5 4 3 2 1

In memory of Patrice Duvic.
Dors bien, mon ami.

THE
LOST ONES

liver Bascombe paced his dungeon cell, wondering when his captors would decide to kill him and how they would do it. Public execution? Swift murder? Torture? Or perhaps they would simply feed him to the Battle Swine and let those filthy porcine warriors bite off his head and strip the flesh from his bones.

In the two months and more since he had first been clapped into the crumbling stone cell with its iron-grated windows and heavy wooden door, he had come to understand that there were only three things a prisoner in the royal dungeon of Yucatazca could do to pass the time—imagine dying, imagine escaping, and work his body hard enough to hurt, just to remind him that he was alive. In all his life, Oliver had never been so strong. He could not escape the irony that despite all of his newly gained strength and discipline, he had also never been so powerless.

A stained sleeping mat was the room's only comfort. Unless

he was sleeping, he kept it rolled up in the center of the cell. With that out of the way, he could walk the perimeter of the room unimpeded by anything but the small sink and the hole beside it that was the closest thing he had to a toilet.

He didn't have space to run; no way to get up any momentum in a cell twenty feet by twelve. The best he could do was walk and so he did that, swiftly and consistently, for at least an hour when he rose and another hour after dark. After dark, Oliver needed to keep his body occupied because his mind became busiest then, as well. Back in the ordinary world, he had always believed that there truly were things lurking in the dark, but now he knew for certain. In the world of the legendary, everything was possible.

No, more than that. Everything is real.

This morning, like every other, he knew the day had begun by the lightening of the cell from black to gloomy gray and from the passage of silent guards out in the corridor. The two small grated windows never received direct sunlight and offered no view of anything but stone and shadow. Beyond the outer wall of the dungeon was a slotted canyon built into the king's palace by its architect. He supposed he ought to have been grateful for that little bit of light that allowed him to keep track of the passage of night and day, but Oliver had no gratitude in his heart.

Only ice.

In the absence of Frost—whom he suspected was alive, despite all evidence to the contrary—he had become a kind of winter man himself.

If not for the presence of his sister, Collette, and his fiancée, Julianna Whitney, in the cell across that stone corridor, he knew his heart would have become ice entirely. What saved him was the ability to hear their voices and catch glimpses of their faces through the grated windows in their parallel door. Instead of slamming his palms and fists against the stones, building callus, he might have rammed his skull into the wall and been done with life.

Instead, he lived.

In between his morning and evening walks, Oliver did sets of push-ups and sit-ups. He'd built up the muscles in his arms and shoulders quite a bit, and his abdomen was tight as a drum. This development did not stem solely from his exercise regimen, but also from what he'd come to think of as the "dungeon diet." He, Collette, and Julianna lived on pitiful meals of crusty bread, water, and a thin stew obviously made from whatever others in the palace had not cared to eat. He tried not to think about the origins of his food and never left a drop in the bowl. It would keep him alive.

"Oliver."

He paused beneath one of the grated windows and glanced at the door to his cell. It seemed to him that the voice had come from the corridor, but he was keenly aware of the possibility that he'd imagined it. Claustrophobia had never been a problem for him, but it had crept into his head over the past two months, and sometimes the walls seemed to close in around him and he imagined shadows moving in the corners. Hallucinating voices seemed a likely addition to the menu.

"Oliver?" the voice said again.

He grinned, feeling like a fool. The voice belonged to his sister.

Silently, he crossed the cell and craned his neck to peer through the iron grate set high in the door. Collette and Julianna were in the opposite cell. Jules was tall enough that he could see the upper part of her face through the grate in their door, but Collette had to pull herself up to peer through, like a child trying to get a peek at the world of grown-ups. Even worn and filthy and half-starved, he thought they were both beautiful. His sister's eyes had a mischievous light in them that had not been extinguished by their incarceration. And his fiancée's gaze was unwavering.

"Morning, Coll," he said. Then he locked eyes with Julianna. "Morning, sweetie."

It ought to have felt odd to use such an endearment under the circumstances. But it didn't. He didn't love her any less after the time they'd spent imprisoned here. In a thousand ways, he loved her more. They'd had perfect, boring lives in the ordinary world as attorneys for the law firm their fathers had helped to found. Oliver had always lived in the shadow of his father and the life the old man had wanted for him.

As a boy, he'd wanted to be an actor, had believed in magic and imagination, but as he'd grown he'd slowly succumbed to his father's efforts to stifle such dreams. When he and Julianna had gotten engaged it had been both the best and worst thing that had ever happened to him—the best because he loved her utterly, and the worst because their wedding would cement him forever into the role his father had laid out for him. Oliver had had his doubts, but they'd been fleeting. If Julianna would be his wife, that alone would provide enough magic for him to survive.

Or so he'd thought.

But that was before the magic he had always hoped to find had blown in through his window in a blizzard of ice and snow, on the night before his wedding, and torn his life apart. He'd traveled between worlds since then, met creatures of myth and legend from dozens of cultures—some of them allies and some enemies—and he and Collette had discovered that they themselves might have a bit of the legendary in their blood. Their father had been murdered and they had been hunted on both sides of the Veil that separated the fantastical from the mundane, drawn into a conspiracy to destroy an age-old peace between the Two Kingdoms. Men and legends had died. Julianna had followed Oliver through the Veil and was now trapped here, in this world, unable to return.

And now they were prisoners in the bowels of the king's

palace in Palenque, capital of Yucatazca, accused of regicide. In truth, Oliver *had* murdered King Mahacuhta, but there had been...extenuating circumstances. At the time, he'd been under a glamour that had caused him to believe the man he stabbed was Ty'Lis, the Atlantean sorcerer who had engineered all of his and Collette's misery, and so much more.

Ty'Lis had tricked him into murdering Mahacuhta—with the sword of Hunyadi, King of Euphrasia.

No news had trickled in to them from the outside, but he had no doubt that the Two Kingdoms must be in open war by now.

Yet in spite of all of that, he stood at the door of his cell and looked across at the eyes of the woman he'd loved since childhood, and somehow found the faith to believe they'd get out of this.

"Are you all right?" Julianna asked, brows knitted in concern.

"Fine. Why?"

"You were kind of muttering to yourself when you were walking."

Oliver leaned his forehead against the bars, smiling. "Stir crazy. We'll take turns, okay? Rotate breakdowns, so at least one of us is sane at all times."

"That's not funny, Oliver," Julianna said.

He lifted his gaze to meet hers. For a moment, he felt strong enough to rip the doors away and tear down the walls that separated them.

"I'm sorry, Jules. You're right. I'm just trying to keep my mind active, stay ready."

Collette poked her head up beside Julianna again. Through the bars in the small window of their cell door, she looked so small and fragile. It was an illusion. Collette had survived as a prisoner in the castle of the Sandman. Compared to that horror, this was like a resort hotel.

"Ready for what?" she asked.

"We'll know when the moment presents itself," Oliver replied.

He had no idea when opportunity would arrive, but he had to have faith that it would. Otherwise, they might as well all curl up and die. The one thing they weren't going to do was try something stupid like pretending to be sick to draw in the guards and catch them by surprise. That sort of thing worked well enough in the movies, but they'd agreed it was damned unlikely to work for real. And even if it did work, where would they go? In addition to the Atlantean instigators Ty'Lis had sewn into the fabric of the Yucatazcan military and court— soldiers, Hunters, giants, and sorcerers—there were the people of Yucatazca itself. As far as they knew, the monarch of Euphrasia had sent Oliver and his friends as assassins to slay their king. Even if they managed to get out of the dungeon and fight their way out of the palace, then what? Leaving the city of Palenque alive seemed a dubious prospect.

"Maybe you're not the only one going a little stir crazy," Collette replied.

As the words left her mouth, she and Julianna exchanged a worrisome glance. Oliver frowned.

"What are you talking about? Are you two okay?"

"We're all right," Julianna said quickly, staring at him again across the corridor between their cells. "It's just . . . something weird."

Oliver pulled his face as tightly against the bars as he could and looked left and right along the dungeon hallway. The guards would arrive soon with stale bread and water for breakfast, and perhaps some morning gruel.

"What is it?" he whispered, locking eyes with his sister now. "Don't try anything. We'll never get out of here without a plan."

"I'm not sure about that," Collette replied.

Panic hit Oliver. "What've you got in mind, Coll? If we're going to act, we've got to work together."

But Collette shook her head. "Nothing like that. Just listen."

Now it was Julianna's turn to peer up and down the corridor. When she was sure no guards were nearby, she took a breath. "A little while ago, we felt cold."

Oliver frowned. "It always gets a little cold down here at night."

"More than that," Collette said. "The temperature must have dropped thirty degrees. There were ice crystals on the wall. And I thought I heard—"

"Whispering," Julianna said.

Oliver stared at them for a second and then pushed away from the door. He paced the cell's perimeter, running a hand over the thick beard that had grown over the past two months.

The only one of their allies not to escape after the assault on the king's chambers and the accidental murders of King Mahacuhta himself had been Frost, who Oliver often thought of as "the winter man." He had been the first creature from the world of the legendary that Oliver had met. Frost had interceded when a monstrosity called the Falconer had been sent to murder Oliver and Collette—though he had lied about the reasons for his presence there and about the Falconer's target. Still, despite those lies, Frost had saved Oliver's life many times over.

Magicians of a hundred cultures had gathered together and woven spells to create the Veil, crafting a barrier that would forever separate the legendary from the ordinary. From time to time, human beings slipped through the Veil into the world of the legendary, but once touched by the magic of the Veil, they could never return. There were Doors set into the Veil, few and far between and always under heavy guard, but only the legendary could pass through a Door.

But the Borderkind didn't need Doors. They were creatures of legend who could travel back and forth through the Veil whenever they pleased. At the time of the barrier's creation, human beings still had enough faith or fascination for them that they could continue to slip through. Sometimes Oliver thought

there was more to it than that—that some of the legendary became Borderkind not because humanity loved them, but because they loved the human world too much to succumb
completely to the spells that wove the Veil.

Ever since discovering that Frost had kept so much from
him, Oliver had nursed resentment and anger. Had his supposed friend been truthful, things might have turned out quite
differently.

"No," Oliver said, shaking his head, gripping the grate. "If
he's still alive, and he's found some way to communicate, how
does that help? If he can't get out—and get us out—then we're
no better off."

"Oliver, I know you feel like he deceived you. Maybe he did,"
Julianna said. "What's his big sin, though, really? He didn't trust
a human being enough to take you into his confidence?
Learning the truth at the wrong time might have cost your life
anyway."

"He lied," Oliver whispered.

Collette banged the door with her palm. "So he played you a
little. Treated you like a little kid, the way Dad always did. But
Frost isn't Dad. I didn't travel with him the way you did, so I
can't know how you feel. All I know are the facts, and—"

"Stop," Julianna said.

Brother and sister fell quiet, listening. Somewhere, water
dripped loudly, echoing off the stones of the dungeon corridor.

"We don't have time to argue this, Oliver," Julianna went on.
"All we wanted to do was tell you what happened, because it got
us thinking."

"All right. What're you thinking?"

"That Frost is the opportunity we've been waiting for,"
Collette said.

Julianna stared across at him. "The moment might never
come for us to act, so we're going to have to make our own moment. From what happened this morning, it seems pretty certain

that Frost is still alive, and close. We don't have to get out of the palace, Oliver. All we have to do is get out of these cells and get to Frost. If we can free *him*, then he'll get us out of here."

Oliver shook his head. "You don't know—"

Collette shushed him. All three of them stopped again to listen, and this time they heard a clanking of metal as the upstairs door to the dungeon was unlocked and swung open. Heavy boots clomped down the stone steps.

The guards were arriving with breakfast. The conversation was over.

For now.

Which was fine. Oliver needed to think. Maybe they were right; maybe it was time to make their own opportunity. It seemed far more likely they would be able to free Frost than that they could escape from the palace themselves. It might be their one chance at survival.

If Frost could be trusted.

Dark clouds hung pregnant above the battlefield just north of Cliffordville, but the rain did not come. The past few days had been blisteringly hot; rain would have been a blessing. But the gods would never bless an abomination such as this.

Blue Jay flew above the clashing armies, the humid air heavy on his wings. He heard the clang of blades on armor and the cries of the wounded and dying. The blood of humans and legendary alike stained the ground. In the distance, he could see the smoke rising from the ruin that the Yucatazcan forces had made of Cliffordville. Most of the residents had been evacuated before the enemy had arrived. Those stubborn few who had remained were likely charred corpses now, adding to the black smoke that furled upward from the remains of the town.

Some amongst King Hunyadi's forces had wanted to lay in wait in Cliffordville and set a trap for the invaders. Neither the king nor his chief advisor, Captain Damia Beck, would hear of it. There would be no honor in such close fighting, and it would mean spreading their troops out into small pockets. If one side achieved the upper hand in the battle, the others would not be able to see what was happening. Hunyadi wanted his enemies to see what they were up against, when the time came.

As a trickster, Blue Jay liked the idea of springing a trap on the invaders, but he saw the king's point. There were too many variables. Not that it was up to him in the first place. After all, he and his fellow Borderkind were only volunteer soldiers in the army of Hunyadi. More than anything, he knew that the king wanted him and his kin to be visible in the battle. In the two months since the war had broken out they had made every effort to spread the word into the south that the Atlanteans were the true enemy, that Hunyadi had not had any hand in King Mahacuhta's assassination.

And nothing would show the human troops the truth more clearly than the fact that nearly all of the surviving Borderkind were fighting on the side of the kingdom of Euphrasia. Even Yucatazcan Borderkind had joined the troops of King Hunyadi. That ought to be evidence enough that the whispers about Ty'Lis were true.

Blue Jay let a gust of wind take him higher, and then banked west, toward the ocean. He came around in a long arc, moving behind the invaders, then descending until he flew less than eighty feet above the battle.

The combat had begun shortly after dawn, with the Yucatazcan force marching out of the ruins of Cliffordville, up a long slope to the northeast that would take them to Boudreau and Hyacinth, and then to the small city of Dogwood. Hunyadi's forces had come down out of the hills and waded into the invading force. The Yucatazcans had suffered enormous early casualties, but now the battle had become a bloody melee with new corpses falling on both sides.

The little blue bird darted over the battle lines. He saw

perhaps two dozen Atlantean soldiers amidst the humans and the handful of legendary creatures fighting on the side of Yucatazca. There were Jaculi amongst them, tiny but savage winged serpents. A small cadre of Battle Swine—tusked boar-warriors whose hair was matted with fur and gore—held firm. Not one of them had fallen as yet. A single Atlantean giant still lived. Two others had stood with the greenish-white-skinned monstrosity, but they were dead now. Archers took cover behind them and loosed arrows at the enemy.

At the center of the area that had become the muddy, bloody battleground, a sphere of death radiated outward from a strangely silent, elegantly choreographed skirmish taking place amongst magicians. Seven Mazikeen—the Hebrew sorcerers who had allied themselves with the Borderkind—stood arrayed in a semicircle, electric golden light crackling in arcs from their fingers and eyes, lancing across the open space that separated them from a quartet of Atlantean sorcerers, whose own spells and hexes burned the air in black and blue tendrils. Not a single living soldier or warrior—human or legend— came nearer than twenty feet from this war-within-a-war.

Blue Jay thought it appeared, for the moment, to be a stalemate. That did not bode well.

Nagas slithered on serpent bodies through the battle. Their upper halves were humanoid and they swung swords and fired arrows, cutting down whatever human soldiers got in their way. The Lost Ones of Yucatazca were not their focus, however. They were slaying as many of the enemy legendary as they could.

More blood spilled.

Pointless. A dreadful bitterness welled up in Blue Jay. He had always been a trickster, a mischief maker, but this was different. The schemers of Atlantis had manipulated the Two Kingdoms into this war so that they could reap the rewards. The Lost Ones on both sides were dying because they did not know the truth. They were all humans, no matter what part of the ordinary world they—or their ancestors—had originated from. To see them massacring one another was an abomination. To watch the legendary kill one another was even worse. There were only a few Borderkind still allied with the Yucatazcan forces, but what did that matter? Whether they could cross the border between worlds or not, legends were legends. Like the humans, they were all kin.

Taken together, the two armies had something less than a thousand sweating, stinking, exhausted soldiers remaining from the forces that had engaged in the battle of Cliffordville. Skirmishes had been taking place on the Isthmus of the Conquistadors—and on both sides of that thin strip of land that separated Euphrasia from Yucatazca—ever since the regicide in Palenque. But now the war had begun in earnest. Other Yucatazcan forces had already moved across the Isthmus and into Euphrasia, headed for locations to the far east and to the north, where they would find Euphrasian army detachments awaiting them under the command of Hunyadi's top officers.

But this area had been the king's focus. This attack route was the one whose path would take the enemy most directly toward Perinthia, Euphrasia's capital. For symbolic purposes, this battle had to end in a decisive victory.

At the moment, that hardly seemed a foregone conclusion.

The Atlantean giant snatched a Naga from the ground, gripped the warrior by his serpent torso, and used him as a club to first sweep several Euphrasian soldiers aside, then to hammer at one of them, killing both the Naga and his human comrade in the process. Blood sprayed the giant's face and the upturned, enraged countenances of the soldiers who attacked him.

Blue Jay flapped his wings quickly and rose into the sky. He scanned the dark clouds above him, still wishing for rain, but more important, wanting to be certain that none of the winged Atlantean hunters, the Perytons, would arrive as reinforcements. He also watched for Strigae, the black birds who acted as spies for Ty'Lis and his masters in Atlantis.

Atlanteans. Blue Jay's feathers ruffled as he glided on air currents. *The bastards are going to pay.*

The smoke still rising from Cliffordville provided a dark backdrop for an odd phenomenon. The very fabric of the air began to tear, not in one place, but in a dozen, spreading out across the rear flank of the enemy troops. Long, shimmering slits appeared, starting from the ground and rising to varying heights, some only a few feet and others scraping the sky.

From the largest of the tears in the Veil there came a gigantic flying shape—a huge, white pachyderm with broad wings and tusks like ivory spears. Hua-Hu-Tiao had arrived, and many other Borderkind followed, flooding into the world, slipping from the ordinary realm into the land of their kin. Blue Jay saw so many that were familiar to him—monsters and giants, beasts and heroes. Chang Hao, the King of Snakes, slithered through and darted forward to snatch two Yucatazcan soldiers into his maw, swallowing them without chewing. Even from the sky, Blue Jay could hear them scream.

Blue Jay had friends amongst the newly arrived force. He saw Cheval Bayard, the kelpy, in her equine form. Her hooves thundered on the ground as she galloped toward her enemies, silver hair streaming. Leicester Grindylow sat astride her back, long apelike arms wrapped around her neck. He looked gangly and foolish atop the kelpy, but Blue Jay knew that Grin would be deadly the moment he leaped into the fray. His strength and swiftness were well-tested, and his savagery in battle was only equaled by his quiet courtesy to his allies and friends.

Then there came Li, the Guardian of Fire. Once he had ridden a beautiful tiger. But when his tiger had been killed by the Myth Hunters, Li had been diminished in some way that Blue Jay still did not understand. The fire in him burned nearly as strong, but he could not control it the way he once had. His flesh had burned away so that now he existed as a walking pile of embers, forged in the shape of a man. Li would never be able to pass in the human world again. But he was Borderkind, and he wanted vengeance on those who had murdered so many of his kin and slain the tiger who had been one half of his spirit and his legend.

Blue Jay fluttered his wings, rising higher. The storm clouds seemed to hang lower than ever, yet still would not release the mercy of rain. He watched the warriors, gleaming with sweat and glistening with blood, as they became aware that the tide had turned. They were surrounded by their enemies. The Yucatazcans were filled with what they thought was righteous fury at the murder of their king, but they were not prepared for the Borderkind.

Without the legends that could cross the Veil, King Hunyadi's troops might have driven the invaders back eventually. It would have been a near thing. Now the Yucatazcans had no chance. The Borderkind swarmed in from behind, burning and tearing and shattering the enemy, and the Euphrasian forces moved in from the front.

Only the killing remained.

Blue Jay wheeled away from the battle, turning back toward the top of the hill, where the tents of the commanders had been pitched in a sparse wood that had once overlooked the quaint little village of Cliffordville.

He scanned the tents and did not see the black cloak of Captain Beck. A tremor of anxiety went through him. Troubled, he flew quickly toward the hill and then spread his wings to slow himself. As he did, the trickster changed. Wings became a blue blur beneath outstretched arms. Blue Jay began to spin slowly, dancing on the air, and he alighted upon the ground with a soft tread, the bird replaced by the mischief man. The breeze rustled his long hair and the blue feathers he kept tied there.

Worried, he glanced around. Commander Torchio and two of his subordinates stood just inside the tree line, but there was no sign of Captain Beck. He started toward them, about to inquire, when the flap of the nearest tent opened and an ebony-skinned hand thrust out.

"Jay. Come in."

A smile touched his lips as he stepped up and took her hand. The trickster slipped into the tent and into her arms. The thin cotton of her black tunic and trousers whispered as he pulled her against him. Her dark eyes widened but, before she could speak, he silenced her with a brush of his lips upon hers.

Then he whispered her name.

"Damia."

Captain Beck grinned, her elegant ebony features alight with mischief that made him feel she was a kindred spirit, even though she was entirely human. She arched an eyebrow.

"It's lovely to see you back in one piece, Jay. But perhaps you might hold your enthusiasm a few minutes."

He blinked, and only then did he sense the presence of another inside the tent. Blue Jay turned, as sheepishly as a trickster could manage, and found the imposing presence of the wanderer, Wayland Smith, filling nearly all of the available space. That was one of the many puzzling things about Smith. He always seemed larger than he was. Most of the tricksters called him uncle, treated him as one of their own, an elder. And yet if he was a trickster, he was from an earlier age, an earlier kind of legend. There were many names for him. The Wayfarer. The Traveler. All Jay knew was that he was a journeyman, wandering the worlds, as well as a magician, and that he could forge weapons that always found their mark. Or so his legend claimed.

Smith had not removed his broad-brimmed hat, though he had set aside his walking stick, which was capped by a brass fox head. His rust-colored beard seemed to have gone more gray than Blue Jay recalled. From the shadows beneath the hat brim came the glint of stony eyes.

"Hello, Jay," said Wayland Smith, inclining his head.

"Wayfarer," Blue Jay replied. "We haven't seen you in more than a week."

"It could not be avoided," the wanderer said. "I have been searching for questions."

The trickster cocked his head. "For questions?"

"You cannot find an answer until you have discovered the question."

"Of course," Blue Jay replied, bowing his head in respect. "And did you find what you sought?"

"I have a great many questions and, indeed, some answers as well."

Damia Beck slid up beside Blue Jay and put an affectionate hand at the small of his back. "He says it's time."

Blue Jay saw the excitement in her eyes, then turned back toward Wayland Smith. "Time for what?"

Even through his thick beard, the wanderer's smile was unmistakable. In the shadows under his hat brim, Wayland Smith's eyes kindled with a lightness of spirit Blue Jay had never seen in that face before.

"Why, time to rescue them, of course. Frost and the Bascombes, and Oliver's fair lady. Now that the war has begun in earnest and the eyes of Atlantis are focused on Euphrasia, it's time to retrieve your friends and draw together the skeins of fate. Then we'll have begun it, Jay."

Blue Jay frowned. "Begun what?"

"The beginning of the end."

"Damia," Blue Jay said, reaching down to take her rough, soldier's fingers in his own. "Do you understand any of this?"

She nodded. "The magician says it's time to get them out of Palenque. Hunyadi has been waiting for the Borderkind to do that ever since their capture. There will still be loyalists who believe anything that Ty'Lis says, but already the rumors have spread that Oliver and Collette are Legend-Born. If we have them in our camp, the Lost Ones on both sides of the war will at least have to listen to what they have to say." Captain Beck put a hand on the grip of her sword. "All I want to know is, when do we leave?"

"Shit." Blue Jay sighed and looked at Wayland Smith. "Apparently we're going to Palenque?"

"You are."

Blue Jay laughed and shook his head. "So you're sending us off on a suicide mission, but you won't be able to join us. That about right?"

"More or less. Hunyadi has plans for Damia, and I have other business, but I'll see you to Palenque safely. I have an errand to take care of first, and then we'll depart. But before I go let's sit a few moments—I'll share my pipe, if you like—and we'll talk of palaces and kings, of heroes and legends, and of the Legend-Born."

The trickster glanced at Captain Beck a moment, then turned once more, uneasily, to Wayland Smith.

"So you believe that story, then, about the Bascombes? You think their mother was a Borderkind?"

Smith nodded solemnly, drawing a pipe out from inside his jacket.

"Of course. Melisande was their mother. And their father was a human. She loved him fiercely until the day she died. She had to give up her essence, her magic, so that she could bear children to the man she loved."

Blue Jay crossed his arms and could not prevent the dubious look that spread across his face.

"And just how the hell do you know all of that?"

The weight of grief and the past lay heavily upon the Wayfarer, leaving no trace of mischief behind.

"How do I know?" he asked, looking up at Blue Jay and Captain Beck. "I know because I brought them together."

CHAPTER 2

willig's Gorge was a river canyon, boxed on either end by sheer stone cliffs. The Sorrowful River flowed into and out of the gorge through tunnels that went right through the base of a mountain, so the settlement inside Twillig's Gorge was well-hidden. Sentries stood guard where the river entered and exited the gorge, and many more lined the rim of the canyon. The cliffs were steep all around, and there were only a handful of safe ways to descend into the settlement, either by various ladders and footbridges that hung above the river, or by one of two sets of stairs carved from the rock face.

On either side of the river, there was a stone walkway lined with shops. There were taverns and bakeries, a florist and a butcher's, and even several dress shops for the ladies. Grand homes had been built across the gorge, high up on the walls like arched bridges. The inn spanned the river as well. Dwellings had been built into the cliff face, excavated from the rock.

Others clung like spiders to the sheer walls of the gorge, propped on support beams that seemed entirely insufficient to hold them up. Wooden stairs and walkways and swing bridges lined the sides of the gorge like scaffolding.

Over the ages, Twillig's Gorge had become something of a legend itself. It welcomed legendary and ordinary alike. All varieties of creatures had settled there, including Borderkind and Lost Ones. It was a sanctuary for anyone who wished it. The rules were simple. *Live and let live.* Courtesy and peace were the principles upon which the settlement at Twillig's Gorge had been founded.

But the war had begun to change all of that.

Many of the legendary and Borderkind had left the settlement, presumably to fight under the banner of King Hunyadi. Others remained, working with the Lost Ones in the Gorge to improve defenses and add to the armory, preparing just in case their sanctuary might be disturbed by the predations of war.

Coyote sat on a walkway above the eastern promenade, smoking a cigarette and watching the bustle of activity down in the Gorge. He drew a lungful of smoke and then blew it out, tapping the ash from the end of his cigarette.

When the Myth Hunters had been scouring Euphrasia for Borderkind, killing as many as they could find, Coyote had gone into hiding. Frost and Blue Jay and a number of others had fought back, and a lot of them had died as a result. Coyote knew most people thought of him as a coward, but he didn't worry much about perception. It could be difficult to tell the difference between courage and stupidity. Similarly, what others considered cowardice, he thought of as mere common sense.

Now, though, the situation had grown more complex. Many of his friends and kin had been brutally murdered. No doubt Ty'Lis had the support of the rulers of Atlantis, and that meant the real war hadn't even started yet. It could still all end with King Hunyadi dead and all of the Two Kingdoms crushed beneath the boot heel of Atlantis. But at least it was going to be a fight, now. He meant to stay out of it for as long as he could, but even a coward could be driven to bravery when people he loved were dying.

Bastards, Coyote thought, taking another drag of his cigarette.

Down at the river's edge, on the cobblestoned promenade that passed in front of the shops, Ovid Tsing rallied a group of men and women who were gathering around him. Even from above, Coyote could hear Ovid's pleas. He wanted the people of Twillig's Gorge to join the fight, to rise up and throw in with Hunyadi's army, just as so many of the legendary had.

Ovid had a grim aura—all damnable seriousness, dark eyes, and prominent jaw. He was the kind of man other humans would follow. Some of the Lost Ones were listening, but others hung back, obviously wishing they could skulk away unnoticed. Coyote understood. Skulking away was a sensible option. It had always worked for him.

Coyote narrowed his gaze and twisted around on his perch to get a look at the front of the bakery that was owned and run by Ovid and his mother, Virginia Tsing.

He spotted the old woman instantly. As expected, she stood just outside the bakery door, watching her son with concern. The two had been sparring ever since Frost and Bascombe and the others had passed through the Gorge some months back.

A figure moved just behind the glass of the bakery café's front door, a tall silhouette in a broad-brimmed hat.

Curious, Coyote tossed his cigarette down from the catwalk and raised an eyebrow. As he stood, his long cotton shirt whipped against his body in the breeze. His dark brown trousers were torn at the knees and he was barefoot. He preferred that, enjoying the feeling of padding along the rocks and cliffs.

He tilted his head back and sniffed at the air, and there it was.

Wayland Smith.

With one hand on the railing of the wooden walkway, Coyote flipped over the side. He dropped twenty feet to a suspension bridge below. He'd barely alighted when he sprang again, leaping from the bridge to a rocky ledge that was a balcony of sorts for a family of trolls, currently away at the war. Like butterflies, dozens of purple and yellow pixies took flight from the darkness inside the cave, darting out over the river and south along the gorge.

A ladder had been bolted into the cliff face outside the trolls' cave. He gripped the sides of the ladder and slid all the way down to the promenade. Agile and cunning, Coyote had a knack for not being noticed. But by now he had spent so much time in Twillig's Gorge that even those who might normally observe him would barely take note of his actions. Even the sentries did not so much as glance at him.

Only when he walked hurriedly past the small militia that Ovid Tsing was trying to recruit did anyone pay attention to him. Ovid himself cast a wary, mistrustful glance his way. Coyote sneered at the intense young man. Arrogance ill-befitted a human in a world of legends.

Outside the door of the café, Virginia cleared teacups and plates from a table, piling them onto a tray. As he strode up, she pretended not to see him. Some of his kin seemed to have been able to shake the general mistrust that so many had for tricksters. Blue Jay had practically become respectable, and Kitsune had earned herself a part of the new legends being formed around the Bascombes.

Of course, that was only because the Lost Ones didn't know she'd run off and left them to die in the king's chambers in Palenque.

Coyote grinned. So much for respectability.

"Hello, Miss Tsing," he said.

The woman might be old, but still she was beautiful; a creature of the Orient. Asian, they would have said in the ordinary world. There were other cultures in her bloodline, but Coyote didn't care enough to discover what they were.

"Coyote," she replied, inclining her head in the curt approximation of a bow.

"Your son will have all the Lost Ones of Euphrasia marching for the border soon," the trickster said, his grin widening.

Virginia smiled, in spite of herself. "I doubt that. Ovid means well, and some will answer his call to arms. But it will take more than his voice to make the people rise up."

"Legend-Born, for instance," Coyote said merrily.

Another woman might have thought herself mocked, but Virgina only nodded. The past few weeks, her debates with her son had spilled onto the promenade, playing out for patrons of their café and anyone passing by. Virginia Tsing had assured her son a hundred times that the only way the Lost Ones who were not already part of the army would rise up would be if the invaders were marching toward their homes, or if the Legend-Born had truly come.

"If the Bascombes reveal themselves as Legend-Born," the old woman said, "the Lost will stand with them against the treachery of Yucatazca or Atlantis. Men and women will rise up by the thousands to fight in their name, but not in the name of any king."

Coyote figured she was right, but since the Bascombes were in the dungeons at Palenque, the old woman was out of luck, and so was Hunyadi.

On the other hand, Coyote had a feeling that perhaps Virginia knew more than she was letting on.

"You had a guest a few moments ago," Coyote said.

Virginia gestured to the people dining at the café's patio tables. "I have many guests."

Coyote tapped the side of his nose. "Ah, but this one had a scent I recognized. A unique scent. And I caught sight of him inside. You can't trick a trickster, old mother."

A smile touched her lips. "Your nose is keen."

"What did the Wayfarer come to say? When he visits, he usually brings new refugees to the Gorge. This time, he came in secret and whispered to you."

The old woman bumped open the door to the café with her hip. She paused, halfway inside, to glance back at him.

"A squirrel perched on my shoulder this morning, Coyote. It told me that perhaps soon a story would become reality. It might be that my son will soon have far more men and women to lead into battle than he could ever imagine."

"You're saying the Bascombes are alive? That the Wayfarer means to free them?"

Miss Tsing raised an eyebrow. "Would you like a cup of tea?"

Coyote nodded once out of respect. "My thanks, but not just now."

The door swung shut behind her. Coyote turned and left the patio. On the promenade he passed Ovid and his growing militia as they began a series of exercises. But he had no interest in causing mischief for Ovid Tsing at the moment.

Swiftly, he scrambled back up the ladder to the trolls' balcony and then climbed a rope, swinging himself up onto the suspension bridge. He raced across, fleet as ever. On the other side, he moved from ladder to catwalk to the wooden struts holding up a little house that jutted out from the sheer cliff face of the western wall of the gorge.

Coyote slipped through an open window. The place had been his since shortly after he'd arrived in Twillig's Gorge, won in a card game from an aging demigod and his satyr mate. They'd left the Gorge not long after. The blustering demigod had been an arrogant prick, and few seemed to miss him.

There were only four small rooms, including the kitchen, but at the rear of the little hanging house, Coyote had found a door, and beyond the door was a tunnel that led to a cavernous hollow that must have been excavated at the time the Gorge had first been settled. If the candles and blood spatters were any indication, it had once been used for worship. Black soot from burnt sacrifices painted the rock walls.

But that had been long ago. Now it was a den. There were new candles back there. As Coyote slipped through the door into the tunnel, he could see the flickering of yellow light on the walls. Inside the cavern, there were far more shadows than the candle flames could dispel. Darkness shimmered with the dancing light. He smelled food—the fish he'd brought the night before, most of it uneaten—and sighed.

On the floor of the cavern lay a huddled figure, sprawled on blankets and reading by candlelight. Reading was all she seemed to want to do these days. He understood that. Coyote rarely felt guilt, but on those few occasions it had been easier to slip into other worlds than to live in his own.

"You've got to eat," he told her.

In the candlelight, Kitsune's jade eyes gleamed brightly and her coppery fur flickered like fire. Her silken black hair framed her face and he caught his breath. They had never been lovers, always more like squabbling siblings. And tricksters could never trust one another when lust entered the picture. But her beauty was enough to make even his deceitful heart ache.

"I ate," she replied without looking up.

"More than that."

She sniffed and ignored him.

Coyote sat beside her and reached out to push the book down, forcing her to look at him. "I'll be the last one, cousin, who ever calls you to task for hiding from things you don't want to face. But it isn't like you."

Anger flared in those jade eyes. Her jaw clenched and un-clenched and then she softened. Fury—at herself, at Oliver Bascombe, and at the world—smoldered until it became sorrow. "You know what I did. I betrayed them. I betrayed him."

"You're a trickster."

"It's different. I'd made a vow. A bond."

"If you'd stayed behind, you'd have been killed, or Ty'Lis would have you in his dungeon, too," Coyote reminded her.

Kitsune lifted her book and began to read again—or at least make a show of it.

"Is that why you're hiding here?"

The fox woman ignored him.

Coyote stood up and brushed off the seat of his pants.

"Wayland Smith visited Virginia Tsing today."

Kitsune flinched, then looked at him over the top of the book. "*Only* Virginia Tsing?"

"So it seems. But if you wanted to make promises about the future of the Legend-Born, there's no one better to talk to than that old woman. All of the faithful will listen to her."

Jade eyes narrowed. "What are you talking about, cousin?"

Coyote grinned. "Isn't it obvious? Uncle has a plan to free the Bascombes. Your friend Oliver may survive this war, Legend-Born or not. I wonder if you'll be happy to see him, should you come face-to-face. Even better, I wonder if he'll be happy to see you."

Kitsune set the book down and slowly rose to her feet. "You never know when to be quiet, do you?"

"Gets me in all sorts of trouble," he agreed. "So, what now, cousin?"

Her anguish lay revealed for a moment, and then she composed herself, her expression turning grim.

"I don't know. But if Oliver's going to be free, then it's time I freed myself as well. It's time I did something to burn away my regrets. But we'll stay away from him, cousin. It gnaws at me, but I don't ever want to have to see my reflection in his eyes."

Coyote nodded appreciatively. "The truth. It's usually so unbecoming in a trickster, but it works for you."

Kitsune strode toward him. "It's our nature to be selfish. But this is too much. I've used your weakness to shield me, but the

Atlanteans have slain too many of us, and they mean to murder the rest. They won't stop until all the Borderkind are dead. It's time to fight or die, Coyote."

He raised his eyebrows. "Are you sure? I was hoping to put it off for a while."

"I'm sure. But we have another task before we can go to war."

"And what's that?"

"There are others like you, hiding, or simply trying to stay neutral. They're fooling themselves, thinking the war isn't theirs to fight. The time has come to disabuse them of that notion."

Coyote sighed.

It had been a perfectly lovely, lazy day. Now Kitsune wanted him to play hero—a role never designed for a trickster.

"Shit," Coyote said. "Couldn't you have simmered in your self-loathing for a few more days?"

Kitsune smiled and slid a hand behind his head. She pulled him toward her and their foreheads touched.

"Good dog," she said.

He cursed at her, and she laughed as she preceded him from the cave. Despite his pique, he was elated to hear that sound. Kitsune had been her own prisoner for too long. Now she would run free, and wild.

Wayland Smith walked between worlds. He had always done so and hoped that he always would. This was his power and his legend. The Borderkind thought him one of their kin, and he never argued the point, but he was not like them. They could walk in two worlds, while he could travel in many.

Yet over the ages, it had become more and more difficult for him to cross those borders. What the sorcerers had done in creating the Veil was unnatural, and it had begun to erode his ability to pass from one world to the other. This alone might not have alarmed him, but he feared that it would only be the beginning.

There were myriad other realities and worlds layered one upon the other—a great many of which he had yet to explore. If the magic used to create the Veil could wear away at his magic, he worried that he might one day find himself trapped in one of them, unable to journey beyond. Perhaps those unaware of the existence of the worlds beyond could be content with such restriction, but he was the Wayfarer, and it would be his death.

The Veil had become his bane, and long years ago, Smith had made up his mind to bring it down.

Now the Atlanteans and their damned ambitions were interfering. Whichever members of the High Council were behind the actions of Ty'Lis, they wanted to seal off the legendary world from the ordinary forever, to exterminate the Borderkind and destroy the Doors. Wayland Smith simply could not allow that.

Whatever it required, he had to see that King Hunyadi was victorious and that the Bascombes survived to fulfill their destiny. *One of the Bascombes,* he thought, correcting himself. Not that he wished harm to befall either one of them, but as long as one lived, his plans could still bear fruit. He had spent long years laying the foundations. He would not be thwarted now.

Smith strode along a mist-shrouded path, one of the Gray Corridors that wound in and out of the worlds, allowing him to move not only between parallel realities but between locations in a single world.

The Wayfarer paused. Mist clouded his vision. He raised his cane and, like a dowsing rod, it tugged him forward and to the left, and he could feel that he was close to his destination.

After a dozen steps, the mist cleared and he found himself standing in a copse of trees whose branches kept off the worst of the southern heat. The battalion led by Captain Beck was on the march, dust rising as they moved northward. For a moment he just watched them go past.

Then Smith emerged from the trees, the brim of his hat providing his only shade, and set off toward the troops. Soon, a small group of soldiers broke away from the battalion and started toward him. Several archers nocked arrows and drew back their bows, prepared to fire.

The Wayfarer kept moving.

One of the archers loosed an arrow—by dint of nerves rather than purpose, he surmised—and Smith knocked it from the air before it struck. A shout came from amongst the troops, and then he saw the tall, lithe form of Damia Beck emerge. She waved the defenders back into the ranks, then stood waiting as Smith approached.

A moment later, Blue Jay extricated himself from the marchers. One by one he was joined by others of his kin—first Li, the Guardian of Fire, and then the odd pairing of Cheval Bayard and Leicester Grindylow. Cheval wore her human face and shape, and her silken gown clung deliciously to her figure as the breeze caressed her.

Smith did not pick up his pace. The four Borderkind and Captain Beck waited patiently for him. He stopped perhaps eight feet away and let several moments pass as the rear flank of the battalion marched past.

"You're ready, then?" Smith asked Blue Jay.

The trickster nodded, his features grim. The feathers in his hair twirled in the breeze.

"You're certain this is necessary?" Captain Beck asked. "My battalion is marching to intercept an invasion force headed for the Oldwood. We need every advantage we have against the invaders, especially if the rumors are true and Ty'Lis is adding more Atlanteans to their ranks."

Smith stroked his beard, studying her. "The enemy will find the Oldwood nearly impossible to take. As for the Atlanteans, you'll find that in a few days whoever they've put in to rule as regent for the young prince Tzajin will announce an alliance with Atlantis. Then the flood of reinforcements will arrive and the real invasion will begin."

"You're sure of this?" Captain Beck asked, horror etched upon her features.

The Wayfarer cocked his head to one side. "I've just learned of it," he lied. How else to explain that she and the other commanders ought to have seen the development coming themselves?

"Suffice it to say, Captain, that if Blue Jay and his companions are swift in their efforts, they may return when you will truly need them, having performed a service far greater than any they could provide in a single battle."

Blue Jay shook his head, crossing his arms and staring at Smith. "Do you ever come right out and say something, or does it all have to be a fucking mystery?"

Smith smiled. "Espionage is usually best conducted in secret, don't you think? Details now could cost your lives later, and the Bascombes'. And then, perhaps, cost John Hunyadi his kingdom."

The trickster glanced at the other Borderkind he had recruited for their task. It was Cheval who met Smith's gaze. Her silver hair seemed to glow almost white in the sun.

"We are at your service, monsieur."

Smith nodded. "Excellent. We ought to depart, then. Good luck, Captain Beck."

The old wanderer began to turn away, but then paused and looked back at Li. His legend called him the Guardian of Fire, but he had lost much of his control over the flames. Every inch of his skin had become black, burning embers. He had no hair, no clothes, no features at all to speak of save for his nose and mouth and the dark orange blazing pits where his eyes had once been.

"Not him, though. You others will blend in, but Li will be far too conspicuous."

The grindylow stood up straight, speaking before Blue Jay or Cheval could summon the words.

"We're mates, aye? That means we stick together, or we don't go at all. You let us worry about keeping our secrets. We've done all right so far. The four of us, we left our friends behind in Palenque. Always figured we'd go back for 'em, and now the time's come, so we'll go. The four of us. You got that?"

The Wayfarer studied the water bogie more closely. "All right, young Master Grindylow. Just so you know it's a problem you will have to solve."

Blue Jay lifted his chin. "You're not the only clever one, Smith. We'll see to it."

Smith nodded and took a final look at Li. The Guardian of Fire only stared back at him with those burning pits and said nothing.

"Say your good-byes, then," the Wayfarer told them.

Cheval Bayard fixed him with a venomous stare, but said nothing. The grindylow stood close by. Li held himself apart. None of them had anyone whom they ought to bid farewell, but Blue Jay turned to Captain Beck and they exchanged smiles only lovers could share. Smith approved. He had spent generations persuading Borderkind that there was no sin in loving ordinary people. Of course, Damia Beck was the descendant of Lost Ones, and so even if they were to have children, their offspring would not be Legend-Born. Such children had to be the product of love between a Borderkind and a human from the other side of the Veil.

Still, it touched him to see the way they looked at one another. Wayland Smith had lived through eons almost entirely alone. Most of the time he felt as though he had nothing but callus where his heart ought to be. Once in a while, however, he felt a small twinge that reminded him that he still could feel.

"You know," Captain Beck said to Blue Jay, "if you succeed, you might well hasten the end of the war."

"One way or another," he said, mischief sparkling in his eyes.

"In our favor, of course," the captain said, ebony skin shining in the sun. Then she kissed him, letting her lips linger a moment, not caring that the others saw. Blue Jay returned her kiss tenderly, and when Damia stepped back from him, she was breathless.

"I wish you better luck than on your first journey to Palenque," Captain Beck said, glancing around at the gathered Borderkind.

The grindylow snorted. "Well, we could hardly do worse."

But Blue Jay and Captain Beck were not listening. Their fingers touched in a final lingering farewell, and then the trickster moved toward his kin and nodded to Smith.

"Let's go."

"Indeed. Swift through the Veil, and careful on the other side. The ordinary world has been too long without proper legends. We must do our best not to disturb them."

"We've all been across before, old man," Cheval Bayard sniffed. "We're all Borderkind."

With a nod, Smith reached into the fabric of the Veil. It took him a moment to grasp it—something that happened more often of late—but when he did, it was simple to draw the curtain aside, to open a path through the barrier for them all.

Li went through first, and quickly, as though he had wished for any reason to leave the legendary world behind. Cheval and Grin followed. Blue Jay spared one last glance at Captain Beck. She nodded gravely to him, and the trickster grinned. Then he stepped through.

Silently, as he too passed through the Veil, the Wayfarer wished the lovers whatever destiny they desired for themselves.

As long as it did not interfere with his own.

CHAPTER 3

The guards always opened the door to Julianna and Collette's cell first. Every morning and evening, a quartet of guards arrived. When they had first been captured, a larger contingent had been in attendance, but soon the number had dwindled. Apparently, someone had decided that the threat they represented had been exaggerated.

All along, Collette had wanted to try for escape and Oliver had dissuaded her. Julianna had never quite understood his strategy, but now she realized that Oliver had been right. Since the reduction in the number of guards, they had never given their captors any reason to suspect that they would *dare* attempt an escape.

"They're coming," Collette whispered.

Julianna took a deep breath and let it out slowly. Collette dropped away from the door, letting Julianna take a look through the grate. As always, the two Yucatazcan guards came first, swarthy soldiers carrying trays of food. They were followed by a pair of Atlanteans. They wore the same uniforms as the Yucatazcans, but there was no mistaking the greenish-white cast of their skin.

The Atlanteans were armed with both sword and dagger. The first soldier came to the door and Julianna stepped back a bit as he braced the tray against his hip and fumbled with the keys. She glanced through the grate and across the hall, where she could see Oliver watching her from his own cell.

The key went into the lock and she could hear the clank of the tumblers. The door swung open half an inch.

"Back away!" the nearest of the two Atlanteans shouted, drawing his sword. "Away from the door!"

Julianna flinched and put on a frightened look. It was not pretense, though normally she would not have allowed them to see her fear. She took a few steps back and raised her hands.

The Yucatazcan guard sighed and glanced at her apologetically, rolling his eyes a bit at the Atlantean's hostility. He didn't even bother trying to hide the look from his prisoners. *Perfect.* Let them see that these two ordinary young women presented no threat at all.

The guard carried the tray in a few feet and then knelt, setting it down on the floor.

Out in the corridor, the other member of the king's guard unlocked Oliver's cell with his own Atlantean escort looking on. Julianna held her breath. Some days, their cell had been closed and locked again before the guards opened Oliver's, but other times they had been lax. She and Oliver and Collette had been waiting for this.

Silently, she said a prayer for the man she loved.

The guard opened Oliver's door and stepped inside the cell. Oliver rushed him, slamming the tray of food up into the guard's face and, in a single motion, twisting the man around to face the open doorway. As the guard began to shout, Oliver wrapped his hands around the man's throat, choking him.

The Atlantean escort raced into the cell, sword drawn. Oliver did not wait for barked commands or threats. He ran at the Atlantean, driving the Yucatazcan guard forward with such force that the swordsman could not pull his blade away in time, and the Yucatazcan was impaled.

Upon instinct, the second Atlantean began to move to help the first. The moment he did, Collette attacked the guard who had brought their tray. The man tried to defend himself, but she had learned to fight years ago. Collette feinted with her left, then shot out her right hand, palm flat, and broke his nose. Then she punted him full-force between the legs.

That left only the two Atlanteans still standing, and both of them were trying to get at Oliver. Julianna raced out into the corridor just as the second Atlantean started to realize his mistake. Julianna collided with him, driving him bodily into Oliver's cell. He stumbled into Oliver and the other Atlantean, who were now grappling for the sword.

Collette came out behind Julianna, slamming the door.

"Oliver!" she shouted. "Come on!"

Julianna started into his cell, but Oliver looked up, panic on his face. They'd known it would be difficult. After being imprisoned so long, the only advantage they had was surprise. But that had lasted only seconds and in Oliver's expression Julianna saw that it hadn't been enough. The Atlanteans were too fast.

They weren't all going to get out.

"Close the door!" Oliver shouted. He tore the helmet off of the dead Yucatazcan guard and began beating one of the Atlanteans about the head with it, still struggling over the sword.

Collette froze outside the door. "Oliver, no!"

But Julianna knew they were out of time. She slammed the cell door and turned the key, then tossed the ring of keys down the corridor. In all her life, she'd never done anything more difficult than locking Oliver in that cell.

But she didn't hesitate.

This might well be their only chance to leave the dungeon

alive. She grabbed Collette and pulled her along beside her. Together, they ran. If they could get to Frost, they could still come back for Oliver, but only if they were quick.

Julianna forced herself to focus. Oliver had not felt the chill in his cell that she and Collette had noticed in theirs. That meant Frost had to be imprisoned nearer to them. She and Collette hurtled down the corridor and reached the archway that led to the stairs. The gate at the top would be locked, but it didn't matter. They weren't going up.

Frost's cell had to be behind theirs, meaning that there must be a second corridor in the dungeon. Julianna ducked her head through the archway and looked to the left. An arched hallway ran parallel to the one where they'd been imprisoned. Only a few sconces burned down that way. But there was a breeze that made her shiver and raised gooseflesh on her arms.

Frost.

"This way," Julianna said, turning to Collette.

"We can't just leave him."

"We won't."

Shouts reverberated through the dungeon, bouncing off of the walls. She cursed silently, glancing around. Heavy footfalls were pounding along the corridor they'd just left. The Yucatazcan guard had recovered from Collette's attack.

A quick glance up the stairs told Julianna they still had a few seconds left. But that was all. Whatever guards were standing sentry at the gate up there, they would hear the Yucatazcan and raise the alarm in a moment.

She bolted along the darkened corridor and Collette followed. The cold air enveloped them as they slipped into the shadows between the splashes of light provided by the sconces. Then she heard the shouts grow louder. Collette grabbed her and the two of them pushed themselves against the wall, hidden in the shadows.

The Yucatazcan ran past at the end of the corridor, but didn't pause. Instead, he went up the stairs, assuming they'd gone that way as well. How many seconds, Julianna wondered, before he got to the gate at the top and realized that there was no way they could have gotten out that way?

They hurried. At the first sconce, Julianna paused in a pool of torchlight and stared at the door set into the wall. Collette went on a few feet, then stopped to stare back at her, eyes frantic. But Julianna was trying to figure out how far they had come down the hall. She stepped up to the cell door and looked through the grate into darkness.

"Frost?" she whispered.

There was no reply. A frisson of fear went through her, and then she felt foolish. He wouldn't be able to reply; not really. He was caught in a spell. Julianna heard more shouts, but distant.

"Go," Collette whispered.

Julianna nodded and they ran on, hurrying to the next cell and peering inside. Quickly they moved on, glancing through the grate in each door in search of Frost. Another gust of frigid wind whipped up and Julianna shivered, her teeth chattering.

"He's got to be here," Collette said, her elfin features frantic.

"I know," Julianna said. "But which one? Where the hell—"

She paused. Further along, just past the next splash of torchlight, a dim blue glow emanated from the grate in a cell door. She hadn't noticed it before because of the illumination from the sconce. It reminded her of the light from a television, seen through the window of someone else's home.

"There!" a voice bellowed behind them.

"No," Collette whispered.

Julianna glanced back to see guards filling the archway at the bottom of the stairs. There had to be half a dozen of them, and she felt sure most would be Atlantean. The Yucatazcan had gone up and brought back help. They should have taken the time to lock him in. Collette should have kicked him harder. So many should-haves, but they had no time for self-recrimination.

Despite the chill, heat flushed her skin as she and Collette began to run. Footfalls like a stampede followed them. Julianna and Collette hadn't been diligent about exercise the way Oliver had. They were exhausted and malnourished. Their flight was a headlong lunge, barely controlled.

As they passed through that next pool of torchlight, she saw that ice had formed on the stone walls.

"That's enough," a voice rumbled close behind them. Julianna felt the pressure of the guard's presence.

A hand grasped at her hair and she shrieked, tugging herself away. Collette glanced back, reaching out to pull her along.

Then Julianna began to slip. She felt the loss of traction an instant before she realized that the stones laid into the floor had also been covered with ice. Julianna pinwheeled her arms, trying not to fall, but then her feet went out from under her.

Powerful hands caught her, clutching her tightly.

She stared up into the face of an Atlantean guard. His touch felt clammy and repulsive.

"Jules!" Collette shouted. She lunged at the guard, but others swarmed around them, and then they had her as well.

So close. They knew where Frost was, now, but would never reach him.

Despite herself, Julianna forced a smile. "Thanks for that. Slippery when wet. You guys should put up a sign."

The Atlantean snarled and tightened his grip, twining his fingers in her hair so that Julianna let out a cry of pain.

Then he swung her by her hair, smashing her head into the icy stone wall. Pain blossomed into fireworks in her mind, and she began slipping down into darkness.

Down and down, and then she was alone in the shadows of her soul, and cold. So very cold.

The smell of blood filled Oliver's nostrils. He sat on the floor, back against the stone wall of his cell, and tried to clear his throat. Even that hurt. His left eye had swollen shut, and the cheek below felt like it had been tenderized. Once the

Atlanteans had gotten hold of him, they'd given him the beating he'd known was coming. Knowing didn't make it any easier. The scent of blood in the cell might have come from the guard he'd killed, but he had a feeling it was his own, soaked into his shirt and still trickling both on his face and inside his mouth.

"Fuck," he rasped, wishing his face would stop throbbing or that the pressure around his swollen eye would go away. He reached up and gingerly pressed his fingers against his cheek, then hissed in pain.

What was it about people that they had to do that—probe their injuries to see just how bad the damage was? Foolish didn't begin to describe it. But the temptation was too great to resist.

Another guard had come to let out the two Atlanteans that Julianna had locked in here with him. They'd left Oliver behind, along with the Yucatazcan he'd killed. The corpse lay on the ground, cooling, and he tried to avoid looking at it.

Wincing, he put one hand against the wall and rose. A sharp pain in his side reminded him of the single blow he'd taken to the ribs, and he wondered if any were cracked or broken.

Oliver shuffled over to the cell door, dragging his boot heels to wipe off the dead guard's blood. In the back of his mind, he felt the dim awareness of the fact that he'd killed a man. It troubled him that he was not more upset by this. Once upon a time, he knew he would have been crippled with the horror of having taken a life. Now it only seemed necessary.

It occurred to him that he had never understood war until now.

A clanking of metal came from down the corridor. Oliver turned to peer to his right and his face brushed against the grate. A hundred tiny needles of pain stabbed him.

Careful not to repeat his mistake, he looked through the grate. A chorus of boot heels greeted him. Then he saw the first of the Atlantean guards and found himself frozen, hands against the door.

Atlantean guards and soldiers passed his cell. Their marching had a thunderous rhythm, like horses drawing a carriage. A
grim-faced Yucatazcan paraded Collette past him, her head
hanging in defeat, her neck red and swollen.

"Coll?" he said.

She glanced at him, but the guard shoved her through the
still-open door of her cell. Collette fell to the stone floor, cursing quietly.

Oliver ought to have been relieved. His sister was still alive.
But still he waited to exhale, wondering what had become of
Julianna. Had she freed Frost, or had the Atlanteans killed her?

The guards ignored Collette, standing at attention, weapons
held at the ready, and that was when Oliver saw her.

Julianna floated along the corridor, dangling from thin, oil-
black tendrils that held her aloft like the strings of some horrid
marionette. Some of them wrapped around her arms, holding
them behind her back, wrists tied together. They encircled her
waist and throat, and a single tug might be enough to end
her life.

Oliver saw all of this. He saw the bruised and bloodied left
side of her face—an injury startlingly similar to his own. Yet he
focused on her eyes, which were wide with terror. Her chest
rose and fell, and a reedy whisper of air slipped in and out of
her lips—all the breath she could draw with the black smoke
tendrils around her neck.

His lips silently formed her name.

Behind her came Ty'Lis. The sorcerer bore the physical sig-
natures of Atlantis with his narrow face and greenish-white
skin, but his golden hair was striking and he wore his yellow
beard in a thick braid. In black robes with crimson trim, he
seemed like the devil of some alien Hell.

He held his left hand up and from his wide sleeve flowed the
black strings in which Julianna had been tangled.

The sorcerer grinned, showing jagged teeth as green as his
skin.

"I swear to God," Oliver began, his voice a primal snarl that he himself did not recognize.

Ty'Lis held up his free hand, the grin growing wider. A Cheshire Cat grin. A hungry tiger's grin.

"Hush, Bascombe."

A horrid smell filled Oliver's nose, eradicating the scent of blood. It was putrid, sewer stink, like the unwashed death-smell of an entire end-stage cancer ward.

In the cell across the corridor, Collette retched.

"I will speak. You will be silent. Otherwise, your lover will die," the sorcerer said.

Oliver obeyed. In the opposite cell, he thought he heard his sister whimper. But that couldn't be; Collette Bascombe didn't cry. Only the destruction of her marriage had ever broken that part of her resolve. He heard her muttering quietly, perhaps a prayer to whatever gods might hear her on this side of the Veil. He hoped that the Atlantean would not think of this as disobedience. His command had been to Oliver.

"I have little time to spare for you, so I will speak plainly. Some attempt to escape was expected, of course. Perhaps you have learned better, now, and perhaps not. Regardless, I won't kill you. It may be that the High Council will have use for you, yet. However—"

As he spoke, those black tendrils pulled Julianna toward his outstretched hand. He wrapped long talon fingers around her neck. The strings tightened and she wheezed. Where her face had been scraped and bruised, droplets of fresh blood dripped down her cheek. Julianna stared at Oliver. He wished he could just tear away the grate, break down the door, only to touch her.

"If you try to escape again, I will kill her. The High Council wants you and your sister left alive, for now. But this one... there is no need for her to live. I could strip her flesh and shatter every bone. I could bathe in her blood and they would not care. I could give her to the guards or, better yet, to one of my giants. I keep her alive only for leverage."

The sorcerer tossed Julianna aside. She crumbled to the ground like a rag doll, gasping for air. Two Atlantean guards dragged Julianna into the cell with Collette and left her there. As they departed, she sprang up and charged at them, mad hopelessness in her eyes.

They slammed the door in her face, expressionless.

Ty'Lis moved his face to within inches of the grated window in Oliver's door. Oliver wanted to thrust his hands out, to tear at the sorcerer's eyes or throat, but he did not dare.

"Behave," the monster whispered, that stench wafting into the cell from his nearness, making Oliver gag.

Ted Halliwell tried to tell himself he wasn't dead.

He could see and hear, though both only dimly and distantly, as though he was submerged in shallow water. At times it seemed he broke the surface and those two senses became sharper.

For the most part, those were his only senses. Yet there was a third—the tactile—that troubled him. Perhaps it would be more accurate to call it a sensation. He could see hands reach out—long fingers with sharp talons—but he could neither control their movements nor feel what they touched.

In the dark, he approached a small military encampment. Horses grazed nearby, and they whinnied as he passed, a shiver running up their flanks. They snorted, spooked as hell, and the terror in their eyes was wild. But he passed by and the sounds of their skittishness faded.

Tent flaps danced in the breeze, as did the banners flying the colors of King Hunyadi. Halliwell had met the king, once, and had felt an immediate loyalty to the man. He had been strong, yet fair and wise—a man Halliwell himself would be willing to follow into war. In another world. In another era.

Now he couldn't follow anyone.

He could only drift along behind the eyes of another. What

troubled him most, however, wasn't what he couldn't feel, but what he *could*. There was no weight to him, none of the burden of flesh he'd felt all his life. But he still felt as though he had substance, and within that substance, he could feel sand, shifting. It eroded his bones, sifting against his insides.

Impossible, of course.

Ted Halliwell couldn't be the Sandman.

But he felt as though he existed only behind the monster's putrid lemon eyes. Somewhere within the creature's mind, he could feel a third presence. He knew that it could only be the Dustman.

Halliwell had come upon the brothers while they were attempting to destroy one another. Like a fool, he had interfered.

Now he slid through the night toward the military encampment. Sentries marched the perimeter but did not see him. If they heard anything, it was a whisper on the breeze. Through the Sandman's eyes, Halliwell saw a sentry yawn, widely, and he wondered if this was the presence of the monster or mere coincidence. For this was no storybook Sandman, gently easing children off to sleep. It was the savage fiend of older stories who punished little ones by plucking out their eyes and eating them.

Halliwell tried to tell himself that he was alive.

He was aware. From that bit of information, he deduced that he couldn't possibly be dead. In the ordinary world—before crossing the Veil in pursuit of the answers he'd thought Oliver Bascombe could give him about a series of murders and disappearances—he'd been a sheriff's detective. Now his old life had been erased and he wished that he had not needed those answers so desperately. Trapped beyond the Veil, Halliwell had come to care only about returning to make amends with his estranged daughter, Sara. They had fumbled their relationship badly, and Halliwell wished for another chance.

But he couldn't go back.

That truth had broken something inside of him, so that

when he finally caught up to the Sandman, he had attacked the creature on his own. The Sandman had been in the midst of a savage battle with his brother, the Dustman. Halliwell had gotten between them.

The biggest mistake he had ever made.

He could still feel the way the whirling sand and dust had scoured his flesh, stripping meat from the bones. He had tried to scream, sand rushing down his throat. Then, for the longest time, *nothing*.

Awareness had returned slowly. At first it had all been darkness, and then he had begun to see, and to hear. From time to time that skittery whisper of the Dustman had come to him as though from the black shadows at the bottom of a well.

Halliwell had no idea if the Sandman knew he was alive, inside. All he knew was what the monster felt, and that was hatred. Oliver and Kitsune had turned his own brother against him and then, for a time, destroyed him. Now the Sandman wanted vengeance. No matter what his former masters asked of him, he had no desire other than the murder of Kitsune and Oliver Bascombe.

And now he hunted.

The Sandman cascaded across the ground between tents, peering at the few of Hunyadi's soldiers who sat in a tight circle, smoking cigarettes and sharing the grim talk of war. How far they were from the battle front, where this camp was in relation to the few other places he'd been in the Two Kingdoms, Halliwell had no idea. Not that it mattered. The Sandman moved from place to place with a hideous ease. His sandcastle still existed in multiple locations through the kingdoms, replete with doors that allowed him to travel to a thousand points on both sides of the Veil simply by passing through.

Through the monster's eyes, Halliwell saw a tent ahead. The king's banner flapped overhead. For a terrible moment, Halliwell feared that this would be the tent of King Hunyadi himself, but then he sensed what the monster knew, and understood that this was simply the tent of the commander of this battalion.

With a swirl of dust around his feet—and it could have been that just for a moment this was not sand, but dust, because after all, the Dustman was in here as well—he paused at the rear of the tent. The night seemed quiet save for the distant susurrus of conversation and the flapping of the tents. The Sandman reached out a clawed hand and sliced the fabric. It split like flesh, pouting open.

Halliwell wanted to scream, to try to shout through the Sandman's mouth in hopes that the commander would hear him. But he didn't dare, for certainly the Sandman would hear him, too.

So he kept silent. Just in case.

No. Act. Stop him, the Dustman whispered in his head.

Halliwell ignored him but could not prevent himself from hearing. Just as he could not prevent himself from entering the tent. As the Sandman twisted his body to duck through the tear in the fabric, he felt the grit scraping against his bones again, felt the sand all around him, and wished the Dustman could understand.

He was powerless to do anything but bear witness.

He wondered if his daughter, Sara, was asleep somewhere in another world, and he prayed that she had found some peace.

The commander was not sleeping. As the Sandman entered, the man looked up, forehead creased in a frown at the intrusion. Realization shot like lightning across his face and he started to rise, opened his mouth to shout even as he reached for his sword.

Halliwell felt hatred and disgust well up within him and tried to exert some kind of control, to reach his consciousness out into the Sandman's hands and stop what was to come.

He could do nothing.

The monster clapped a hand across the commander's

mouth, forestalling any cries for help. With his other hand he disarmed the man, breaking bones in his wrist and arm.

"You know what I am?" the Sandman whispered.

The commander, wincing in pain, nodded. Halliwell wondered if he recognized the Sandman from his legend, or was merely aware that death had come for him.

"Excellent," the monster rasped. He bent and darted out his tongue, running it over the commander's left eyeball. The tongue was rough with grit, like sandpaper, and the commander screamed into the hand covering his mouth.

"You will tell me, sir, of the war between the Two Kingdoms, and especially anything you know about the Legend-Born filth called Oliver Bascombe, and Kitsune of the Borderkind. You will speak softly. If you fail in either of these, I will suck the eyes from your face and chew them while the nerves are still intact."

The commander whimpered.

The Sandman pulled his hand away.

The man trembled as he began to speak.

When it was over, the Sandman did precisely what he had threatened. The commander had not disobeyed him, but the monster simply could not resist.

Halliwell had spent weeks on the precipice of madness. He teetered there once again.

itsune stood on the corner of a cobblestoned street in the Latin Quarter of Perinthia. Loose stones and cracks made the road treacherous. Since the last time she had come to the city, only months before, this neighborhood seemed to have crumbled even further into ruin.

Most truly old cities in the ordinary world had their equivalent of the Latin Quarter—a bit of self-contained ancientness that predated the rest of what sprawled around it. Perinthia was the capital of the kingdom of Euphrasia, and the city reflected its origins. It was a mishmash of bits and pieces, of cultures and legends from all over Europe and Asia and North America in the human world. Far to the east there were places in the kingdom of Euphrasia that were older, but in the capital city, the Latin Quarter was it.

There were narrow alleys and several broad boulevards, but most of the buildings lining the streets were partially collapsed.

Some were entirely ruined. Others only stood like withered corpses, their windows the sunken orbits of desiccated skulls. Columns lay fallen across the roads. Plants had grown up through cracks and in amongst the ruins. These buildings came from the legends of ancient Greece and the Roman Empire, and had been shifted from the ordinary world to the realm of the legendary when the Veil was raised.

Despite their appearance, however, it was not safe to assume that the buildings were deserted. No one quite knew how many people still lived in the Latin Quarter—no census had ever been successfully taken.

Kitsune had thought that the Quarter seemed sparsely populated the last time she had been there. Now, though, it felt deserted. From the corner where she stood—at the end of a street with no name—she could see stalls and awnings and wagons that had once been part of the marketplace. Wooden boxes were scattered about, some of them shattered, and there were the pulped and rotting remnants of fruits and vegetables on the cobblestones. As for vendors, however, she could see only a single, lone girl with a small cart, its meager offerings of apples and oranges hardly enough to feed even her.

Impatient, the fox woman looked over her shoulder, down a curving alley to her right. Coyote stepped from the shadows, zipping up his pants. She wondered at his brazenness. Like her, he was a trickster. Like her, he had senses far greater than a human's. By scent alone he would know that the buildings and ruins weren't as deserted as they appeared to be. So why he would risk the wrath of the Latin Quarter's denizens by seeming to mark his territory so publicly was a mystery to her.

"Can we continue now?" she asked, looking down her nose at him.

Coyote raised an eyebrow and glanced at her. Taking his time, he reached into the pocket of his battered leather jacket and withdrew a small cigarette case. Coyote rolled his own, of course. He pulled out one he had fixed that morning, tucked it between his lips, and then produced a lighter. It flared briefly and he inhaled, then let out a long swirl of smoke from each nostril.

Kitsune didn't even see him slip the cigarette case back into his jacket.

Months in hiding, stewing in guilt and mourning her own image of herself, had dulled her senses. Or perhaps she simply didn't care so much anymore. Her black clothes were loose beneath her red fur cloak, and her hood shaded her eyes. In her heart, she knew that anyone looking at her would not see the mischief that had once danced in those eyes. She simply did not feel it anymore.

Her cunning might remain intact, but she found no merriment in its ownership.

Coyote drew in a lungful of smoke from his homemade cigarette and blew it out, then started down the street, boots clicking on cobblestones. Given their origins, some might presume a similarity between Blue Jay and Coyote, but the two could not be more different. One was a proud spirit, soaring overhead, and the other was a scavenger, preying on the weak.

They kept close to the western side of the street, slinking along as though they might remain unobtrusive in a place where even a mouse would be conspicuous. Kitsune caught the scent of cooking meat on the air, and spices and garlic, and she knew that their journey had not been for nothing. The knowledge sped her along and lightened her heart a bit—a difficult feat of late.

Coyote tipped his nose to the sky. "I smell sex," he said, with a predator's grin.

Kitsune frowned, but then understood. He could not have missed the scent of cooking, but there was, indeed, a musky, sexual smell in the air beneath the stronger odors of food.

"That building, there," she said, nodding toward a run-down palazzo ahead on the right. "It's a brothel."

Coyote laughed softly. "More life in the Quarter than I'd

begun to fear. People have to satisfy their hungers. But still, it doesn't mean there's much society here."

"We don't want society. We don't want the people at all."

"Speak for yourself. The smell of the veal frying's got my stomach growling. I'd be more than happy to eat some people right now."

Kitsune glanced at him, presuming he was joking, but didn't bother to call him on it. If Coyote was serious, she didn't want to know.

They moved down the nameless street, surrounded by buildings with darkened windows. The fox-woman felt the skin prickle at the back of her neck and glanced around at the rooftops. They were being watched, but she could not locate their observer.

Past the whorehouse stood a building with open windows and accordion doors that could be drawn back on pleasant days. Once upon a time it had been a Roman bathhouse. In the center, Kitsune recalled, was a patio where patrons could dine beneath open sky. Smoke rose from the chimney at the rear where the stove must be.

"Lycaon's Kitchen," she said. Once, in ancient Greece, the owner had been a king. Then he had been made a monster.

"Is it true?" Coyote asked. "His legend?"

"That he was a cannibal, or that he tried to feed human flesh to Zeus?"

"Both."

Kitsune smiled in spite of herself and ran her tongue over her small, sharp teeth. "Aren't the legends all true? In any case, does it matter? Whether Zeus was responsible or not, Lycaon is the original werewolf. He's eaten his share of human meat, but it's not on the menu here."

Coyote grunted, low in his chest. "What makes you think he'll have any interest in this war?"

The fox woman laughed softly. "He doesn't. But neither did you."

At the door, she did not hesitate. If there had ever been time for such pretensions, it had passed. Kitsune pulled the door open and stepped inside, eyes quickly adjusting to the darkness of the restaurant. Gray daylight spilled through the opening in the roof, but barely permeated the shadows of the corners. Coyote followed, moving off to one side so that they could not be attacked by the same foe.

Two withered, bent crones sat at a table in a far corner with a slim young man who stank of perfume. Kitsune knew them right away as madams from the adjoining whorehouse, which meant the slender man was one of their prostitutes. He was weeping quietly.

A quartet of gruff-looking men—warriors or even legendary heroes from the look of them—had gathered around a table off to the left. A thin tree-creature shuffled toward them with a tray bearing platters of meat. There were others already on the table, festooned with bones and fat that had been sliced away. Even seated, it was impossible not to notice that one of the men was taller than the others; some sort of demigod, Kitsune presumed. He studied Coyote a moment before giving her an appreciative appraisal. Then a shadow passed over his features and he merely nodded in greeting.

She nodded back, but only to be courteous. Her attention was otherwise occupied by the man sitting alone at a table in the patio at the center of the restaurant. His back was to them, but though she had only seen him once she would never have mistaken him for anyone else. He had wild, unruly hair and massive hands that seemed capable of crushing the skulls of his enemies effortlessly. He sipped at a large tumbler filled with ice and amber liquid that could only have been Norse mead. It was a rare import. Whatever remained of the Nordic legends endured beyond the shores of the Two Kingdoms. It was rare to find them, or their worshippers, here.

Kitsune and Coyote strode up behind him, stopping just outside of the range of his arms.

"Lycaon," she said.

He made a noise that might have been a scowl or a laugh. "I wondered how long before one of you returned to recruit me."

Coyote sniffed derisively. "Yeah. You seem to be in high demand, but we're not here to recruit you."

The man stiffened. Kitsune saw the hackles rise on the back of his hairy neck. Lycaon drained the rest of his mead, ice tinkling in the glass, and stood.

For just a moment, those bestial eyes pinned Coyote and then Lycaon dismissed him, staring instead at Kitsune.

"Have you come for a fight, then? You want to try to kill me?"

"We're not here for trouble," Kitsune said. She drew back her hood and shook out her raven-black hair, letting Lycaon's eyes linger on her a moment before she fixed him with a stare as dark and brutal as his own. "But your business does seem to have dropped off, Lycaon."

He let out a long breath, relenting to the inevitability of their conversation. "Many legendary have gone to help King Hunyadi, along with the few Borderkind who had been hiding away in the ruins." He nodded toward the table of heroes. "Those warriors are leaving tonight, joining their swords to Hunyadi's cause. The Lost Ones have begun to move out of the Quarter. Some want to be in the center of the city, among more of their own kind. Others have retreated further to the north and east, away from the war. But many have joined the king's army."

"Not you, though," Coyote said.

Lycaon growled a low warning, but did not turn to look at him.

"You said 'Hunyadi's cause,' " Kitsune observed, studying the werewolf's face. "Isn't it also your cause?"

Lycaon knitted his thick brows. "Why should it be?"

"I know you haven't been through the Veil in a great many years, but you are still Borderkind. The conspirators in Atlantis do not care if you want to cross the Veil. All that concerns them is that you *can*. One day, they will come after you."

Lycaon rattled the ice in his glass, staring down into it. "Hunyadi has legions. What help can one old beast be?"

"King Mahacuhta is dead. Murdered. The Yucatazcans have been manipulated into war by Atlantis," Coyote said with a passion that surprised Kitsune. "With both kingdoms allied against him, Hunyadi will need all the help he can find."

Kitsune took a chance, reaching out to touch his arm. Lycaon sneered but did not pull away. She met his gaze.

"Others are dying to protect you. Not only legends and the Lost, but your kin. Soon you will be sitting alone in this place. The fires will be dark, and the mead will be gone. What then?"

Lycaon seemed to hesitate. "I thought you weren't here to recruit me."

Kitsune released him. "We're not. If you would rather die alone and hunted than on a field of battle, there's little I can do to convince you."

The beast seemed diminished by her words. He spoke quietly. "I know about wars, kings, and murder. I promised myself, when I opened the doors of this place, that those things were all behind me."

Coyote stepped nearer to him. All the mockery had gone from his face. "You put them behind you, Lycaon. But they've caught up."

The werewolf flinched, but kept quiet, lost in reverie.

"When we go, you're welcome to come along. That will be for you to decide. But no matter your choice, there is something we need from you."

Lycaon frowned and glanced up at Kitsune.

Coyote cleared his throat. "The old gods."

The beast looked askance at him. "They're dead. You know that."

"No one has ever believed they were all gone, Lycaon, no matter how they wished their legends would end."

"And if I refuse, then what? For millennia, people have called me a monster. The word is not inaccurate. Do you think you can force me to help you?"

"We are not enemies, Lycaon," Kitsune said. "If we succeed— if those rallying behind Hunyadi succeed—you will benefit. If they do not, you will die. All three of us here will die. So understand me well when I say that if you do not cooperate with us, then at least one of us will not have to wait for the Atlanteans to end our lives. You will have to kill us both, or we will be eating your black heart for our dinner, cooked upon your own stove."

"I've never responded well to threats," the beast-man said darkly.

Kitsune shrugged. "As you like. But I wager your response to death would be even less favorable. We'd rather have you as an ally than a corpse. No matter how hungry Coyote might be."

Coyote took a final drag from his cigarette, then dropped it to the floor and crushed it under his boot.

For long moments, Lycaon said nothing.

Then, at last, he nodded. "I'll take you to the old gods. But do not be so deluded as to think we are now allies, or that the old ones will trouble themselves with the likes of you."

Kitsune nodded. "Lead on, then," she said, as she raised her fur hood, hiding her face once more.

When Wayland Smith led them through the Veil into the human world, Blue Jay felt strangely at home. He had traveled all through the Two Kingdoms and to other lands in the legendary world, but he'd never felt quite so at ease as he did in the badlands of America. The people who'd believed in him and who still told his stories . . . this was their land, no matter who supposedly owned it now.

When they stepped into the world, they found themselves in an arroyo that hadn't seen rain in months. The sky had been the deep indigo that only came in the small hours, long after midnight. The moon hung low and cast its light across a hard-scrabble land of tangled brush and cactus. Far off, a mesa thrust up from the flat earth, its striated layers lit up by the moonglow.

Blue Jay would have given anything to stop here, just for a while. He could have been at peace.

But Smith wouldn't hear of it.

They started off immediately. Blue Jay danced into the sky, transforming into a small bird not usually seen at night. Cheval had likewise changed, shifting her form from exotic woman to silver-maned, green-tinted horse. Jay had never met another kelpy, but he wondered if they were all so tragically beautiful. Grin rode astride Cheval's back. Li spread his arms wide and fire erupted from his hands. From it he forged a flaming tiger, which he mounted and rode as he had with the tiger who'd been his flesh-and-blood companion.

That had left only Smith, who meandered along with his cane. Blue Jay watched the old wanderer, who seemed to move far more slowly than the other Borderkind. Yet every time he glanced down, Smith was no further behind than he had been. The trickster had to remind himself that Smith was a magician of sorts, and the Wayfarer's power had a great deal to do with his journeys.

All through the night they walked, traveling for hours across the rough country of the southwestern United States and making more progress than an ordinary man on horseback could have ridden in several days. They journeyed through small, sparse towns and over high passes, and Smith gave them not a moment's rest.

Blue Jay felt many times during those long hours that he had traveled these lands before, but only when he saw the lights of a city to the east did he become certain they were in Arizona. The city was Tucson. The Mexican border was not far away.

Perhaps an hour before dawn, they came over a rise to find a barbed wire fence before them. The ground here was rough and tufted with spikes of prickly grass. Blue Jay circled above their heads and watched as Wayland Smith gestured to Li.

The burning tiger reared back and the Guardian of Fire raised a fist of glowing embers. When he opened his hand, fire rushed from his palm and blew the fence apart, charring wooden posts and scorching the ground.

Smith led the way across the Mexican border. Blue Jay flew in wide arcs, watching for the border patrol, but no one came. He felt a profound relief at that, because he knew that they would not have allowed themselves to be stopped by humans with guns. Innocents might have died.

They walked south into Mexican territory, but less than ten minutes into their journey, a buzz filled the air. Blue Jay sailed down from the sky, spun into a blur of blue light, and alighted upon the ground as a man once more. His cotton shirt and blue jeans felt soft and comfortable after so long on the wing.

"What's that, then? That odd drumming?" Grin asked, still astride Cheval. The kelpy glanced up with wide, eloquent eyes.

Li stood there on that rough earth, burning, and stared at the sky.

But Blue Jay stared at Smith. "A helicopter. Maybe more than one. Border Patrol, I assume."

Smith nodded. "Our friend Li is not the most inconspicuous. We'll cross back over now. No one owns this land, except perhaps the Mexican government. We can breach the Veil from here."

"Seems a shame," Grin said. "Got nearly an hour till daybreak. No telling how much further south we could get in that time."

"No, he's right," Blue Jay said. He caught sight of the lights of the helicopter in the distance. "When we cross over, we'll be in Yucatazca. The war will be north of us."

He didn't mention that they'd have to avoid reinforcements that Ty'Lis would no doubt be sending along the Isthmus of the

Conquistadors to aid the invasion of Euphrasia. Yet, when the quintet of Borderkind had slipped once more through the Veil into the sunlit world of the legendary, Blue Jay was surprised to find they met no resistance at all.

At first he thought this might be extraordinary luck, but as the hours passed, he began to suspect it had more to do with the fact that Wayland Smith was leading them. It seemed that his path took him only where he wished it to. Somehow he found the most remote areas of Yucatazca for them to journey through. Once, flying above a rain forest mountain with his comrades trekking below, Blue Jay saw an army detachment at least two thousand strong marching northward toward the Isthmus, but they were miles away.

When they camped that night, he asked Smith about it.

The Wayfarer just smiled. "I choose my steps carefully."

The next morning they resumed their journey at speeds far greater than Blue Jay had ever managed while he, Frost, and Kitsune had been traveling with Oliver Bascombe. Many of the legendary had magic within them that granted them a certain swiftness, and others were simply faster by nature than human beings. On foot, and over short distances, neither Li nor Grin would have outpaced a reasonably fit human. But on a journey that spanned the borders between worlds and kingdoms, and with Grin astride Cheval and Li upon his burning tiger, they covered ground in a fraction of the time.

Cheval had suggested that they find a branch of the Winding Way, but Smith insisted that the detour would actually slow them down.

As the day wore on, Blue Jay found himself glad that he was not walking with the others. They were in thick jungle now, with hills and ravines and clouds of insects that seemed to be waiting for unsuspecting travelers. There were creatures in the tangled jungle, of course—some of them ordinary beasts and birds, but others figures of legend. Smith stopped at the edge of a stream to talk to something the blue bird couldn't quite make out from the sky. Most of the legendary they passed were wild things, however, that would not want anything to do with war or politics or the city of Palenque.

In the middle of the afternoon, Blue Jay saw a glint of gold against the horizon. As he scouted ahead, flying nearer, he saw the terraced buildings and gleaming rooftops of Palenque. Exotic and elegant, it seemed like a city of gods. And perhaps it once had been. The city itself had been designed as a kind of maze, the streets turning in upon themselves over and over. As one walked deeper into the city, trying to reach the palace at the center, the streets became so narrow that it was almost necessary to walk single file. For centuries, the kings of Yucatazca had used their own capital city—and its people—as their major defenses. An army could never take Palenque that way.

No, any attack that was to succeed would have to come from within.

With one last glance, he flew down in a long arc, gliding between the trees. Spreading his wings, the bird became the man, and Blue Jay stepped down out of the sky to stand beside Wayland Smith.

Li turned his great, burning tiger around, staring at the trickster with cinder eyes. Blue Jay beckoned to him, even as Cheval cantered up behind him. Grin slid from the kelpy's back, and with a wet, cracking noise, she took on her alluring female form once more.

"We're near the end of the jungle," Blue Jay said.

Smith watched him calmly.

"This isn't the same approach we used the last time," Cheval Bayard said, her accent lilting. She shook out her silver hair, but there was nothing sensual in the action, or in the grim expression on her face. On their last journey to Palenque, her companion, Chorti, had been killed in battle with the Perytons and the other Myth Hunters.

"Right," Grin agreed. "If I've got it sussed, we're coming in from the northwest this time."

Li said nothing, the crackling of fire his only audible contribution.

"Remember the mountainside on the west end of the city, with the homes built right into the slope?" Blue Jay said. "We're going to come in right at the top. The city will be down below."

"It will not be a simple thing to climb down unseen," Cheval said.

Blue Jay turned to look at Smith. "There isn't an approach to Palenque where we could go unnoticed. But that's why you're here, isn't it, Wayfarer?"

Wayland Smith arched an eyebrow and ran a hand over his full beard.

"Follow me."

With that, he raised his fox-headed cane and opened a path through the Veil. For the second time in as many days, their strange quintet crossed through into the ordinary world.

On the other side, Blue Jay spun around, staring in every direction, eyes wide in confusion.

"It's exactly the same."

And it was. The jungle, the trees, the insects.

"What the hell's this?" Grin demanded. The bogie rounded on Smith, staring up at him with a warning in his eyes. "We haven't gone anywhere."

Li tapped the tiger on its shoulder and it lowered its flaming head so that the Guardian of Fire could reach down and touch the ground. He felt the dirt between two burning fingers.

"Actually, we have. This is the human world," Li said, looking around at them with those eerie, furnace eyes.

Smith said nothing. He turned and continued southeast through the jungle. They all followed, moving more slowly and warily now. Soon, however, they emerged from the trees and found themselves gazing out across a breathtaking vista. There were mountains in the distance, and hundreds of miles of rain forest.

But twenty yards ahead, they found themselves at the edge

of a cliff, staring down at an ancient ruin. All but two or three small structures were unrecognizable as buildings. Walls were little more than strewn stone and earth. But it was clear—once, this had been a city.

"What is it?" Blue Jay asked. "Incan? Mayan?"

"Atlantean," Smith said.

The trickster stared at him. "What?"

The old wanderer actually smiled. "They had ambassadors in ancient days as well, my friend. This was a colony. Before they became treacherous and were driven from the world."

Then he turned his back again. When he began to descend the long slope, where indents in the face of the mountain showed that once there might have been caves, they had little choice but to follow.

Smith led them to the nearest of the three remaining structures and through the arch that might once have been a door before more than a thousand years of erosion had been at work.

There was no exit.

Cheval's green dress swayed around her as she entered, the last of them to follow. Grin rested, apelike, on his fists. Li knelt to whisper to the burning tiger and then slowly reached out his hands and reabsorbed the creature's flames into himself.

Slowly, they all stared at Smith.

"Well?" Blue Jay asked. "What next?"

"Now you cross over."

"Us? What about you?" the trickster asked, suspicion flaring in his mind.

"I've told you from the beginning I wouldn't be going with you. Nothing has changed. Your infiltration begins now. If you are fortunate, and as clever as I think you are, you will return with the Bascombes."

Grin snorted. "Is that supposed to cheer us up?"

Wayland Smith looked at him, thunder in his ancient eyes. "No."

For a moment, they were all quiet.

Li was the first to raise his hand and pull at the fabric of the world, opening a passage for himself through the Veil. He stepped out of the realm of the ordinary, and back into legend.

Blue Jay cast one final, doubtful glance at Smith, and then went through after him.

The sun had crept nearly to the horizon, with dusk less than an hour away, when Damia Beck heard the shrill whistle of her advance scout. She spurred her horse forward and raced along beside the infantry soldiers in her command. At the outset of the war, only weeks before, she'd begun with two cavalry regiments under her. King Hunyadi had hesitated to part with Damia, but had recognized that she would be more use to him in the field. With the assassination of one of his commanders, the king had given her command of a company of infantry as well. Now, after her performance in the Battle of Cliffordville, the king had transferred an additional three companies to her control, making her the only captain in the history of the King's Guard ever to be made commander of an entire battalion of the Euphrasian army—one thousand men.

Some of her fellow commanders, particularly Maggiore and Boudreau, had made their disdain for her promotion clear. Others had welcomed her. Sakai and Alborg had gone so far as to salute her. And then they had all gone off to war. Word had come that Maggiore had already been slain by some kind of Yucatazcan monstrosity. Despite the way he had treated her, she regretted his passing. He had been a capable commander.

In addition to her original two cavalry regiments, Damia had a platoon of legendary warriors taking orders from her. There were five ogres who had come down from the northlands, a storm spirit called Howlaa, a trio of Naga archers, a Japanese oni called Gaki, whose red skin and horns would have given him a demonic air even if he did not have the head of an ox and a hideous third eye in the center of his forehead.

The last of the legendary platoon was an ancient, twisted-looking Englishman with ruddy cheeks called Old Roger. His legend had something to do with apples, and from what she understood, he'd been one of the Harvest gods, once upon a time. He had since fallen out of their good graces. Blue Jay had told her that the Harvest gods would fight the Atlantean conspiracy, but thus far, poor Old Roger was all she had seen of them. What help he might be in battle she could not say, but she appreciated his loyalty.

How many of them might be Borderkind, she did not know. The distinction between the legendary who were anchored on this side of the Veil and the Borderkind was mostly lost on her. Oh, she knew the difference, but not on sight. To most of the Lost Ones—both newcomers and those like Damia who had descended from humans who'd crossed the Veil in centuries past—there were humans and nonhumans. Whether they could or couldn't cross the Veil was an issue that concerned only the legendary, because the Lost Ones could never go home.

A smile touched her lips as she rode past the troops. She had been near the back when the scout's whistle had reached her. Dust swirled up from the dirt road, raised by the tramping boots of her soldiers. She wiped grit from her eyes and cleared her throat.

Home. What a strange way for her to think about a place she had never been—never seen. Neither had her mother, or her mother before her. Damia descended from a Nubian mother and a Euphrasian father, but they themselves had ancestors who had crossed the Veil from Africa and from America. Her mother's people had been Sahelian and her father's Sioux, many generations ago.

Yet she still thought of the human world as home.

They all did. How could they not, when the legendary never called them anything but the Lost?

Which made her wonder if what everyone was saying about Oliver and Collette Bascombe was true. Were they Legend-Born? Would they lead the Lost Ones home? And if they could, would she want to go?

Again, she cleared the dust from her throat. Men and women looked up from the ranks as she went by and some saluted, though it certainly wasn't required when the commander was merely riding past. They were courageous and loyal, and she knew they would fight to the death. The rest of Euphrasia might not yet believe that an Atlantean conspiracy was behind the breaking of the Truce and the war between the Two Kingdoms, but the army had no doubt.

King Hunyadi had declared it.

Blind obedience to any leader was unhealthy, but Hunyadi had earned it from them, and from her.

The only thing missing now was Blue Jay. Damia had grown up fighting. Her mother and father had both been soldiers, loyal to Drago Hunyadi, the grandfather of the present king. Love had always been a secondary concern to her. She had taken men into her bed, but never her heart. It had never even occurred to her that a man could set up residence there, or that his essence could fill her so completely. Even had she imagined it, she would never have thought that she could love a legend. And a Borderkind, no less.

In a matter of weeks, Blue Jay had stripped away all of the presumptions she had ever made about her own capacity for emotion. They had fought side by side, arguing all the while, in the moments following the assassination of Commander Kharkov and the attempted assassination of the king himself. And Damia had found herself catching her breath every time she looked at the trickster. His eyes danced when they looked at her, sparkling with mischief.

Tricksters were known for their cunning, she told herself. For their deceit.

But she could sense no deceit in him on the night they had first kissed. The light in his eyes when she took him to her bed was no more than joy. She trusted him, in spite of all she had ever heard of tricksters.

Gods, how she wished he were here with her now. Not to fight alongside her—not because she felt she needed his help—but simply because she missed him.

Her horse began to slow and she spurred him on faster. The Oldwood was just ahead and, once they reached it, the horses would be able to rest a while.

Damia rode past three companies of infantry and both cavalry regiments. When she came abreast of the first line of cavalry she raised a hand. Her lieutenants did the same, calling orders back amongst the ranks, and the command rippled through all her gathered warriors. The platoon of legendary had been at the rear of the march all along, sometimes straying but always returning, watchful for ambush or spies.

Soon the rolling thunder of hooves and boots came to a stop. Lieutenant Fee, a grimly serious blond woman who led the Dawn Regiment, dismounted at the same time as Commander Beck. Damia handed the reins over to Fee and nodded as the lieutenant saluted.

They had come to a stop forty yards from where the road narrowed and disappeared into the cool, quiet shadows of the Oldwood, where the most ancient, most primitive, and most stubborn legends still lived wild.

Her scout, a swift-footed legend called Charles Grant, stood just out of reach of the last rays of sunlight. Dusk was now only perhaps forty minutes off, probably less.

"Hello, Charlie," Damia said as she approached, her hands in full view, her sword and guns banging against her hips, still sheathed. Charlie could be skittish.

He watched her guns warily. There were very few guns in Euphrasia. They were the sort of thing the Veil tended to screen out, somehow. From all she had heard of the ordinary world, Damia had long since figured out that there were a lot of things the Veil kept out, even when Lost Ones wandered in.

"Charlie?" she ventured.

The fleet-flooted boy gave a low toot on his whistle. That instrument—carved of bone—was the only method of communication she had ever heard him use. She didn't know if he could talk, but no one she had ever asked had heard his voice.

"Is he there?" she asked.

The boy nodded.

"Waiting for me?"

Charlie gave the tiniest blow of his whistle, looking out of the corner of his eye as though he was afraid the forest itself would come creeping after him.

"All right," Damia said, glancing up to study the darkness of the road through the Oldwood and the thickness of the forest on either side. The master of the forest had answered her summons. Now she had to go and speak with him. "Go and wait with—"

A breeze rustled her black cloak.

Commander Beck blinked when she realized that Charlie Grant was gone. Arching an eyebrow she turned to see the boy already standing with Lieutenant Fee, running a hand along the flank of her horse.

Taking a deep breath, Damia entered the Oldwood, wondering if she would ever come out.

usic played low on the radio in Jackson Norris's car. Sara had ridden with the sheriff several times since coming back to Maine, and she'd never gotten used to that. Sure, his police radio squawked, but there was nearly always music playing as well. In the movies and on TV, the cops never had their regular radios on.

Sting's song "Fields of Gold," began. The irony was there, in the back of her mind, but she had to concentrate for a second before she dredged it up. Right—Sting had been the front man for the classic rock group the Police. *There you go. Irony.*

Sara earned strange looks whenever she got out of the car with its cop paint job and the light bar on the top, never mind the Wessex County Sheriff's Department logo on the doors. But at least she wasn't riding in the back in cuffs.

Not that she gave a shit what people in Kitteridge, Maine, thought.

She didn't care about much, these days.

"You know you don't have to go back to Atlanta," Sheriff Norris told her, his tone gentle.

"You know I do, Jackson."

A burst of static came from the police radio.

"I can't just hibernate in that little house, waiting for my father to come back. I'll go insane. How long do I wait? What if he never—"

Sara couldn't finish. Her throat closed up and she felt her face flush. Out of the corner of her eye, she saw the sheriff looking at her. After a moment he returned his focus to the road. It had been warm the week before—unseasonably warm for Maine, though it was late winter. Today the sun still shone, but the cold was back. The snow had all melted, but somehow that made it worse, icy wind whipping across frozen tundra. It got down into her bones.

Atlanta would be beautiful by now. Soon, the whole city would blossom.

She had to go home.

"You could be a photographer up here, you know," the sheriff said.

"For who, *Downeast* magazine? I don't think they're looking for a fashion photographer."

Sheriff Norris smiled. "Who knows? You could meet a guy . . ."

He let the words trail off, having brought the topic up several times over the past few months, the way an uncle might. Sheriff Norris had always been a sort of uncle to her. A sweet man, but he had never been that quick on the uptake. Since subtlety didn't work, she decided it was time for the direct approach.

"Jackson?"

The sheriff glanced at her. "Yeah?"

Sara waved at him. "See me? Over here? Gay. I like girls."

He blinked. To his credit, he hid his astonishment well. The thought had never even occurred to him.

"Oh," he said after a moment. "Well, then, you've got a hell of a lot better chance of meeting someone nice in Atlanta than up here."

With a laugh, she drew herself across the front seat and kissed his slightly stubbled cheek.

"Thank you," she said.

"For what?"

"For being a good friend to me and to my father."

A sadness came over the sheriff then. He felt at least partially responsible for Ted Halliwell's disappearance and it weighed on him.

"You really have to go, huh?"

"I really do."

They rode in silence for a while, tires crunching on sand left over from the snowmelt.

After years away from Maine, she had come home when word had reached her of her father's disappearance. Yet months had passed without any sign of his fate or clue as to how he'd vanished in the first place. She had flown to Bangor just before Christmas, her schedule clear until after the first of the year. When she called her clients—most of them advertising and fashion people—during the first week of January and explained her situation, they had all been understanding. They didn't want to use another photographer, but they would make do until she was back in town.

Now it was the middle of March, and her phone had been ringing for weeks. It wouldn't do to abandon her clients so long that some fell so much in love with her replacements that they abandoned her. That was pretty much what had happened in all of her relationships—she'd gone off on some assignment and come home to find her latest girlfriend had moved on.

But she had to earn money to live, and maybe a return to

Atlanta and her friends and her routine would help to stave off her sorrow.

Before she went, however, she had asked Sheriff Norris to arrange a meeting for her.

He signaled for a left and then took the turn, following driving regulations without even thinking about it. The heater whirred, though it wasn't very effective, and Sara huddled deeper into her thick winter coat. The trip to Freeport had been one of many distractions she had engineered in the past two months. None of them had been terribly effective.

Sting stopped singing and an ad for the local television news came on. The DJ hadn't identified the song. Sara could remember when they had always told you what song you had heard and never could understand why they stopped doing that. If you liked it and wanted to go buy the CD—or if you wanted to download it—how were you supposed to know what it was called?

Sheriff Norris pulled into the driveway of a beautiful home, the kind of place she always wished she could live but knew she never would. Sara made an excellent living as a photographer. Maybe one day she'd even have enough money to think she was rich. But she didn't think she was destined for a place like this.

The car went silent. She blinked and looked over to see the sheriff taking the key from the ignition.

"You all right?" he asked.

Sara smiled. "If we wait for that, I'll be sitting in this car the rest of my life."

She popped open the door, shut it behind her, and led the way up the walk toward the front door. The sheriff had to hurry to catch up. On the steps, Sara reached out to ring the doorbell, but before she could, the door opened.

The woman who stood inside had been beautiful once. In some ways, she still was. But despite the elegance of her clothes—a counterpoint to the blue jeans, boots, and bone-white turtleneck Sara wore under her coat—she looked faded, like dried flowers or antique furniture. Her lips were folded in a tight line, so that when she blinked and smiled, she looked as though the act pained her.

"You must be Sara," Mrs. Whitney said. "Please, come in. You too, Jackson. It's freezing out there, and I've made hot cocoa."

"Thank you," Sara replied, stepping inside. "That sounds perfect for a day like today."

The sheriff followed her in and, while Mrs. Whitney closed the door behind them, they took off their coats. She hung them in a closet so as not to mar the immaculate house. It looked more like a museum than anything else.

"I'm afraid that my husband was called away at the last moment to meet with a client," the woman said. "So it will just be the three of us."

Sara glanced at the sheriff, who didn't seem at all surprised. It was Saturday morning. She suspected that Julianna Whitney's father simply didn't want to talk to a stranger about his vanished daughter. Though Sara did not like the pretense this forced on Mrs. Whitney—the poor woman shouldn't have to lie for her husband—she understood.

"That's all right. We won't take up too much of your time, anyway," Sheriff Norris said.

"Oh, please," Mrs. Whitney said, waving away his concern. "Time is all I have, these days."

She brought out a tray with a pot of cocoa and a plate of shortbread cookies. Sara had never tasted better hot chocolate. It had to have been made from scratch and she let it warm her. Very little could.

When they had all sipped at the cocoa for a few minutes and the sheriff was on his third shortbread cookie—this strange pantomime of civilized behavior a soothing mask over their grief—Mrs. Whitney fixed Sara with her gaze.

"I'm glad of the company," she said. "But I think perhaps it's time for you to tell me what it was you wanted to talk about."

Sara managed a smile as she set down her cup. "More than anything, I just wanted to meet you. I'm...well, I'm making plans to go back to Atlanta soon. That's where I live. I don't think there's anything else I can do here, and I have responsibilities."

"Of course you do," Mrs. Whitney said kindly, but there was a kind of sad envy in her expression, as though she wished that she too had responsibilities that would take her away from this place and the specter of her daughter's disappearance.

As she tried to continue, Sara's breath hitched and she paused, fighting not to cry.

Mrs. Whitney reached out and laid a hand over hers. Whatever differences were between them—age, social status— none of it mattered. As of last December, they were now far more alike than they were different.

Sara nodded, though the woman had said nothing.

"I just thought maybe you could tell me a little about Julianna," she said, studying Mrs. Whitney. She gnawed her bottom lip a moment, then shrugged and gave a soft laugh. "I guess I thought if I knew her, knew who she was, I mean, then I'd feel like maybe my dad wasn't out there alone. Wherever he is."

Julianna's mother put a hand across her heart. Her eyes were moist.

"I think that's a lovely idea."

Jackson Norris sat and sipped cocoa and ate shortbread cookies while the two women talked. They shared stories about Julianna, and about Sara's father, and before they knew it more than an hour had passed.

Sara saw the clock and sighed.

"We should go. I really wanted the sheriff here to introduce us, but I hate to have taken so much of your time, and his."

"Oh, Jackson doesn't mind," Mrs. Whitney said. "Do you, sheriff?"

"Not at all," he said. But Sara knew that the man had other

things to do. There were politics involved in his position, but there was police work as well.

"Still, we should go."

Mrs. Whitney stood up with them and fetched their coats. As the sheriff put his on, the woman's hands fidgeted.

"I presume there's nothing new, Jackson?" she said.

Sheriff Norris zipped his coat. "It's on my mind every day, Margaret. And it will be until I find them."

The woman nodded, and then a frown creased her brow.

Sara noticed. "What is it, Mrs. Whitney?"

One hand fluttered in front of her. "Nothing, I'm sure. It's just that I've been thinking lately about Friedle."

"Who?" Sara asked, turning to the sheriff.

"Marc Friedle," he replied. "He was the Bascombes' household manager; basically, the butler, valet, driver, and everything else in one. He hired and fired gardeners, cooks, painters, that sort of thing."

The sheriff looked at Mrs. Whitney. "Margaret, you know I looked into Friedle. We have no reason to suspect him of anything. His fingerprints were everywhere, but he practically lived in the house. There's no evidence he had anything to do with Max Bascombe's death or the disappearances of Max's kids."

The woman nodded. "I'm sure you're right. But more and more, lately, I've been thinking about him, and about how odd it seems to me that he rushed out of Kitteridge so quickly when Max Bascombe was killed. Oliver and Collette had vanished, and everyone was searching for them frantically. But Friedle was the manager of the house. It was his responsibility, and he left so fast it was almost like he was the one person who never expected them to come back."

Sara turned toward Sheriff Norris. A dark twist of suspicion began to tighten in her chest and she knew the moment she saw the sheriff's brows knit together that he had the very same feeling.

It seemed her return to Atlanta might be delayed after all.

Halliwell felt the anger burning inside the Sandman. The creature had no veins through which poison might flow, but the anger churned in him just the same. It was part of the storm of his essence, just as Halliwell himself had become part of the Sandman. He was integral to the creeping, murderous thing, and its iniquity stained his soul. The Dustman was still there as well, a grave voice rising up from within Halliwell's own mind like an echo down a canyon or a conscience long subdued.

Subdued, Halliwell thought. *Is that it? Have I been subdued?*

The question rankled. He had never been subdued in his life. Oh, he'd taken orders from superior officers and employers, certainly. But he had never kept silent when the situation called for someone to speak up. He wondered if that had changed. Between discretion and cowardice, where did one draw the line?

At murder, his conscience told him. Or perhaps it was the voice of the Dustman, the monster's grim, less savage brother. *One draws the goddamn line at murder—at the bloodthirsty mutilation of children.*

Of course. Such a thing should not even have had to be considered. What kind of man would hesitate to agree with such an assertion?

But he was adrift within the Sandman's essence and powerless. Briefly, when he had realized his fate, Halliwell hoped that perhaps he would be the poison that would infect and cripple the monster. But the Sandman didn't seem even to notice his presence, or that of the Dustman.

It was the worst horror imaginable. It was Halliwell's own poison, twisting his heart with hatred and his mind with hopelessness. He had heard the screams of the Sandman's victims and seen the terror in their eyes—seen the monster reflected in the mirror of children's eyes, just before he plucked them out and placed them between his teeth.

The nightmare had no end. He could not command the

hands that murdered or the black lips that pulled back in a leer. In every way that mattered, he was the Sandman. The atrocities were not within his control, but he suffered through each moment, mind screaming in silence.

Lemon-yellow eyes glanced upward at the sky. The moon was a sliver, the heavens sable black. The stars seemed withdrawn, as though they dared not come too close to the world of the legendary in these ugly days. The monster had learned that Oliver Bascombe was being held in the dungeon at the king's palace in Palenque. Bascombe wasn't going anywhere, so he would kill Kitsune first. He would shred the fox-woman's flesh, just as soon as he found her.

A rasp accompanied the Sandman as he slipped through the nighttime streets. The village slept, but fitfully. Spectral, little more than a wraith, he moved toward a building whose first floor was a candy shop. A soft glow illuminated the eyebrow windows set into the gables of the roof—an attic room, a candle still burning.

There would be children here.

Halliwell felt the thrill run through the Sandman, so much like lust. Were those terrible lemon eyes his own, he would weep.

The Sandman clambered up the side of the shop as though carried by the wind. His cloak billowed around him and then he collapsed into a flurry of sand, slipping through the open window. Once within, the sand skittered across the wood floor and the small throw rug at the center of the room. Grain by grain, he reconstructed himself, a shell that now housed three beings.

A small boy slept beneath a freshly laundered blanket. His face was so beautiful in repose, cheeks flushed, lips open slightly. His brown hair was tousled and wild on his pillow. Lovely, heartbreaking innocence.

Halliwell was sickened to realize that the Sandman saw the same beauty in that innocence. He tried to grasp at any straw of hope that his imagination could muster. The child was sleeping. The legend of the Sandman spoke of him punishing only those young ones who were still awake when he arrived, claiming their eyes in return for their insolence.

But the monster had taken sleeping victims before. Simple enough to torture them to screaming wakefulness.

In a single stride, the Sandman stood beside the bed and reached long, narrow talons down to slowly draw back the covers. The blanket smelled of lavender soap.

The sleeping boy sighed and his brow creased, troubled, until he turned onto his side and pulled his knees up to his chest, his body aware of the missing blanket.

The Sandman went still. Awareness prickled. Somehow, he had heard Halliwell scream. Or felt it. Inside the monster, Halliwell could not move. His soul had gone rigid with fear unlike anything he had ever known—a terrible denial that would drive him fleeing into the darkened streets if only he had legs with which to run. Shame cloaked him, now, but he drew it tightly around himself as though it might shield him.

This was death and dream and anguish. How could he not flee?

After a moment, the Sandman moved once more, attention no longer turned inward. With the relief and release Halliwell felt there came bitter fury both at the monster and at himself.

This had to stop.

Then the voice, welling up from the depths of their shared psyche. *Fool,* said the Dustman. *You have told him we are here.*

The anger stirred in Halliwell again. *Who the hell are you to judge? What have you done but hide?*

For a moment, he thought the Dustman had gone. The terror that struck him at the idea that he might be trapped within the monster alone was almost worse than the attention of the Sandman. But then he spoke again. Halliwell could not see him—he saw only through the lemon eyes of the monster—

but he could feel the Dustman coming closer and his memory supplied an image of the legend—the old London gent with bowler hat and thick mustache, the collar of his greatcoat turned up, the gray dust and dirt texture of his clothes and flesh identical.

Shut your gob and listen, the Dustman whispered in Halliwell's mind. *Come down into the dust with me, Detective. It's time we had a chat.*

The Sandman snatched the little boy from his bed, dangling the child by one arm. The boy's eyes snapped open and grew wide with terror. He opened his mouth in a shriek, legs twisting and kicking as he tried to pull himself loose from the Sandman's grip. The wraith only held him more tightly, and the child cried out in pain.

The bedroom door crashed open. The father stood silhouetted in the doorway, the mother in the hall behind him, both frantic with worry.

Then they saw the monster that held their son. The mother screamed. The father backed up a step, grabbed hold of the doorframe to steady himself.

Come, Detective, the Dustman whispered. *Nothing you can do for them. Not yet. Turn away.*

I can't.

Turn away. The voice was insistent.

All along, Halliwell had been afraid that if he allowed his tenuous hold on the world—his view through the Sandman's eyes—to go dark, he would be adrift forever in the swirl of darkness in the creature's venomous heart. But the Dustman beckoned him deeper.

In the child's bedroom, the father demanded that the Sandman release the boy. The monster's laugh skittered along the floor like errant grains of sand. The mother rushed past her husband, hands raised, fingers hooked into claws to save her son. The Sandman let her come and, as her fingers dug furrows into him, covered her face with his free hand. Her scream was muffled. Sand filled her throat. His hand expanded, covering her face, scraping . . . eroding.

When he dropped his hand, the mother's face had been scoured away, leaving only bloody muscle, gleaming bone, and screams. The monster batted her aside and held up the struggling boy as his prize.

"What do you want?" the father screamed.

The Sandman crouched low, holding the boy to him as though the child were precious.

"There is a secret place nearby," the monster rasped. "A haven for Lost Ones and old legends. Twillig's Gorge, they call it. I would know where it is."

The father only gaped in despair and confusion.

"You've heard of it?" the Sandman growled.

"Yes. Of course," the man said, desperate, trying to ignore the whimpers from his wife, trying to keep his son alive. "But I don't know where it is."

The Sandman narrowed his lemon eyes.

Halliwell tried to look away. The Dustman called to him.

The monster's rasp was barely louder than the scratch of sand upon the floor as the breeze rose again.

"Pity," the monster said. "Now I will have to ask another father. Another mother."

Hopeless, now, Halliwell surrendered. He released his hold upon the world and let his spirit drift down into the maelstrom of the Sandman's heart, where the Dustman whispered to him of will and grit and bone.

The gods of wine and depravity lived in bloated torpor in the ruined cellar of a palazzo in the Latin Quarter. The openings that led down beneath the ruin were treacherous. Grape vines—half withered—had grown over some of the shattered columns and fallen arches and stone blocks of the palazzo.

"Here?" Kitsune asked.

The sky had cleared and the sun beat down on the stones and made the grape leaves curl on the vines. Her copper-red fur was a part of her, but it felt too warm now, too close. Still, she would not remove it. To do so would make her feel less the fox and more human, and she was feeling too damnably human as it was.

She hated the Atlanteans and the Myth Hunters for what they had begun. She wished she had never met Oliver Bascombe. More than anything, she wished she could tear out the love in her heart.

No. No more thinking about Oliver.

Easier said than done, however. Particularly when all of her efforts now sprang from having known him. She would like to think that she might have stood and fought against the enemies that would destroy her and her kin—that would shatter the Two Kingdoms and take down fair and wise monarchs—even if she had not met him. But Kitsune could not have said that with any certainty, and this troubled her most of all.

"Here?" she repeated, turning to Lycaon.

Not even the old gods, it seemed, could escape time.

"So much for Olympus," Lycaon said, his voice a growl. He did not look at Kitsune, or at Coyote, who climbed across the rocks, trying to keep up with them.

Kitsune stared at the opening that Lycaon expected them to climb into. "There must be others whose circumstances are less dire."

"None who'd welcome me, or see you because I asked," the monster replied.

"Cousin," Coyote began.

Kitsune silenced him with a look. He sighed and came to join her in the rubble. With a glance back at Lycaon, they started down. A slab of stone shifted under her feet. If not for her natural agility, Kitsune would have tumbled into the hole.

Just a few steps lower, however, they found the original

stairs that led to the wine cellar. The stink of fermenting grapes rose from below, powerful enough that the small hairs on the back of her neck rose and she was forced to breathe through her mouth. Drunken laughter rippled up from below.

Before she had even seen them, she knew the wine gods would not join them in their campaign against the invaders.

At the bottom of the stairs she found a heavy wooden door, but it hung open. She glanced back at Coyote. In the gloom, his eyes gleamed with a hint of red and gold. He nodded, urging her onward. Beyond him, Lycaon hesitated. Kitsune wondered if he would betray them, but the beast would not have bothered to rouse himself from his kitchen just to lead them into trouble. No, that was the trickster's nature, not the monster's.

Pushing the black velvet curtain of her hair away from her eyes, she knocked loudly, but there was no reply.

"Just go in," Coyote said.

His impatience seemed to free something inside of her, so Kitsune pushed open the heavy door and stepped through.

A dozen steps took them down into a cavernous underground chamber whose walls were lined with racks and old wooden casks. Many of them had shattered or rotted away, and the dirt floor of the cellar was muddy with old wine.

Fresh grapes grew in huge quantities in the dark, far corner of the cellar, as though they could survive in that sunless hole. They did survive, of course; the wine gods made sure of that. Blocks of stone that had once been a part of the palazzo upstairs had been brought down to construct a dais in the center of the chamber. Upon the dais, on filthy velvet tapestries that might once have been art, the two gods sprawled. Each must easily have been seven or eight feet tall when standing, but they looked as though they had not bothered to climb to their feet in some time. Bacchus and Dionysus, of the Roman and Greek pantheons, respectively, looked very little like gods of any age or culture.

They were naked and dirty, their beards overgrown tangles of gray. One of the stinking gods sniffed the air, taking in the new scents that had entered the cellar, and then sat up. When he saw their visitors, he grinned.

"What have we here, brother Bacchus?" he said, slurring his words. "A pretty thing come to the party. Strip off your garments, girl, and make your offering."

Kitsune blinked. Then, unable to help herself, she laughed. At the sound, Dionysus gazed at her blearily. He seemed more confused than insulted. But Bacchus struggled to raise his bulk. He had a jug of wine in one hand and accidentally spilled it across his chest.

"Do you mock, girl?" Bacchus demanded. He sneered, but his head swayed with the muzzy numbness of the besotted.

Neither of the gods had even acknowledged the presence of Coyote or Lycaon. They were discarded deities, living in filth, and yet their arrogance remained. Perhaps it was all that had kept them alive.

"No, Lord Bacchus. I wouldn't dare. I have come on an issue of dire importance, with news that threatens all of Euphrasia, an insidious evil that will find its way even here, in this haven you have made."

Bacchus gazed doubtfully at her.

"We are gods, little fox, not merely legends. What might frighten the Lost or the legendary means nothing to us."

Kitsune hesitated. She would have loved to correct him, to tell him that most of the beings that had once been gods were no more powerful, and sometimes far less so, than many of the legends she had met.

"Lord Bacchus," Coyote interjected, perhaps sensing her pique, "Kitsune speaks the truth. Atlantis has betrayed the Two Kingdoms. They've coerced and deceived Yucatazca and murdered its king. War has begun. Invaders swarm into Euphrasia. If the races of Euphrasia don't come together now, it will be too late."

The Roman god belched loudly. Burgundy spittle ran down his chin.

"Get out," Bacchus sighed.

"You're not listening," Kitsune growled. "You can't just wait here to die."

Dionysus laughed. The Greek god had apparently not forgotten they were there after all. He glanced at Kitsune.

"Little one, we've been waiting to die for a thousand years. Until then, we pass the time. But perhaps some of our brothers and sisters will take a greater interest in survival. They've lived this long, after all. So many have scattered throughout the Two Kingdoms and beyond—far beyond—and twice their number have died. But there are still a few who might listen."

He glanced at Bacchus, as though for approval, but the other god ignored them.

"Lycaon," Dionysus said.

The monster flinched. Strange to see the beast, the cannibal, so cowed. "Yes, Lord Dionysus?"

"You brought them?"

Lycaon lowered his head. "Yes, lord."

"Good," Dionysus said. "Each morning, go to Lycaon's Kitchen and wait. If any from our pantheons wish to hear what you have to say, they will find you there."

"Wait?" Coyote asked, taking a step toward the dais. "For how long?"

Dionysus laughed. "Until the gods deign to see you."

CHAPTER 6

ollette Bascombe lay on the thin mattress that was all she and Julianna had by way of comfort in their cell. It stank and there were stains on it that she did not wish to consider, but still she was grateful. When she thought of a dungeon, she imagined sleeping on cold stone. That would have been far worse. Yet even that would not have been as terrible as her captivity in the Sandman's castle, with the roasting sun above during the day and the creeping chill after dark.

Had they taken the mat away, she would have survived. But Collette was glad to have it, both for her own sake and for Julianna's. Her friend—and her brother's fiancée—had never been much afraid of anything in her life. But during the nights that had passed since their attempt to reach Frost, Julianna shivered with the cold and, perhaps, with fear that they would never leave those stone cells again. They'd had their chance at escape, and failed.

There had been periods of silence and some of tears. Conversations had been whispered, particularly those held across the corridor with Oliver. They were wary of being over-heard. Not that they had developed any real plan, but the guards were cautious, now. What else could they do but wither here and wait to die?

Collette did not share these thoughts with her brother or with Julianna, but she knew her friend could see the doubt in her eyes.

The thought made her shiver. Julianna huddled close to her on the mat, sharing warmth. Collette wondered if she was awake or if the gesture was instinctive. She did not turn to find out. Sleep was a precious commodity recently, and if Julianna had managed it, Collette did not want to wake her.

Instead she lay there, trying to breathe through her mouth to avoid the stink. The bruises she had received from the guards were healing, but there was still an ache in her side where she feared their kicks had cracked her ribs. They would heal as well, but more slowly. The swelling on her face had gone down, but the flesh was still tender and Julianna had confirmed that her jaw still had a greenish-yellow hue. Her blood had stained the mat, but it had long since dried.

Curled on her side, she let her right hand trail off the edge of the mat. Her ragged fingernails traced the lines of grout be-tween the stones in the floor. In the dark, she could not see them, but she could feel the difference in texture between the smoothness of the stone and the rough mortar.

Then her fingernail scraped something up off of the mortar groove between two stones.

In the dark, Collette frowned. She ran the ball of her finger over the same spot and felt the loose grit again. With her nail, she dug between the stones and the grout came away, not in chunks but in a soft powder, as though whatever adhesive qual-ity it had once had no longer existed.

A tremor went through her.

She sat up, rubbing the grit from her finger with the tip of her thumb. In the dark, she bent forward and tried to see the section of floor she had been scraping. Her fingers ran over the stones and the grooves again. She found the place where she had done her small excavation and brushed away the loose powder. Once more she tried to dig between the stones.

Now, though, nothing happened.

"Shit," she whispered, some of the hope that had begun to rise in her slipping away. Collette tried the grooves between the other stones in the floor of the cell, but found only a few grains of loose grit, normal erosion.

"What is it?"

With a sigh, she turned to regard Julianna. In the dark, all she could see was the outline of the woman sitting up on the mat. Some tiny bit of illumination must have filtered in from the corridor, because Julianna's eyes had a wet gleam.

"I'm sorry if I woke you," Collette said.

"I wasn't really sleeping. What's wrong?"

Collette gnawed her lip for a moment, wondering if she should say anything. Then she forged ahead.

"Do you remember when I told you about escaping from that pit the Sandman kept me in? What I did with the sand?"

She could still remember the way her fingers had dug into the walls. One moment they'd felt like concrete, but then they'd given way under her touch and she had been able to create handholds and footholds and climb out. Once before that and once after she had dug right through the walls of the sand-castle.

"Of course," Julianna said. "You and Oliver figured it had to do with your mother being Borderkind."

"Melisande," Collette replied. Speaking her mother's real name—if, indeed, that legendary creature had been their mother—still felt strange to her.

"That's how you two were able to destroy those sand-things so easily, and when you hurt the Sandman—"

"Yeah. Exactly," Collette interrupted. "It was like we could undo the things the Sandman had built. Unmake them."

"Unravel . . ." Julianna said.

In the dark, Collette reached out to take her hand, afraid to hope. "I was just lying here, scraping my fingers on the floor, and I dug up some of the stuff between the stones. It might've just been loose. Probably that's what it was, since I tried again and now it's all pretty solid. But for a second, it felt the way it had at the sandcastle . . . like I was just, what did you say? Like I was unraveling it, somehow."

Julianna squeezed her fingers and started to stand, pulling Collette to her feet.

"What are you doing?"

"You've got to tell Oliver."

Collette hesitated. "It isn't working, though. It's probably just loose mortar."

"What if it's not?"

The question echoed in her mind. "This isn't the first time I've thought about it, Jules. Ever since we ended up here, I've been thinking about the time I spent down in that pit. I've tried it. Maybe Oliver and I are half-legend and maybe we're not, but we don't have any special magic in us. We're not myths. We're people."

"But you weren't thinking about it this time, were you? You're hurt and exhausted, like you were then. It just happened, like before."

Collette took a breath, then nodded. "Maybe."

Julianna pulled her toward the door of the cell. Collette put her hands against the wood and stood on the tips of her toes to see through the metal window grate.

"Hey," she whispered. "You awake?"

A tiny bit of light filtered down the corridor from the torches that must have been burning up the stairs where the guards stood sentry. It gave her enough illumination to make out the door to her brother's cell.

His voice came from the darkness within.

"Who can sleep with you two gossiping over there?"

Collette smiled. Still, after all they'd been through, her little brother could tease her. Maybe there was hope after all. She and Julianna had been whispering, but Oliver had overheard them. That meant he had been unable to sleep as well.

"You heard?"

"Yeah."

"What do you think?" Julianna asked.

In the dark, behind that door, Oliver hesitated. Collette felt the regret coming from him, even with the space between them, and suddenly she knew what he was going to say.

"You've been trying too," she whispered across the corridor.

"Not recently. Not much," Oliver replied. "But I did when we were first thrown in here. How could I not, after what you did, Coll? I tried a million times to loosen the stones around the door or the window. No such luck."

Collette came down off of her toes and rested her forehead against the door. She ran her hands over the wood and traced the frame with her fingers. Closing her eyes, she tried to remember the feel of the mortar giving way, the grit of that soft powder.

Her eyes opened.

"Oliver?" she said, raising her voice so it wouldn't be as muffled by the door.

"Yeah?"

Collette looked at Julianna. In the slight illumination that came through the grate in the door, she saw her friend's determined expression.

"Keep trying," Collette said. "It wasn't my imagination."

"This was a mistake," Blue Jay said as he and Cheval threaded their way along a narrow, curving alley alive with music and chatter and the drunken stumblings of the citizens of Palenque.

Cheval took his hand and leaned into him, smiling as though they were lovers. Blue Jay grinned. The kelpy might be a beast in truth, but her human mask was exquisite and sensual.

"What are you talking about?" she asked.

"Taking you with me," he replied, and felt her stiffen at the insult. "Your beauty is far too conspicuous. You draw attention when what we wish is to pass unnoticed."

Cheval squeezed his hand. Her touch was cold. "I will choose to take that as a compliment," she said. "And I shall endeavor to be uglier."

The trickster couldn't help laughing. "That would be helpful."

His good humor faded almost instantly, however. Cheval had never shown the slightest romantic interest in him, but he did not want her to think he was flirting. For only the second time in his ageless existence, he had taken responsibility for another's heart. He would do nothing to hurt Damia Beck.

Other troubles loomed larger, in any case. The day before, at Smith's instruction, they had stepped blindly through the Veil having only his assurance that they would emerge somewhere safe from prying eyes. He had been as good as his word. They had arrived in Palenque in an apartment on the second floor of a building that overlooked one of the narrow streets of the labyrinthine inner city.

But were there allies here in Palenque, or only enemies?

It was a question he would find an answer to while they found a way to free the Bascombes and Julianna Whitney from the palace dungeon.

But their work had just begun, and already he believed he had made a mistake. Bringing Cheval along truly had been an error. They had left Li and Grin back in the apartment because they could not pass as humans and their appearance might lead to trouble. If they were identified as Euphrasian Borderkind, someone would report their presence, and Blue Jay was determined that there would be no blood spilled until the moment of his choosing.

He had removed the feathers from his hair and tied it back. Within minutes of his first excursion from the apartment he had persuaded two street gamblers to part with their billfolds and purchased a colorful serape for himself and a peasant dress for Cheval. The gossamer gowns she favored would not do. But even in that ragged dress, she still seemed far too beautiful to be one of the Lost Ones. One look at her, and a man would have to presume she was a goddess or a legend.

Foolish Jay, the trickster thought now, as he steered them both through the busy street.

Not all of Palenque was alive like this. When last they had walked these streets, the whole center of the city had been undulating with life, the air filled with the aromas of alcohol and tobacco. From what Blue Jay and Cheval had seen, the war had dimmed the spirits of the Yucatazcans somewhat. Shutters were drawn. Some doors bore a strange, batlike symbol painted upon them in red, representing mourning for sons and daughters killed in battle.

Yet here, on Calle Capiango, it seemed the laughter had never stopped. Perhaps this was the place where Palenqueians came to hide from their fears, or perhaps those who dined in the calle's restaurants and tavernas simply had no reason to fear.

A man stood on a street corner playing a guitar. His long hair was slick and his features dark and smoldering. Women who passed him let their eyes linger, hoping to get his attention, but he saw only his guitar.

Until Cheval walked by.

Damn it, Blue Jay thought.

He took her by the hand and hurried along the street. He bumped into a large man and apologized, but the man cursed at him. Blue Jay swore under his breath, scanning the street and the mouths of the small alleys around them.

At last, he saw what he'd been searching for. The alley seemed indistinct save for the small blue birds painted on the shutters of an apartment on the third, uppermost floor. He led Cheval to the corner as casually as possible, then ducked into the alley.

She grabbed his arm and spun him to face her. Her eyes seemed as silver as her hair. Cheval stared at him, her lips and cheeks flushed pink from the rushing of her pulse.

"What are we doing, exactly?"

"Meeting some old friends."

Cheval narrowed her eyes. "Old friends? I do not understand. We are supposed to infiltrate and recruit some assistance. If we had old friends here, surely we would begin with them."

"That's exactly the plan."

"But Smith said nothing about old friends."

Blue Jay smiled and pointed at himself. "Trickster, remember? I've been in contact with allies here in Palenque for weeks. The underground Smith wanted us to build—I started long before he asked. The Wayfarer may have my respect, but he does not have my trust. I don't think he's loyal to anyone but himself. That's fine, if we have the same goals. And maybe we do. But I didn't tell him all my secrets, and I'm damned sure he didn't tell me all of his."

"What secrets?" Cheval asked. Her eyes grew stormy. "Perhaps you do not trust Smith, but you had better trust me, monsieur. What old friends are we meeting?"

Blue Jay hesitated. He had kept secrets, certainly. Tricksters always did. But he remembered that Frost had kept secrets from Oliver and the trouble that had caused. Cheval might be volatile, but she had proven her loyalty as a friend.

"Sorry. I should've said—"

Above them, something scratched against the side of the building. Metal clanked softly. Out on the main street, Blue Jay would never have heard the sound, despite his acute senses. But there in the alley it was all too loud. He and Cheval turned as one to look up. In the moonlight, they saw a creature hanging from a windowsill by its tail. The thing had a body like a monkey but a canine head and snout with damp nose and bared teeth. The tip of its tail split into digits like fingers and it clung to the windowsill as though it had a hand there.

Cheval uttered a breathy French curse.

Blue Jay tensed, prepared for an attack.

The thing growled, but it didn't look at them. It stared back down the alley toward Calle Capiango. Blue Jay forced himself to tear his gaze from the little fiend to see what had caught its attention.

Two men stood in the mouth of the alley, even as a third stepped in behind them. They moved slowly toward him and Cheval, staring at her with hungry eyes. One carried a crude blade etched with arcane symbols. He gestured with it and snarled orders in a language that Blue Jay had heard before but did not understand. *Mayan,* he thought.

"What did he say?" the trickster asked.

Cheval moved nearer to him. She had been friends with Chorti for many years and had spoken his language.

"Do you really need me to translate? You were right—I draw the wrong attention."

Above them, the creature had gone silent, but Blue Jay could hear it shifting against the alley wall, perhaps preparing to spring. The three men formed a blockade and began to move nearer, cautious, glancing at Blue Jay.

"Tell them they should know better than to challenge a legend."

Cheval said something in Mayan and the man with the ceremonial dagger laughed and replied in a burst of staccato syllables.

"They like legends best of all, he says," Cheval translated, her voice tight. "The king is dead and the eyes of the authorities are all turned toward war. No one will notice what happens here."

Blue Jay smiled thinly, and without humor. That made it easier. He did not have to worry about whether or not these men survived to emerge from the alley. The trickster spread his arms and began the stiff, ritual steps of an ancient dance. The air at his sides blurred, tinting the darkness blue.

Cheval sniffed in disdain, glaring at the man with the dagger. The three Lost Ones did not even have the sense to be frightened. Blue Jay felt the presence of the creature above them keenly, wondering when it would attack, and why it would be aiding these men.

As if in answer, the creature growled and leaped from the wall. But it lunged not toward him or Cheval. The creature dropped down onto the ugly, unwashed Mayan. It barked loudly and growled, and the man screamed as it clutched at his head. He drew his dagger, but the creature lashed out with its tail, and the three fingers at its tip gripped his wrist, stopping the weapon. The man cried out at the strength of that strange hand, but he could do nothing. With a low growl, the thing forced the man's hand down until the dagger stabbed into the killer's own throat, twisting and tearing.

The man dropped to the ground, blood gouting. The creature leaped from his head, still brandishing the dagger at the end of its tail.

Cheval and Blue Jay could only stare.

The other two men cried out in fury and rushed at the Borderkind and their bizarre ally. Even as they did, crackling tendrils of mystic energy wrapped around them, lifted them off of their feet, and slammed them against opposite walls of the alley. The sickening sounds of bones breaking echoed around them.

At the mouth of the alley there stood a pair of familiar, cloaked figures whose gray skin and long knotted beards were almost identical to each other. Golden light still crackled around their fingers. When they moved deeper into the alley, the shadows seemed to slide away from them. They did not walk so much as glide.

"Mazikeen," Cheval said.

The brotherhood of Hebrew sorcerers had joined with them in the fight. Several of their number had lost their lives to the Myth Hunters, but each of them seemed to know everything the others had experienced. Blue Jay presumed they shared an extraordinary rapport, almost a kind of hive mind—a group telepathy that made them each part of a greater whole.

"These are the friends I mentioned," Blue Jay replied. "Like I said, the insurgence is already beginning."

The creature capered across the alley to the two Mazikeen. It leaped from the ground into a sorcerer's arms and then ran up to perch on its shoulder, uttering two soft happy barks. With its tail, it handed over the dagger. The Mazikeen slipped the blade up inside one of its sleeves.

"What the hell is that thing, anyway?" Blue Jay asked.

"Ahuizotl," the Mazikeen answered, two voices in unison. "He is Borderkind, like you."

Cheval shook her head in amazement. "That creature is Borderkind?"

Ahuizotl growled at her. Cheval hissed in return and the creature ducked its head behind the Mazikeen.

"We should get moving," Blue Jay said. "We have a lot of work to do."

"The work has already begun," one of the Mazikeen said. "We have allies amongst the people and the legends. They are prepared to spread the word."

"Glad to hear it," the trickster replied. "But let's talk about this elsewhere, don't you think? We have brought allies with us as well, and they're going to need your help before they can participate."

"Masks?" the other Mazikeen asked.

Blue Jay smiled. "Something like that."

"Lead on," said the Mazikeen.

Ovid Tsing did not give his recruits false hope. Some of them had never struck another in anger, much less fought with swords or daggers. What he promised them was camaraderie, faith, and loyalty. Twillig's Gorge had been founded by those who did not want outsiders interfering with their lives. Those who settled there believed in liberty, both for themselves and for others. He did not have to make fiery speeches to rouse their ire. Whether it was the current rulers of Yucatazca or the High Council of Atlantis, as some rumors said, did not matter to them. Whether or not Oliver Bascombe had assassinated King Mahacuhta was quite beside the point.

All that mattered was that an army had invaded Euphrasia. King Hunyadi had never tried to exert his will over the residents of Twillig's Gorge. Not a man or woman believed that the southerners would offer the same freedom.

They would never have gotten involved with the workings of the Two Kingdoms—the people of Twillig's Gorge did not even communicate much with nearby communities, except for necessary trade—but Ovid had convinced them that the threat was simply too great. So many of the legends and Borderkind in the Gorge had already gone to fight under Hunyadi's command. They could do no less.

Ovid stood at the rim of the gorge. Behind and below him, life went on as it always had. His mother would be down there making pastries and baking bread, serving coffee at the café. He had been frustrated with her of late, but he still hated the idea of parting from her.

Yet if he stayed, it would only be a matter of time before the routine in Twillig's Gorge would be shattered forever. Someone had to fight.

The wind whispered across the plateau. Sentries stood guard at the top of the stairs down into the gorge nearby. They were Lost Ones, however. The Nagas, who had always acted as sentries for the Gorge, had already gone off to war. Ovid wondered who would guard the rim when he and his militia marched away.

His recruits were arrayed across the plateau twenty yards away. Ovid had chosen three lieutenants—two men and a woman who had soldiered in the past—to oversee their training. Vernon led a platoon in hand-to-hand combat trials. The recruits had learned how to pull their punches and kicks easily enough, but the real test would be when they had to execute such moves in battle. LeBeau taught them swordplay. Or, rather, he tried. Some of them simply had no skill with the blade. The woman, Trina, taught small weapons combat, gauging the recruits' skill with daggers, axes, and cudgels.

Ovid himself had plucked seven of the recruits for his own special unit of archers. Some had learned from the Nagas when they were younger and others, like Ovid, had a natural skill.

He watched them all now, going through their paces. Perhaps he ought to have lied to them. Some would die on the first day of fighting. Many would never return to Twillig's Gorge. He had never been in war himself, but he had met enough warriors to know the truth of it. Some would survive because of their skill, and others through sheer luck. Many would die the same way.

His archers were working with Trina at the moment. When enemies came too close, it was vital that they be able to defend themselves with whatever they had at hand.

Ovid had his bow slung across his back with his quiver. He started away from the gorge toward the recruits. Trina would be through with the archers soon, and then he would continue their training. The sun felt warm on his shaven pate and he ran a hand over the top of his head.

When a voice called his name, Ovid turned and saw two large figures standing on the ridge. From their jagged silhouettes, it was clear they were not human.

"Archers at the ready!" Trina snapped.

Ovid spun and glared at her. "No," he commanded. "They are Jokao. Our neighbors. Their village is only half a day's walk from here."

"Stonecoats?" Trina asked. "I've heard of them. But I've never seen one before. They've never come to the Gorge."

That much was true. Ovid started across the plateau toward the far ridge. As he passed between the other two platoons, LeBeau touched his arm. Ovid turned to look at him, barely aware of anything but the sight of those rough creatures on the slope.

"They are legends, not Borderkind," LeBeau said. "How do you know they are not in league with the southerners? They might have come to destroy us."

"Two of them?" Ovid said. "I don't think so. But if they kill me, destroy them before they can get down into the Gorge."

LeBeau's reply was a grim nod.

Ovid did not spare another glance at the rest of his recruits as he strode up the slope toward that ridge. As he drew near to the Jokao, he realized that their outer husks were the same texture and color as the stones that thrust up from the ground. They were called Stonecoats because their bodies were entirely covered in a rocky armor. Their eyes were like pure quartz crystal. Whether there was flesh beneath their Stonecoats was the subject of great conjecture. Ovid himself had only ever seen Jokao once before, and then from a distance, while he'd been on a trade excursion for his mother.

"What do you want?" he asked. Perhaps he ought to have been more courteous, but that was not his way.

One of the Stonecoats—whose chest was scored with three deep furrows that had been painted a deep red ochre—raised his chin imperiously.

"Stories travel far," the Jokao said, with a clacking of rock jaws. "We have heard that you prepare an army to fight Atlantis."

Ovid frowned. How could these creatures have heard of his militia, and how had they gotten the truth so skewed?

"Not an army," he replied. "Only a small force of soldiers. Soon, we'll march south to join the king's forces. But we aren't going to fight Atlantis. We only wish to stop the invaders."

The Jokao cocked his head. Stone scraped upon stone. "To stop the invaders, you must fight Atlantis. The Truce-Breakers."

"I'd thought that only a rumor."

The stone warrior shook his head. He reached out and touched one of the rocky projections that jutted like teeth from the ground.

"No. The stones know. Stories travel fast. The Jokao pass them through the ground. The invaders have Atlanteans commanding their armies. Once we were slaves, and Atlantis our master. When you march south, we will be with you. We will not be slaves again."

Before Ovid could begin to reply or even to make arrangements, the Stonecoats turned and started across the plateau. He considered calling after them, explaining that it would be days before his militia was ready to march. They were storekeepers and fishermen and carpenters, and they were not ready yet.

But then he realized that the Jokao knew precisely what Ovid had been doing, there in the Gorge. Somehow the stones had told them. And when the militia marched south, the Stonecoats would know.

Unnerved and confused, he turned and went down the slope to where his recruits and lieutenants all waited. The questions began immediately. They wanted to know what the Jokao had said.

"We have allies," he told them. "Continue your training. If we want to make a difference in this war, we must leave soon."

And with that, he departed, descending the stairs and ladders into Twillig's Gorge. So many of the homes were empty, now. Some of the shops had been closed up. He missed the smell of fresh fruit that had always risen from the market, and the delicious aroma of spices and roasting poultry from Taki's restaurant.

He crossed the Sorrowful River on a footbridge twenty feet

above the water and then scrambled down a ladder to the promenade on the east bank. This time of day, the café normally would be alive with patrons sitting on the patio and sipping coffee, sharing gossip from throughout the Gorge. Now only a single, older couple—Giovanni Russo and his wife, Lucia—sat at a table, eating pie and drinking black coffee. Ovid nodded to them as he stepped inside the café.

His mother stood behind the counter, moving sweet rolls from a hot baking tin onto a tray in the display case. When she looked up, Virginia must have seen something in her son's face, for her brow creased with worry.

"Ovid? What is it?"

How could he explain without offending her again? He still did not believe in the Legend-Born. The idea that some predestined figure could deliver the Lost Ones seemed so much like a dream. Besides, wouldn't such beings have appeared long before now? Other legends were solid and verifiable.

No, the Legend-Born were nothing more than a story. But his mother believed in them with all her heart. He could not challenge her faith again, and had no desire to spend the few days they had left together arguing.

Yet he had been wrong once already. He had not believed the rumors that Atlantis was behind the invasion of Euphrasia, the murder of King Mahacuhta, and the shattering of the truce between the Two Kingdoms. The Stonecoats were legends themselves. Ovid knew he should not simply take their word for it, but still he found himself believing the Jokao.

And if the Atlantis conspiracy turned out to be true, then it seemed Oliver Bascombe had not assassinated Mahacuhta after all. That did not mean he and his sister were Legend-Born, but it was curious, indeed.

"What is it?" his mother asked again. She looked almost frightened.

Ovid smiled and reached over the counter to take her hands. He raised them to his lips and kissed her fingers.

"Nothing, Mother. Only that I love you. No matter how we disagree, that will never change."

Virginia nodded. "You have always been a good son, Ovid. Too serious, sometimes, but good. The Lost need to rise. The future depends upon it. I'm proud that you will help to lead them."

"Only a few."

"A brave few. And more will follow. They must."

Ovid nodded. "On that, at least, we can agree."

he cell door swung open.

Oliver stood leaning against the opposite wall beneath one of the grated windows. A light rain had started to fall, and even those few droplets that the breeze blew in were refreshing. The coolness of the dungeon could not compete with the heat of the day.

"You're late this morning, guys. Breakfast is to be served promptly at eight A.M. on the Lido Deck."

Two guards stepped inside—both Atlantean. One carried a tray of something that resembled gruel and a piece of crusty bread. Two other guards waited in the hall. They wouldn't open the door to Julianna and Collette's cell until Oliver's was locked up again. Since the escape attempt, he hadn't seen a single Yucatazcan guard in the dungeon. Only the pale, grim bastards from Atlantis.

The one carrying the tray sneered.

The other stormed across the cell and reached for Oliver, who did not bother trying to elude him. Where could he hide in this cell? The guard grabbed him by the front of his shirt and backhanded him across the face. His lip split, stinging in the warm air, and fresh blood dripped down his chin. It happened regularly. The guards didn't leave him alone long enough for the lip to heal properly.

"And good morning to you," he mumbled over his swollen, bleeding lip.

The Atlantean sneered at him. Either he was bald or his hair had been shorn almost to the scalp, for not a single strand poked out from beneath his helmet. Like many of the soldiers of Atlantis, he seemed an entirely different breed from the sorcerers—taller and broad-shouldered, but his features still had that narrow sharpness and his skin the greenish-white cadaverous hue. His eyes were dim and cruel.

Oliver did not react. He simply returned to his position against the wall, and waited while the other guard set down his tray and the two of them withdrew from the cell. During the last skirmish, he had given a good accounting of himself.

When the guards had locked him in once again, the keys jangled as Julianna and Collette's cell was opened. Oliver tensed inwardly, hoping that there would be no beating for them. On the day after they had tried to reach Frost, Julianna had been groped by a guard. Had she been raped, Oliver would have attacked the next Atlantean to come into his cell, even knowing that it might mean his life.

But they hadn't raped her. Yet.

She and Collette had both reassured him that they were okay. But that night he had heard Julianna crying and forged a new hate inside him.

Today neither his fiancée nor his sister met the guards with wisecracks, the way Oliver had. That was for the best. He did it because he couldn't help it, and because the pain they gave him in return helped to keep the furnace of his hate burning. But Collette and Julianna kept quiet and the guards did nothing but leave their food and lock the door to their cell again.

Boots scuffed the stone floor as the soldiers marched back up the corridor, then up the stairs out of the dungeon. And they were alone again.

Oliver sucked on his split lip and spat some blood onto the floor. He pushed away from the wall and walked to the door. Atlantis had bred strange people, some of them stealthy and cunning. The guards did not normally fall into this category, but he had learned caution. Oliver peered through the grated window but saw no one. He heard his sister and Julianna speaking to one another quietly but could not make out the words, nor could he see any sign of them through the grate in their door. They were still choking down their food.

He ran his fingertips along the mortar grooves between the stones that made up the wall of his cell. Eyes closed, Oliver cleared his mind. Sometimes he tried this trick on the outer wall, tempted by the sunshine. But if Collette was right—if what she'd done at the sandcastle hadn't been some strange fluke—then just getting outside wouldn't solve their problems.

If Collette was right... Oliver knew his doubt had to be a problem, but he could not seem to put it behind him.

"At it again, huh?"

He opened his eyes. Julianna was peering at him from the cell across the corridor. Oliver smiled, drawing a sharp pain from his split lip. A flicker of concern passed over Julianna's features. Her face was filthy, her hair tangled and wild, but her eyes had a light that woke something in him, just as it always had. With just a look, she could remind him of all the things he had always dreamed of being.

"Yeah. Not much else to do."

Julianna looked back into the gloom of her cell. Her fingers wrapped around the grate.

"Collette, too. She's getting frustrated."

From within the cell, Oliver heard his sister's voice. "Of course I'm getting frustrated. This is bullshit. We can do this. We can get out of here."

Oliver grinned, hissing with pain and touching his bleeding lip. "Yeah. We're so out of here."

Julianna frowned, angry with him. "Maybe it's your attitude that's keeping us here."

"Hey—"

"Hey, nothing, Mister Bascombe. You two are special. Your mother was a legend. Borderkind. All your life, your father tried to drum that out of you. He pretended magic didn't exist to try to convince you of the same thing."

Oliver scratched his fingers against the mortar. "But it does exist."

"Of course it does!" Julianna replied. "Don't you get it? That's why he acted the way he did. To protect you."

A knot of ice formed in Oliver's gut. This was nothing he had not already considered, but to hear Julianna talking about it, to have the thoughts spoken out loud, troubled him.

Nobody who had known Max Bascombe before the death of his wife could ignore how drastically the man had been changed by his loss. As young as Oliver had been at the time, he could still recall his parents laughing together often. He cherished the memories he had of them together, dancing at the New Year's Eve party they'd thrown at the house, picnicking on a blanket on the back lawn with the Atlantic Ocean stretching endlessly in front of them, and a handful of times he had entered a room to find them embracing or locked in a kiss.

Her death had extinguished a light inside Oliver's father. From that time on, he had become more sentinel than parent, grimly watching over his children, but seeming to take little joy in them. Oliver, in particular, had vexed the man. His father had steered him away from fanciful movies and discouraged cartoons. On one birthday, Julianna had given him a magic set. Oliver had played with it for hours, but when he woke in the

morning it had vanished. He had ransacked the house searching for it, thinking Friedle or the cleaning woman had put it
away, but no one could recall having moved it at all. It had
taken Collette to make him see the truth—their father had gotten rid of it.

Later, other items vanished in similar fashion. Neither father nor son would say a word, but the gulf between them
widened. His complete set of *The Chronicles of Narnia* disappeared a week after Christmas, the year he turned fifteen. When
his high school English teacher had assigned Charles Dickens's
Hard Times to the class, Oliver had found a distressing echo of
his own relationship with his father. The diatribe that opened
that book had remained with him all of these years: *Facts alone
are wanted in life. Plant nothing else, and root out everything else.
You can only form the minds of reasoning animals upon Facts:
Nothing else will ever be of any service to them.*

Oliver had taken to hiding away in the town library, reading
mythology and fantasy and all sorts of other things his father
would never have approved of. And whenever he had a part in a
play in school, or with the Kitteridge Civic League, his father
would never be in attendance. More than once, he had forced
his son to quit the drama club, only to relent when teachers in-
tervened on Oliver's behalf.

And Julianna thought his father had done all of those things
to protect him?

"It's true," a softer voice said.

Collette had stopped trying to take the wall apart. On tiptoe,
she looked at him through the grate.

"She died because of what she was, Oliver. It's the only thing
that makes sense," Collette said. "Dad was afraid we'd end up
dead, too. He feared what we were because he didn't want to
lose us."

"Funny way of showing it."

"Do you remember when I gave you *Phantastes*?"

As painful as the memory was, Oliver laughed softly.

"How could I forget?"

As cold and distant as his father could be, it had given him a certain amount of pleasure to piss the man off. Any kind of emotion revealed that his father was still human, even anger.

Collette had read George MacDonald's nineteenth-century fairy tale—about a man who slips from the ordinary world into one full of magic and fairy courts, a tale that now resonated powerfully with Oliver—for a college course, and had brought it home for her brother on a break from school. One morning, Oliver had come down to the kitchen to find his father standing by the table, reading the back cover of *Phantastes*. Oliver had left the book there the night before, forgetting to return it to his room.

His father had glanced up at him, his expression almost bewildered. Anger had flashed in his eyes and he had held the book up and begun to tear pages in half.

"Enough," he had said. "Haven't you learned by now? That is enough of this shit. You keep your head in the real world, son, or you're never going to have much of a life. No more of this dreck in my house. I'm telling you now, and you'd better believe I'll tell your sister as well. No more."

Oliver had snapped, then. Years of hurt and rage over things that his father had made vanish bubbled over. He had screamed at the man and called him a dozen vile names. When he ran out of steam, his father dropped the book—in two halves now— onto the table, crossed the room, and grabbed Oliver by the front of his shirt.

"You may not like it, but I'm your father. I'm all you've got. You curse and shout all you like, but a father's supposed to look out for his children, and that's what I'm doing for you and your sister. If you want to hate me, there's little I can do about it, and it won't keep me from doing what I think is best for your future. Take your head out of the clouds. Wake up, Oliver."

Collette called his name.

Through the grate in his cell door, he stared at her.

"All this stuff about Melisande...it gives that morning a different perspective, don't you think?" Collette said.

"Maybe it does," he admitted. Julianna and Collette were right. It would be foolish for him to try to deny it, especially to himself. All his life, he'd nurtured bitterness and resentment toward his father, and loved him in spite of it. Now he knew his father had had reasons they never could have guessed, and that only made both his love and his resentment grow. There must have been a better way for him to protect his children.

"Keep trying the wall," he said.

Julianna smiled at him. Oliver closed his eyes, fingertips finding the grooves between the stones again.

Night fell. Damia Beck went on foot into the Oldwood. Sprites and pixies flitted up in the branches of trees, giving off glimmers of light like multicolored fireflies. The colors were soft and lovely, a bright bouquet of butterfly wings that danced through the darkness and then disappeared.

Things snorted in the undergrowth, rustling in the tangled branches, but did not emerge. Her hand gripped the pommel of her sword, but it seemed as though the creatures that lived in the Oldwood had been warned away from her.

Dark shapes watched from the branches and from the darkness of the thick wood. Some were low to the ground and misshapen—little goblin things with gleaming eyes—and others were clearly animals, or legends in the skins of beasts. Many of the animals in the Oldwood were not what they seemed. Some were legends, but others would be ancient demigods, wood deities. In a world full of legends, many were little more than names to her, and there must be countless things on this side of the Veil that she had never heard of at all.

But the master of the forest—that legend was quite familiar.

Damia tried to ignore the lurkers in the dark. She had set off at a steady pace, working her way through the woods on a westerly course. At some point, she would meet the one she had summoned, but when? Damia had begun to grow impatient.

"Hello?" she said, into the trees.

Leaves rustled. No path had opened before her, so she forged her own, relying on her instincts to keep on course. An owl cried mournfully above her and she glanced up. Something growled just off to her left.

When she focused once more on the trees in front of her, moving between two tall rowans, she saw a tiny man in a blood-red cap. He had a thin beard and leaned against a tree with his arms crossed, a grim expression on his face.

Damia cocked her head and studied him. "You're not—" she began to say. Then, fearful of causing offense, she started again. "Are you the master of the forest?"

It was all she could do to keep the disdain and doubt from her voice.

The little man snorted with derisive laughter, shook his head, and turned away, disappearing into the Oldwood.

Frustration growing, Damia continued. For a time the ground trembled with the footfalls of something enormous, and she heard branches snapping loudly in the distance. More owls cried, and she tightened her grip upon her sword.

Back on the road, three-quarters of her battalion awaited. Likely they would be wondering why they were sitting around. Doubt filled Damia. Had Charlie misled her? Was this simply a waste of time? Images filled her mind of a Yucatazcan ambush falling upon her battalion while they waited on the road.

"Damn it," she whispered.

Still, she forged on. She had committed herself to this rendezvous and would not turn back unless she had real reason to believe she had been deceived.

Damia walked on. Roots seemed to shift themselves underfoot as though trying to trip her. Branches scratched at her arms and face. Then she noticed something that troubled her.

The owls had fallen silent.

Not only the owls, but all of the creatures of the forest. Nothing moved in the branches or the underbrush. Even the wind seemed to have gone still. For the first time since embarking on this journey, Damia Beck took a step backward.

"Hello?" she said, her voice echoing back to her.

From the corner of her eye, Damia glimpsed motion. She turned, but saw only trees. Then something shifted near the trunk of a thick oak and she frowned in confusion. It seemed that the tree itself had started to move. Branches became arms and fingers. Bark took on a shape, rough and jagged. It was a woman, naked and thin, but her flesh had the texture and color of the tree. Or perhaps it truly was bark.

Something snapped behind her. Damia spun to see another tree-woman peeling herself from the trunk of an oak. Her eyes opened like a newborn's, gleaming black in the moonlight that filtered down through the branches.

Damia drew her sword and backed away. But a wet, cracking noise came from behind, and again she spun to find a third tree-woman standing in the shadows. The creatures were unsettlingly sexual, their bodies ripe and alluring in spite of their rough texture. As they circled her—and a fourth and fifth appeared—their flesh grew smoother and lighter, until they almost could have passed for human in the darkness.

"I am Commander Beck," she said. "I travel the Oldwood under the seal of the King of Euphrasia—"

"Not our king," one of the dryads said, her voice sultry and full of warning. She extended one long, ragged finger. "Our king is *here.*"

Sword held before her, Damia turned. The dryads had surrounded her, but now two of them stepped back to make way as a huge, gleaming stag came toward them.

She blinked. It was no stag.

He had a pelt of thin, sleek brown hair, but a body like a

man. Huge and gloriously muscled, he towered over her. Atop his head was a massive rack of antlers that would have tangled in the branches of the trees...if they had not drawn back from the path of the Lord of the Oldwood. In ancient times, the Celts had called him Cernunnos, and that had served as his name ever since.

Cernunnos stood gazing down at her with hard, intelligent eyes of the brightest green. His antlers threw criss-cross shadows over Damia's face.

"You are the Lost girl who summoned me?"

For a moment she hesitated. Then she cursed herself silently for becoming so enchanted. She stood up straight and sheathed her sword, then bowed her head in respect.

"I am, Lord Cernunnos. You honor me and my king by agreeing to meet here."

"I avoid involvement with the lands beyond the wood," the master of the forest said, his gaze sage and a bit sad. "But my people are afraid. They whisper of a dark time beginning. They fear war and fire in the wood. Are they right to be afraid?"

Damia raised her chin, meeting his gaze without wavering. "Yes, milord. They are. Atlantis has betrayed the Two Kingdoms. The truce is broken."

Cernunnos waved a hand in the air. The trees seemed to sway away from him. But when he spoke, it was as if they leaned in to catch his every word.

"That has nothing to do with Oldwood. The legends here care nothing for kingdoms or kings."

Still, she did not waver. "Would that they could continue to live without caring, sir. But the war will not leave the Oldwood unscathed. The armies of Yucatazca have invaded, with spies from Atlantis amongst their ranks. They will come. And those prophecies of fire may well come true. You will be a part of the war, whether you wish to or not.

"If you want to keep the Oldwood safe, you must help us. I have sent a portion of my soldiers to the west of the forest. The southern army will see them and will pursue them. My troops hope to retreat into the Oldwood, to draw the invaders in. We'd like to fight them here, in the wood."

All the quiet wisdom went out of his eyes. Cernunnos's face darkened with rage. His lips peeled back from his teeth and he quaked with anger.

"You dare much, Lost girl," he sneered. "The war might have passed us by, and instead you ask to bring it here?"

The dryads hissed and circled closer, fingers hooked into talons. From the branches and the underbrush came a stirring of bestial sounds and the snapping of twigs. Eyes glowed yellow and red in the darkness, hidden behind trees and in bushes.

Damia steeled herself. "And what will you do then? Eventually, they will come to subjugate you and all of Oldwood. As angry as you are, you should recognize an ally when you see her. Hunyadi does not interfere with you. Do you think Atlantis will afford you that courtesy?"

Cernunnos scowled at her, his nostrils flaring. Then he held up a hand and the dryads withdrew.

"And how much time do I have to prepare?"

"Tomorrow, with your permission, a company of my soldiers will lead the invaders into the Oldwood from the west. I have three more companies, making a full battalion, waiting on the eastern road, with two regiments of cavalry and a platoon of Borderkind. I'd like to move them into the forest tonight.

"But I need to know, milord. When the battle begins, will you help?"

Cernunnos took a long breath, then nodded, his head heavy with those wicked-looking antlers.

"Yes, Commander Beck. We shall help kill your enemies."

A shudder went through Virginia Tsing's sleeping form. Rising almost to wakefulness, she drew her blanket up to her neck and huddled under it. This far north and east, the nights could get chilly, but she enjoyed sleeping with the windows open. Her bedroom was above the café and faced the Sorrowful River. Sometimes she felt she could hear the gentle sigh and weep of the waters, but usually it was only the soft rush of the river rolling by. The sound comforted her, eased her mind when she lay down at night.

Again she stirred. Half aware, she frowned and reached up to rub at her eyes. Her nose wrinkled. The place was always full of the smells of the café—of coffee and baking bread, of cinnamon and moon cakes—and underneath it all the thick, starchy odor of dough and flour.

Without opening her eyes, she tried to discover what had woken her. There had been a sound that was not the river, and a smell that was not the café. The odor had an earthen quality to it and it tickled her nose.

She burrowed deeper under the covers. The aches of an old woman's body pained her, but when she settled down again, they retreated. Her breathing was steady, but her forehead had not lost the crease of the frown she wore.

The sound came again. Not the creak of a floorboard or the sound of voices that might have reached her if Ovid had a lady friend visiting late. This was not the river. It had a scratchy quality, skittering across the floor.

Virginia's nose wrinkled again. Her breath hitched and she brought her hand up, but could not prevent herself from sneezing. When she sneezed, her eyes flew open.

And there he stood.

Death had come for her, a hooded figure that seemed to shift and rasp with each movement. Its body flowed with motion and she realized it was made of sand.

The Sandman stared at her with bright yellow eyes. It smiled, showing sharp black teeth.

"What do you want?" she asked.

The creature slid toward her, its tread scouring the floor.

"Kitsune," it rasped. "The Borderkind who traveled with the Legend-Born . . . the Bascombe. I am told that the fox is here, and that you will know where."

Her heart fluttered with fear. Those eyes were dreadful to see. But Virginia Tsing would not crumble. She was far too proud. Perhaps that was the thing she had most in common with her son. Even terror could not break her.

"She's no longer among us," the old woman said softly. Her voice did not sound as strong as she had hoped it might.

It reached down with one hand and laid its palm across her mouth. She felt the sand spilling into her throat. Her eyes widened, and her heart began to race. Terror gave her the courage to reach up and grab its wrist. She felt the sand shifting beneath his cloak as she stared up into those awful yellow eyes.

Virginia gagged as the sand reversed direction, returning from her body to the Sandman's.

"Where?" he asked.

"Perinthia," she rasped. "Kitsune's gone with Coyote to Perinthia, to see the old gods."

The Sandman bowed his head as though in thanks, the hood of his cloak obscuring his eyes.

"You won't stop the Legend-Born," she persisted. "Their time has come."

The monster laughed. "I don't want to stop them. Only to kill them."

As though it were a promise, he lowered himself toward her. Virginia cried out, her scream blotting out the sound of the river. Strangely, in that moment she could smell all of the aromas of the café—the coffee, the cinnamon, the flour.

The Sandman dipped its talons toward her eyes.

She studied its face and realized she had seen it before. Once, that face had belonged to a man, a Lost One, who had passed through Twillig's Gorge.

"Halliwell?" she asked.

The Sandman plunged his fingers into the corners of her eyes and plucked them out. Virginia shrieked and he silenced her with a flow of sand that clogged her nose and throat once more. He flooded her skull with sand and it spilled from the empty sockets where her eyes had been.

Inside the Sandman, Ted Halliwell screamed.

The monster heard his voice, and only laughed in return.

Halliwell knew he existed only as a thought, now. He saw what the Sandman saw, heard what the abomination heard. Yet Virginia Tsing had looked up into the face of her death and she had seen Halliwell himself. Frozen in horror and grief over the woman's murder, he shivered at the realization that, looking up into the sand sculpted into his own features, the woman had died thinking that Halliwell himself had murdered her.

And yet, as much as that weighed on his heart, he quickly realized it had other implications. Somewhere in the eyes of the Sandman, Virginia had *seen* him. Had some part of his essence come to the surface in that moment? *If enough of me still exists in here for her to see me, is it enough to exert some influence?*

Sickened as he was by the old woman's death, he found in it a glimmer of hope.

When the Dustman had drawn him down into the dark storm at the core of the Sandman, he had shared a terrible truth. They were all one, now. Three spirits in one form. The substance of the Sandman had changed. Now it was sand, and dust, and Ted Halliwell's bones, ground down to a fine powder by the scouring of the sand.

They were one. The teeth that bit into Virginia Tsing's eyes were *their* teeth. The claws that ripped at her flesh were *their* hands.

"I'm sorry," Halliwell said.

It might have been that the words came from the Sandman's lips. And, if so, what else might Ted be able to do down there in the dust, and the sand, and the powder of his own bones?

Ovid woke to the sound of his mother's voice. As he blinked, clearing his vision and his mind, he realized it was still early. What was his mother doing awake? Yet, now that he listened, he realized there was another voice as well—an inhuman rasp that made the hairs on his arms stand up.

He vaulted from his bed, legs tangling in the sheets. As he extricated himself, he heard his mother coughing. Ovid's heart beat faster, his skin warming with the heat of panic. He ran to his wardrobe. His sword hung in its scabbard from the door. The metal sang as he drew the blade.

"*You won't stop the Legend-Born,*" he heard his mother say, coughing. "*Their time has come.*"

Whatever menaced her, it laughed. It didn't want to stop them, it claimed. Only to kill them.

Ovid froze. The thing—whatever it was—had just confirmed his mother's belief. The Legend-Born *were* real.

Then his mother began to scream.

"No!" he cried, and bolted from his room.

Sword in hand, he raced down the corridor. He had recently begun to insist that she lock her bedroom door at night. As she shrieked in agony he tried to work the point of his sword between the door and the frame. His blood boiled with bitter irony.

At last he reared back and began to kick the door, just beside the knob. Again and again he kicked, until at last the wood splintered and the door flew open.

Only then did he realize that her screams had ceased. He peered into the darkened room. His mother lay on the bed, her throat crushed, broken, and bleeding. Her chest had been caved in. Where her eyes had been there were bloody, ragged holes.

THE LOST ONES   113

Above her stood a thin figure in a gray cloak, its body shifting and flowing, its flesh in motion. But it was not flesh; it was sand. For a moment, he recognized that face, and it was not the face of a monster but of a man he recognized...a man to whom he and his mother had given their hospitality. Ovid even remembered his name. Ted. Ted Halliwell.

Then the sand shifted again and the face became the monster's. The Sandman turned to gaze at Ovid as it licked its bloody fingers, which were thin as knives.

Ovid screamed and ran toward it, anguish overcoming reason. He raised his sword—grief a hollow pit in his gut—and swung the blade as he lunged for the Sandman.

The sword passed through it. Ovid felt a tug against the metal and heard it hiss as the sand scraped against it.

The Sandman collapsed, losing all cohesion. A wind rose from nowhere and swirled and eddied the sand across the floor and out the windows into the nighttime peace of Twillig's Gorge.

When it had departed, all that remained for Ovid Tsing was the gentle sound of the river passing by outside.

On a street in Palenque's inner maze, just outside the great plaza where the king's palace thrust up from the city's heart, a small bar called Brasilia provided the pulse of the capital. A pair of musicians played steel drum and guitar, sometimes adding flute and trumpet. The couples who dined or drank on Brasilia's patio were young and beautiful, with complexions the color of caramel or cinnamon. The waitresses were even younger and more beautiful. Everyone smiled and laughed, and once in a while someone passing by the patio would begin to dance to the music.

The scent of flowers carried on the breeze from a nearby florist. A father swung his daughter up to perch on his shoulders and made the snorting sounds of an angry bull, scraping his shoe against the cobblestones as though about to charge. The girl squealed in delight.

Leicester Grindylow watched all of this from just inside the bar. He sat on a stool from which he could take in both the inside of the bar and the bright, glittering nightlife on the patio and beyond. Inside, however—where the serious drinkers were—things were not so bright, and the patrons were far less beautiful. They had not come for dinner or music, but only to stare into their drinks and to argue bitterly about things upon which they mostly agreed.

Had they been able to see him for what he was, they would not have spoken so freely. Had they realized he was a spy—for what else could one call his present occupation?—they likely would have beaten him bloody. But there was no way for the Lost Ones in Brasilia to recognize his true nature. They would see an ordinary man instead of a long-armed water boggart. When he spoke, they would not hear English with the London accent he had acquired over years of visiting the ordinary world.

The Mazikeen had seen to that.

When Blue Jay and Cheval had first returned to the apartment where the Borderkind had holed up in Palenque, Grin had been dubious. Yeah, the Mazikeen were powerful. But a pair of sorcerers weren't going to have enough magic between them to take the palace and free Oliver, Frost, and the others. For that, all the Mazikeen in the Two Kingdoms might not have been enough. Ty'Lis had enough sorcery on his own to take out several Mazikeen, at least the way Grin had heard it. And even if Ty'Lis had sent most of the other Atlanteans off to the north to conquer Euphrasia, they had no way to know what kind of forces he had in the palace, or what surprises he had waiting.

But it turned out Blue Jay hadn't shared the whole plan with any of them. Part one of their mission didn't have a thing to do with getting Oliver out of the dungeon. A bit of espionage was the first order of business.

The Mazikeen had lined them up—not just Grin, Cheval, and the burning Li, but a bunch of local Borderkind the sorcerers had organized in secret in Palenque. There was a bloke with a massive mouth in his belly, and half a dozen Pihuechenyi—tall, winged, serpent-men with wicked fangs.

Yucatazca didn't seem to have a lot of cute, furry Borderkind, or even a lot of pretty tricksters. Not a happy lot.

But they needed allies, and the old saw about beggars not being choosers was never far from Grin's mind as he spent time with the group the Mazikeen had gathered.

One by one, the Mazikeen had taken them and cast a glamour over them. They called it something else, but Grin had learned a bit about magic over his long life, and he knew a glamour when he saw one. The sorcerers disguised each and every one of them as humans, Lost Ones. They could see through one another's glamours, but no one else could. If a magician grew suspicious, she might be able to use magic to get a glimpse of their inner selves, but otherwise, they were completely hidden.

Ever since, they'd been out in the city of Palenque, mixing with the people. Listening. And talking.

"You don't really believe that," said the bartender now, a woman slightly older but no less beautiful than the waitresses who served the fashionable young people on the patio. Perhaps her extra years meant the managers of the bar thought her only fit to deal with the grim drinkers in the gloomy interior.

"I certainly do," replied a nattily dressed man with wispy white hair and a thin mustache. The others called him Professor, though Grin didn't know what had earned him the title.

A portly fellow with several days' growth of beard slapped one hand on the bar. "That is shit. Traitors talk like that, Professor."

The professor's eyes narrowed and he stared at the man. "So I am a traitor, now, Enrique? On the contrary. I am a patriot. I have taught the children of kings. Government is never perfect, and there are things they do in secret that we are all better off not knowing. I understand this. It isn't our king or our government I'm speaking against, but our enemies. Our true enemies."

"Atlantis," Grin said.

All eyes in the bar turned on him. For a moment, he felt sure they could see the northern Borderkind that they would all call enemy, but then the professor just nodded.

"Precisely." He gestured around the room, first toward Paola, the bartender, and then to some of the other men and women gathered there. They were no longer quite so interested in their drinks. "You have all seen them. I know that you have. The Atlanteans were here in Palenque before good King Mahacuhta was slain. On the day of his murder, some of you were in the plaza. There were giants on the palace steps, fighting the northern intruders. Atlantean giants."

"Why? What were they doing here?"

Enrique grunted. "Guarding the diplomats. Don't you read the newspaper, Professor? The giants and the others were guarding the diplomats from Atlantis. They were already working to forge an alliance with us—that is why the dog Hunyadi sent his assassins to murder Mahacuhta."

From a small table in the back, a woman spoke up. She might have been fifty and her face was weathered. She sat with a younger man whose face bore the scars of battle, yet who sat up straight and had about him the air of a soldier.

"Don't believe everything you read, sir," the woman said.

Eyes narrowed again, and this time they were focused on the woman and her son.

"My son was a captain in the King's Guard. When Ty'Lis began to put Atlantean soldiers into their ranks, he questioned the order. They whipped him, beat him, and cut out his tongue. They stripped him of his rank and threw him in the dungeon for thirty days."

Even the professor blanched at these words. "Atlanteans in the King's *Guard*?"

After a moment, Enrique cleared his throat. When he continued, some of his confidence was gone. "So, what are you suggesting?"

The professor sighed. "You know what she's suggesting, Enrique. Don't be obtuse. We've spoken of the rumors before. Why did the entire city of Palenque stand by and let the northern Borderkind pass when they came to challenge the king? Hunters had been sent out to exterminate the Borderkind all over Euphrasia, and some in Yucatazca as well. But they left Palenque alone. Why? So that the Borderkind here would not rise up and fight beside their kin against the Hunters until it was too late."

"Conspiracy shit," Enrique muttered.

"Hush," said the bartender. She looked troubled, almost sick, but she nodded to the professor to continue.

"He's right," said the woman. Her son looked as though he would have spoken, had his tongue not been cut from his mouth.

"The whole city let it happen, that terrible day," the woman went on. "Some of us hid in our houses and pulled the shutters. Others lined the streets and cheered them on, thinking that Mahacuhta had betrayed the truce and sent the Hunters north. But we should have known better. The Atlanteans had been infiltrating for months. Ty'Lis is behind it all."

Enrique stood up and took two steps toward her, glancing at the door that led to the patio. "Watch yourself, woman. Talk like that could cost your life."

The professor smiled, but there was no humor in it. "There. You've said it yourself. If she speaks against Ty'Lis, an advisor to the king, she is doomed? Is that the kind of kingdom this has become?"

"That's enough," said another—a disheveled, bearded man

who'd been drinking with Enrique. "You are all traitors. Prince Tzajin is going to be crowned soon enough, but already he rules in his father's place. He has declared war against Euphrasia. He has issued edicts calling the legendary and many Lost Ones to enlist in his army. Tzajin leads us, now, and to question his rule is treason."

A chill went through the bar. Waitresses hurried from the kitchen out onto the patio with drinks and trays of food. The woman tending bar stared at Enrique, but he did not meet her eyes. Even the professor seemed frightened by the prospect.

Leicester Grindylow turned on his stool. He tipped his beer glass back and took a long sip, then wiped his mouth with the back of his hand.

"How can it be treason," he asked, "when the throne is here in Palenque, and Prince Tzajin is issuing his edicts from Atlantis? The boy is the guest of the High Council of Atlantis, surrounded only by the scholars who have been teaching him. The edicts are released here in Palenque by Ty'Lis, who has been behaving like a regent instead of an advisor. Only a blind fool would not at least ask the question, my friends. How do we know that Tzajin declared war, or issued those edicts? How can we be sure the prince even knows that his father is dead?"

They stared at him in horror. Some shifted uncomfortably and looked away, but the mute soldier only nodded in dark approval.

"There's a more horrible question," the professor said. "How do we know Tzajin is still alive?"

The soldier knocked on the table to get everyone's attention.

"He wants you to consider another question," the mute man's mother said. "Who really killed King Mahacuhta?"

"Now that is enough!" cried the bearded man who'd lectured them about treason.

Enrique shook his head. "So now you want me to believe the Atlanteans murdered the king?"

"How can you not believe it?" the woman asked, her voice

weighted with grief. "You've heard all of the rumors. The only reason that you haven't made that connection is because you don't want to. But it's the only thing that makes sense. Otherwise, why hasn't the prince come home, yet? We are at war, for the gods' sake! Where else should he be, if not in the palace, commanding our fate?"

Her dark-eyed son stood, arms crossed. He opened his mouth and even in the gloom the vacant hollow inside was evident.

"Then what of the assassins in the dungeon?" the bartender asked. "If they weren't sent by Hunyadi to murder Mahacuhta, then who are they?"

Grin stood and set his glass down on the bar, drawing their eyes one last time. He turned to take in every man and woman in the bar—twenty-two souls; he had counted.

"Why did Ty'Lis send the Hunters out to slaughter Border-kind if not to cut off all contact with the ordinary world, to separate the Lost from our ancestral home forever? Maybe the so-called assassins in the palace dungeon are exactly what all of the whispers say they are. Maybe they're the Legend-Born, come to take us home."

He turned and strode through the door, out onto the patio. The laughing beauties of Palenque took no notice, but he felt the attention of those inside the bar until he had vanished from their sight.

As they infiltrated the city, Grin and the other Borderkind had found just what Blue Jay had hoped and predicted. Many of the Lost Ones of Palenque were not blind or stupid. They might be afraid to make unpleasant connections, or speak up, but they were not fools.

If they could be forced to face their own suspicions, the Borderkind would have more allies than they could ever have imagined.

CHAPTER 8

liver could not sleep. He had tried, fidgeting
awkwardly on the mat, searching for the least
torturous position. Then he had gone to the
window and stared out at the wall across from
his cell, wishing he could see the sky. A view of the stars would
have lifted his heart.

At length, he walked across the cell and stood in front of the
door. Out in the corridor, nothing stirred. Torchlight flickered
somewhere down the hall, giving the walls a wet glow. Beyond
the grate in the door to Julianna and Collette's cell, there was
only darkness. He might have heard a low, troubled snore, but
that could as easily have been his imagination.

He pressed his forehead against the cool metal of the grate
and peered into the corridor. No one stirred. Idly his fingers
brushed over the stones in the wall and traced the mortar
grooves, just as he'd been doing almost since the moment
they'd been locked up. Collette had been doing the same.

How many people believed they were Legend-Born? Thousands? Millions? And if all of those people believed, did that make it true? Once, humanity had believed their world was flat, but they had been proven wrong. How disappointed all the Lost Ones would be if they found out it was all bullshit.

And it had to be bullshit, didn't it? They'd been in these cells for going on nine weeks and hadn't been able to summon up a single bit of magic. If their mother was Borderkind—if they were supposed to fulfill some kind of prophecy—why did he feel so damned ordinary?

Or maybe not completely ordinary.

He chewed on that for a second. Ever since coming through the Veil for the first time, he'd felt the way he always did when giving a closing argument in court, or acting onstage. Like what he did was fulfilling some role in a grand plan.

Just a little full of yourself, aren't you?

Maybe he was. But that didn't change the way it felt.

And what if it's true? That was a question he'd asked himself a thousand times ever since Ty'Lis had first talked about the Legend-Born. If it was true, that changed everything.

Could their mother really have been Melisande, a beautiful creature with dragon wings and a serpent's lower body? Oliver had photographs of her and his memories, and she had always seemed ordinary. She had been sweet and kind, with a light of joy in her eyes. But he had seen Blue Jay and Kitsune and other legends transform themselves easily enough, and it might be possible that Melisande could do the same.

He had also thought about what Julianna had said about his father. If their mother had indeed been Melisande—if he and Collette were half-human and half-Borderkind—that went a long way toward explaining the way Max Bascombe had treated his son. Oliver had longed for magic, all of his life. And yet . . .

Dad didn't want you to reach for it. He was afraid of what you might find. Or of what might find you.

Oliver drew in a long breath and bit his lower lip. All his life, all he'd wanted was for his father to love him and for himself to be able to put his resentment aside long enough to return that love.

But his father was dead, now, and that would never happen.

If only the old man had told them the truth, when they were old enough. Yet he'd kept it from them, trying to protect them. Otherwise he might still be alive.

Oliver froze, staring out into the corridor. A frown creased his brow. If Melisande had been his mother, and they had inherited some kind of magic from her legendary blood, what would that be? How did Collette's escape from the pit at the Sandman's castle make sense? She had torn the wall of her prison apart, but that didn't seem like their mother at all. If their mother had magic in her, it wasn't a magic of destruction. Yet whenever he had tried to dig at the mortar, he'd been thinking about pulling the wall apart with magic. Obviously, that wasn't working.

The stones beneath his left hand shifted.

Oliver held his breath, then glanced over at his hand. Mortar sifted like dust from the grooves between stones.

"Holy shit," he whispered.

It's not about destruction. No, it wouldn't be. Not if they were their mother's children. Which wasn't to say that they would have magic similar to hers. From what he'd heard, there seemed no real pattern to the magic that developed in the offspring of legends, and no known precedent to indicate what magic might occur in a child half-human and half-Borderkind. Still, instinct told him that his mother's magic would not have been cruel or terrible.

All creatures had delighted her. She had loved her garden, right down to every beetle. Her magic, he felt, must have been in beauty and life. In growth. Yet when autumn came and the garden began to wither, she had seemed equally as content as she'd been when the flowers were in full bloom. Oliver hadn't learned the word entropy until he was in high school, but later, he'd understood it. Things fell apart, lost their cohesion. Everything had its season.

And if you could speed that process along...

Slowly, but firmly, he pushed his left hand forward, and dry, discolored mortar sifted down like powder. The stones began to fall outward.

Oliver drew back his hand and watched as the wall collapsed into the corridor.

He heard Collette and Julianna talking in low voices and knew they didn't have long before the noise of the collapsing wall summoned the guards.

"Jules! Collette! We're going now."

"Oliver?"

Julianna's face appeared at the grate.

He jumped into the corridor and went up to their door.

"What'd you do?"

"It worked." His eyes sought his sister in the darkened cell. He saw Collette pulling on her shoes. She stared up at him.

"How?"

"It's all real, Coll. Melisande was our mother. I went over it a million times, and it's the only thing that could be true. We crossed the Veil, sis. All the legends are real, here, and we're one of them. No way would the Atlanteans have gone to such trouble to deal us out of the game if they didn't believe we were Legend-Born."

He smiled, then glanced at Julianna, who gazed at him in wonder.

"Now, stand away from the wall. We're out of time."

Oliver placed both hands on the stones, ran his fingers and palms over them, and again thought about entropy. About the loss of cohesion. More than anything, he thought about his mother, and wished he could have known her true self.

Once again, the mortar sifted down. He gave the wall a shove and the stones tumbled into the cell. Oliver stepped over the rubble and into the cell.

"I've tried," Collette said.

Their eyes met. He took her hands. "It isn't about breaking things. It's about letting them rest. Making them surrender."

"What the hell does that mean?" Julianna asked.

But Oliver kept his focus on Collette. "You did it before, when you weren't thinking about it, or when you were so exhausted you couldn't think straight. Now you've just got to . . . no, believe isn't enough. You've got to *know* what you are."

He went to Julianna and slid one hand behind her head, fingers tangling in her hair. They kissed, and he felt like he could just crumble into her arms.

"You ready to go?"

Julianna stiffened, eyes full of pain. "I can't cross the Veil. You know that."

"Screw that. We're out of here, one way or another."

He turned to Collette. Pointed to the wall behind her. "You take care of that wall. We've got maybe thirty seconds, if that, to do something. I'll be right back."

"Where are you going?" Julianna asked.

But Oliver had already jumped back into the hall. His heart raced and he could not erase the grin on his face as he sprinted down the corridor. He ran so quickly that when he had to slow down to make the turn toward the stairs, he nearly lost his footing. But he recovered, and a good thing, too, for as he went through the arch toward the bottom of the stairs he heard the iron gate slam open above and the shouts of Atlantean soldiers berating the Yucatazcan guards.

Oliver ran to the stairs. He took them two at a time, and made it halfway up before a guard rounded the curving stairwell above him and shouted. Oliver heard the scrape of metal upon metal as the Atlantean drew his sword.

He laughed, crouching, and reached out to lay his hands on the stairs just above him. They started to shift and crack immediately. Oliver scrambled backward down the stairs, dragging his hands over the stones as he went.

And the stairs gave way, leaving an empty pit behind.

Oliver leaped the rest of the way to the bottom, but the soldier fell through the gap. The others rounded the corner on the stairs and stopped short, staring at the chasm that separated them from Oliver. He grinned and shot them the middle finger, then ran back down the corridor toward the cells.

Julianna and Collette weren't there, but the rear wall of the cell had collapsed. Oliver whooped with joy and ran through the opening into the next cell. That one had been opened as well, but in this case it had not been the wall that Collette had taken down. It was the door.

Oliver stepped into the far corridor. The hall was filled with a cold mist, and the stone walls were rimed with ice. He shivered, teeth chattering, as he turned to see Collette and Julianna standing in front of a door that glistened with ice crystals.

Frost.

Collette put her hands on the door and hissed, pulling away from the ice that must have seared her. Julianna glanced at Oliver—past Oliver—and he knew she was remembering the last time she'd been here, and the horrid promises that Ty'Lis had made if they were ever caught again.

Collette tried again, putting her hands against the wall of the cell instead of the door. Oliver ran to join her. The guards would figure out a way to reach them soon, he was sure.

He put his hands on the door. The ice was so cold it burned. His eyelashes stuck when he blinked and his breath plumed in front of him. But the metal bands on the door fell off, and the bolts holding the hinges on pulled loose from the frame. Where Collette touched the wall, the stones began to shift.

"Push," Oliver said.

Together, they brought down the whole front wall of the cell, door and all. Stones and wood crashed inward. Ice shattered. Frigid air rolled out, and then the three of them stood staring at the winter man. Frost had been placed in a kind of stasis within a dark sphere of magic. At least three quarters of the sphere had been covered with an outer layer of ice and snow. Deep within, where the sphere was not covered, they could see Frost. From what Oliver could tell, he did not look shattered anymore.

"What's going on?" Julianna asked. "Is he trying to get free?"

"Repairing himself, maybe. And working his way out," Collette said.

Oliver shook his head. "We don't have time to wait." Hesitating only a moment, he glanced back at Julianna and then put his hands on the purple-black sphere.

It crackled at the touch.

Nothing happened.

"What's wrong?" Collette asked.

Oliver frowned. He could try to concentrate, but what little he knew of the power he and his sister shared told him that it didn't work like that.

"I don't know."

"Magic," Julianna said, sounding almost dazed. She stared at them both. "You've dealt with things that have a real substance before. The sand. The walls. Maybe magic isn't like that."

Collette threw up her hands. "Great. What now?" She poked her head out into the hall to scout for guards.

Oliver worked his way around, peering through the sections of the sphere that weren't covered in ice. Finally he found an angle at which he could see the winter man's face.

Frost glared at him with blue-white eyes. Long, dagger fingers seemed aimed at a place where magic and ice met. Oliver took a closer look, and saw that that ice seemed to have passed through the sphere at that point, slicing like a knife, instead of having simply formed outside the sphere.

He put his hands on the ice. They were still numb from the door, and now he could barely feel them at all.

Entropy took hold. The ice began to crumble and sift into a fine, powdery snow. With a loud crack, a fissure formed in the thick ice shell. It ran down through the mystic sphere, cracking the ice inside as well.

A frigid wind burst through that fissure and knocked Oliver to the ground. He sprawled there, looking up as wind howled in the cell. All of the ice seemed to flow into the air at the center of the room, churning into a tiny blizzard that drew all of the snow and ice from both within the sphere and without, and from the walls as well.

The blizzard slowed and took form.

The winter man glanced at Collette and Julianna, then stared down at Oliver. He cocked his head, long, icicle hair clinking together.

"Another week and I would have been free," Frost said.

"Yeah. You're welcome," Oliver replied, climbing to his feet.

"From your entrance, it seems you've claimed your inheritance. Excellent. Now we must—"

"No time," Oliver interrupted. Julianna and Collette flanked him, so that the three of them stood before Frost as though trying to bar his exit. "Julianna can't go through the Veil. Collette can. Take her with you, now. Get back to Euphrasia and help Hunyadi against Atlantis."

Collette looked at him sadly, but did not protest. She had known this was coming. There was no other way.

Julianna took his hand. Oliver squeezed her fingers in his own.

"And what of you?"

"Don't worry about me. I'll figure something out. Anyway, you only need one of the Bascombes to fulfill your prophecy, right?"

Frost blinked, then glanced away, and Oliver was surprised to see that the winter man even had the capacity to feel guilt.

"You don't understand."

Shouts came down the corridor. Collette looked out. "They're coming."

"Go!" Oliver shouted.

Frost reached out and opened a rift in the Veil. It seemed so simple for him, like parting curtains. Oliver felt the lure of that easy safety, but he tightened his hold on Julianna's hand as Frost and Collette stepped through.

"See you soon," Collette said. She blew him a kiss, and then they were gone.

Oliver ran to the rear wall of Frost's cell. He pressed one palm against it, took a breath, and pushed. Powder and stone crumbled and then they were running through into the cell behind it. Opening that door was simple enough. Then they leaped out into the corridor where they'd been imprisoned only minutes before.

The pounding of heavy boots crashed down the hall, followed by loud cursing. Oliver glanced to the left and saw the first of the Atlantean guards emerge through the archway. It was the one he'd skirmished with in his cell. Hate fired his blood, but now wasn't the time for payback.

He let go of Julianna's hand and put both hands on the wall in front of him. Before long they were at the rear wall of the dungeon, and outside was the city of Palenque.

The wall crumbled easily. Fresh air rushed in—cool night air still rife with the warm smell of spices from the restaurants around the king's plaza. Oliver pulled Julianna forward and they dropped onto the grass below. Twenty yards away was an iron fence, and beyond that the cobblestone plaza.

"Run," Oliver told her.

"Hurry," she replied, and then she did as he'd asked, bolting for the fence.

Oliver faced the palace. He put both hands on the shattered wall. Breathing evenly, he felt for the integrity of the wall. He could sense its age and all of the places where the stones were already loose, where the mortar had cracked.

One such crack ran up the wall to his left. Oliver nudged it and a portion of the palace wall thirty feet high and twenty wide caved in, burying some of the soldiers alive.

He raced for the fence and grabbed it with both hands. Two of its upright bars rusted and then fell down onto the cobblestones with a clang. Julianna clutched his hand, then they were through the fence and sprinting across the plaza to the nearest alley, disappearing into the maze of Palenque's streets.

They were lost and friendless in a city whose citizens believed they were assassins who had murdered the king.

But they were free.

And Oliver was Legend-Born.

One morning, the gods came to Lycaon's Kitchen.

Kitsune had nearly lost track of the days. She and Coyote had been sleeping in an abandoned marble and granite home a quarter of a mile from the restaurant. Bitterness still lingered between them. She knew she ought to forgive Coyote his past cowardice and recognize the courage it had taken him to overcome it, but bitter barbs had been exchanged between them long before the Myth Hunters had begun to kill their kin. And tricksters—like elephants—had long memories.

So she kept to herself and she did all that was in her power to avoid thinking of what danger Frost and Oliver might now be in—if they were even still alive—and the looks on the faces of Collette Bascombe and Julianna Whitney when she had left them all behind.

Yet all of her efforts to avoid thinking about Oliver and the others meant that they were all she did think about.

Until that dismal gray morning when the gods walked in out of the rain. There were three of them. A tall, voluptuous goddess with braids of dark hair and lavender eyes carried a spear and wore a heavy sword at her hip. A war goddess, from the look of her, she had a rusted chest plate and a dented helm that seemed to have served her well long ago. Beside her came another goddess, a slender creature whose pale flesh was textured with scales and whose hair had a greenish hue. Her smile was radiant. The third of their number had the bedraggled dignity of a Romany traveler or a paladin. An aura of light surrounded him, pulsing, mesmerizing.

"Kit," Coyote murmured, staring at them.

"What?"

But he had nothing to say. They both stared at these faded gods, and wondered what marvels they must have been at the height of their glory.

Lycaon came out of the back with a tray of sausage and eggs that he had fixed for their breakfast. The old gods glared at him, and the cannibal slid the tray onto the table in front of Kitsune and Coyote and made a hasty, silent retreat.

"You are Kitsune of the Borderkind?" asked the goddess.

Kitsune stood, clumsily. These beings were no greater than a thousand legends she had met—no greater than she was. Yet here she was acting as though they were her superiors. But she couldn't help herself. It was something in the way they carried themselves, their austere dignity.

"I'm Kitsune," she said. "This is my cousin, Coyote."

The warrior goddess nodded to him in greeting. Kitsune liked that. At least this one hadn't ignored him the way the wine gods had.

Coyote stood and bowed his head to them.

"I am Bellona, goddess of war," she said. *Roman,* Kitsune thought, trying to keep the two pantheons separate in her mind, though so many of them were facets of one another's legends.

"This is Salacia, my sister, goddess of the sea," Bellona went on. A small smile touched her lips. "And you have already noticed our Greek brother, Hesperos, the evening star."

Kitsune could not look at him, he was so beautiful.

"We know why you have come," Salacia said, her voice a soft lilt. "But we would hear from your own lips all that you know of the war."

Hope flickered inside Kitsune.

It was Coyote who asked the question. "Then you'll help us?"

Bellona shook her head. "That will be a decision for Artemis."

Kitsune shivered. Her own legend was from the far east, but

the name of Artemis still resonated. The daughter of Zeus, she was goddess of the wilderness and the hunt, goddess of the wild animals. Kitsune felt a kinship with this being she had never met, but more than that. Instinctively, she knew that she would follow Artemis to war without question.

"She lives?" Coyote asked.

The old gods turned dark eyes upon him and he looked away.

"Artemis is not what she once was," Salacia replied. "None of us are. But Artemis bears the scars of time and battle and the betrayal of her father, himself now dead. Her mind often drifts, but our brothers and sisters follow her word. If she agrees to aid you, then those who are willing may join the fight. If she does not, your time has been wasted."

Hesperos said nothing, but Kitsune felt his gaze upon her. Her skin felt flushed with warmth, and she told herself it was the nearness of the aura of starlight that surrounded him.

But the stars were supposed to be cold.

He distracted her, but she shook it off. All that mattered now would be the decision of Artemis.

"And if she agrees, how many do you think will come?"

Bellona opened her hands. "We three, at least. Perhaps others who still wish to feel alive, or who still have enough pride to punish an enemy who dares threaten us."

Three, Kitsune thought. If only she had time to go east, to try to persuade the gods of Asia to join them. Many of the legends from the eastern lands had begun to come west to aid King Hunyadi, but the old gods were sleeping, there.

Still, three would be better than nothing. And perhaps there would be more, if Artemis allowed it.

"Do you think I should speak to Artemis myself? I could tell her the tale of what transpires, try to convince her—"

"Not if you value your life. She would not trust you for a moment. The animals turned on her, once, and she has never forgiven them."

The tale filled Kitsune with revulsion, but she only nodded.

Together, she and Coyote began to tell the old gods all they knew of the war and its origins and the threat of the Atlantean conspiracy.

When they had finished, Bellona made her a promise.

"If Artemis wills it, we will meet you an hour past dawn tomorrow on the southern road, in view of the city walls, with all of the gods who will join us. For my part, I hope to see you again. It has been far too long since I have seen war, and I yearn for it."

ebellion simmered in Palenque, and Blue Jay relished every moment of it. According to the Mazikeen and to the other Borderkind and legends who had joined their underground movement, dissent and suspicion had begun to spread through the city. No matter what official edicts came from the palace, many of the citizens of Palenque weren't going to believe a word unless they heard it from the lips of their next king himself.

"Every day that the prince does not return from Atlantis, suspicion grows," Li said.

Jay nodded. "But now we've got to focus on getting our friends out of that dungeon."

"It's time, then?" Li asked.

"Yeah. I think it is. We've done Smith's work. There are hundreds of legends in Palenque—dozens of Borderkind among them—whose hatred of Ty'Lis is rising. Time to get Frost and the Legend-Born out of Atlantis's hands."

He almost mentioned Julianna, Oliver's fiancée, but Li didn't have a personal relationship with Bascombe the way Blue Jay did. None of them had been a part of the original group that had fled across the Veil when they'd been betrayed in Perinthia. Kitsune and Frost would understand.

Oliver might be Legend-Born—he might have some destiny that made him greater than ordinary men—but to Blue Jay, he was just a courageous, resourceful companion, a man who always seemed to lighten moods and hearts.

He was a friend.

Glancing away from Li, Blue Jay took in several of the other Borderkind who had gathered in that room. A Mazikeen stood motionless in the corner. He and his brothers shared an empathic and perhaps telepathic rapport. If anything were to happen within the apartment—if soldiers or Hunters were to attack—the others would learn of it instantly and be able to react, either getting themselves to safety or coming to the rescue.

At a small table, a jaguar-man sat gnawing on a leg of lamb beside an Ewaipanoma. The latter was an odd, headless thing with a wide mouth in the center of its chest. The mouth panted and its tongue traced its teeth from time to time. Otherwise it seemed entirely without intelligence or purpose. Blue Jay had learned this was far from the truth. The Ewaipanoma ate mostly vegetation and small rodents—rarely humans—and were both perceptive and fierce in battle.

The trouble was, the thing gave him the creeps.

Blue Jay smiled softly and turned to Li again.

"The sun will be up soon. We should wait until tonight. Pass the word to Grin and Cheval. I'll speak to the Mazikeen and the others who've volunteered to help."

Li nodded. "Tonight. Good. I grow impatient."

"Me too, my friend. Me too."

Then a wave of dread passed through Blue Jay. What if Frost wasn't there when they went to break Julianna and the Bascombes out? Hell, what if they were all dead?

"Blue Jay? Are you unwell?" Li asked.

In the corner, the Mazikeen glanced up, perhaps in concern. It was almost impossible to tell what they were thinking.

"Just hoping nothing goes—"

He was about to say *wrong* when the door of the apartment swung open. The timing sent a chill of dread up his spine.

A vampire serpent—one of the Pihuechenyi—slithered through the door, tall as a man, its wings pinioned behind it as it glanced around the room, searching for threats. Cheval Bayard entered behind the creature. When she stepped into the apartment, her face glowed with uncharacteristic excitement. At her side, she carried a leather satchel, and she seemed more alive than he had ever seen her, a lightness sparkling in her eyes and lifting her step.

Blue Jay rose from his seat. "What's going on?"

The kelpy laughed. "Half the work has been done for us, my friends."

"What do you mean?"

Cheval reached out and touched his cheek. "It appears that we will no longer need to break our friends out of the palace dungeon, Jay. They have done it without our help."

The trickster stared at her. "You're serious?"

"Completely."

The Mazikeen moved to stand beside Blue Jay, motion so fluid he seemed to flow.

"What, exactly, have you heard?"

The other Borderkind all began to gather around. Li, eyes now churning with such fire that Blue Jay felt certain his glamour would be burned away, crossed his arms imperiously.

"Three or four hours ago, a large section of the western wall of the palace collapsed, revealing part of the dungeon," Cheval explained, swinging her satchel. "Frost and Collette Bascombe escaped through the Veil. Oliver's fiancée is Lost, but he would not have left her. Bascombe and Julianna Whitney were seen running through the plaza into an alley."

"The damage could have been caused by anything," Li said. "Even if our friends tried to escape, we have no way to be certain they succeeded. Did anyone see Frost and the Bascombe woman cross the Veil? And this witness who saw Oliver and the other fleeing, do we have reason to believe it? Have any of our allies seen anything at all that would support the story?"

Cheval seemed irked. She sniffed and focused on Blue Jay. "The very questions I asked myself. I would not have come in so happily if I did not have answers."

The kelpy bared her teeth in a different sort of smile, then reached into the leather satchel and drew out the bloody head of a soldier of Atlantis. The soldier's head had been torn from the body and so its neck was a ragged stump, trailing several inches of spine.

"All that I have heard, I confirmed with this handsome soldier. That, and more. The official alliance with Atlantis will be declared today. Hordes of Atlantean troops will join the war against Euphrasia. And Ty'Lis's handpicked guards witnessed Frost and Collette crossing the Veil with their own eyes."

Blue Jay felt a strange lightness. "And Oliver and Julianna are out there, somewhere, on the streets of Palenque?"

The kelpy dropped the soldier's head back into the satchel and let it fall to the floor. "Yes. Somewhere."

Blue Jay smiled and looked around at the gathered Borderkind. "All right, then, spread the word to friends and allies. Everyone get out there. Let's find them before Ty'Lis does."

King Hunyadi's encampment was arrayed along the ridge of a bald hill, a dozen tents comprising the field headquarters of his army. One open tent held the map of the Two Kingdoms upon which he and his commanders kept track of the troop movements for both their own forces and that of their enemies. To the north, at their backs, lay Jamestown. Many of its people had evacuated, to stay with relatives in other towns and cities. They knew without being told that their hometown was ripe for the plucking. There were bigger cities to the west and the northeast, but as the crossroads of midwestern Euphrasia, Jamestown had become the core of the kingdom.

If the Yucatazcans and the Atlanteans could take Jamestown, the rest of the kingdom would feel as though nowhere was safe. King Hunyadi could not afford such a loss. He needed the people to rise, to fight against the invaders. If Jamestown fell, they might flee instead, thinking the war unwinnable.

Reinforcements had been trickling in, and Hunyadi would take them all. With every thrust northward that the invaders made, his commanders were reporting heavy casualties, thanks in large part to the presence of Perytons, Atlantean giants, and Battle Swine in the southern ranks.

This morning, however, he began to believe that the tide might turn.

Jamestown will not fall today.

King Hunyadi stood on the hill outside his tent. With a telescope to his eye, he gazed at the broad trade route that ran south from Jamestown. More than a mile to the south, the road curved westward. There, the armies of the Two Kingdoms were at war, staining the ground with blood.

Through the telescope, he watched a sphere of green flame slingshot into the sky—Greek fire, deadly in battle. It struck a Peryton and the Atlantean Hunter plummeted to the ground. The wind had turned, and Hunyadi thought he could hear the creature shrieking as it fell.

Swords flashed. This battalion had come with a single giant and it had been slain at the outset of this morning's fighting. The Battle Swine—stinking, tusked, boarlike creatures who walked on two legs and were savage in combat—swept through Hunyadi's men like the reaper at harvest time. But the Euphrasian forces had the advantage of greater numbers. One by one, at a cost of a dozen men for each, the Battle Swine were being felled, leaving stinking, putrid corpses on the road.

Three horsemen rode up the road and then cut across open ground, moving up the hill toward the camp. Hunyadi's personal guard moved to intercept them—the deadliest and most faithful soldiers in his service—but when they recognized Commander Sakai they parted to allow him to pass. A pair of personal bodyguards attended the king, and they stepped up behind him, now. Sakai had proven himself loyal, but in a world of magic and deceit, it would be foolish to take risks.

Sakai dismounted. For a small man, he carried himself with immense dignity. Hunyadi had always marveled at how unremarkable he was, both physically and in his features. His face did not betray any particular cunning, and yet Sakai had proven to be his greatest commander.

"It goes well, I see," the king said.

Commander Sakai bowed his head and then looked up. "Very well, Majesty. We suffer great losses, but their spirit is weakening and their numbers are dwindling faster than ours, now that the swine are mostly dead. We will turn them within the hour, and then have all day to drive them south."

Heartened, the king nodded. "You'll be pleased to hear that couriers have brought word from Boudreau and Alborg. They haven't had our success, but they have stopped the invasion from advancing. Alborg feels certain he'll turn them back by tomorrow."

"And Commander Beck, Majesty? Have you word from her?"

The king narrowed his eyes. "Nothing yet, Hiro. But don't concern yourself. Damia will stop them at the Oldwood."

Sakai said nothing, but his lips were tightly closed and he breathed through his nose.

"Something you wanted to say, Commander Sakai?"

Again, the little man bowed his head. "Once we turn this attack away, Majesty, I thought you might want to send reinforcements to aid Commander Beck. If the division Ty'Lis has sent northeast is not stopped, we will never reach them in time to stop them from attacking Perinthia."

Hunyadi considered for a moment, and then shook his head. "They would have to cross the Atlantic River and travel many long hours. If it came to that, we could catch them. And the city has many sentries. The towers would not fall before we arrived. But trust that it will not come to that. Commander Beck will stop them. I would not have put my faith in her unless I was certain."

"Of course, Majesty. If she has your confidence, I am certain she will prove herself worthy of it."

The king nodded. "As am I. Your counsel is ever appreciated, Hiro. Now, though, return to battle. The troops need their commander. We have the upper hand, and I want to take advantage of it before the invaders receive reinforcements."

Commander Sakai withdrew. His aides had not dismounted. As soon as he had climbed back into the saddle, the three soldiers turned and rode south at a gallop.

The king watched through his telescope for several more moments, then turned to walk toward the tent where his map of troop movements was laid out. From the corner of his eye he saw a dark shadow pass before the morning sun, and looked up to see Wayland Smith standing on the east edge of the camp, just beyond the king's own tent. His dark clothes and wide-brimmed hat seemed to harken back to another age.

The Wayfarer started toward Hunyadi and not a single one of the King's Guard moved to stop him. They did not even seem to notice him.

Hunyadi forced himself not to shudder. He felt grateful Smith was an ally; he would make a deadly enemy.

The king went into his tent. A moment later, Smith followed him inside. The Wayfarer rested on his cane—an affectation, the king thought, for he did not believe Smith needed it—and inclined his head.

"Good morning, Your Majesty."

"And to you, Mister Smith."

"Your brave men and women performed admirably today."

"They do, as ever," the king said. In moments like this, he wished he were back in Perinthia. Better yet, he longed to return to his summer residence at Otranto, where he could drink ale with the local men and spend his days fishing in the lake or riding his mare, Nadia, in the hills.

Wayland Smith held up his cane and studied its fox head as though he had never seen it before.

"You come with news, I presume?" the king prompted him.

"Some of each variety, in fact."

Hunyadi studied him, curious now.

"It will please you to learn that the Legend-Born have escaped."

The king stared, a smile spreading across his features. "Truly?"

Smith nodded. "I received word from the Mazikeen. Frost and Collette Bascombe crossed the Veil. Oliver and Miss Whitney are on the run in Palenque."

"We've got to help them—"

"If they can be helped, they will be. There are many voices, eyes, and hands doing your work in Palenque now, John. You need to remain focused on driving the invaders back. The Atlantean troops will not be so easily beaten."

The king glanced toward the battlefield. From inside the tent, he could see nothing of the melee, but he could picture its savagery in his mind.

"Nothing easy about it, Smith."

"It's going to get more difficult."

Hunyadi frowned, a knot of ice in his gut. "You said Atlantean troops?"

Smith nodded. When he looked up, a storm brewed in his gray eyes. "Difficult news, but not unexpected. This morning, the newspapers in Yucatazca announced an alliance between their government and the High Council of Atlantis. There are statements from Prince Tzajin. Falsified, we must presume, for he remains in Atlantis. The High Council promises to send at least three full divisions of Atlantean army forces to the Isthmus of the Conquistadors before the week is out, to aid in the war against you. Of course, they continue to claim it is only justice, since you broke the Truce by having Tzajin's father assassinated."

Hunyadi scowled. "Ty'Lis is quite the puppeteer."

"It is not merely Ty'Lis," Smith replied. "He answers to the High Council. He's little more than a puppet himself."

"How can you be sure of all of this? Are we certain that Prince Tzajin is under their control? It may be that he is in league with Atlantis. I have little faith to put in anyone of late, I fear."

For the first time, Wayland Smith seemed less than sure of himself. "The High Council must be commanding Ty'Lis, or they wouldn't have struck this alliance. They wouldn't be sending an invasion force. As to the prince, why would he turn on his father? Mahacuhta was not a young man. If Tzajin wanted power, he only had to wait for the old man to die."

"Youth can be so impatient," Hunyadi replied.

Smith lowered his head, the brim of his hat obscuring his face.

"Perhaps it is time you paid a visit to Atlantis," said the king. "I know you'd rather not involve yourself any more than you have to, Mister Smith, but with Atlantis revealing themselves and declaring open war, knowledge of what the High Council is planning may be the difference between the destruction of the Two Kingdoms and survival. And if Atlantis prevails, the Veil will be sealed forever. You know that is their intention."

The Wayfarer knitted his brows. He stared at the ground and then met the king's gaze with much consternation.

"I am not a soldier, John. I am not in your service."

"No. But you are a friend and ally, Smith," Hunyadi replied.

"If nothing else, we need to know if Prince Tzajin is collaborating with Atlantis, or if he is held against his will. The answer might well be the way to trump the High Council. If Yucatazca could be turned against Atlantis . . ."

He did not have to finish the thought.

"Understood," Wayland Smith said. "I will return."

Hunyadi watched him leave the tent, cane in hand. A moment later, he followed, but the Wayfarer was gone, as though he had never been there at all.

Oliver woke to the warmth of Julianna's body pressed against him. For several moments, her nearness was all he knew. Then, in a rush, other stimuli crowded into his mind. His neck itched. The air was warm and close, and filled with the smells of hay and horseshit and leather. A horse snorted and he opened his eyes.

He found himself spooned against Julianna in a nest of hay they'd found before dawn. For hours they had slipped from one hiding place to another, moving through alleys and hiding under wagons and underneath the tables on taverna patios to avoid being seen. Ty'Lis might not have many soldiers still in Palenque, but there were enough. They would be hunting the escapees. And if the Lost Ones in the city hadn't heard yet, they would learn as soon as morning arrived.

With dawn approaching, they had made it perhaps half the distance to the edge of the city. They had to find a place to hide out for the day where they might have a chance of going undiscovered. Homes and shops would not do. As the sky began to lighten, Oliver and Julianna even considered a dark alley where a carriage had been abandoned, thinking to hide underneath it. But then, not far away, they had come upon a large building that combined a stable and tack shop. The rear windows of the stable had been open to let in fresh air, and it had been a simple enough thing to sneak inside.

Exhausted and filthy, they had climbed into the loft and laid down together. There had been some talk about taking turns staying awake, and Oliver had taken first watch. But lying there with Julianna snuggled up against him—perhaps the most sublime moment of his life—had been too seductive.

Now sunlight streamed in the windows below. He shifted slightly and saw bits of dust and hay dancing in the shafts of light. Oliver nuzzled the back of Julianna's neck and kissed her ear. They had survived. From the angle of the light, he guessed it was late morning. The days lasted longer on this side of the Veil, so it was possible they'd had as much as five hours' sleep. That would have to do. They couldn't leave here until dark, but they needed to be vigilant, now.

He kissed Julianna's neck. With her in his arms, he felt hopeful, even peaceful, for the first time in so long. He wished for a shower and clean clothes and a soft bed upon which to make love to his fiancée. But all of those things would come, in time. First, they had a war to fight. Whatever this power was that he and Collette had, the legend said it came with a destiny. But at the moment that was the least of his concerns.

More awake, now, he discovered an ache in his neck and in his lower back. He reached up and wiped the grit of sleep from his eyes. Julianna made a soft moan of complaint, still mostly asleep, and nestled back against him.

Oliver smiled.

With a clank and a long creak, someone opened the door.

His heart raced. He laid his head down, then froze, not wanting to rustle a single piece of hay. Voices carried up to the loft. They had been lucky so far. When he'd woken and realized they had not been discovered, he had begun to think the tack shop was closed for the day. Someone would come to tend to the horses, of course, but the city would be on edge. He had dared to think the fact that they hadn't been disturbed yet meant they would be all right.

Julianna took a deep breath and let it out. Slowly, her eyes fluttered open.

"Sweetie, listen," Oliver whispered in her ear, hoping the men's conversation and the stamping and chuffing of the horses down below would cover his voice. "We're not alone."

She stiffened against him, and glanced back to meet his eyes. Together, they lay there and listened. The men spoke in the local language, or some other Yucatazcan tongue. Oliver didn't understand a word, and he knew Julianna wouldn't, either. He heard two voices and hoped there were only two men. If they were discovered and had to fight, they might be able to overcome them. If worse came to worst, he could bring down half the barn. But where would that leave them? On the streets of Palenque in broad daylight.

He held his breath, heart pounding in his chest. Hay prickled his neck and arms. The men laughed together and he could hear them moving around below. Something shifted, and from the sounds he realized that the horses were being fed. So they weren't soldiers. That was one piece of luck, at least. They weren't Ty'Lis's warriors, out hunting for the escaped prisoners.

One of the men snapped angrily at the other. Though Oliver didn't understand the words, he gathered this was a command of some sort, and perhaps an admonishment as well. The other replied with a placating voice . . . that began moving closer.

Julianna stared up at him, desperation in her eyes. He read the question there, but didn't have an answer.

Then he heard the creak of wood and saw the top of the ladder that came up into the loft shift slightly as the man began to climb. Oliver took a long, silent breath. It had all been too good to be true. They would have to fight, now, or risk being discovered.

His eyes narrowed and he stared at the top of the ladder. Julianna saw his intentions and she began to move, as slowly and quietly as she could. Oliver did the same. The men had stopped talking to one another and surely any moment the one climbing the ladder would hear them. But nothing could be done. If they tried to bury themselves in hay, he would hear them for sure.

Eight feet away, a pitchfork leaned against a tower of hay bales.

Oliver rose into a crouch.

The ladder shook and creaked.

He saw the top of the man's head—black hair powdered with gray—and then he bolted for the pitchfork. The man shouted in surprise. Julianna went over the side of the loft, hung by her hands, and dropped. Oliver could not think about what she was doing, only that she was in motion. Their lives depended upon one another.

His hands closed around the pitchfork and he swung it up, its tines pointed at the man who now stood at the top of the ladder. The man's eyes were wide and frightened, and whatever he said must have been a curse or a prayer. Oliver gestured with the pitchfork and the man leaned against the edge of the loft for balance and raised his hands as though he were being robbed.

"Ixchel!" the other man shouted from below.

Oliver moved closer to the edge. He saw the second man—rotund, with a dramatic mustache—coming out from one of the stalls. Julianna appeared, then, from beneath the loft. Relief washed through Oliver; she was unharmed from her drop. Then he saw the leather bridle in her hand.

The man on the ladder glanced from his friend to Oliver. A stream of words came from his mouth. One of them, Oliver felt sure, was "Bascombe," and it formed part of a question.

Oliver nodded. For better or worse, he would never again deny his identity. He was his mother's son, and his father's as well.

The man smiled, which threw him off.

Down below, his friend began to shout at Julianna. She started to swing the bridle in her hand. Oliver realized what he saw—a tall but thin woman, pretty, no threat to him. And perhaps he was right. Julianna could defend herself, but this was a large man, used to working with his hands.

"Jules, don't!" he called. "Keep away from him."

The man on the ladder—perhaps "Ixchel" had been his

name—turned and called down to the other. In the stream of words, he heard his own last name again, more than once. The way he said it, it seemed he thought it would calm the other man, but instead the man spat on the ground and shouted something. Oliver could imagine what it was. "Assassin," perhaps, or "murderer." Ty'Lis had all of the Two Kingdoms believing Oliver had killed King Mahacuhta.

"Hey," he said to the man on the ladder. "I didn't do it. I didn't kill him. Atlantis is your enemy, not us."

With a shout, the rotund man rushed at Julianna. Silently, she sidestepped and whipped him in the face with the bridle. He cried out and reached toward his eyes. She swung it again, slapping his hands away, and then she backpedaled.

Furious, the man kept after her.

On the ladder, Ixchel called to him. Then he glanced at Oliver with regret, and started to hurry down the ladder.

"Hey. Wait! Stop!" Oliver shouted, but the thin, graying stablehand had already dropped out of sight.

"Shit," he snarled.

Only one thing to do.

"Jules!" he called.

She spared a quick glance over her shoulder. As she did, Oliver dropped the pitchfork. It landed half a dozen feet away from her and Julianna raced for it, snatching it up and turning it on her pursuer.

Oliver went over the side. He dangled for just a second, glancing down to make sure he wouldn't break a leg, then dropped. The impact jarred him, and he went down hard on his ass. He scrambled to his feet and turned, almost at the same moment that Ixchel reached the bottom of the ladder.

But the stablehand barely looked at him. He started toward his friend, hands in front of him, and an argument began between them. Ixchel, incredibly, seemed to be telling the other man to back off. Both men grew more and more insistent.

"What the hell's going on?" Julianna asked, glancing back at Oliver.

The fat man lunged at her. In that moment of distraction, he grabbed hold of the pitchfork and tugged it from her hands. Then he started toward them both. Oliver grabbed Julianna by the hand.

"Get ready to run," he told her.

"What? Don't do anything stupid."

"Too late. Just get ready to run. I'll distract him."

Only when Oliver saw Ixchel did he realize he'd momentarily lost track of the other man. The stablehand stepped up behind his friend and swung a shovel. The man staggered and went down on his knees, eyes rolling up in his head.

He fell on his face, nearly impaling himself on the pitchfork. A trickle of blood ran down his temple.

Ixchel, regret and worry on his face, knelt at his friend's side and felt for a pulse. When he stood, he seemed satisfied.

Quickly he ran to the stable doors, cracked them open to glance outside, then closed and barred them. Oliver and Julianna could only watch in amazement, still shocked at what he had done. Then Ixchel turned to look at them.

"Bascombe," the man said.

Oliver nodded slowly, curiously.

Ixchel smiled. He gestured to Oliver and said a few words in his own language. Then he shook his head in frustration because he knew they didn't understand.

"You," he said, finding the word. "Legend-Born."

CHAPTER 10

The gods came out of Perinthia at dawn, just as they had promised.

Kitsune had been sitting on a rock beside the Truce Road, thinking back to the last time she had been here, sneaking into the city with Oliver and Frost after their mad flight on horseback from Bromfield Village with the Myth Hunters in pursuit. Those had been anxious days, but they had been sweet as well. Their intentions had been pure, their understanding of one another uncomplicated.

It had all gone wrong since. Kitsune wished that she could go back. But there was only forward, now, to war—and to whatever life held for her on the other side.

Boredom had forced Coyote to shed his human form and to chase voles across the rough landscape on the outskirts of the city in the hour just before dawn. But as the horizon had begun to lighten and the city of Perinthia began to awaken, the coyote had come and laid down at Kitsune's feet, gaze locked on the archway that led into the city. The arch connected two watch-towers. Dark figures appeared from time to time atop those towers, but Coyote's attention was on the arch itself. On the road.

For her part, Kitsune tried her best not to look at the arch, superstitious that if she stared in that direction, the gods might never come. But when Coyote made a soft growl in his throat and rose from his haunches, then transformed fluidly from animal to man, standing almost at attention despite his usual slouch, she knew that they would not march alone.

The war goddess, Bellona, came first through the arch, one hand upon the pommel of her sword, chin high with salvaged dignity. Only steps behind her came a god all in black. The ebon armored chest plate he wore gleamed in the dawn's light, as did the helm upon his head. His eyes were hidden in shadow, but Kitsune could see the thin line of his mouth and she shuddered. Never had she seen a being so grim.

"Ares," Coyote muttered.

Kitsune shot him a look.

"It must be," he whispered.

The fox-woman agreed. The god of war had come. How could he have resisted?

Salacia and Hesperos followed, but Kitsune's lingering gaze was broken by a blur that swept past Hesperos and Salacia, darted around Ares and Bellona, and raced toward her with such speed that she barely had time to raise her hands in self-defense before he came to a stop in front of her. His narrow face and thin limbs trembled as though with terrible age, and there were lines upon his face. Yet despite the wisps of white hair, she knew this could only be Mercury.

His eyes were alight with youth and power, with speed.

Then he vanished in a blur, racing off along the Truce Road toward the south—toward Bromfield and the Atlantic Bridge and toward war.

"Where the hell's he going?" Coyote said.

"To scout ahead," Bellona replied.

Kitsune turned. The golden gleam of the morning sun made the gods seem almost like figments of her imagination. But the rust on Bellona's chest plate and the dents in her helm were not illusions.

Ares walked past Kitsune and Coyote without a word, not even pausing to be introduced.

Another god came along behind Hesperos and Salacia, a fair-haired male in a pale blue robe who floated several inches above the ground, a small wind swirling up a dust devil underfoot.

"Thank you for coming," Kitsune said.

"Where are the others?" Coyote asked.

"Most of the old gods are tired," Bellona said, glaring at Coyote. "But there are those of us who refuse to be forgotten."

Kitsune shot Coyote a hard look.

"And we're very grateful," she told Bellona.

Placated, the war goddess gestured around her. "Mercury and Ares have gone on ahead. Salacia and Hesperos you know." She put a hand on Kitsune's shoulder. "Notus, this is Kitsune of the Borderkind and her cousin, the trickster Coyote," Bellona said, and nodded toward the floating god. "And this is Notus, the south wind."

Kitsune bowed her head. "We are honored to have you with us."

A gentle wind caressed her face, perhaps whispered something in her ear, and then was gone. Notus smiled at her, then continued along the road.

Kitsune glanced at Coyote, but saw that her cousin was not watching Notus, nor was he gazing at either of the beautiful goddesses who had joined them. His eyes were locked upon the watchtowers at the city's edge and at the archway between them.

Head bowed, a giant lumbered through the arch, the road buckling beneath the heels of his leather boots. With his shaggy

THE LOST ONES 151

beard and dusty clothes, he looked like one of the carnivorous giants who lived along the Sorrowful River, eating wayward children and crushing their parents underfoot.

Frantic, she glanced around for cover. Not all of the Myth Hunters, it seemed, had gone to war.

But Bellona laughed softly and both Hesperos and Salacia turned to smile lovingly at the giant.

"Have no fear," the war goddess said.

"It is only Cronus," Hesperos added.

Kitsune shook her head in confusion. "Cronus?"

Salacia stepped up beside her, looking almost sickly in the morning sun despite her beauty. Her green-hued skin had an almost Atlantean caste, but the dawn light gave her a kind of jaundiced, cadaverous appearance.

"A Titan. They were forerunners of the gods. Cronus is the father of Zeus. His mind is not what it was, once, but he is fearless and savage in battle."

Coyote stepped close to Kitsune. "I don't doubt it."

Kitsune watched the Titan as he lumbered toward her. His head was still bowed and she looked at his eyes, expecting them to be cruel but finding only lost innocence there.

Cronus smiled at her. "Pretty fox," the Titan said.

Bellona stood straighter, hand gripping the pommel of her sword.

"Shall we go?" the goddess asked.

Kitsune bowed with a flourish of her copper-red fur cloak. "By all means."

The morning had been gray and bitter, but as the lunchtime crowd began to make the pilgrimage back to their offices, the sky allowed a tantalizing glimpse of spring. In the passenger seat of Jackson Norris's new Jeep—his personal vehicle, since it wouldn't be very subtle to sit there in a car emblazoned with the logo of the Wessex County Sheriff's Department—Sara

Halliwell gazed up at the blue sky peeking through the clouds above and thought about the hope that spring inspired. Spring, she had told more than one girlfriend, was what made people believe in God and the afterlife. The seasons followed the arc of human life, and when men and women hit autumn, they began to fear the snowfall. Come winter, brittle and white and cold, people were desperate to believe in spring.

Sara didn't know if she believed in an afterlife—in a spring after human winter—but she had no doubt that when she reached her own autumn, she would wish for a little faith.

"Doesn't this guy ever eat lunch?" Sheriff Norris said.

Slouched in the driver's seat, he stared over the top of the steering wheel at the façade of Bullfinch's, a small used book shop two blocks out of the center of Chesterton, Connecticut. They had been there since shortly after ten A.M., and Sara had to pee, but mentioning this to Sheriff Norris seemed like a bad idea. This was supposed to be a stakeout. But the man they were waiting for would have to leave the bookshop at some point to eat lunch.

Wouldn't he?

A terrible thought struck her, and she couldn't stop herself from giving voice to it. "What if he brought his lunch to work?"

The sheriff sighed and glanced at her. "I've been trying not to think about that. I really don't want to have to sit here all day. My butt's already asleep and before long I'm going to need the bathroom."

Sara grinned. "Thank God. Me too."

Jackson looked through the windshield again. "Let's give him half an hour. If he doesn't come out, we'll take turns for bathroom breaks."

"Deal." Sara nodded. Then she glanced at him. "Are you sure you don't want to just go in there and talk to him?"

"For a dinky little bookstore, they've got some healthy traffic. Seems like there's nearly always someone in there," the sheriff replied. As if to punctuate his words, a pair of fortyish women came along the sidewalk carrying cups of coffee—office workers still on break—and entered the store. "I really don't want to be interrupted."

Sara felt a twinge of sadness for Marc Friedle. "We're just going to ask him some questions. You talk like he's the one who killed all of those kids."

A furrow wrinkled the sheriff's brow. "Nothing like that. But the more I think about it, the more I'm sure Friedle knows something that he didn't tell us. Kind of pisses me off. I wonder what we would have done differently if he'd been forthcoming with us from the outset. I wonder if your father would still be around, bitching to me about some policy change or other."

Just like that, she didn't feel sad for Friedle anymore. She laid her head against the cold glass of her window and watched the door of Bullfinch's Books, willing the man to emerge. Sara had known Jackson Norris most of her life, but she had never envisioned spending long hours in a car with him. They had exhausted topics of conversation two-thirds of the way into their trip to Connecticut and she had no idea what they would talk about on the way back. But for now, silence was just fine.

Chesterton had a certain appeal. Forty minutes south of Hartford, it wasn't quite close enough to the ocean to be considered seaside, and was neither large enough to be a city, nor small enough to be called a village. Yet Chesterton was clean and upscale enough to almost be considered gentrified. The locals cared about their town. A banner that hung over the street announced that the Spring Fling Festival would be held the first weekend of May.

There were many places Sara had been that she'd felt could be summed up with that classic bon mot, "It's a nice place to visit, but I wouldn't want to live there." Chesterton seemed like it would be a wonderful place to live, but visitors would be bored out of their skulls.

"Here he is," Jackson said.

Sara's eyes popped open and she drew in a long breath,

realizing she had begun to drift off to sleep. It took her a second or two to interpret the words. Sheriff Norris stared out through the windshield and Sara followed his line of sight to discover a small, almost dainty-looking man standing in front of Bullfinch's Books with a ring of keys, locking the door. Doubtless when he stepped away, there would be a "Back in thirty minutes" sign or something similar on the glass.

Friedle started along the sidewalk toward them. Sara reached for the door handle.

"Wait," Sheriff Norris said, one hand on her arm. "Not until he passes."

So they watched him go by. Sara studied him out of the corner of her eye. He had thinning hair and a vaguely European look, but his distant gaze and despondent air diffused some of her antagonism toward him.

When Jackson opened his door, Sara did the same. She stepped out onto the sidewalk, her muscles throbbing at the change in position. They closed their doors simultaneously and the sheriff moved swiftly around the back of the Jeep. Sara fell in beside him and the two of them quickened their pace, catching up to the neat little man.

"Mister Friedle?" Jackson said.

Sara thought it odd that, instead of stopping, Friedle walked on a couple of paces, then slowed, halting with his back still to them. He seemed to deflate.

"I wondered when you would come for us," the man said, his voice a strange rasp.

Then he turned toward them. Sara flinched back, horrified. His face had changed. The pale, somewhat effete countenance had become a twisted, ugly thing with leathery furrows and jagged, broken teeth. She stifled a small cry and then blinked—

And the illusion had passed.

Illusion? That didn't feel right, but how could it have been anything else? She glanced at Sheriff Norris, but he didn't seem fazed at all. If he had caught a glimpse of that ugly, inhuman face, he gave away nothing.

"Us? Who do you mean by 'us,' Mister Friedle?" Jackson asked.

Now, though, more than one mask had come up to cover Friedle's features. A caul of suspicion pulled tight across his face as he studied the two of them.

"I'm sorry. I thought you were someone else."

Jackson pulled out his identification wallet. As he took a step nearer to Friedle, he glanced around to make sure no one was paying attention.

"We've never met, Mister Friedle, but you probably know my name. I'm Jackson Norris, the sheriff from up in Wessex County."

The man blinked, and a different kind of sadness seemed to burden him than had troubled him when he'd strode past the car.

"I know the name, Sheriff. Mister Bascombe spoke highly of you."

"And of you, Marc. Which is why I'm confused about a few things."

Friedle's eyes narrowed. "What things might those be?"

"Is there somewhere we could talk?" Jackson asked.

The man arched an eyebrow and looked at Sara. She realized that it was the first time he had focused on her since she and the sheriff had walked up behind Friedle together. A shudder went through her. Already the details of that face had begun to fade from her mind. She had caught only a momentary glimpse and it had disappeared in an eye blink. Sara had to consider that it had only been her imagination, the stress of the past few months, and her inner conviction that Friedle was some kind of monster.

But she'd never had hallucinations before, nor seen visions, so she couldn't brush it off so easily.

"I had just been going to the café for a sandwich and coffee. You're welcome to join me, and I'll answer whatever questions you've come so far to ask. But, first, who is your lovely companion?" the man asked, and his accent became stronger. Where did you get an accent like that? Switzerland? Denmark?

"This is Sara Halliwell," the sheriff said. "Her father was—is—my best detective. He's gone missing, just like Oliver and Collette Bascombe."

Friedle gave her a sympathetic look. "Ah, yes. He'd gone to England with Julianna. I'm very sorry. It appears that I must add your name to the list of people I have failed."

Sara stared at him. "What do you—"

Jackson shot her a look that reminded her that he was the sheriff and would ask the questions.

The man they had come so far to speak with saw the moment of tension between them and nodded as though in approval. "Perhaps you could both do with a bite to eat as well. We can find a comfortable booth and discuss all of the mistaken assumptions that have been made about Max Bascombe's murder, and the fate of those who've vanished."

That sounded good to Sara, in spite of the fact that she did not want to move any closer to the man who sometimes had the face of a monster.

But Sheriff Norris took insult at the man's words.

"What mistaken assumptions?"

Friedle did not smile. Instead, he gnawed his lower lip and such sadness came over him that his eyes grew moist and a tear slid down his cheek.

"Oh, nearly all of them, I'd say. Come along, my friends. I'll give you the truth. You won't accept it, but telling it is the least I can do. I owe them all that much."

The man turned and started away from them. After a few steps, he glanced back and Sara flinched, afraid she would see that hideous face again. But he looked perfectly normal, now.

"Come along, Sheriff, Miss Halliwell. It's a story that

could cost my life, and it's what you came for, so you'd best pay attention."

The Twillig's Gorge militia marched southwest on the Orient Road, dust rising in their wake. They were a motley crew of men, women, and legends, carrying a broad array of weaponry, but still Ovid Tsing felt proud of them.

They would follow the Orient Road toward the Isthmus of the Conquistadors, and the moment they found a detachment of Hunyadi's army, they would pledge themselves to the commander of that force. Whatever it took to defend Euphrasia, they would do. In all his life, Ovid had never done anything as important. The Atlanteans had attempted genocide against the Borderkind. They had shattered the Truce. They had murdered the King of Yucatazca and invaded the Two Kingdoms.

They had to be stopped.

The Jokao marched behind the Twillig's Gorge militia. The Stonecoats had rendezvoused with them when they left the gorge, coming across the plateau with a rumble that shook Ovid's heart in his chest. Some of them had designs engraved in the stone that armored their bodies, dyed deep, natural colors. He had not been with them long enough to recognize any hierarchy dependent upon these sigils, but knew their leader from the three ochre-painted furrows on his chest.

Ovid would have preferred to have the Jokao at the front of their force, but the Stonecoats' thunderous passing raised a great deal of dust. Also, their presence seemed to unnerve the human members of the militia. Legends were often formidable, but rarely came in such large numbers. There were perhaps one hundred and fifty Jokao marching with them—an enormous number, far greater than Ovid had hoped—and they had sworn the same vow as the militia had, to drive the Atlanteans from the Two Kingdoms.

When the last of his militia had passed, Ovid nodded at the

leader of the Jokao and fell in with the final line of his re-cruits—the seven archers he had helped to train. They greeted him cheerfully, and that gave him heart. The march had already been long, but enormous distance still separated them from the Isthmus. It gladdened him to see that none of the militia were flagging.

They marched on. From time to time he saw someone sip from a water-skin. In another hour, they would stop for a brief rest and dry rations. No full meals would be eaten until they camped tonight. It had been planned fairly well, he thought. The help he'd received from his lieutenants had been invaluable, but he would be relieved to hand over command of the militia to the king's army. They would know how best to utilize volunteers, as well as how to keep them fed and armed.

Such thoughts occupied much of Ovid's thinking as his feet rose and fell. The march became a numb monotony, but they were traveling to war, and there would be no monotony once the arrows began to fly and the steel to sing.

The day grew warmer. As they continued southwest, the heat would only increase, but he didn't mind. Ovid liked the way heat settled into his skin and then down into his bones. It made him feel alive and vital. Death always seemed close by when the snow fell.

A voice shouted his name, shaking him from his reverie. Ovid glanced to his left and saw LeBeau, the swordsman among his lieutenants, hurrying along at the edge of the road even as the militia marched on. The troubled expression on the swordsman's face forestalled any greeting.

"What is it?" Ovid demanded as he stepped out of the ranks.

"Another army awaits us on the road ahead. A rabble, I'd say, but I don't see Hunyadi's colors anywhere."

"Damn it." Ovid slipped his bow from where it had been slung across his chest, then caught up to the other archers who made up his personal guard. "Come with me."

The archers hurried out of the marching ranks. Ovid and

LeBeau led the way, running alongside the rest of the militia. As they neared the front of the march, Ovid shouted for them all to halt, waving his bow in the air to draw their attention over the stomping of the Stonecoats at the rear. Men and women, and the handful of legends that'd joined them, came to a stop. Some watched him curiously, but the front line knew exactly why Ovid had halted them.

Two hundred yards ahead, an army camped on the road. They flew no colors that might have proclaimed their allegiance to any king, but there were a great many of them—perhaps three hundred—and a third of those had horses. Where in a thousand Hells had they come from?

"What will you do?" LeBeau asked.

Ovid stared at the men and women blocking their path. The horsemen were all mounted. Some of the foot soldiers, however, had been resting on the side of the road as he arrived at the front of his volunteers. Now they all began to rise. From what he could see there were no legendary among them, only Lost Ones.

"Bows," he said.

His seven archers unslung their bows and drew arrows from their quivers, preparing to fire at his order.

"LeBeau, with me," Ovid said, slipping his own bow across his back once more. "Archers, if we fall under attack, you are to respond in kind."

"Yes, sir," Yangtze replied curtly. Of all of the archers, he was the only one with any military training.

Ovid studied the road ahead, tempted to bring the Jokao up to approach this motley army with him. But he worried that the approach of Stonecoats might incite violence, and he wanted to find out if these were enemies before slaughter ensued. He had certainly not expected to meet armed resistance until they had traveled much further south.

LeBeau fell into step beside and slightly behind him. The lieutenant did not draw his sword, but kept his hand upon the pommel of the weapon. Ovid held his own hands out, palms up, in a gesture he hoped would be seen as peaceful. Together they crossed half the distance between his militia and the soldiers who blocked their path. There, he stopped. LeBeau shot him a quizzical look, but Ovid ignored it.

They waited.

After perhaps twenty seconds, a woman—an officer, it seemed—dismounted from her horse and handed the reins to another. A gray-haired, bearded man kept pace with her and the two walked out to where Ovid and LeBeau waited. Wariness flickered on their faces; they weren't any more certain what to make of this meeting than Ovid.

The woman and the gray-bearded man approached. Ovid could feel the combined attention of the soldiers on both sides, and knew he was just as much a target as those he now faced.

"We are in range of your archers," said the graybeard. His accent was unmistakably Spanish, tinged with humor. "I hope that you do not intend for them to kill us."

Ovid raised his eyebrows. "We are soldiers and citizens, not killers."

"I am pleased to hear it," the older man said. He executed a small bow. "Do I have the honor of addressing the leader of the Twillig's Gorge militia?"

Surprised, Ovid blinked. "You do. Ovid Tsing, sir. My lieutenant is Andre LeBeau."

The man inclined his head. "Then we are in time, after all. I had begun to fear you had passed by before we arrived. If it pleases you, sir, I am Cristobal Aguilar, Mayor of Navarre."

In confusion, Ovid stared at the man. "You have me at a loss. Do you mean to say you've been waiting for us?"

"Indeed," Mayor Aguilar said. "Word reached Navarre of your militia. Many of the men and women of our town had been talking about volunteering for the king's service. When we learned of your march, it...how do I say it? We were inspired. Preparations were swiftly made, and now we are here, General."

Ovid shook his head. "I am no general, Señor Aguilar."

"Ah, but it seems you are," the mayor replied, gesturing to the troops aligned behind Ovid. "We offer you our services, if you will have us."

For a moment, nothing seemed real. Ovid glanced at the army ahead and the one behind. He wondered how word had traveled so fast, and if it was spreading. Would other Lost Ones—other ordinary subjects of King Hunyadi—come to join the fight when they heard?

A smile touched his lips. His mother had been right all along, and now her dream was coming to life. He only wished she were alive to see it.

"We're honored to call you allies and friends, Mayor Aguilar."

Damia Beck let out a battle cry. Her sword flickered in the shafts of sunlight that came down through the branches of the Oldwood. All through the forest around her, combat raged. The company of soldiers she had sent to bait the southern invaders into the wood had succeeded. Cernunnos had commanded that the creatures of the Oldwood allow them to pass, waiting to attack until Commander Beck herself gave the word.

Now the word had been given. Blood flew, dappling leaves and soaking into the ground. The stink of the Battle Swine filled her nostrils. She had never been so close to one of them before and the stench nearly crippled her. The Swine brought its axe around in an arc meant to cleave her head from her shoulders. Damia grunted with effort as she dropped into a crouch, avoiding the blade, then rolled out of the way as the stinking, sweating boar kicked her. Its heavy boot caught her in the side, but added to her momentum as she rolled away.

The commander leaped to her feet. Pain spiked through her side where the Swine had kicked her, but she ducked behind a tree even as the boar swung its axe again. The blade bit deep into the wood and lodged there. The Battle Swine squealed in rage.

"Die, wretched beast!" Damia snarled, and drove the point of her sword toward the Swine's throat.

It dodged enough that the blade only slashed the side of its neck. Blood flowed over the heavy, leather armor that covered its chest. Its eyes gleamed yellow in the shade of the tree and it glared at her, snorting breath even more rancid than the stink of its body.

It lunged. Damia sidestepped to put the tree between them. Branches shook and leaves drifted down. A flutter of bright, tiny creatures darted into the shade—some breed of pixies whose wings were lavender, bottle green, and eggshell blue. They attacked the Battle Swine's eyes, distracting it. The idiot thing squealed and batted at the pixies, striking itself in the face.

Damia glanced around in search of help. A single human soldier against a Battle Swine might as well be suicide. But there would be no help coming. Corpses littered the forest, some in the colors of King Hunyadi and many more in the uniforms and helmets of the army of the south. Some of the dead, clad in Yucatazcan garb, had the unmistakable features of Atlantis. Dead goblins had been flung against trees or broken beneath the tread of the invaders. Strigae had been shot from the sky with arrows, plummeting to the ground as black-feathered lumps. Other wild things from the Oldwood lay dead as well, but far more—brownies and hobs, owl-men and a massive spirit bear—continued the fight alongside Damia's own troops.

Horses thundered through the wood, splintering branches and driving up divots from the earth. Her cavalry hacked at the Yucatazcans with their swords. As she spotted a handsome young horseman from Galacia, a Battle Swine emerged from between two trees and took hold of his mount, dragging soldier and horse together to the ground, hacking downward with his axe.

No help. Not now. Not in time.

Pixies shrieked and died. The Swine she'd been battling snatched one from its snout and thrust the brilliant little creature into its mouth. The pixie died between its teeth even as the Swine swept the others away and launched itself at Damia. Blood still flowed from the wound on its neck.

Weaponless, it threw itself at her. Damia raised her sword and, as the Swine attacked, she struck. Her blade sliced cleanly through the the massive beast's throat, but its momentum was too great. Even as it died, it fell upon her. By instinct, in its dying moment, it lowered its head and tried to gore her with its tusks. One of those yellowed ivory tusks plunged into her shoulder, rending flesh.

Damia Beck screamed in fury. She ground her teeth together as she pushed upward on the Swine's massive head. A sucking noise came from the tusk as she lifted it out of the wound in her shoulder. Her body quivered with shock and pain and she felt a terrible chill go through her.

A moist grunt came from behind her. Not far from her head came a thump upon the ground that could only be another heavy boot. She had killed a Battle Swine in hand-to-hand combat, but now as she rose to her knees, three others surrounded her.

"Bitch," one of them snarled.

Damia nearly laughed. She didn't think the rancid beasts capable of speech. Why the Battle Swine—legends from the Northlands of Euphrasia—had fallen in league with Atlantis, she had no idea. They were brutal, savage things fit for nothing but killing. Perhaps they simply hadn't had much opportunity for war and bloodshed of late. No matter. They were the enemy, now.

"Traitorous pigs," she sniffed.

The three Swine laughed, then began to move in around

her. Commander Beck raised her sword and tried to figure out how to survive. From the few glimpses she had gotten, her battalion stood poised to triumph. But she would not live to see it.

One of the Battle Swine lifted its axe and started for her. Damia shifted, held her sword across her body, and shot a kick at the nearest boar. As she did, she extended her sword in the other direction, stabbing through the hand of the attacking swine. It squealed and dropped its axe.

Her heart raced. Sweat dripped down the back of her neck and trickled between her breasts as she steadied her breathing. The trio of Swine glared at her with their little piggy eyes, and she knew they saw her as a threat for the first time. They would not play with her, now. They would just kill her.

Damia smiled. She would not make it easy for them.

Both hands on the grip of her sword, she glanced back and forth between two of the Swine, keeping track of the third in her peripheral vision. A single second stretched into eternity, and she felt them move even before they began to attack.

Then a massive gust of wind blew down on top of them, staggering Damia and pushing the three Swine back a single step. A shadow blocked out the sunlight that streamed through the branches, and then a body struck the ground, driven down by the supernatural wind. Bones cracked. Green feathers danced on the breeze. Antlers snapped.

The Peryton that had scouted for the Yucatazcan battalion lay dead, separating Damia from two of the Battle Swine. The Atlantean Hunter's green wings were folded beneath it. Arrows had been shot through its chest and neck, but it had been the strength of the wind that had slammed it to the earth and killed it. Dark ichor leaked from the broken Peryton in a spreading pool.

A low grunt and a scuffle came from behind her, and Damia spun to face the third Battle Swine only to find it already dead. Gaka, the Japanese oni who served in her Borderkind platoon, had come up behind it. The ox-headed oni held the head of the

Swine by its matted hair. Gaka had twisted the beast's head right off.

Damia nodded to him. Gaka blinked all three of his eyes as he nodded in return. The commander glanced around to see the remains of her Borderkind platoon closing in. Four ogres had survived, though one had grievous wounds on his side and face and a broken arm. Two Naga archers slithered across the ground, bowstrings drawn back, arrows aimed at the remaining two Battle Swine.

The wind spiraled down and took human form as Howlaa, an impossibly tall, impossibly thin, blond female, clad in white fur. The elemental wind spirit came from the Northlands, like the ogres and the Battle Swine. Howlaa spat at the Swine. One of the ogres, huge war hammer in one hand, cuffed a Swine with the other. They felt betrayed by these other legends from their homelands.

Damia waved off the Nagas. The archers lowered their bows.

The Battle Swine grunted and one of them laughed. Neither had dropped its axe.

"Take them," the commander said.

She turned her back, having been witness to more than enough death for one day. As she did, Old Roger stepped from a tangle of underbrush. His flesh seemed more like knotted wood than she remembered and his ruddy cheeks were red as apples. She wondered how effective he had been in battle, but that was before she looked past him and saw the three Yucatazcan soldiers who had been impaled from the ground up, with branches growing out of their sides and faces. Apple blossoms tipped each branch.

"All over but the tears, eh, Commander?" Old Roger asked.

Damia glanced around. Her soldiers had begun to come together in small clusters. Some were tending to wounded, others gathering the weapons of their fallen enemies. Goblins scampered up into trees. Pixies darted off and disappeared, normally unwilling to be seen by the Lost Ones. All sorts of other Oldwood creatures had aided them in this battle, but most of them had hidden themselves away again.

"So it appears," Damia replied.

A cavalryman cantered through the trees toward her.

"Report," she said.

The soldier bowed his head. "From what we can tell, Commander, none of the invaders who entered the Oldwood made it out of the forest alive."

"Excellent." Damia glanced at the wind spirit. "Howlaa, take a look. Do not allow yourself to be seen. If there are others to the west of the Oldwood, we'll wait until dark and attack. If they march north to try to go around, we'll pursue them and still have the element of surprise."

Old Roger made a small noise.

"What is it?" Damia asked.

"You don't think either of those things is going to happen."

"True. I believe they will retreat southward and wait for reinforcements before making any further attempt to reach Perinthia. There are too many unknowns for them here, and they have just learned their forces aren't sufficient to overcome them."

Howlaa smiled, and the wind whipped around her, sweeping her up into invisible nothingness. The trees rustled and she was gone, off to observe the enemy's movements.

"Their forces aren't sufficient," a shrill, grating voice said, "but they will be soon."

Damia glanced around and saw the swift-footed Charlie Grant leaning against a tree as though he had been there for hours. Behind him, Cernunnos, lord of the forest, stepped out from the daylight shadows, his antlers crusted with dripping gore. Damia held her breath. Apparently the lord of the forest had engaged in battle himself.

But it had been the boyish Charlie who had spoken.

"You can talk?" Damia said, studying him.

The little man took out his whistle and gave it a toot. "I like the sound of this and despise the screech of my own voice. Once I had a beautiful voice. You should have heard me sing. Women swooned. Men laid down their weapons. Then I bedded the daughter of a witch, and the hag punished me thusly."

Damia understood. His voice made her skin crawl. The whistle was vastly preferable.

"If you have news, Master Grant, you'd best announce it," Damia instructed.

Charlie nodded grimly. "Dire news, but not unexpected, Commander. The alliance has been struck between Atlantis and Yucatazca. Of course, the High Council presents it as though they are only now coming to the aid of Prince Tzajin against Hunyadi, blaming Hunyadi again for the murder of King Mahacuhta."

Frustrated, Damia sheathed her sword with a sharp click. "Do the people of either kingdom believe that? How could anyone?"

"Some will," Charlie replied. "Many in Yucatazca, of course, but far more in Atlantis. And the governments of Nubia and other lands are not going to get involved if they can at least pretend the war is just. The invasion force has been driven back in many places, but a single, massive battle front has formed thirty miles north of the Isthmus."

Her infantry and cavalry had begun to gather around her. Damia forced herself to put on an air of confidence she did not feel.

"Then we have not a moment to lose. Hopefully more troops will come from the north and east. Until then, we must do all that we can."

She studied Cernunnos. He shifted, muscles rippling under his pelt. There was grace and majesty in the lord of the forest, but grim disdain as well.

"What of you, milord? Will you and the wild of Oldwood help us to defend Euphrasia?"

Cernunnos scraped the ground with one hoof. "I have told you that we will not leave here. If the invaders pass through, we will stop them. But the Oldwood will not fight Hunyadi's wars for him."

"Even though your help could mean the difference between victory and defeat? If we fall, you will have no allies to defend your own land."

Many of the wild things in Oldwood had emerged once more to hear her speak. Goblins and owls watched her closely. A hideous hag-woman with blue skin stood only a few feet from Cernunnos, shaking her head as though angry at the idea of any further alliance.

"We will survive," Cernunnos said.

"Yes. Until they come and burn down the whole wood." Damia sighed. "Whatever you wish, milord. I only hope we're able to defeat the invasion without your help. Otherwise, by the time the war comes to you for the last time, you'll be on your own."

The lord of the forest studied her a moment from beneath the rank of antlers that sat heavy upon his head like a crown.

"You will want to bury your dead, I presume?"

Commander Beck nodded. "Yes. If it's no trouble, and their remains won't be disturbed."

"They will be left at peace," Cernunnos replied. "They died with courage and as our friends. But leave the corpses of the invaders to the animals. The forest has to eat."

awn had broken over Ecuador. Light rain fell, and Collette Bascombe lay her head back and let it sprinkle her face. Hidden away in the thick of a banana plantation, clad in the stale clothes she had worn for months in the dungeon, she would have given almost anything for a shower and clean clothes. And perhaps she would get them, soon. For the moment, though, she was just grateful to be back in her own world.

Your world? Really?

The words came unbidden into her mind and the voice of her conscience had an edge. She and Oliver were children of two worlds, the living embodiment of everything the Veil was not. They were human and legend together. But this ordinary world was hers. And still felt like home.

The rain fell. The wind blew. People worked and played, lived and died, and it was all completely ordinary. Little people weren't likely to come out of the jungle. Monkeys weren't prone to transforming into men and speaking riddles or holding grudges.

The legend said that a child of human and Borderkind—someone like her, or Oliver—was destined to tear down the Veil between the ordinary and legendary worlds. At the moment, Collette thought this was a spectacularly bad idea. She liked her world just the way it was. Boring. Ordinary. Life had enough peril and ugliness without adding all of the problems of the legendary world to it.

She wished she could stay here. Not hiding among the banana trees—although even that would be preferable—but here in the mundane world. Even a few days' reprieve would have filled her heart with joy. But there would be no rest. No break at all. Her brother and Julianna were still there, on the other side of the Veil. Julianna would be there forever, it seemed, trapped by the magic that had created the godforsaken barrier between worlds.

Oliver and Julianna were caught in a war zone, and Collette was going back, not just for them, but because—no matter how nice it felt to be in her own world—they all had a score to settle. In life, there were some fights you could never walk away from. Not and forgive yourself.

Yet for the moment, Collette tried to let the peace and quiet of the plantation soothe her. The rain fell warm and gentle. The breeze smelled delicious and earthy. She and Frost had learned they were in Ecuador as soon as they had reached the outskirts of the city. A garbage can by the side of the road had given up a dirty, torn newspaper. They were in Machado, and just a few miles away was Puerto Bolivar, its sister city.

In the night, they had stolen along the perimeter of the city and eventually found the banana plantation.

Collette didn't want to spend a minute longer than she had to with Frost. The winter man said little. His blue-white eyes issued a kind of cold mist and his expression was grim; a crack in the ice made up his mouth. At the moment, she enjoyed his absence.

Then the light rain turned to brittle, frozen sleet, and she swore under her breath and sat up. The banana trees rustled and a gust of wind blew snow and ice across the sky. Impossibly fast, the small blizzard built itself into a man.

"Time to go," Frost said.

He glanced around, as though afraid they might be discovered. His hair—like dreadlocks made of ice—clinked together when he moved.

Collette climbed to her feet, feeling tiny beside the winter man. She had never been tall. With the spray of freckles across her nose and her petite stature, she had often had to fight extra hard for people to see her as something more than just "the cute girl." Now, all of that life was in her past. Her job, her friends in New York, all done with. She tried not to think about whether she would ever be able to go back.

"You found an American Express office?"

Frost narrowed his eyes, ice cracking. "No. We haven't time for that."

"That's the only way out of here," Collette said. "I need identification. I need money. And you said it's too dangerous to try to cross back through the Veil so close to Palenque."

"All true. So come with me."

The winter man turned and started along a path between two rows of banana trees. The top of the main plantation building could be seen in the other direction. Collette stared at his back a moment, then hurried to catch up.

"Look, it's going to take weeks—"

"We don't have weeks!" Frost said, spinning on her. The air around Collette dropped thirty or forty degrees. Her breath fogged and her eyelashes stuck together when she blinked.

"Listen—"

"No. Collette, stop. You haven't been thinking properly since we crossed the Veil. Perhaps it's because you're back in your world and you think, suddenly, that means that you need to follow the rules of humanity. But you can't think that way. Authorities all across your world will be looking for you, now. You vanished, remember? After your father was murdered."

"So, now I'm a suspect, the way Oliver was?"

The look on Frost's face chilled her.

"Perhaps. That does not matter at all. Regardless, you will be questioned. They will want to know where you have been. All of that will take time, during which Oliver and Julianna—and many thousands of others, both of your kind and mine—may lose their lives."

Collette shivered, then shook it off and faced him. She'd been tormented by the Sandman, kept as his captive, and escaped only to fall into the hands of Ty'Lis and end up in the dungeon at Palenque. In that time, she had learned a great deal about herself. She had found the magic of her mother's heritage inside her and a strength that came from her own heart. Home had a powerful allure, but the time hadn't come yet to indulge that.

Still, she studied Frost closely and did not care that he took offense at her scrutiny.

"You doubt me," he said.

"Why shouldn't I?"

"Our goals are the same, Collette. They always have been."

"Including when you brought Oliver across the Veil and left me to be murdered by the Myth Hunters?"

Frost cocked his head. "They did not kill you."

"True. The Sandman took me. There were times I would rather have died. Just because Oliver and I are both still alive doesn't mean you did the right thing," Collette snapped.

"This is foolishness," Frost said. He started walking again, but something wavered in his tone and aspect that said he might not be as confident as she had always thought. Collette didn't know whether to be heartened or frightened.

"Frost—"

"It might not have been the right choice, but it was the only choice. It kept you both alive. Oliver and I owed our lives to each other, several times over."

Collette caught up to him again. "And through all of that, you never trusted him enough to tell him the truth?"

Frost kept walking. "He was safer not knowing."

"But he deserved to know. *We* deserved to know."

"And now he hates me," Frost said.

Collette paused. Frost went on several steps under the banana trees, soft rain pattering against his slick, icy form. Then he stopped, but did not turn. Collette had heard the weary sadness in his voice. Maybe all he'd said was true. Perhaps he had thought of Oliver as his friend, and the rift between them pained him.

"No," she said, softly. "I'm the one who hates you. I'm the one you left behind. Oliver only resents you. Maybe he'll forgive you, one of these days."

Slowly, the winter man turned. For the first time, his face—all sharp lines and edges—looked almost human.

"And you?" Frost asked.

Collette shook her head. "You and I were never friends."

After a moment, the winter man nodded. "Fair enough."

He turned and strode more quickly along the path. In silence, Collette followed. A little over a minute later and they had reached a fence that ran around the perimeter of the plantation. Frost reached out and froze a section of the fence, then, with a fist, he shattered it.

On the other side they came to a dirt road. Nothing moved along that road—neither person nor vehicle—but twenty yards to the left a small gray truck sat on the shoulder. Rust had eaten away part of the front end and the sides of the truck were spattered with dried mud.

Frost started toward it.

"What the hell is this?" Collette said, hurrying to get a better look at the truck. Anxious, she glanced up and down the road, but they were completely alone. Frost moved with purpose, and that worried her.

"What've you done?" she asked.

At the truck, the winter man paused and glanced back at her. Mist rose from his eyes, drifting on the breeze. The rain around him turned to sleet and pelted the truck with a metallic prickling.

"I've become a thief," Frost said. Perhaps he smiled as he said it. "But not a murderer, if that is your concern."

With a gesture, he indicated the roadside. Under the trees lay a brown shape, and it took her a moment to recognize it as some kind of canvas tarp. Beneath it, she realized, lay the driver of this truck.

"He's not dead?"

"He'll live," Frost replied. "Get in the truck and drive, please."

"Where are we going?"

The winter man opened the passenger door, climbed in, and closed it, just as if there were nothing strange at all about a creature made entirely of ice and snow riding in a rusty old truck.

Collette did as he asked. The keys were in the ignition and the truck started instantly. The windows were open. Several times Frost simply evaporated out of his seat, drifting up into the sky, a twisting storm cloud rushing ahead of the truck, only to pour himself back into the seat a minute or two later with directions. They stayed north of the city, though Collette got several glimpses of it through her window; she was surprised at how modern it seemed. The truck rattled along plantation roads and then what might have passed for a main road. For a mile or so it seemed they might actually drive into Machala, and then Frost directed her to take a narrow, rutted turn to the northwest.

Moments later, they came in sight of the water. To the south, she could see the port and was stunned to find not only fishing boats but elegant pleasure craft and huge shipping vessels. They bounced through a pothole and she had to focus on the road, but she could still glimpse the port in the rearview mirror. On the left, they rolled past a massive seaside operation that a sign identified as a shrimp farm.

"You really think this is going to work?" she asked.

"What?" the winter man said.

"We're just going to take a boat? Obviously that's your plan, because there's no way anyone is going to let me on a plane with no identification, even if I had the money. Which means we're stealing a boat."

Frost glanced at her, his hair clinking together again. "I have already stolen it. The men I stole it from had guns. The hold was full of bags of white powder I assume is cocaine."

Trying to process this news, her mind snatched one question out of a dozen. "You know what cocaine is?"

The winter man scowled. "I have been crossing the Veil since its magic was first woven. I have seen the best and worst of humanity. One of the men is dead, shot by another and fallen into the sea. The others are incapacitated."

"You did all of this in a couple of hours?"

Frost looked back out through the windshield. "Time is short. They were evil men."

As though it was that simple. And, Collette realized, perhaps it was. Four or five miles up the coast, the winter man directed her into a narrow drive that led into a wooded, rocky piece of property. Whoever owned the place was wealthy by any standard. Her father had been very well off, but the house that perched on the edge of the ocean here was twice the size of the Bascombe home.

They drove up and parked right in front. Collette felt wary as they got out of the truck. The front door hung from its frame. Several windows were broken. Nothing moved except the door, which swayed loosely with the breeze. Part of her wanted to go inside and see the chaos that Frost had wrought.

Instead, she hurried around the side of the house, following a path that led to a dock. Two men lay bruised and bleeding and unconscious on the beach, several feet from the dock. One of them had an arm twisted at the wrong angle, clearly broken.

Collette paused to stare at him, thinking that no matter what this man had done, they ought to call someone. If his injuries were bad enough, he could die.

"We are at war," Frost said. His voice felt like a chilly whisper against her ear. "If our war took place here, these men would be our foes."

She took a breath. Much as she still hated Frost for leaving her to the Sandman's mercies—and much as she had lived her entire life by the laws and morals of her own people—she could not disagree with him.

They walked out onto the dock and boarded the boat. As a child, she had watched reruns of *Miami Vice* voraciously. Drug lords and cigarette boats. They called them something else, now, but she couldn't think of the word. Didn't matter. If those little, slick, swift craft were cigarette boats, this one was a cigar.

Less than an hour ago, she'd been lying beneath the banana trees and thinking how nice it was to be back in her world, where things felt more real. But now, nothing about this felt real. Or maybe it was just that Frost was right—they were at war—and in war, the old rules no longer applied.

"You never asked me if I could drive this thing," she said as she investigated the instrument panel on the boat. She ought to go below and look at the food and water stores, but there wasn't time even for that. If she needed something, Frost would provide. She might hate him, but she knew that he needed her, now.

He needs me, because Oliver stayed behind, and if Oliver dies...

She shuddered. Of course. Frost had done it to them again. Oliver had insisted he stay behind to protect Julianna, because she couldn't pass through the Veil. So Collette couldn't blame Frost for that. But the truth could not be denied. Once again, he had left one Bascombe behind to live or die, content with the knowledge that he had the other in his safekeeping.

Yet as perverse as it seemed, Collette found some comfort in this. She was Legend-Born. Frost couldn't afford to let her die. Too much relied upon the Bascombes. The Lost Ones would follow them into war, or fight on their behalf. The Borderkind who feared Atlantis's efforts to seal off the Veil forever would fight all the harder, knowing the Legend-Born lived.

"You can drive it, can't you?" the winter man asked.

The salt wind off of the water scoured him, but he seemed to enjoy it, somehow.

"Yes. How did you know?"

Frost cocked his head, as was his habit. "Perhaps Oliver told me. Or perhaps I assumed it, given your background. Your father's money provided many luxuries."

Collette sighed and started up the boat. The engine purred. "Right, then. Cast off."

Frost went to see to the moorings. Collette looked at the water, wondering what had become of the man who'd been shot and fallen in. His corpse would be floating down there, somewhere.

As the winter man breezed up beside her, she glanced at him.

"You know someone will come after us, right? If not the police, then the military. Or other scumbags like the ones back there on the beach. Even if they don't catch up, we'll run out of gas long before we reach the California coast—if I haven't starved to death by then."

"We should go," Frost replied.

Collette stared at him. "You're making this up as you go, aren't you?"

The winter man said nothing, just retreated into the cabin to get out of the sunlight.

Collette checked her instruments and pushed up on the throttle, pulling away from the dock. Oliver waited for her an entire world away, and she would do whatever had to be done to get back to him.

Ixchel brought them a hose that must have been used when the horse stalls had to be cleaned out, and Oliver and Julianna transformed an empty stall into a makeshift shower, taking turns cleaning off the grime and stink of the dungeons. Their new friend—whose entire knowledge of the English language was Oliver's last name—made several trips out into the city for them. He brought back soap, clean clothes, and food.

Oliver didn't think he had ever been so grateful to anyone.

When Ixchel helped him bind and gag the other stable worker—whom Oliver figured might also be the saddle maker—the man's face was heavy with regret. Julianna and Oliver tried to use the tone of their voice to thank him, and Ixchel nodded his appreciation, but when the other man regained consciousness and glared at his former friend, there could be no consolation.

Perhaps three hours after they had first been discovered, Ixchel went out again. This time, he did not come back right away. Oliver and Julianna busied themselves feeding the horses, avoiding any conversation about what to do next. Eventually, they could put it off no longer.

"He's been gone a while," Julianna said.

She'd tied her hair back with a strip of cloth. The shirt Ixchel had gotten for her was too small and the pants too large, but Oliver thought she looked adorable.

They met in the middle of the stable. The smell of leather and hay filled their nostrils. Oliver took her hand and leaned over to kiss her.

"He'll be back."

"How do you know?" Julianna asked, forehead creased with worry. She had not feared many things in her life. It troubled him to see fear in her eyes now.

"Jules, you've got to let it go."

Her gaze hardened and her nostrils flared. "Let what go?"

Oliver took her face in his hands and stared into her eyes. "I'm not leaving you here. If you have to stay, then I stay. We'll both survive it."

A sad smile touched her lips and he knew that—though she would always remember the girl she had been—this moment they had built a wall between past and future.

"We start from right now?" she said.

Oliver nodded. "From right now. We get out of here. We go north and hook up with King Hunyadi somehow."

"I like him."

"I know you do. If this is our world, now, we'll live in it together."

Julianna squeezed his fingers in hers, and Oliver knew that his fiancée wasn't the only one who had gone through a door that had closed forever behind her. The man he'd been, once upon a time, no longer existed. He would not grieve, though. For better or worse, he'd become who he had always been meant to be. His mother's son. His father's son. Himself.

A soft knock came at the stable door. They darted together into the stall they'd used as a shower, even as one of the front doors creaked open. Ixchel entered with another man—a thin, distinguished-looking fellow with silver and black hair. They spoke rapidly and Oliver had the distinct impression the other man was demanding to know why Ixchel had dragged him here.

Ixchel pointed toward their hiding place. "Bascombe," he said.

Oliver stepped out of the stall, holding Julianna by the hand.

The newcomer stared at them in something like terror, and then his face slowly transformed into a smile.

"You," the man said, in thickly accented English. "You are really him? You are Oliver Bascombe?"

"I am. And you?"

The man clapped Ixchel on the arm, then rushed forward to shake Oliver's hand. "I am Lorenzo Baleeiro. Many call me Professor, because I have worked as a scholar and teacher."

"Professor—" Oliver began.

"Lorenzo, please."

"All right. Lorenzo," he agreed, taking the man's hand before gesturing to his fiancée. "And this is Julianna Whitney. We're both very grateful to you for coming. I admit, we were a little anxious given how long Ixchel was gone."

Lorenzo waved this away. "You have nothing to worry about for the moment, my friends. Like many of us, Ixchel believes in the Legend-Born. It is our honor to be able to give you whatever assistance we can provide."

Oliver glanced at Julianna. She shivered, obviously as unnerved by this statement as he was.

"Look, Professor...Lorenzo," he said, "I appreciate it. We both do. But I'm no savior, y'know? I've been on this side of the Veil for a while now and I know how much stories and legends mean, here. But I've also learned that every legend has a core of truth. Monsters and heroes all have their own true nature that sometimes doesn't have a damn thing to do with the stories people tell about them."

He ran a hand through his hair, enjoying the sensation of being truly clean for the first time in months, though his mind whirled as he tried to determine their next move.

"Truth is," Oliver said, reaching out for Julianna's hand, "we're just people in trouble."

Lorenzo smiled warmly. "You may feel ordinary, Señor Bascombe, but trust me, you are not. Unless you are not truly Legend-Born?"

Oliver fought the urge to hide from the truth. Instead, he met the professor's gaze firmly. "I'm told my mother was a French legend, a Borderkind named Melisande. My sister and I are being hunted for that heritage. I'm not sure if we're ever going to be able to bring the Lost Ones home the way the prophecy says, but there are some things that Collette and I can do, things we've discovered, so we know we're not as normal as we always thought."

The professor chuckled contentedly, nodding. "Excellent. We really have been waiting for you for ages. Belief in the Legend-Born is one of the few things that the Lost Ones in Euphrasia and Yucatazca have in common. Which leads me to the obvious question."

Oliver raised an eyebrow.

Julianna stepped closer to the professor. "What might that be?"

"Why, what to do now, of course. You didn't escape from the dungeon just to spend the rest of the war stashed in the hayloft of an old stable, did you?"

A grin split Julianna's face. "I sure as hell hope not."

"I thought not."

Oliver hesitated to discuss their plans with anyone, yet he felt he could trust this man. "We thought we'd wait until nightfall and slip out of the city. I want to travel north and find King Hunyadi. Someone has to tell him that Atlantis is responsible for all this."

The professor's eyes went grave. "That has been the rumor. Do you confirm it, now? That Atlanteans are the cause of the war?"

Oliver nodded, and Ixchel started asking questions. Lorenzo quickly translated. As the two men spoke, Julianna moved closer to Oliver.

"Do you have any idea what you're doing?"

Oliver fixed her with a glance. "Something. I'm doing something, Jules. Maybe for the first time in my life. My father—no matter how benevolent his motives—took this from me. And I'm taking it back."

Julianna reached behind his head, fingers curling in his hair, and kissed him hard. When she broke away, both of them a bit breathless, she wore a small, suggestive grin.

"I guess you are. And y'know what? It's kinda sexy."

Oliver shook his head, smiling, and together they turned to face their newfound friends once more. Ixchel and the professor were talking rapidly now, hands gesturing too quickly to follow. They nodded to one another in agreement.

"Lorenzo."

The professor looked up.

"We don't want to interrupt, but we need to get out of here," Julianna said. "And not just out of Palenque, but out of Yucatazca completely. We'd appreciate any help you could provide."

Lorenzo looked stricken. Ixchel tapped the older man's arm and asked a question in his native tongue. The professor ignored him, staring at Oliver.

"You cannot simply slip away in the dark, my friend. There is so much good you could do here, not only for Yucatazca, but for yourself. The Atlantean scum who have usurped our throne claim that you murdered King Mahacuhta. They deny the existence of the Legend-Born. They send us to war against Euphrasia. But already many do not believe the edicts that are issued from the palace in the name of Prince Tzajin. If you were to speak to the people—to stand and speak the truth—many in the city would believe you, and others would at least begin to doubt."

"Wait, what about the prince? If they're doing all this in his name, where is he?"

"In Atlantis," Lorenzo replied. "Once, I was his teacher, but Ty'Lis convinced the king that the boy should learn at the feet of the scholars of Atlantis. Now with Mahacuhta dead, we do not even know if Tzajin still lives and, if he does, if he knows of his father's murder."

Julianna looked sick. "So this boy who should be king now is basically a prisoner in Atlantis?"

Ixchel watched them all impatiently. Oliver understood how frustrating it was to be surrounded by people speaking another language, but the conversation ran too fast for Lorenzo to translate.

"Yes," the professor replied. "That is what I believe. I know Tzajin. He was my student. If he were here, this war would not be taking place. The boy would have made certain of the truth before breaking the truce and attacking Euphrasia."

Oliver took both of Julianna's hands in his. They shared a long moment of unspoken communication. He knew her determination and her courage, and she knew that his years of bending to his father's will had made him unable to turn away from a fight that didn't involve his old man.

Ixchel muttered something to Lorenzo and the professor replied quickly. The stablehand turned to them and spoke as though they could understand him. When he finished, he gave Lorenzo a pleading glance.

"What is he saying?" Julianna asked.

Lorenzo took a breath, defeated. "He says we must help you leave the city. There are still Borderkind here. Ixchel believes there are some from the north, working in secret with people and legends in Palenque. But Palenque is uneasy. As you said, soldiers were in the streets this morning looking for you. Many people shouted at them and even threw things. Several were arrested."

Oliver narrowed his eyes, studying the man.

The professor surrendered. "As Ixchel says, you must leave. Your safety is in our hands. I believe I know a place—a bar—where many meet who could help us find the Borderkind. It will be up to them to see that you reach the north. Tonight, we will go to this bar. I will take you there myself."

"Or we could just go right now."

Julianna stared at him. "Oliver, no."

"The place is a powder keg," he said. "If we can set it off before we leave here, all the better. Whatever Collette and I are supposed to do or be, there's an opportunity here that you and I can't ignore. We want to help Hunyadi win this war, and make sure Atlantis doesn't take over the Two Kingdoms. And we can't do it from the shadows."

"Are you sure about that?"

Oliver touched her cheek. "I've spent too many years in the shadows as it is."

Julianna hesitated, then looked at Ixchel. "Saddle us some horses."

Lorenzo translated the request. Ixchel's eyes lit with excitement and he ran to comply.

"We're horse thieves, now?" Oliver asked.

"No. Apparently, we're fucking heroes."

"Do you kiss your mother with that mouth?" he teased.

But once spoken, the words could not be taken back. Julianna would never see her mother again.

The light went out of her eyes and her smile vanished. Powerless to soothe her, Oliver could only pull her close and hold her tightly. He kissed her temple but did not bother trying to summon any words of comfort. Nothing could be said.

everal minutes after he and Julianna had left the stables on horseback—with Lorenzo leading and Ixchel following—Oliver began to wonder what the hell he'd been thinking. Courage and stupidity could often be confused for one another, and he had a feeling perhaps this was one of those times.

The horses' hooves clip-clopped on the cobblestones of the narrow, curving street, drawing attention as they passed. At first, no one seemed to make any connection between them and the two prisoners who had escaped the palace dungeon, but then they began to earn strange looks. People whispered to one another when they passed. More than one of the murdered king's subjects darted off into shadows or back the way they'd come, perhaps hurrying to alert the soldiers that the assassins were trotting down the middle of the road.

Julianna shot Oliver a worried glance. He smiled, faking it badly.

"How far, Lorenzo?" he called.

The professor held up a hand. "Not far."

Whatever the hell that meant.

Their exchange did not go unnoticed. As soon as Oliver spoke in English, other faces appeared. Shutters opened. An old woman came out on her balcony and stared in such horror it seemed as though the devil himself were passing by. But then two other women—younger, if no prettier—stepped from the darkened interior of a house and started to keep pace with them, hurrying as they followed alongside the horses. A man came out the door of a tavern, eyes widening when he saw them, and popped back inside, shouting. Half a dozen others emerged with him and they, too, fell into step behind the horses.

Children laughed and ran ahead. A young girl—a beautiful creature in the prettiest dress—started to knock on doors as she hurried to keep in front of them. As they entered a wider street, people stood up from the patio of a restaurant and stared. On the corner, a man with a guitar stopped singing in the middle of the song.

A man shouted something at him from the restaurant.

"What was that?" Oliver asked.

"He wants to know if you're the one, the Legend-Born."

Oliver gripped the horse's reins and glanced at Julianna. "Tell him I am."

Lorenzo beamed. He announced it at the top of his voice.

A cascade of reactions swept around them. Some people laughed. An old man began to cry. Others were not quite so pleased.

A beer glass sailed through the air from the patio. Oliver pulled the horse's reins taut, stopping the animal just in time. The glass shattered on the cobblestones.

"Murderer!" someone shouted in English.

Other voices were raised as well, and now the crowd began to shout at one another. They spoke different languages, but Oliver understood even those whose words were not in English.

Some believed he had come to deliver them home at last and others that he was a fraud and an assassin.

"Ride," Julianna said.

Oliver spurred his horse and they began to canter down the road. Lorenzo shouted at the people as they passed, loudly announcing his identity. He recognized his name in the flow of the foreign tongue, spoken again and again. Oliver Bascombe. Ixchel joined in, shouting at the crowd, but his voice was joyous. He seemed to be exhorting them to action.

They came to a switchback in the road and took it, slowing only as much as was necessary. A huge crowd now followed, filling the street behind them. Lorenzo rode ahead, leading the way into an even wider road where vendors had set up a market. Fresh fruits and vegetables were on display. Shops with open doors sold hand-sewn leather bags and clothing and marionettes and a hundred other things. A girl with a basket of flowers watched them pass.

The word had preceded them into the market square. People spilled into the streets, gathering on either side to watch them pass.

"The bar is just there, across the square," Lorenzo called back over the ruckus of the crowd. "Those who are whispering rebellion into the ears of the people must be nearby."

You hope, Oliver thought. Otherwise, he was about to die.

A group of men and women barred their way. Lorenzo brought his horse to a halt. Oliver's own mare snorted and reared back before he reined her in. More calls of "Murderer" reached him. Some in the crowd screamed for his blood. He saw the same pretty girl who'd been running ahead of them catch up, her face etched with hatred. She wanted him dead. The idea sickened him.

Oliver sat up straight on his horse and raised both hands to quiet them.

Whether they hailed him or hated him, they complied. Only a low muttering of voices filled the square, now.

"In a few minutes, soldiers are going to try to take us back to the dungeon," Oliver said, raising his voice so that they could all hear him. Lorenzo translated as he spoke. "I don't plan to let them do that. The sorcerer, Ty'Lis, has promised to torture and murder the woman I love."

All eyes shifted to Julianna. She did not shy from them.

"My name is Oliver Bascombe. My father was an ordinary man named Maximilian Bascombe, and my mother was a legend, a Borderkind named Melisande."

The gasp of the crowd was audible. It had been one thing for them to hope for the truth, but it was another thing entirely for him to confirm it. Catcalls came from the crowd calling him liar and worse. Oliver ignored them.

"If you believe in the Legend-Born or not, that is up to you," he told them, and Lorenzo continued to repeat his words in the language of Palenque, though many of the people seemed to understand English perfectly well. "I can't and won't tell you what to believe, because most of the time, I don't know myself. So I won't try to explain what I believe. Instead, I'll tell you the things I know.

"The High Council of Atlantis wants to seal the Veil forever. On their orders, Ty'Lis sent Myth Hunters out across two worlds to track and murder the Borderkind, and sent the Falconer to murder my sister and me in our home because Atlantis believes that we are Legend-Born, and that we threaten their plans. With help from the Borderkind, we both survived. But the slaughter continued. You see, the High Council had a brilliant plan. If they could kill all of the Borderkind, and us, they could seal the Doors and close off the human world completely."

He paused, glancing at Julianna again and then surveying the crowd. They were listening. But what could he say? In truth, the king had died by his hand, but it had been the sorcerer's magic that had led to that tragic moment.

"I carried the Sword of Hunyadi with the blessing of the

King of Euphrasia," Oliver called across the square. "But Hunyadi did not send me here, and I am no assassin. The blood of your king is on Ty'Lis's hands, not mine. Atlantis has used us all! They want to see the Two Kingdoms torn apart by war so they can come in like vultures and pick at your remains. Now, Ty'Lis has the Sword of Hunyadi hanging on a wall in the palace, and Yucatazcans are killing and dying at the whims of Atlantis!"

Shouts rose. New voices. More people had flooded the square. Something moved on a rooftop and Oliver glanced up to see the strangest creature, a thing that looked as though it were part dog and part monkey, with a grasping claw at the end of its tail. Balconies filled. In the crowd, other legends began to appear—bizarre creatures with the heads of alligators or with mouths where their chests and bellies should be. Snake things slithered over cobblestones. A massive pachyderm stood on two legs at the entrance to a side alley.

"Give us proof!" a voice cried in English.

Before Oliver could say anything, Julianna stood up in her stirrups.

"Proof? What more proof could you want than this?" she demanded, arms thrown wide. Though clean, her hair still looked wild and her exquisite beauty and the edge of her fury made her seem like Eve, freshly evicted from the Garden.

"Oliver could have left Palenque in the middle of the night!" Julianna shouted. "Instead he's right here, in front of you. Unafraid. Could any of you say you would've done the same? Would you have run, or would you have given yourself over to your accusers?"

There's the lawyer coming out, Oliver thought. And he realized that he had been doing the same thing.

A scuffle started. A monstrous thing with eyes like a spider's all over its body tried to reach Oliver. Men and women—Lost Ones—intercepted the creature and drove it back. It began to screech, shouting at him in that foreign tongue.

"The Lost Ones want the Veil destroyed," Lorenzo said, edging his horse closer to Oliver's. "But most of the legends do not."

"Is it true?" a voice cried, cutting through the noise.

Oliver glanced up and saw an aging, bearded man on a corner, keeping out of the hot sun in the shade of a bookshop. His clothes made Oliver think that this man had crossed the Veil himself, not descended from some long-ago ancestor who'd come through, and that he might not have been here many years at all.

"Can you really tear it down?" the man called, desperation in his voice and his eyes.

Quiet fell upon the square. Oliver had felt this scrutiny from juries and from theater audiences many times, but it had never mattered this much. Some of what he'd said thus far had been a performance, even a small deception. But now he could not find it in himself to give them anything but honesty.

"I don't know," he said, quietly at first, and then he repeated it louder. "I don't know. I haven't tried to touch the Veil. My sister and I...there is magic we inherited from our mother, or from whatever magic brought her and my father together. But whether it works that way, I don't know. I'll tell you this much, though. Even if we can bring the Veil down, there's no way in hell we're going to do it with this war going on. No way."

An arrow sang through the air and took Lorenzo in the throat.

Julianna screamed.

The professor brought up a hand, eyes wide with surprise, and touched the feathers on the arrow's shaft even as blood leaked around it. With agonizing slowness, he tumbled from the saddle and fell to the cobblestones. People backed away and he hit the street with a thump.

Oliver spun in his saddle and saw the soldiers. The King's Guard had been alerted. To his mind, it was a miracle that he'd had the few minutes he did. Perhaps the size of the crowd had slowed them. Soldiers shouted and shoved people out of their way. No doubt they were telling everyone that he had to be arrested on the orders of the king.

Most of the crowd began to back away. But some pushed forward and attacked the soldiers.

Oliver glanced at Julianna. Her expression was grim. Ixchel still held the reins of his horse and gazed numbly down at the corpse of the professor. Not that they could have ridden away now. There were too many people crowded around, and Oliver counted fifteen or twenty soldiers coming up the street. Half a dozen more appeared from a side alley.

"Shit."

Julianna shot him a look. "Is that the best you can do?"

"You got anything better?"

"Hell, yeah." Again she stood in her stirrups. Cupping her hands to her mouth, she screamed at the top of her lungs. For a moment, all of the commotion stopped as everyone turned to look at her. Even the soldiers paused.

Julianna pointed at the larger group of soldiers. "Who gave them their orders, today? They're going to tell you that the king commands them, but where is the king? Who is your king, now? Is it Ty'Lis? Is an Atlantean the king of Yucatazca, now? Or is it Prince Tzajin? Because if Tzajin's the king, then where is he? His father is murdered and he doesn't even show up to bury him? He doesn't come back to Palenque to see to his people and to be crowned king? Bullshit! Tzajin isn't here because he's in Atlantis, and they won't let him come back! So who are these soldiers taking orders from? Who are you *all* taking orders from now? Atlantis?"

Seconds of silence followed.

Then a massive serpent rose up from the crowd, wrapped around one of the soldiers, and crushed him. Two men fell upon a second and tore off his helmet.

Beneath it were narrow features and greenish-white skin that was almost translucent. The soldier was Atlantean.

A thunderous roar went up from the crowd. Like a wave, they turned on the soldiers. In amongst them, some legends and even some humans fought against the rebellious mob.

"I'm glad I never went up against you in court," Oliver called to her.

"You should be," Julianna replied.

Neither of them smiled. Lorenzo had aided them, and now he was dead.

"Ixchel!" Oliver said, yelling to get the man's attention. "Let's go!"

He spurred his horse gently, trying to lead the way, to break through the crowd. Getting out of the city remained a priority. He had lit the fuse here in Palenque. The powder keg was exploding, but this wasn't his battle to fight. It belonged to the subjects of King Mahacuhta. Oliver and Julianna had to get out of Yucatazca and join Hunyadi. More than anything, they had to reconnect with Collette and Frost. Oliver knew his sister would go to Hunyadi as well. If he wanted to see her again, that's where he would find her. And that's where the next phase of this war would take place.

As to what that next phase would be—a grim certainty had begun to form in his mind. Oliver Bascombe was no hero, but he had a plan. And for that plan to work, he would need all the help he could get.

The square erupted in chaos. People attacked one another. The soldiers were dragged down. Swords flashed in the sunlight. Oliver closed his eyes against the glare and edged his horse closer to the other side of the square, where the road would eventually lead out of Palenque. He glanced over his shoulder and saw that Julianna followed right behind him, and Ixchel behind her.

Then a figure swam up out of the crowd—a creature covered with spider eyes—and grabbed Julianna by the leg. She shouted and kicked out at the monstrosity. Oliver called her name and grabbed the pommel of his saddle, prepared to dismount, knowing only that he had to protect her.

Someone slapped his leg to get his attention.

"That's enough of that stupidity," a curt voice said.

Oliver shot a hard look. He blinked in astonishment. For a moment, the face looked unfamiliar, but now he knew it. There were no feathers in that dark hair, but the ragged blue jeans and cowboy boots were still intact.

"Blue Jay!"

The trickster smiled, eyes sparkling with mischief. "Damn good to see you, Oliver. And I'm not alone."

"How did you find us?"

Blue Jay laughed. "How could we not? You're not exactly being subtle."

A shriek went up from behind him and Oliver turned, fear stopping his heart, only to find that the scream had not come from Julianna. The spider-beast stood impaled upon a dozen tall needles of white substance that looked like spun sugar—or spiderweb. On either side of him stood a Mazikeen sorcerer, faces lost beneath their hoods, but a welcome sight just the same.

"Oliver?" Julianna asked.

"They're friends," he said.

The relief in her eyes made him realize just how vulnerable they had made themselves.

He turned to look down at Blue Jay. "I assume you can get us out of here?"

Again, the trickster smiled. He shouted something. A small figure dropped from the top of a building and landed on Blue Jay's shoulder—the weird monkey-dog creature he'd seen before. Several creatures Oliver presumed to be Borderkind started to clear a path. The air in the square rippled with a tremor of magic and several of the people around the horses transformed. One became a long-armed bruiser that Oliver was sure he'd seen before. Another he recognized immediately as the kelpy, Cheval Bayard. Oliver had met Cheval only once, on a night in Twillig's Gorge when Frost had gathered a handful of Borderkind to discuss striking back at Ty'Lis. Her silver hair gleamed in the sunshine.

Near Julianna's horse, a glamour was lifted to reveal a short man who seemed to be on fire, his skin blackening and burning, even though he walked calmly alongside them.

There were others. Some kind of cat-men. Tall things with wings and serpentine bodies and long fangs, blood smeared on their faces from where they'd drunk the blood of those who tried to attack them.

The Mazikeen passed Oliver, stepped in front of his horse, and together the two sorcerers gestured. Pushed back by the invisible hands of their magic, the crowd parted.

"Go!" Blue Jay shouted.

Oliver spurred the horse and snapped the reins, then just held on. He heard hoofbeats behind him on the cobblestones. Julianna and Ixchel had been freed from the crowd as well.

Then they were all riding, the Borderkind running and flying and capering beside them, keeping up as they navigated the twists and turns of the labyrinth of Palenque's streets.

Behind them, the chaos spread. The rebellion had begun.

The coffee had gone cold in Sara Halliwell's hands. Though she did not look at him, she felt Jackson Norris beside her in the booth at Veronica's Café. The sheriff's presence lent her some assurance that her mind had not begun to slip. And when his voice chimed in, low and menacing and more than a little bit angry, she could have kissed him, even though he was much too old and male for her.

"You're talking about fairy tales," Sheriff Norris said.

Sara didn't take her eyes off Friedle, partly because she couldn't believe the words coming out of the man's mouth, and partly because—as much as she kept telling herself she couldn't possibly have seen what she thought she had—she wondered if once again the mask of his face would slip, letting her see the ugly, frightening countenance beneath.

Friedle sighed. "Not fairy tales. Not the way that you mean, Sheriff. Honestly, I'm not quite certain which came first—legends or the legendary. Did the stories create us, or did we always exist? Time fades memory, even for ephemeral creatures such as yourselves."

Her hands clutched the sides of her coffee mug. Sara hadn't moved in minutes. They'd come all this way, and they had ended up with some fruity nut bar? Friedle paused to scrutinize them, perhaps to see if his words were getting through. Sara glanced at Sheriff Norris, wondering what was going through the mind of her father's old friend.

Ephemeral creatures?

He means us, she thought. *He's talking about human beings.*

Which crystallized the impression he'd been giving all along, talking about them as though they were an entirely different species. They existed on the ordinary side of this thing Friedle called the Veil, and his homeland was on the other. In his version of reality, all of the creatures of myth and legend, as well as all of the civilizations and lands and peoples, had once been a part of the world as Sara knew it. At some point, maybe a thousand years ago—more or less; Friedle wasn't sure—magic had been used to separate the ordinary from the legendary, to put a barrier up between them and give each their own lands. In the mundane world, humans didn't remember any of it, except in stories. But sometimes people wandered through to the other side by accident, or were brought through.

He'd also talked about legends called Borderkind, who could pierce the Veil at will, and humans called Lost Ones, who were trapped on the legendary side. People in the café went about their business. The waitress refilled coffee cups and brought lunch to various tables. A couple of fortyish moms chatted at the next booth, happy to have a day without their kids, and paid no attention at all to the insanity unfolding right beside them.

Then, to Sara's astonishment, the story had become even crazier. Friedle believed that Oliver and Collette Bascombe had been abducted by creatures from across the Veil, and that Sara's father and Julianna Whitney had tried to follow them and gotten trapped on the other side. Lost.

She shook her head, staring at the man. "How the hell did you manage to run a household for the Bascombes with all of this stuff in your head?"

The words came out before she could stop them, but she did manage to plug in "stuff" instead of "lunacy" or "crazy shit."

Friedle arched an eyebrow. "Please, Miss Halliwell. I understand that you're distraught. I'm merely giving you what you came here for. You wanted to know what happened to your father, and I'm giving you the answer. When I've finished, if you've got a theory that fits the facts more than the truth I'm sharing with you, I'm quite certain you'll ignore anything I've said that doesn't fit within your worldview."

Stung, Sara stared at him. In all her life, no one had ever accused her of having a narrow worldview. With her lifestyle, openness and acceptance usually came with the territory. So many people were cruel and intolerant to her, the last thing she wanted was to do the same. But either Friedle had a genuine mental disorder or he was fucking with them.

I don't need this.

"Let's say, for the sake of argument, that some or all of this is true," Sheriff Norris began.

Sara shot him a dark look. "You can't be serious, Jackson."

He quieted her with a glance. She relented. He was the cop. Maybe he approached lunacy with a different attitude. Or maybe he thought there was still something they could learn from Marc Friedle.

"It is," the man replied.

"All right," Jackson agreed. "You still haven't explained who you are, and what you have to do with the Bascombes, and why they were abducted and their father was murdered. Care to shed light on any of these things?"

The little man sat straighter, a glint in his eyes. Something dark flashed there and Sara winced, remembering the frightening face she'd thought she had seen when he had first turned toward them out on the sidewalk. It had been a trick of light and shadow, or of her own imagination, of course. He seemed nothing but ordinary now. That fidgety normalcy made his story even more ridiculous.

Now, though, his eyes took on a kind of ancient wisdom that belied his features, and he did not seem quite so ordinary.

"For more than two hundred years, I served in the house of Melisande. Most times, she was a creature of rare elegance and beauty, but when her mood turned dark or she yearned for the water, the lower half of her body became that of a serpent. When the Veil was raised she became Borderkind, and could travel with ease between this world and that, and sometimes I traveled with her.

"My true name is Robiquet," he said. "And my true face is something you do not wish to see."

When he spoke those words, he looked hard at Sara as though they were meant for her. She flinched. Had she really seen something, then?

No. It's just grief and hope and confusion. This can't be true. It couldn't be, because if she believed this little part of what Friedle—or Robiquet or whoever—was telling her, then she had to believe everything. And she couldn't do that.

Friedle smiled. His teeth were small and sharp. "I'm a goblin. What you see is a glamour, magic that Melisande gave me long ago."

Something shattered in the kitchen—a dropped glass or plate—and Friedle clapped his hands over his ears, a sudden flash of terror and pain in his eyes. Then he took a deep breath, squeezing his eyes closed, and when he opened them he wore the most sheepish expression, so that she could not help feeling sorry for him.

"Breaking glass," he said, and then shuddered, as though that was explanation enough. "Just can't abide the sound."

"So, this Melisande?" Sheriff Norris prompted, like this was any other investigation and Friedle just a typical informant.

The little man nodded. He went on at length about Melisande, but Sara found herself only half listening. Despite how unsettled she'd been out on the sidewalk, she studied his face, trying to imagine the features of the other one she'd imagined she'd seen. What had happened at that moment, when they had come up behind him?

"—introduced Melisande to Maximilian Bascombe. I'd always loved the ordinary folk and visited whenever I could. Melisande came to love you people as well, and this world, and more and more we would journey here amongst you. Many Borderkind did. Some still do. There are places we meet, taverns and inns and baseball parks and such."

For once, the sheriff seemed taken by surprise. He held up a hand, chuckling and shaking his head.

"Baseball parks?"

Friedle frowned deeply and stared at him, eyes so dark that Sara thought she might be seeing the goblin underneath. "We love baseball."

The sheriff wasn't smiling anymore. "Right. Sorry. I may have read that somewhere, actually."

That made Friedle's mood lighten. "Quite possible. You love to write about us. Always have. Even before the Veil went up."

He brushed at the air as though erasing the tangent the conversation had taken. "In any case, Wayland Smith introduced Melisande and Max."

"Who's this Smith?"

Friedle seemed almost surprised that they had to ask.

"Wayland Smith. The Wayfarer? Traveler, some call him.

One of a kind. I suppose he's a legend, but there's more to it than that. Rumors abound. No one's precisely certain who he is or where he comes from, but he walks between worlds easily enough. Melisande encountered him while in this world and he brought her to a masquerade. Max was a very serious man, even then, but he loved to dance. They fell in love that night— genuine love, though some say such a thing is impossible between the ordinary and the legendary. But how could it have been anything else? She gave up her world for him, surrendered to everything ordinary."

"Meaning what?" Sheriff Norris asked.

"Well, she didn't look human, did she? Not in her natural form. To remain with him, she wanted to permanently alter her appearance, to become human in all ways. Smith aided her, and there was a magician who helped. Melisande had lived centuries as a creature of beauty and mystery, and she gave all of that up for love. She could no longer travel beyond the Veil. Oh, she could still sense the nearness of the legendary world, but if she had crossed over, the magic would unravel and she would return to her mythical appearance, perhaps forever. That was just as well, because she bore her husband children, and the legendary would have killed them on sight, had they known about them."

"What? Why?" Sara asked.

The waitress arrived. The three of them fell silent.

"Get you folks anything else?"

Sara smiled. "My coffee's gone cold. Could I get another cup?"

The waitress held up a finger, took a few steps over to the coffee station, and returned with a clean cup and a carafe. She filled it up and Sara wrapped her hands around the mug, grateful for the warmth that flooded into her and the aroma that seemed to clear her senses.

"Anyone else?"

"I think we're set," Sheriff Norris replied, and the woman

scribbled something on their bill, left it on the table, and sailed away. She hadn't given them so much as a glimpse of personality thus far, and Sara doubted she would reveal one.

When the waitress was gone, she and the sheriff stared at Friedle—or Robiquet, if that was his name.

"Why would the Bascombe children be killed?"

Again, Friedle gave them that look, the one that said these were all things everyone should know.

"They're half-human and half-Borderkind. Legend-Born, we call that on the other side. The Lost Ones believe that someday a child born of human and Borderkind will tear down the Veil and they'll be able to return to this world again."

Sheriff Norris massaged his temple, as if he had a massive headache coming on. "Hold on. If there are people on the other side—the Lost Ones you keep talking about—there must have been other children that were half-human, or whatever."

Friedle nodded. "Certainly. But the Lost Ones have already been touched by the magic of the Veil. For a child to be Legend-Born, the human parent has to have been born on this side, of entirely ordinary heritage. Max Bascombe had never been touched by magic before Melisande came along, I can assure you of that."

"But Oliver and Collette can't be the first ones," Sara said.

"No. Sometimes they've been killed. Other times they've lived out their lives undiscovered. But as far as I know, Melisande's children are the first ever to cross the Veil."

"So you believe they're supposed to fulfill some kind of prophecy?" Sara asked.

"I do. Most of the Lost Ones believe it, of course. And I suppose the legendary believe as well, or they wouldn't be so afraid of a half-breed being born. Wayland Smith knew it, of course, when he introduced Melisande to Max Bascombe. But by the time Max learned that his children would be seen as saviors by some and a threat by others, his wife was already dead."

Emotion strained his voice when he said this last and he had to look away a moment.

"Max hated us all, after that. The Veil. Legends. Magic. Anything of the sort, and Smith most of all. He blamed the Wayfarer for not telling him the truth before he and Melisande had children. Max feared for them. He kept me around because his wife had been fond of me and because he thought I could help him if Oliver and Collette exhibited any strange behavior or physical attributes. He grieved horribly, and at the same time, he worked to extinguish any spark of legend in his children, so that they would never wander afar, never discover what they were, never be revealed to those who would do them harm. He failed, of course. And I failed. I promised Wayland Smith I'd look out for Melisande, and then I promised her that I would look after her children if anything happened to her. I failed them all.

"I don't know how they learned of Oliver and Collette's existence. The only one who knew of them was Wayland Smith, and he'd practically orchestrated their parents' meeting, so he'd have no reason to expose the truth.

"But someone knew. Someone who wanted them destroyed. The Sandman came to kill them—killed Max and took his eyes, and lots of others after him, since someone was stupid enough to free him. Now they're both across the Veil, on the run—if they're even still alive—and Julianna and Detective Halliwell, your father, miss, are trapped there."

Sara found she had been holding her breath. She trembled a bit as she inhaled. "Trapped for now, you mean. If all of this is true . . . if any of it is true . . . then the Veil might not last forever."

Friedle nodded, practically bowing his head. "As you say."

"Sara?"

Sheriff Norris had turned to stare at her.

"What?"

A cop wouldn't speak his mind while the object of his investigation was sitting right there in the booth with them. Sara knew that. The fact that he'd questioned her at all with Friedle present had been a lapse and now Jackson tried to wave it away. But Sara knew what that one word—her name—had been asking. She understood the question. Was she buying any of this? And if she was buying it, was that only because it gave her hope that her father hadn't been murdered, that whoever had torn out Max Bascombe's eyes hadn't done the same to her dad, and left him lying in a ditch somewhere?

Sara stared at the sheriff. "You've got a hundred little mysteries wrapped up in this case, Jackson. You and the FBI and the police and governments in half a dozen countries. All this stuff is connected. You know it is. And you all know—every goddamn one of you knows—that you're not going to find the answers to any of them. If you were going to, you would've figured it out already. You think about those mysteries, Oliver popping up in foreign countries with no record of travel, the kids all over the world killed the same way as Max Bascombe, what happened on that island in Scotland, and dozens of other little questions—and you tell me this...can you explain any of them? Even one?"

Sheriff Norris stared at her a moment, shifted his gaze to Marc Friedle, and then looked at her again. "You know I can't."

"But the story we just heard explains them all."

"It's impossible, Sara. All of it."

She couldn't argue the point. The sheriff was right. Impossible. But the story they'd heard was also the only thing so far that seemed to make any sense.

"Maybe when the questions are impossible to answer, that's because the answers themselves are impossible," she whispered.

Friedle smiled.

"Let me ask you something," she said. "When we first came up behind you on the sidewalk and you turned around, you said something about somebody finally coming for you. But you said 'us.' Who's us?"

His smile faded. He looked around, as though despite all of the wild things he had told them, this was the one thing he did not want anyone else to overhear.

"Some of us—Borderkind—we don't ever want to go back. We want to live here forever, in the ordinary world. We like it here. But whoever wanted the Bascombes has been sending Hunters into this world, killing my kind. After what happened in Maine, I came down here to stay with friends. All of us at Bullfinch's, we're Borderkind. I thought you were Hunters, come for us."

Sara studied him. "So you have this other face; your real face."

Friedle glanced away, perhaps ashamed of his true self. "Of course."

"Can we see it, just for a moment? Just so we know what's real?"

"Here?" he asked, glancing around.

Sara looked at Sheriff Norris. He seemed genuinely baffled, but he focused expectantly on Friedle.

"Here," she confirmed.

The glamour dropped for a single eye blink, but that was enough. The waitress screamed, then looked embarrassed at the attention she had brought upon herself. Confused, she kept looking over at them, trying without luck to confirm that she hadn't had a hallucination.

Sara looked at the sheriff, but Jackson only stared at the goblin sitting across from him.

"All right," Sheriff Norris said. "What now?"

"What do you mean?" Robiquet asked.

"You made a promise. You screwed up. But as far as you know, Melisande's children are still alive. We want to find them, and Julianna and Sara's father, too. You said there were Doors."

The human-faced goblin shook his head. "Oh, no. The Doors are always under guard."

Sheriff Norris smiled thinly, a little bit of strain around his eyes. His understanding of the world had just been broken into pieces, so Sara didn't blame him. She knew she must look much the same, but her own worldview had been shattered slowly, over the weeks since her father had vanished and she'd had to come to terms with the possibility he might never return and she might never know his fate.

Maybe that had changed.

"Under guard?"

Robiquet nodded.

The sheriff left forty dollars on the table to cover their lunch and stood up. He glanced at Sara, then at the goblin.

"That's what guns are for."

hey fought their way out of Palenque. Black pillars of smoke rose above the city—fires burning somewhere near the palace.

Cheval Bayard had forsaken her human form and now the kelpy galloped along the cobblestones. Hours had passed since Oliver and Julianna had escaped from the dungeon, and the word had spread.

A full-scale rebellion had erupted in the heart of the city. It would spread, just as the smoke and fire would spread. But here at the edges of Palenque, the spirit of revolution had yet to arrive. A single building disgorged a band of Encerrados—horrid twisted little creatures whose mouths were crusted with gore—and the monsters rushed through their human neighbors to get at the escaping Borderkind. Cheval crushed one of them under her hoof with a sound like the bursting of rotten melon. Li stepped forward, fire roaring up from his eyes, and held out both hands. The very air around the little cannibals exploded into flame, charring their flesh instantly.

Cheval Bayard sideswiped a huge serpent. It coiled around her legs and brought her hard to the ground. Blue Jay would have gone to her aid, but Leicester Grindylow arrived before him, swinging a stolen battle axe with ruthless abandon. Grin had once been a sweet, amiable fellow, but in these past weeks a darkness had come into his eyes. The water boggart hacked the serpent's head off and helped Cheval to her feet. She neighed and tossed her head, and he took that as a signal, grabbing hold of her mane and throwing one leg over to sit astride her back. They charged together along the widening cobblestone street.

Blue Jay saw it all.

He lagged back, letting others take the lead, so he could keep close to Oliver and Julianna, who were still on horseback. A pair of soldiers—some kind of city guard—came from an alley toward the exodus. Blue Jay spun, dancing in a swift circle that lifted him from his feet. He whirled around, summoning mystic wings that blurred the air beneath his outspread arms. When the soldiers tried to attack him, his wings sliced through bone and meat and muscle, severing reaching hands. With a final twist, he swept his wings out and cut off their heads.

Savage, but swift, and right now quickness was the only thing that mattered. Though he was a trickster, Blue Jay did not have a callous heart. He grieved for these men, who likely had no idea they were following the commands of Atlantis, but this had become a war. In war, death decided the outcome.

Blue Jay stepped up into the air, riding the wind and transforming into a bird. Wings spread, the little bird rose higher and circled above the running melee below. As they'd stampeded through the labyrinthine streets, they had attracted both rebels and crown loyalists. Lost Ones fought one another in the ripple current of their passing. Blood splashed the cobblestones.

Jaguar-men and the vampiric, serpentine Pihuechenyi shoved and slithered and leaped through the crowds to reach the legends who dared to try to stanch the flow of the rebellion that carried Oliver and Julianna toward the city's edge. Other Yucatazcan Borderkind had joined them. Back toward the center of the city, the blue bird saw the pillars of fire rising into the air, still pluming black smoke. The turmoil continued, and would spread. Suspicion had run rampant long before he and his comrades had arrived to foment rebellion. All they had done was set a match to the fuse. Their work here was done.

He soared higher, dipped a wing and wheeled around to see that they were only one curve in the road away from the outer limit of Palenque. Beyond the city's edge there was a long stretch of grassland and—past that—nothing but jungle and mountains.

"Bastards!" Oliver shouted from the saddle, down below.

Blue Jay began to descend and spotted Oliver immediately. He had a sword of his own—no replacement for Hunyadi's blade, which still hung in the palace—but it would do. A couple of human thugs grabbed hold of Julianna and began to pull her from her saddle. Lost Ones had formed a protective wedge around Oliver's mount, just trying to get him out of the city. But he spurred the horse past them, and then jumped down into the crowd, sword in hand. On foot, now, he went after the thugs who were dragging Julianna into the midst of the fray.

Panic shot through Blue Jay. They'd gone through too much for Oliver to be killed now. Much as he hated to admit it, the symbolic victory Ty'Lis would achieve if the Legend-Born were killed was too much too allow. It didn't matter that Collette still lived, somewhere. Blue Jay counted Oliver as a friend, but more than that was at stake.

He darted toward the ground, wind whipping his feathers as he pinned his wings back. Fifteen feet above the heads of the crowd, he transformed again from bird to man. Dancing in the air, he dropped down into the chaos.

Even as he did, Blue Jay saw Julianna grab a fistful of the

long hair of one of her attackers. She drove her forehead into his nose, yanking him toward her by his scalp. The unwashed warrior staggered back, hands going to his bleeding, broken nose, and Julianna drop-kicked him in the groin.

She spun, ready to face the other.

Oliver reached her then, stepping between her and the pot-bellied man. The fool laughed and raised a cudgel in one hand. Oliver slashed the man's arm, severing tendons and breaking bone, then turned the tip of the sword and followed through with a lunge that drove the blade through the man's right shoulder even before his cudgel could hit the ground.

Blue Jay whipped through a small group of Lost Ones and a pair of creatures who looked like knotted masses of black sea-weed, their tentacles whipping at his face. Blood and green ichor flew into the air as his mystical wings cut them down. The trickster no longer hesitated.

"Well done," he said as he stepped up to Oliver and Julianna.

"How much further?" Julianna asked, her voice sharp.

"One more turn."

Oliver brandished his sword, keeping a black, wraithlike creature at bay. "Let's go," he said, and then they were off again, rushing along as though carried on the current of a swift river.

Blue Jay let out a battle cry. The other Borderkind who heard it might not have known the significance, but they recognized his voice and picked up their pace. They were breaking free now, the flow of the exodus too powerful to be contained in this one street.

"You know what I noticed?" Oliver said, glancing at Blue Jay as he ran. "No Perytons. No Atlantean giants."

"Yeah. Good for us. But bad for Hunyadi, I think. Atlantis has sent its worst against Euphrasia."

Oliver had no reply for that but his dark determination turned even more grim. They fought together to the next turn in the road. Another fire had started behind them, likely thanks to Li. The burning man had left a trail of charred and flaming corpses behind them. Blue Jay caught sight of him several times with Grin and Cheval. They had become almost like family to him by now, and he worried for them.

When they rounded the corner, the opposition began to break up. At the end of the road—at the edge of the city—a single person stood in their path. Even from a distance she was beautiful, her long red hair flowing around her shoulders and down her back. Her dress seemed like little more than a thin shift. Sunlight streamed around her, silhouetting her body.

"What the hell is she?" Julianna asked.

Blue Jay grinned. "She's a friend. Keep running!"

When they passed between a pair of three-story white-washed apartment buildings that marked the end of the street, the red-haired woman before them spread her arms wide. Blue Jay grabbed Oliver and Julianna and held them back.

"Give her room."

Fighting, trudging, marching, running, the others came on behind them—friend and foe alike. But then a brilliant yellow light exploded from the eyes of the woman who blocked their path. Blue Jay threw up a hand to shield his eyes. When the brilliance had receded enough that he could lower his hand, he saw the bird of light on the road ahead of them.

"Alicanto!" a voice cried out in alarm.

"You said she was a friend!" Oliver told him.

Blue Jay nodded. "She is. We're done here. Let's go."

Again he issued a battle cry and they rushed forward, moving past the treasure bird. Blue Jay had met Alicanto only once. She did not visit the human world often, but she was Borderkind.

Cheval galloped past him with Grin astride her back. Li rode his tiger. Jaguar-men and other Yucatazcan Borderkind followed. He saw Ahuizotl, the little monkey-dog who had proven both loyal and resourceful. They flooded out of the city along with dozens, perhaps hundreds, of Lost Ones, but their enemies halted and then returned to the city, terrified of facing the primal elemental force of Alicanto.

Julianna's legs ached, her muscles burned, and her throat was parched, but she kept running. Her fingers were wrapped around a long wooden staff that she barely remembered picking up. It had a blade on either end, almost like a rifle bayonet. Her auburn hair blew in the wind, whipping wildly across her face, and she knew she had been bruised and battered by running the gauntlet of Palenque's streets.

But they were out.

She whooped loudly, exultant, and turned to Oliver with a grin on her face. His free hand reached for hers and she took it. How had their lives come to this—lovers racing along a hard-packed dirt road with a city of legends behind them, he with a sword in one hand and she carrying that strange, double-bladed stick?

"You're laughing," Oliver said, his eyes shining bright.

Julianna hadn't realized it, but now she laughed harder. Her long legs stretched and she felt like some wild gazelle as she ran.

"We're out!"

Oliver only smiled. With his scruffy beard and sinewy body, he looked almost like an entirely different man. Julianna had loved him when he had only been ordinary Oliver Bascombe, but he looked like a warrior now, formidable in ways neither of them could ever have imagined. She felt some of this same change within herself, too—and though it frightened her, she also relished it.

This world would never be home. But with Oliver, she could endure. She had always prided herself on her intelligence and the strength of her heart, and if she had to live in the Two Kingdoms, none of that would change. They were in the midst of war, and for the first time she understood that it was her war just as much as it was anyone's. Julianna Whitney was one of the Lost Ones.

"What's going on?" Oliver called to Blue Jay, who ran along beside them, braided hair swaying, the feathers that had been missing before now magically returned, tied there where they belonged.

"What do you mean?" the trickster asked.

"The bird, Jay," Oliver said. "If she's on our side, why didn't she help us before?"

"Alicanto won't enter Palenque, but now that we're out of the city, she won't let any of them follow."

Julianna glanced over her shoulder and saw that he was right. Surprised, she surveyed the sky, thinking an attack might come from there.

"Seriously?" she asked. "Nobody's going to chase us?"

"Not right away," Blue Jay replied.

She let go of Oliver's hand, her weapon becoming heavy. She shouldered it as though it were a baseball bat. "Then why are we still running?"

Blue Jay laughed, leaped and twisted in the air, then came down, still running. "Why? Don't you want to run?"

Julianna found that she did. All of the long days and weeks in the dungeon were being burned out of her. Soon she would have to rest. But now—with the Borderkind and Lost Ones who had helped them escape Palenque streaming out behind them—she just wanted to keep going.

Their pace slowed not long after, and by the time they reached the edge of the jungle, they were moving only a little faster than a walk. As they entered the jungle, she stood between Oliver and Blue Jay and looked back at the city. Smoke still rose from spots all around Palenque.

"Do you think they're still fighting?" she asked.

"I hope so," Oliver said. "And yeah, I think so. Those people want answers. What we started today isn't going to end quickly, and it isn't going to end neatly."

Blue Jay crossed his arms. "We've made quite a mess for Ty'Lis. That's good. But it's only a start. With every day that passes without Tzajin returning, the suspicion and anger will grow. It may be that Atlantis will face a war on two fronts soon."

Julianna glanced at him. "But Ty'Lis may not even be in Palenque anymore. Most of the army has already gone north to fight. They're following orders."

"For now," Oliver said.

Then he took her hand. "Let's go."

For the first time, with the excitement and adrenaline wearing off and her bruised, exhausted body complaining, Julianna realized she had no idea where they were going.

"What's the plan? We're just going to walk all the way back to Euphrasia?"

Oliver shook his head. "No. There's a shortcut."

So they marched.

Twice during their long journey they stopped to camp. Sentries guarded their rear flank and ranged on ahead to make sure they would not be ambushed. Julianna soon became used to the rhythm of their traveling, to the voices of the men and women and the Borderkind that accompanied them. She shared several long conversations with Leicester Grindylow and found the boggart charming and kind. Cheval Bayard shot her chilly looks whenever she talked to Grin, as though she were jealous. Perhaps she was, though not, Julianna believed, in any romantic sense.

Li, the Guardian of Fire, stayed apart from the rest. There were perhaps fifty or sixty Lost Ones and half that number of Borderkind on the trek along with them, but Li kept to himself. Only Cheval and Blue Jay made a point to break away to speak with him now and then. Wherever he walked, his footprints were black, burnt marks in the jungle, but the fire did not seem to spread unless he willed it.

After a blur of time that seemed like an eternity, they came out of the thick woods—no longer as tangled as the jungle they'd first entered—and discovered themselves on the shore of a green, gently rolling sea. For two or three miles they walked north along the shore, and then arrived at their destination.

"The Sandman's castle," Julianna said, a pit of fear knotted in her stomach.

"He's dead, Jules," Oliver reminded her.

She shuddered. "I know."

But the knowledge did not dispel her fear. This was not the sandcastle they had been through before. Its architecture—if a structure made entirely of sand could be thought to have architecture—was quite different. But Julianna knew that the monster had at least three or four such dwellings scattered across the Two Kingdoms, and maybe more in other lands on this side of the Veil. But they were only separate structures on the outside. On the inside, the sandcastles were one and the same. They could enter here and exit through any of the others. The Sandman had also created doors that led to various other locations on both sides of the Veil.

"What are we doing, Oliver? Is there a Door—" she started.

"No Door," he said, staring at the peaks of the abominable place. "We'll go through from here to the sandcastle in Euphrasia. There'll be a lot of traveling ahead from the other side, but we'll be closer to the war than we are now. And once we're on the other side . . ."

He didn't finish the thought. Nor did he need to. Julianna had an idea what he was thinking.

All through their journey, Blue Jay had been conversing with the leaders amongst the Lost Ones who accompanied them and with some of the Borderkind who had helped to build up the underground rebellion in Palenque before it ignited. When Oliver and Julianna stood in front of the door to the sandcastle, the trickster approached them.

"It's just us," he said.

Oliver blinked. "What?"

"Well, the three of us, plus Grin, Cheval, and Li."

"Why?" Julianna asked. "We could use all the help we can get in the war. The Borderkind especially. Don't you think Hunyadi would want those jaguar-men on his side?"

"They are on his side," Blue Jay replied, gaze shifting between her and Oliver. "This is their land. They want to fight for it. They escorted us this far to make sure that Oliver got out of Yucatazca safely, but they're going back, now. If this is going to be a second front in this war, these people and Borderkind are needed here."

"You're right," Oliver said. "Of course."

"You're ready?" Blue Jay asked.

Li strode toward the doors of the sandcastle. Cheval Bayard had long since abandoned her kelpy form and approached them now, silver hair gleaming, as though she were some elegant lady out for a stroll. Grin followed, long arms practically dragging on the ground.

Oliver looked at Julianna. She nodded.

"We're ready," she told Blue Jay.

"Just tell them all to keep back from the castle after we've gone in," Oliver added.

"Why?" the trickster asked.

Julianna smiled and took Oliver's hand. "Just tell them," she said, and they walked through the open doors together.

The quartet of northern Borderkind entered behind them and they found themselves in a great hall of sand. A shudder went through Oliver as he looked around. Despite the Sandman's destruction, the place seemed to breathe with lingering malevolence. Since he had first crossed the Veil, he had been inside three manifestations of the sandcastle. Death had nearly claimed him the first time he had been inside this hall, and it had been here that he had finally found his sister again. Oliver was glad Collette was not with them. She would not have liked to return to the place that had been her prison.

"This place gives me the creeps," Julianna said.

Oliver clasped her hand and nodded. "Agreed. I don't want to be here a second longer than necessary."

"None of us do," Blue Jay said.

Oliver led them to the stairs that rose up on one side of the room, and they followed him into the upper chambers of the sandcastle into a twisting maze of passages until they found the steps that led to the castle's peak. From there, as before, they descended on the other side. At the first window, Oliver saw the landscape of Euphrasia's eastern mountains spread out around the castle, and knew they had to try again. They returned to the peak and began to descend what appeared to be the same stairs they had come up. But this time, at the first window, the view revealed forest and a well-defined way that he recognized as the Truce Road.

Their destination.

"This way," Oliver said.

Twenty or thirty minutes after they had entered the sand-castle in Yucatazca, they stepped out through its massive doors onto the grass of Euphrasia, an entire kingdom away.

Oliver turned and looked up at the castle looming over him. He clenched and unclenched his hands. For what seemed an eternity he stared at it, and then he became aware of Blue Jay and the others gathering just over his right shoulder.

A soft hand touched his left arm and he turned to see Julianna there. She moved her hand to the back of his neck, leaned in, and kissed him.

"Do it."

He smiled thinly and nodded. The sandcastle might be useful, but it was a monument to evil. Instead, he would make it a grave marker for the monster who had constructed it.

Oliver reached out and pressed both hands against the outer wall. At first it felt like concrete. But soon the grains of sand began to lose their cohesion. Entropy took hold and the wall began to break down. The sand cascaded down around him, sifting around his feet.

"Back away," he told Julianna. Then he glanced at Blue Jay. "All of you."

Even as they complied, the entire castle began to tremble. Oliver waited a handful of seconds, then staggered away, picking up his pace and running to join Julianna and the others.

He turned just in time to see the entire castle collapse with a rush of air and a hiss of sand against sand, its substance spilling and spreading on the ground. In the Orient, and in Yucatazca, and wherever else the sandman had built castles, those structures would be doing the same. In his mind's eye he could see the remains of the sandcastle that had stood on the seashore in Yucatazca. It would be crumbled now. The waves would roll in. Over time, they would erase any trace of its presence.

In a hush, they all stood and stared.

What the Sandman had made, Oliver had unmade.

The sun rose on a new day, but Collette and the winter man were still on the water. For much of the previous day they had skipped across the ocean at high speed, burning through the gas in the tank and then tapping the reserve fuel tank and at last moving on to a pair of large plastic gas cans stored in the rear of the boat. Luck had been with them in a lot of ways since their escape from Palenque, but Collette thought stealing the boat of a drug lord topped the list.

They'd kept a north by northwest course all through that day and had spent hours out of sight of any land at all. During the night, she'd seen the lights onshore.

Now, an hour or so past dawn, she studied the coast through binoculars the boat's owner had conveniently stowed on board and tried to figure out where the hell they were. One hand stayed on the wheel, the warm weather long since having melted the ice that had formed on it during the few hours she'd slept and let the winter man drive.

A chill went through her, gooseflesh prickling her skin. The coolness almost caressed her.

"Do you recognize anything?" Frost asked.

Collette lowered the binoculars and turned to him. His jagged features gleamed white and blue in the morning light, but his eyes seemed soft and a light mist rose from them.

"I've never been to Central America. What am I going to recognize?"

Frost cracked half a smile. "You're well-educated, Collette. I thought you might be able to put that education to work."

"Meaning you want me to guess?"

The boat skipped over the waves. She let her knees absorb the rise and fall.

"Essentially."

Collette tried to hate him, but she couldn't stop herself from smiling. "Based on our coordinates and not on any visual confirmation, I'd guess we're looking at the coast of Nicaragua. In case you're unfamiliar with it, let me just say it's not a place I'd want to get stranded."

Frost looked thoughtful. "But we have very little fuel remaining."

"Maybe we'll get lucky. Could still be Costa Rica we're looking at. That'd be better."

The engine coughed.

"Either way, we're going to have to start heading in."

But Frost wasn't looking at her, or at the shore. The winter man had turned around and now stared southward, back the way they'd come. His eyes were narrowed and his brows knitted together with a crackling of ice.

"That might be wise."

Collette felt her spirit sag. "You're shitting me. All day and all night, nothing. And now?"

She turned before he could answer and confirmed her worst fears. Three boats were moving fast toward them from the south, swiftly skirting the tops of the waves. These weren't government boats. Not a single flag fluttered in the wind. They were private vessels, and she had a feeling they had guns on board.

"Crap."

Frost reached out, took the wheel, and cut it toward shore. He grabbed the throttle and pinned it. The boat surged forward and Collette had to grab hold of him to keep from falling. Her palms and fingers seared with the frozen touch of the ice, then she managed to take the wheel from him.

"Hurry," he called to her over the roar of the engine and the cry of the wind.

"And when we hit shore?" she shouted back.

"Then they're my problem," the winter man replied.

Collette gripped the wheel so hard her fingers went numb. The thrum of the engine and the skip of the boat across the surf traveled up her arms and made her bones ache. But she kept on, straight for shore, the wind whipping at her, and she resisted the urge to look back to see how close the other boats had gotten.

The shoreline grew closer. A small inlet lay ahead, not much more than a fishing village. Sails dotted the harbor, fishermen already at work. Collette started toward the inlet, thinking they could lose their pursuers for a few vital moments amongst the other boats there—long enough to find a place to hide or a car to steal. How strange that such things, once inconceivable to her, had become pure instinct. Survival was hardwired.

"Not that way," Frost said.

The winter man loomed in her peripheral vision, a sculpted creature, pointing out across their bow.

"Take us to shore, as close and fast as you can."

"You got it."

A small promontory, little more than a spit of land, jutted out to help block the worst of the surf from the inlet, protecting the village harbor. Collette cut the wheel due east, the boat slewed a bit, and then they were jetting toward the spit at full throttle. Water sprayed up and blew in her face.

A gunshot cracked the air.

"Son of a bitch!" Collette shouted, turning to look.

The lead boat headed for them at an angle. Some asshole in a black T-shirt knelt on the bow, trying to get a bead on them.

The rocky promontory drew closer. They were only a couple hundred yards from shore, now, but the other boats were closing.

"Even if we beat them to land, they're going to be right on our asses!" Collette shouted over the wind.

The engine sputtered. She'd practically forgotten how low they were on fuel. She looked up at the winter man. His icy blue eyes met hers and she saw the determination there, the utter sureness, and she wondered what that meant.

Another gunshot echoed across the water.

"Whatever you have planned—" Collette started.

She never finished the sentence.

Frost flowed toward her, half solid and half storm. He gripped her wrist in that icy touch and the world seemed to ripple in front of the boat, the air turning silvery and opaque. Collette felt herself break through the Veil and then the wind and the human world released her. The boat disappeared from beneath her feet. Side by side, she and Frost plunged into the warm ocean.

She kicked to the surface, sodden clothes clinging, trying to drag her down. Spitting salt water, she wiped her eyes and looked around. They were only fifty or sixty feet from shore.

No boats chasing them. No gunshots.

Several fishing boats drifted further out, but these were sailing ships with an antique flair. The spit of land had vanished. The harbor village as well. The landscape of the coast had changed entirely.

"Where are we?" Collette asked as she struck out for shore.

Frost seemed to float in the water without any effort. What

he did could not rightly be called swimming. He appeared to glide just underwater, only his head above the surface. "Through the Veil."

"I know that much. I mean where. Geography is all different in this world, I gather. But I know there's a loose correlation, right? So we're still in Yucatazca?"

Frost stood up. Collette put her feet down but could not touch the bottom; not much of a surprise, considering her height. She swam a few more feet and tried again, and in moments they were both slogging toward the rocky shore.

"This place is called the Isthmus of the Conquistadors," the winter man said. His jagged body glistened as water ran off of him. "It connects the Two Kingdoms. Whatever troops are coming from the south, they have to take this route."

Collette had been trying to squeeze water out of her shirt, twisting up the bottom to wring the cloth. She dropped it and stared at him.

"So what now? Do we go north a ways and then cross back over?"

Frost shook his head, mist leaking from his eyes again. "The distance on that side of the Veil is too great. We must stay here and make our way as best we can."

She pushed her fingers through her hair, shedding water. As unwelcome as the news might be, she would not argue. What would be the point? They were behind enemy lines and she didn't want to stay here a moment longer than was necessary.

"You're saying there might be troops coming up behind us—"

"Infantry and cavalry," Frost interrupted. "When the invasion force from Atlantis comes, it will be by sea. But it will be on the eastern side of the Isthmus, so we'd do well to stay here on the western shore."

Collette took a deep breath, gnawing on her lower lip.

"It sounds impossible."

"Nothing is impossible."

"And if we run into the Yucatazcan army from behind? Hell, when we run into them—because eventually we'll hit the battlefront—I'm guessing you have a plan?"

Nothing about Frost could be construed to look human. She had been trying to remind herself that she wasn't supposed to like him—he had deceived Oliver, and left her to die, once upon a time. Yet in that moment, his eyes betrayed a vulnerable humanity and a dark humor.

"The word 'plan' might be overstating."

Collette stared at him in horror, and then she laughed, shaking her head. "You're not exactly reassuring me."

All trace of humor left him. His expression became grim once more. "We'll go north as swiftly as we can. If we encounter enemy troops, I will get you past them. And when we catch up with this hideous war, I will carry you over the battle lines and see you safely into the company of friends. You have my word."

Not even a flicker of a smile remained on Collette's face.

"I'll hold you to it."

ven gods needed to rest.

Kitsune walked along the bank of the Atlantic River in the dark, the moonlight glittering on the rushing water, and felt the tug of its flow. She wanted to hurry on to their destination the way the river did. A knot of anxiety had wound into her gut, and it tightened with every moment they spent camped on the eastern bank.

Bellona had insisted they make camp. The war goddess did not seem to imply that they were tired, so much as that a pause in their march to battle was the natural way of things. They stopped to rest because armies were expected to do such things. It maddened Kitsune, especially since she herself trembled with exhaustion, and yet her mind would not let her rest.

Guilt burned like poison in her blood, and emotions warred within her. She felt shamed by her jealousy and by her behavior with Oliver, even as she hated him for the way he had looked at her and touched her hand, his gentleness and the lust she had seen in his eyes. But had she really given him any choice? Kitsune had played the temptress, had nurtured his lust quite purposefully, even as she pretended innocence. She had hungered for him and so tried to lure him into betraying Julianna.

Kitsune had fallen in love with him.

Yet, though tempted, Oliver had never succumbed. He had wanted her—there could be no doubt about that. But he did not love her, and never could. His heart belonged to Julianna. Confronted with that truth, Kitsune had turned bitter, and her trickster nature had emerged. Had she stayed and fought Ty'Lis with them, she would only have been captured herself. But that would have been better than striking Julianna and fleeing for her life. Better than seeing the pain in Oliver's eyes.

Now she would reclaim her own self, her pride and passion. War raged, and she had called the gods themselves out from the heart of Euphrasia to aid King Hunyadi. Oliver might be in a dungeon in Palenque, but if she helped to turn the tide of the war, one day soon he would be free. He and Julianna.

They could find happiness.

It tasted sour in Kitsune's mouth, but she knew their happiness would be the only way she could forget the way she had betrayed them. The war must be fought, the Atlanteans crushed for their deceit and their slaughter of the Borderkind, and Kitsune would do whatever she could to see it happen. She fought for her kin. But if she died, it would be as much for Oliver as it would be for herself.

She'd had enough of hibernating, and enough of guilt.

"Damn you all," she whispered through sharp teeth, turning to look back at the camp the gods had made. "Let's just get on with it."

But they would not. The gods moved in their own time. Perhaps it would have been better had she and Coyote not attempted to recruit them.

A chill went through her, a hint of a long winter to come, though still distant. Kitsune raised her copper-red hood and pulled the cloak of her fur close around her. Immediately, she felt better. More herself. More clever. The fox had none of the heartache of the woman in her; at least, that was what she told herself. But even so, she could not separate the two.

A rumble came from the camp. She glanced over to see dark silhouettes by the fire. Fully a dozen of the old gods of Rome and Greece had joined her, and they were formidable. But they were still shadows of themselves. Once, these few would have turned the tide of the war simply by arriving upon the battle-field. Now they looked to combat as resurrection, a way to make themselves feel young and powerful again.

Notus, the south wind, drifted lazily around the camp. Mercury had gone ahead to scout, unable to stand still. If Kitsune had his speed, she would not be able to control herself—she would have left them all behind long ago and raced to join King Hunyadi on the field of battle. Salacia, Hesperos, and Bellona clung together, like lovers, and she suspected that might be the case. Ares, the Greek god of war, clearly lusted after Bellona despite the nearly incestuous nature of such a coupling. Dark and brooding, old and grim, Ares never spoke except of killing. Kitsune worried that he might not care very much about who or what he was killing, as long as he could make war and spill blood.

Coyote kept mostly apart from the old gods, save for Cronus. The Titan had risen from beneath ruins in the Latin Quarter, destroying what remained of those buildings. Though a lumbering, mad giant, Cronus nevertheless was excellent company. He spoke in a low murmur, gazing into nothingness, rattling off stories about the days before days and the glory of the creation of Olympus. From time to time he spoke to gods and Titans who were not present, as though reliving scenes from his ancient life. He had come along because Ares had summoned him, as though he was some kind of attack dog, and Kitsune wondered what would become of Cronus when they joined the war.

A smile touched Kitsune's lips—rare, these days. The gods had descended from Titans and they from beings born out of chaos. Perhaps by bringing these faded things to war, chaos would be the result. What a gift to Hunyadi that would be.

Then again, what were she and Coyote but tricksters? It might be that chaos was all that they could ever give to anyone.

Kitsune turned her back on the camp and continued along the river, breathing in the cool night and letting the sound of the Atlantic carry her where her legs, at the moment, could not. It brought her a little peace, and she could ask for nothing else—deserved nothing else.

"Evening, cousin."

She paused and glanced around to find Coyote behind her. Kitsune could not be surprised that he had caught up to her so quickly, and without her hearing a step. It was their nature.

"Lost in your head again, I see," he said.

Kitsune nodded. "I cannot seem to escape the predators in there. They wait for me every time I close my eyes."

Coyote sighed and shook his head. His eyes were mischievous as always, but strangely gentle. "It isn't healthy for our kind to think so deeply. Caprice is our great fault and our great salvation."

"Trickster-philosopher, that's a new one."

"One of us has to practice a bit of awareness. Usually, I'd rely on you. But you're not yourself."

Kitsune couldn't argue with that.

"How strange to have come to this moment," she said. "Once, I despised you as the most devious, most cowardly, and least honorable of our kin."

Coyote executed a courtly bow, half mockery and half sincerity. "And in those times, I worked hard to earn your scorn. But you and Blue Jay put aside caprice and whimsy to focus on the threat to all of us, and though it frightened me, I could no longer deny the truth."

"Which is?"

"If I let the world die around me, I would be alone."

A silence fell between them, full of understanding and sudden longing. Coyote wore his lopsided grin, but for once she did not think it foolish.

Then his eyes widened. His nostrils flared and he snarled, gaze locked on something just beyond Kitsune. Coyote bared fangs, ears pricking up, transforming even as he leaped past her.

Kitsune spun.

The Sandman stood on the riverbank, an arm's length away. Terrible lemon eyes glowed sickly in the dark and the moonlight. His gray-black cloak seemed to swallow the night. The sound of shifting sand filled the air and she saw the way the grit of his substance undulated beneath his cloak. And then he flowed toward her, long, dreadful fingers reaching for her, jaws opening, tongue rasping across his teeth.

Coyote flew toward him, meaning to drive him away.

A hand darted up. The Sandman gripped his throat and Coyote lashed out with his paws, clawing the monster, digging furrows in him.

The Sandman pulled Coyote to him, long, rough tongue poking out, and sucked one of Coyote's eyes into his mouth.

Coyote's tortured scream echoed along the riverbank. The monster tossed him away like garbage and turned on Kitsune. His soft, insinuating laughter crept under the fox-woman's skin, and she felt despair take hold of her heart.

"You turned my brother against me," the Sandman whispered. "You and Bascombe. I have hunted you, trickster-bitch. Now you die. You, and then Bascombe. And I'll bring him your eyes so that he knows that you are gone, and that you died screaming."

Kitsune shook her head, terror shuddering through her. "I saw you die."

"Destroyed. Not dead," he rasped. "I cannot die. Not as long as children fight when sleep comes to take them."

He extended a single, knife-thin finger. "Come. Your eyes are the loveliest green. I hunger for them."

Coyote struggled to rise, laid back his head, and howled to the moon and to the gods. Kitsune heard shouts from the camp and the ground shook as Cronus began to move. But they would be too late. If she pulled her fur around her and became a fox, the Sandman would catch her easily. As a woman, she could fight for a few moments. They would be all that remained of her life.

I'm sorry, she thought, but couldn't have said who the apology was meant for. Sand skittered toward her along the ground and then began to rise in a dancing breeze around her, scouring the exposed skin of her hands, face, and throat. She could feel it in the fur of her cloak. And she understood. He would strip the flesh from her bones.

First, though, the eyes.

Kitsune showed her tiny pointed teeth in a snarl. She hooked her fingers into claws.

"Take them," she dared him.

The Sandman came toward her. She tried to fight him, tore at his body and his cloak, dragged fingers through his sandflesh, reached for his eyes, but he batted her arms away. His knife-fingers tore her hood back and twisted in her long curtain of hair, and Kitsune screamed.

She hated herself for it, but she screamed.

Halliwell hid deep inside the Sandman. He had a tactile awareness of a body he no longer possessed. Still the sand seemed to flow over and around him. Nearby he could sense the presence of the Dustman, cold and angry and grim. When he had first learned he had become trapped behind the Veil—that he would never see his Sara again—he had felt like Alice down the rabbit hole. But this was far, far worse. This was a churning, rasping Hell.

His hands were stained with blood. Perhaps the Sandman's murders had not been committed with Halliwell's own hands, but the difference mattered little to him. He was a part of this barbaric, murderous thing. There in the maelstrom at the center of the Sandman, he was sure that he had felt their souls crying out as they died, felt their spirits brush against his own. As vicious and brutal as their murders had been, some part of him had been envious. They were free, while he was trapped with those eternal monsters.

The Sandman's hands. The Dustman's hands. Ted Halliwell's hands.

He hated himself, now. *Show a little backbone, Detective,* he thought. There was a cruel bit of humor in there somewhere, but he hadn't the heart to find it. *Hadn't the heart. There you go again.* He hadn't a heart or a backbone now, of course. But these were spiritual as well as physical things. Heart. Backbone. Courage.

There was a major disconnect in his brain. Courage wasn't the absence of fear, he reminded himself. It was action in spite of fear.

Ted Halliwell visualized himself standing on the riverbank. He saw through the Sandman's eyes, watched the water stream by, watched as they slipped toward the woman in the fox-fur cloak—Kitsune—and the man with whom she spoke.

He knew what would come next.

The Sandman had been looking forward to this moment ever since the three of them all rose together in this single form—sand and dust and bone, three beings in one. Kitsune had to die. Then the Sandman would travel to the dungeon where Oliver Bascombe was imprisoned, and in that darkened cell, they would murder the helpless man.

Halliwell stretched out his fingers. The ground felt solid beneath his feet. But there was what he saw through the Sandman's eyes and what he saw in his mind. The sand still shifted around him as though he had been buried alive. He felt its weight and warmth and texture on skin he no longer had.

In his mind's eye, he turned. In the sandstorm that enveloped him, he sensed the shape of the other—the Dustman, with his greatcoat and bowler hat.

"What are you doing, Detective?"

Halliwell sneered at him. "You know exactly what I'm doing."

"I'm not sure it's possible," the Dustman said.

Halliwell imagined himself breathing evenly. He imagined his flesh rippling with a constant shift of sand. He stared out through the Sandman's eyes and felt with the Sandman's hands as the monster shook Kitsune like a rag doll. She clawed at him and down there inside the Sandman, Halliwell cried out in pain, feeling the ragged furrows she dragged in his/their sand-flesh.

His fingers twined in her hair and he yanked her head back.

The Sandman's fingers twined in her hair and he yanked her head back.

"It has to be possible," Halliwell snarled to the Dustman. "We're all in here. You said so yourself. That means we have a choice. I can't bear any more blood on my hands."

The Dustman hesitated. Halliwell could feel it. Perhaps he didn't believe they could do it or perhaps he was only afraid of his brother. The Sandman's ferocity gave him the strength to subjugate them—or it had, so far.

Halliwell saw the terror in Kitsune's jade eyes. He watched the way her beautiful, elegant face became ugly and twisted with fear, and she opened her mouth and screamed. Her anguish tore at him.

The Sandman thrust out his tongue and licked Kitsune's eyes. Her cry became one of pain as the rough sand obscured her vision. The monster dangled her at arm's length and reached out with one prying, knifelike finger to dig her eyes from their sockets.

"I wish we had more time together," the Sandman said.

At first, Halliwell didn't understand these words. Then noises flooded into the maelstrom and he heard shouts and felt something shaking the riverbank beneath his feet. A low growl came from nearby. The one-eyed coyote rose on his haunches, issuing a menacing snarl. Wind whipped around them suddenly, tearing at the Sandman's cloak. Something loomed against the night sky—a giant, lumbering toward them.

"Alas," the Sandman said.

His talon cut the skin beside Kitsune's left eye.

Halliwell remembered the first time he saw one of the Sandman's young victims, a girl named Alice St. John. He allowed himself to recall, now, the screams and blood and ravaged faces of the victims the monster had taken since their substance was joined.

He could feel the riverbank underfoot, shaking with the giant's approach.

Truly feel it.

Sorrow and fury swept Halliwell forward. He felt as though he were surfacing from a sea of sand. New screams came from inside his mind, but now they belonged to the Sandman himself. Halliwell tossed Kitsune away. She hit the ground and rolled halfway into the river, then shot up to a crouch, staring at him.

I did it, you bastard, Halliwell thought.

The Sandman howled. He could feel the monster inside him, and the Dustman as well. The Dustman remained still, though he had begun to churn and flow, and somehow Halliwell knew the Dustman had begun to move closer to the Sandman, down there in the maelstrom.

For a moment, Halliwell was in total control. He could feel the grains of his substance, the swirl of sand, the wind whipping his cloak. Then pain raced up the back of his neck and a terrible weight crushed down upon his soul, trying to force him into the maelstrom again.

Kitsune stared at him.

"Run," Halliwell told her. "He's going to—"

The coyote hit him from the side, driving him down to the

dirt and glaring down at him from its one, remaining eye, gore still dripping from the crater of the other. The impact jarred Halliwell, and when he tried to move, he could no longer feel the Sandman's body—only his own bones, scoured by the maelstrom. He could see and now he could hear.

You wait and see, a voice in the maelstrom said, the Sandman talking directly to him, and perhaps to the Dustman, too. *Your presumption will cost you dearly. Whatever spark of you remains, it will be extinguished.*

Halliwell expected the Dustman to be troubled by this. Instead, he felt a grim satisfaction coming from him. *"If he could have done so, he would have done it already."*

"All of a sudden you sound pretty sure of yourself."

"Your spark survives. Your spirit's continued existence is proof enough."

So the Dustman had used him to see if the Sandman could be thwarted without repercussion.

"You're an asshole," Halliwell said.

The Dustman did not reply.

Halliwell concentrated on seeing out of the monster's yellow eyes.

A being hung in the air, the center of a blossom of starlight that illuminated the entire riverbank. Halliwell saw the others, now, warriors with hammers and swords and axes, all racing toward him. Kitsune had stepped out of the water, copper fur glittering with droplets, and the coyote trotted to her side to face the Sandman.

Too many, the Sandman's voice echoed into the maelstrom. *I will take her another night.*

They burst into a drifting, eddying mass of sand and floated off across the river, with the shouts of Kitsune's comrades—Borderkind or legend or whatever they were—chasing them into the dark.

You dislike being a killer, tasting the blood that stains the sand of my fingers. There is a village nearby with many young children.

Perhaps we should pay a visit to each and every one. I can almost feel the pop of their small eyes between my teeth now. Can you feel it, Detective?

"I'll stop you," Halliwell replied.

No. I felt it just before you stepped into me. Now I know what it feels like, and I will be on guard. You are a little puppet, mimicking my every move.

Ice gripped Halliwell's heart. Courage seemed far away, now. Where was the Dustman? If he could combat the Sandman, why had he withdrawn so deeply into the maelstrom that Halliwell could no longer even sense his presence?

No. Not the village. A far more satisfying punishment occurs to me, the Sandman thought, resonating inside Halliwell's head. *It will kill what's left of you, extinguish that spark, and you will surrender your soul willingly. You will beg for oblivion.*

Her troops shone with pride and renewed vigor that stemmed from their victory in the battle of the Oldwood, and Damia Beck indulged them such feelings, for now. Her fleet-footed messenger, Charlie Grant, raced from one detachment of the king's army to the next, delivering and retrieving information. In an hour, Charlie could travel ground that would take a soldier on horseback a day or more, and never seemed to tire.

The southern invaders had been routed. King Hunyadi's forces had turned them back at every step, in spite of the Atlanteans scattered in amongst the Yucatazcan army. Now the army of Hunyadi was driving them further and further south, and the soldiers believed that victory had arrived.

Damia tried to dispense with such illusions, but could not bring herself to be brutal with them. Not yet. There would be time enough for that later, when the army of Atlantis began its own incursions into Euphrasia. A few Atlanteans in amongst ordinary troops was one thing, but the army of Atlantis merged with Yucatazcan forces, and the reinforcements that were even now crossing the Isthmus of the Conquistadors—that would be a very different sort of war.

Her cavalry units rode at the front of their southern march. They had suffered a number of casualties at the Oldwood, but more for riders than horses. Half a dozen infantry men and women had been promoted to cavalry. The infantry hiked tirelessly southward, singing soldiers' songs and calling out to one another with ribald jokes and braggadocio.

Soon, when they drew closer to the new battlefront, Damia would gather her troops and give them a speech that would sober them up quickly. She would give them an idea of the odds that they were facing. Hunyadi had sent notes with Charlie Grant, coded messages that detailed their troop strength and indicated where the king felt the true battle would unfold. The facts were clear. With Atlantis joining the war, the odds would be stacked against the king's army.

Damia missed Blue Jay. She wished she could hold him in her arms and stroke the length of his lean, muscular back. The smell and feel of him seemed so distant to her now and she did not want to forget. In his eyes, she'd always seen mischief, but she had also seen adoration. Men had always lusted after her, and sometimes feared her, but no one had ever looked at her the way Blue Jay did.

A shout rang out.

Her fingers tightened on the reins and she spurred her horse on, breaking away from the rest of her mounted troops. Somewhere a bugle sounded—celebratory and playful—and she decided she needed to speak to her troops sooner rather than later.

A single figure stood on the road ahead; a tall, stooped, ugly thing—one of the ogres from her Borderkind platoon.

She snapped the reins, and her mare surged into a gallop. Damia sat forward on the saddle, letting the rush of the moment wake her up from her musings.

"Report!" she said as she approached the ogre.

The ugly northlander did not salute, but Borderkind were not regular army. Such protocol was not required of them.

"We've caught and killed three outriders, Commander."

Damia frowned. "Not together?"

As she spoke, the ogre glanced at the trees alongside the road. Two of his brothers lumbered out from the shade beneath the branches. The Nagas, Old Roger, and Howlaa had been sent in other directions, spread out to search for any Yucatazcan or Atlantean riders who had been left behind or sent back to the north as spies.

"No, Commander. Over the past several hours, we've caught two headed north and one, a messenger we think, headed south."

"Were you able to decipher the message?"

"Afraid not," one of the other ogres said.

Something was wrong. Damia frowned as she studied the three of them.

"So you brought the messenger back, of course," she said hopefully. Their orders were very clear. If a spy had been caught with a communiqué, they were to attempt to decipher it, or to coerce the messenger to decode it. And if neither of those things was possible, they would bring the messenger to her.

The ogres shifted nervously, glancing at one another.

"Not exactly."

The rest of her troops had almost caught up with her. Damia lifted a hand to signal that they should keep going and the cavalry began to thunder by. Damia shifted in her saddle. The mare danced to one side, just a bit, as she looked around at the ogres.

"Where is Gaka?"

A grunting laugh came from the woods. "Slow," came a rasping voice.

The Japanese oni stepped from the trees, a snarl on his face. He carried a corpse in Yucatazcan battle dress over his shoulder. All three of his eyes stared at the ogres for a moment and then he turned to Damia.

"I could not move as quickly as these ugly donkeys, or I would have told the story a bit differently," the demon said, hefting the corpse on his shoulder. "I questioned her, but she would not cooperate. My efforts to coerce her were unsuccessful. I'm sorry to say that I broke her."

Gaka tossed the woman to the ground. Inside the armor, she was a bloody mess of broken limbs, which flopped at terrible angles when she landed.

Damia stared at her a moment, then looked at the ogres. Their eyes were on the passing troops—infantry now, the cavalry had already gone by. The commander turned and saw that her soldiers were staring at the broken, shattered corpse.

"Get her out of here," she told Gaka.

He narrowed his three eyes, but nodded. "Yes, Commander."

As he lifted the corpse, she addressed all four of the Borderkind. "Dispose of the body. When you're through, spread out again. We've got a ways to go and I want all outriders stopped. This was ugly and unnecessary, but they're better dead than free to roam. Next time you find a messenger, though, I expect you to bring her to me alive."

The three ogres actually saluted her.

Gaka nodded solemnly, shouldered the dead soldier once more, and turned to go back into the forest.

Damia watched them vanish into the shadows of the woods, steadied herself, then spurred her horse on. Killing in battle was one thing. Torturing to death a girl who only fought because she'd been commanded to do so by generals tricked into doing the bidding of Atlantis was something else entirely.

She rode to catch up with the cavalry units, not meeting the eyes of the infantry who she knew would be gazing up at her as she passed. All of them would be thinking the same thing.

Ogres ate carrion.

That dead soldier girl couldn't be considered anything but.

Damia could have ordered them to give her a decent burial, but not if she wanted the ogres to continue to fight under her command and in the army of King Hunyadi.

She tried not to think about it as she rode south. After a while, she noticed that the sense of excitement and joy and victory had dispersed. It seemed that her battalion did not feel like celebrating anymore.

The fox and the coyote crossed the Atlantic Bridge side by side, and the old gods of Rome and Greece followed behind. Shaken by the Sandman's attack, Kitsune had transformed not long after they had set off again, preferring animal instinct and the relative isolation of the fox to the questions and concerns she would no doubt have encountered in her more human façade.

When she had begun the long crossing over the bridge, she had been touched to discover that Coyote had also taken animal form. The change that the past weeks had wrought upon him had been subtle at first, but now he seemed a different creature entirely. Her cousin had thrown off the cowardly guise he had worn for so long. He had sacrificed an eye trying to protect her. Though he had cleaned it, the wound was hideous to behold. Yet Kitsune would always see it as a mark of his valor, and a reminder of what he had lost. For a short time, the knowledge that he would be half-blind from then on had weighted her with guilt. But despite his pain, Coyote expressed no regret. He seemed only grimly determined, and so she took his demeanor as her inspiration. Had anyone ever suggested she might look to him for example, she would have laughed. But Coyote had changed. War had changed them all.

He fell into step beside her without a glance or a nudge, offering the comfort of his presence. A kind of relief went through her. In all her life, she had never felt such terror as she had when the Sandman had come for her. Coyote had been there for her then, and he shared the burden of the aftermath with her now.

A strong wind gusted across the bridge. The morning had dawned gently, soft white light on the horizon. Now the sun began to rise in earnest and the sky deepened to a glistening azure. Breathing the sweet air off of the river seemed to ease some of the tension and fear that lingered in the fox, and the further they traveled from the eastern bank, the better she felt.

The pilings of the bridge were set on tiny islands that dotted the river, many of them thick with trees. When the fox came to one particular island she paused a moment to peer into the branches of the many cherry trees that grew there. Once upon a time—not long ago, and yet it seemed distant in her memory—she and Frost had nearly died there at the hands of the demon of the cherry trees. Oliver Bascombe had saved their lives. The demon had been destroyed, but the memory came back to her powerfully. It might have been on that island that she had first begun to realize—even if only in her heart—that Oliver was something more than just an ordinary man.

The coyote nudged her.

The fox glanced at him. She smiled a smile that only an animal would recognize, gave a twitch of her tail, and trotted on. After a few steps she glanced back to see the gods trailing behind. Cronus came last, as always, huge and lumbering with his almost simian gait. Kitsune felt a fondness toward him she would never have imagined. The others were all so aloof, whether grim or giddy, but the simplicity of the Titan bonded her to him.

As the morning wore on, that formidable band of somber ancients arrived on the western bank of the Atlantic River. The moment they stepped off of the bridge, Kitsune altered her form again. With a thought, her fur slipped around her shoulders as a cloak and parted around her face as a hood. When she turned to look, the rangy little coyote had changed as well. He nodded to her, his missing eye a dark pit.

"You feeling any better?"

Kitsune nodded, scanning the bank of the river and the wide expanse of the Truce Road, which rose up the hill to the west.

"He could have killed me," she said without looking at Coyote.

"I thought you told me he was dead?"

"He was. I saw him die. Him and the Dustman and a human called Halliwell."

Coyote pushed his hands into his pockets, glancing back at the gods as the last of them marched to the riverbank. "Then what did we just fight? What did this to me?" He pointed to his missing eye. "And what made him pause like that? He could have broken you apart before any of us could help."

She shivered. A sick grin touched her lips. "Thanks for the image."

Coyote shrugged. "It's just the truth."

"I know. But I don't have any answers."

The gods surrounded her, then. Assurances were exchanged and the march began again. They kept to the middle of the Truce Road and did not encounter a soul along the way, neither Lost One nor legend. In the trees on the roadside, animals foraged and capered, and a trio of hawks circled in the sky perhaps a mile off.

At the top of the hill, Kitsune stopped again.

Below them, the road turned slightly southward. Thick groves of apple and pear trees lay on either side, and other fruits grew there as well. Past the orchards was a broad expanse of crops—corn and wheat and barley and a hundred other things.

"What is it?" Bellona asked, impatience in her voice.

Kitsune turned to look into the dark eyes of the goddess of war. Behind her, Hesperos and Salacia seemed troubled, gazing down across the orchards and crops.

"You've never traveled this way before?"

Bellona shook her head. "But I feel something—a powerful presence here."

"The gods of the Harvest," Kitsune explained. "They linger, gathered together from a hundred cultures. They travel afar, but they have made a kind of home here."

Bellona flinched. She glanced back at Hesperos and Salacia, the closest of her companions, and Kitsune saw anxiety in their eyes. It could not have been called fear—not for beings of their power and history—but their hesitation was plain.

"What is it?" the fox-woman asked.

The goddess of war did not reply, so Kitsune glanced at the others.

"If this is the sanctuary of other gods," Salacia said, "we should not enter without being given leave."

Most of the other gods kept to themselves. Ares, in particular, made no move to approach the conversation the Borderkind were having with his kin. Coyote reached into his pocket and produced a hand-rolled cigarette and then a match with a flourish that drew all eyes to him. He lit the cigarette and drew a lungful, then shook out the match. It vanished in his hand like some parlor trick. Smoke plumed from his nostrils.

"Kitsune and I will go. If there's a concern about going into their territory without permission, it's best you all stay here. Tricksters are expected to break the rules."

Slowly, Bellona nodded. Kitsune thought she might be reluctant to admit Coyote was right, but she had no choice.

"All right," the fox-woman said, glancing at her cousin. "With me, then."

She started down the hill.

"You're the boss," Coyote said, following.

Kitsune wondered when that had happened. Once she'd been nothing but mischief, a little trickster in copper fur, capering in the forests and dallying with men and legends. Now the last of the bitter old gods followed her lead, and the never-reliable Coyote watched her back.

Together the tricksters followed the Truce Road, accompanied only by the sound of the breeze rustling the trees on either side and their own soft footfalls on the hard earth. A loud bark came from behind them. Only when Kitsune turned did she realize it had been the voice of Cronus. He made as if to follow them, perhaps taking her safety as his mission, but Bellona and Ares had halted him.

Kitsune smiled softly. It could not hurt to have a Titan watching over her.

The air filled with the sweet smell of apples and pears at their fullest ripeness. Orange nectar drifted on the breeze. Kitsune shivered with the heady pleasure of those and a dozen other scents all in impossible simultaneous bloom. Her mouth watered.

Coyote began to stray toward a peach tree.

"No," she said, grabbing his arm. "Not without an invitation. Stay to the road."

He nodded, still smoking his cigarette. Its herbal smell mixed with the aromas of fruit, and she realized this was his way of offering peace to the gods of the Harvest even before they had encountered those earth deities. Silently, she approved.

Long minutes passed.

When they at last reached the end of the orchards and the sides of the road turned to field upon field of crops that rippled and swayed in the breeze, they saw the first of the gods moving in amongst the corn. Stalks danced aside as it passed.

On the road ahead, figures began to emerge. Some of them she recognized. There were lovely, ethereal females and animals whose bodies were made entirely of stalks and husks and branches. Twice while traveling with Oliver she had encountered a group of these gods—once upon this very spot—and now she saw the Kornbocke step from the rows, its head high despite the heavy rack of antlers upon its head. The Appletree Man ought to have been back in the orchards, but he was there as well, and shuffled upon thick, knotted roots to the edge of the road.

The hard-packed dirt of that ancient road—once the symbol of truce between the Two Kingdoms—trembled.

"This can't be normal," Coyote whispered. "They don't come out like this every time a traveler passes by."

Kitsune agreed. Something transpired here that she did not understand.

Even as the thought touched her mind, the road ahead erupted with thick cornstalks, rustling against one another.

"What the hell?" Coyote asked, stub of a cigarette dangling in his hand. When he dropped it, roots thrust from it down into the soil of the road, and a tiny garden of herbs grew up on the spot. The ravaged socket of his missing eye had changed his face so that his expression was difficult to read.

Kitsune stared at the herbs, then looked at the corn that grew wild right before their eyes. A trickle of fear ran down her back. Once she had feared very little, but the Sandman had unsettled her.

Determined, she stepped forward.

The cornstalks twined around one another, twisting and layering and building themselves into a tall, humanoid figure.

"Ahren Konigen," she whispered as the features became clear.

Coyote shot a glance at her. "The harvest king?"

Kitsune nodded.

Konigen stood watching them, though he had only blank, shadowed pits where the corn husks that comprised his face were indented to imply the presence of eyes.

The gods of the Harvest gathered round them. Coyote shifted nervously.

"You are welcome here, Kitsune," Ahren Konigen said, his voice a rustle.

The wind rippled the crops. The gods of the Harvest seemed to sigh.

"You have our thanks," Kitsune replied.

Konigen did not seem to hear her. "We have been awaiting your arrival. You travel slowly, for legends and gods."

Kitsune blinked. She frowned and glanced back up the hill to where the old gods of Greece and Rome waited in the road.

"We met with difficulty across the bridge," Coyote replied for her, reaching up to touch the raw flesh at the edge of his empty eye socket.

She turned and saw the knotted brows of the harvest king draw more tightly together, stalks twisting. "The roots have carried the news. We might have come to your aid, but your trouble ended quickly."

"It's kind of you, Konigen," Kitsune said. "And you are right. We do not travel swiftly enough. We journey toward the border to help King Hunyadi repel an invasion—"

The king raised his hands to take in all of the other gods of the Harvest, and the two tricksters as well.

"Do you think word has not reached us?" he asked in that rustling voice. The husks of his face rearranged themselves into what might have been a smile. "Word travels fast along the roots underground, and sometimes on the breeze from tree to tree. We have been waiting for you, Kitsune, because a vote has been taken."

Confused and a bit worried, Kitsune studied him. She glanced at Coyote, trying to form the question that needed to be asked. Konigen did not wait.

"You have been our ally in the past. You and Oliver Bascombe, who revealed the crimes of Aerico and returned Appleseed to us. The schemes of Atlantis threaten us all. When we learned that you traveled this way, in league with the gods of Europe, the Harvest voted. We will join you in this journey. The Harvest will stand or fall with Hunyadi. With Euphrasia. For if Atlantis should win, surely they will burn us to the ground."

Kitsune drew back her hood, staring at Konigen with wide eyes. Her copper fur glistened in the sunlight as the wind billowed it around her.

"Your Highness, I cannot find the words to thank you."

The king of the harvest inclined his head, almost courtly. "There is no need. You have proven your mettle, trickster. We call you friend. And this matter concerns us all.

"Now, call down the gods from across the river and we will all be as one, allied in this cause, with destruction or victory the only possible outcomes."

Kitsune felt the shadow of the night's terror dispelled at last. A vibrant energy surged up through her. She wished, in that moment, that the next turn in the road would bring them to the enemy, so that they could join in the battle that very moment.

"It would be our honor," she said.

Coyote glanced around at the Harvest gods gathered there. Further into the fields, other things moved through the crops. Kitsune wondered how many there were, guessing at least two hundred. Most would not have the power that Konigen or the Kornbocke had, but they were all very difficult to kill and could be cunning and cruel when the need arose.

"Let's be off, then," Konigen said. "I have sent word ahead to Oliver that we would join his band by midday, and the sun is already overhead."

Kitsune froze. The words hardly seemed real. Knots formed in her stomach and her skin flushed as all of her guilt and shame returned.

"What do you mean? Oliver's in Yucatazca. Ty'Lis has him in the king's dungeon in Palenque."

Corn husks twined together on Konigen's face. "The roots bring the truth. Oliver escaped. He travels with his lover and a coterie of Borderkind. They came through the sandcastle that had stood for centuries just south of here, but once they left the place, the castle fell."

Kitsune stared at him. "It fell?"

"Collapsed," Konigen replied. "It is nothing but sand, now. And the roots bring whispers that the same thing has happened to all of the monster's other castles—at least within the Two Kingdoms. They wait for us in the ruin of the Sandman's castle, and from there we shall all march to war."

"And he knows we're coming?" Kitsune asked, mystified that Oliver would be waiting for her, but wondering, as well, if after all of the intervening months he could have forgiven her.

Konigen nodded. "He waits."

Kitsune felt numb. She did not know how Oliver would greet her, what bitterness might have stayed with him during his time in Palenque's dungeon. But how could she hesitate?

"Coyote," she said, "hurry back to Bellona and the others. Tell the gods they have found allies amongst the Harvest."

But even as he ran up the hill, five words echoed in her mind.

He travels with his lover.

CHAPTER 15

liver sat on a huge stone on the side of the Truce Road and gazed southward at the trees that lined that road. When they broke camp and set off, they would pass the trees where he, Frost, and Kitsune had found a little Red Cap murdered and hung for display. It had been the first time he had seen a victim of the Sandman. Only four months had passed since then, and yet he found it difficult to recall the horror he knew he had felt in those moments. Since then, the awful things had piled upon one another until he could barely summon horror anymore. Disgust and fury, certainly. But horror had become almost a constant now, part of the fabric of his life, and he hardly recognized it within him.

The breeze carried a chill and he shuddered. He preferred this weather to the heat of Yucatazca, but a sweatshirt would have been welcome.

"Where are you drifting?"

Oliver turned to find Julianna walking toward him. He smiled at the question and slid over to give her room beside him on the rock.

"Forward and backward," he said. "Wondering what the future holds, and remembering how we got to this point. Still hard to take it all in, even though we've lived it."

Julianna slid her arm through his and leaned on his shoulder, her body forming perfectly to his as it always did. He loved the smell of her hair.

"That's you, babe. Escaping in your brain."

"Escaping?"

Julianna gave a soft laugh. "What else would you call it? I wish I could go into my head the way you do yours. Maybe I wouldn't be so impatient."

Oliver kissed her on the forehead and Julianna looked up at him. Instead of being lost in his own mind, he became lost in the space between them—and then he made it vanish, leaning down to brush his lips against hers. He kissed her again, more fully, and then they pressed their foreheads together.

"I'm not quite so impatient," he said. "I'm not in any rush to make tomorrow come faster. Not when you're here with me right now."

She started to smile, but then a frown creased her brow. "Wait, tomorrow? We're not breaking camp until—"

He laughed. "Just a figure of speech, Impatient Girl. As soon as the Harvest gods arrive, we'll be heading south."

She hung her head, her hair a curtain across her face. "So weird how you can just say that. 'Harvest gods.' Like it's totally ordinary, everyday stuff. Even after what I've seen, it's still hard for me to picture."

Oliver did not reply. The comment did not require a response. No matter how much time he spent here, he knew he would always be adjusting to the amazements the world presented. Julianna was no different.

They sat for several minutes just listening to the breeze

through the trees, watching the Truce Road to the south. He had told her the story of what had happened here and was glad she did not want to discuss it any further. Nightmares were best forgotten. Sometimes—too often—the task proved impossible.

With Julianna beside him, out in the world and away from the dungeon of Palenque, Oliver felt himself relax in a way that he had not managed since the night when Frost first intruded upon his life. He felt content and lucky. His sister, Collette, was off with the winter man in the ordinary world somewhere, and no matter how much he resented Frost, Oliver knew she would be safe with him. The two people in any world that he loved were out of harm's way. He only wished they could go home now and leave the Two Kingdoms behind. But the war concerned them all. If this moment was all he could hope for—at least in the near future—it felt all the more precious to him.

He stiffened at the sound of a voice on the wind.

"What's wrong?" Julianna asked.

But when it came a second time, she heard it as well. The two of them turned, twisting around on the rock, and saw the powerful, apelike figure of Leicester Grindylow barreling toward them.

"Grin?" Oliver ventured, still getting used to the water boggart's nickname. "What's going on?"

But even as he asked the question, he saw the dust rising from the Truce Road to the north, and he had his answer. Oliver slipped from the rock and stood. Julianna did the same, reaching for his hand. Their fingers twined and they started toward Grin.

"Right, you've seen 'em, then," the boggart said. "Figured you'd want to know that the Harvest gods have arrived."

"Thanks. We're on our way."

Grin nodded and turned around, hurrying back the way he'd come. Oliver had thought the boggart might fall into step beside them, but found himself relieved that Grin was in such a hurry to rejoin the others.

Blue Jay, Li, and Cheval stood at the edge of the road several hundred yards to the north, where the wind blew grains up from the ruins of the sandcastle, but all he could focus on was the bizarre parade of legends coming down the slope toward them. He recognized many of the gods of the Harvest, but others were unfamiliar to him. In addition to the men and women and beasts made of wood and leaves and wheat and cornstalks, several thick roots burst from the soil on the roadside and then plunged into the dirt again, moving like worms. Thick as fallen logs, they emerged and then burrowed down again.

Beyond the Harvest gods were legends he did not recognize. In his time on this side of the Veil, Oliver had seen many warriors, but none like these. Many legends were larger than ordinary humans, but this small cadre was somehow also grander. They were formidable and they strode along the Truce Road as though they were some royal family, gathering for the funeral of one of their own. Last of all came an ugly, lumbering giant who seemed at once ancient and childlike. His hands were so large Oliver thought he could probably crush a man's bones to powder with one squeeze.

Yet even with that extraordinary sight, he only glanced at the approaching legends. His focus had begun with—and now returned to—the two figures at the front of that strange parade, a skulking trickster in a denim jacket with a cigarette clenched between his teeth and the familiar, petite form of Kitsune. The sunlight made her copper fur gleam red and orange, as though tiny pinpoints of fire burned on her cloak and hood.

"Did you know she was going to be with them?" Julianna asked.

Oliver turned and saw the hurt in her eyes.

"I had no idea."

"And she just expects us to behave like nothing happened, like she didn't run away and leave us to die?"

Oliver watched as the bizarre foot soldiers arrived at the ruin of the sandcastle. The roots that had been burrowing through the ground thrust up from the sand and became tree-creatures. One of them was the Appletree Man, whom Oliver knew. Cheval Bayard, Grin, and Li moved to meet them. Blue Jay slid past the first of the Harvest gods and went to his cousins—the tricksters. With a nod to Coyote, he took Kitsune in his arms in a tight embrace. From behind, all Oliver could see were the feathers in Blue Jay's hair, dancing in the breeze.

"I guess she does," he said. "The war's on. She's bringing a bunch of warrior legends to fight alongside Hunyadi's soldiers. We're all on the same side."

Julianna stood rooted to the spot, the two of them halfway between the rock they'd been sitting on and the ruins of the sandcastle. "Maybe she doesn't care if we're here or not. Maybe she doesn't think she did anything wrong."

Oliver shook his head. He remembered all of the times Kitsune had looked at him with those jade eyes, the intimacy of her nearness, her lips brushing his own. Even though at the time he hadn't known if he and Julianna would ever be together again, he had not followed through on those temptations. But he had wanted to. He and Kitsune had grown close in so many ways. Their friendship had been intense and passionate, even without the sexual tension that had developed. He would never have imagined her abandoning them to the dungeons of Palenque to save herself.

But that had been willful blindness. Had he given it any thought, he would have been able to predict it. Oliver wouldn't flatter himself by believing that Kitsune truly had fallen in love with him, but the journey they'd gone through together had created a bond between them that Kitsune—a trickster, normally caring for no one but herself—would not willingly surrender or even share. Oliver should have seen her jealousy coming. At the very least, he should have understood it at the time.

Now he did. Not that he forgave Kitsune, but he knew that what happened was nothing more than her nature. Instinct.

"Oliver," Julianna said.

Ahead, at the ruins, the three tricksters were talking even as the other Borderkind and legends began to gather on the road. The time for rest had passed. They were off to war.

Kitsune pulled back from Blue Jay, looking around. Her gaze fell upon Oliver and Julianna and even from a distance he could see the sadness etched upon her face.

"War's like politics," Oliver said. "It makes strange bedfellows."

Julianna cupped one hand behind his head to get his attention and moved closer, locking eyes with him, tearing his focus away from Kitsune.

"It better not," she said.

All along, she must have had her suspicions about what had gone on between him and Kitsune through that long journey. But she had said nothing until now. Oliver smiled softly, reminded how extraordinary a woman this was. Julianna had gauged the situation and put it aside as unimportant, particularly with Kitsune out of the picture. Now, as strong as she was, she wanted reassurance.

"We got very close. But never *that* close."

"And now?"

He shook his head, reached out and touched her cheek. "All I want is to be with you. As for friendship with Kitsune, I could have forgiven her leaving us high and dry. I really could have. But she hurt you, Jules. Whatever bond we had before, she broke it."

Julianna took a deep breath and some of the fire left her gaze. "War makes strange bedfellows."

"Yeah. It does."

"But I'm not going to play nice."

Oliver had no reply to that. Julianna Whitney had never put on a false face in her entire life, except with some of the law firm's clients, and then only under duress from the partners.

In silent agreement, they strode toward the ruins of the castle, which had spilled sand for hundreds of feet all around it as it collapsed. As if on cue, Kitsune extricated herself from Blue Jay and Coyote and walked out to meet them. Blue Jay watched with concern until Coyote said something to distract him, and then the two tricksters studiously attempted to mind their own business. The rest of the gods and legends were making introductions. How strange that in the midst of such wonders Oliver and Julianna should be focused on the personal and intangible.

The breeze blew Kitsune's silken black hair across her face. She brushed it aside and then reached back, as if to raise her hood. As her fingers touched the copper fur, she hesitated and changed her mind, leaving it where it was. She would not hide in the shadows of her cloak, or in the fur of the fox that she was in her heart.

He saw no trace of mischief in her eyes, today. Only regret.

"Oliver," the fox-woman said. Her gaze shifted. "Julianna." She bowed her head in some combination of greeting and penitence and then looked up at them again, finally searching Oliver's eyes. "You know that if I could take those moments back, I would. For a trickster, trust is a gift, whether given or received. I knew...I *know* that I ruined that trust. And I am deeply sorry."

Slowly, Oliver nodded. "You did, Kit. And it means a lot to hear you say that. But you know it can't be that simple."

So much remained unsaid between them but to try to discuss it now would serve no purpose except to hurt Julianna.

Kitsune glanced at Julianna. "I could not have taken you through the Veil. You know that. But I should not have struck you."

Julianna let out a breath that was almost a sigh. In her eyes, Oliver saw a sadness that reflected Kitsune's, full of sympathy and frustration.

"I'd like to punch your lights out," she said, as though the words surprised her. "But I don't know how to be that kind of person. We're going to travel together, I guess, but allies don't have to be friends."

The fox-woman glanced at Oliver and then back at Julianna, bristling at her words. Whatever sadness and shame she felt, it couldn't be easy for her not to react. But instead she pulled her cloak around her like the day had suddenly turned cold.

"We go to war," Kitsune said, her voice low and aching. "In case one or all of us should die, I wanted you to have my apology. Nothing more needs be said. If fate is kind, once we reach King Hunyadi, we will never encounter each other again."

Night fell over Atlantis.

On the spiral dome of the kingdom's great library, the Walker Between Worlds perched precariously and stared out across the city that comprised the entire island. In one hand he clutched the fox-headed walking stick that had become like a totem to him, and with the other he held onto the spire. His dark cloak floated out behind him.

Wayland Smith narrowed his eyes to study the troops that massed in the circular plaza below, then gazed out to the water's edge, where strange ships awaited the soldiers they would take to war. The ships were like spiral palaces set atop Moorish castles, but all made of many-hued glass whose surface billowed as though alive. They floated upon the water like jellyfish, but each had a dozen small masts strung with sails that reflected back the world like silver mirrors.

King Hunyadi would not be pleased.

There had never been any question that Atlantis would attack. But it had been some years since Smith had been to these shores, and he would never have imagined them capable of mustering such an attack. Each separate detachment of troops in the plaza had several sorcerers garbed in black and gold, and at least one Atlantean giant. To the west lay a mountainous, volcanic island shrouded in dark smoke that issued from vents and craters and hid the city of the giants from view. Smith had no idea how many of these ancient monstrosities still lived on that shifting, volcanic rock, but he counted twenty-seven on the main island of Atlantis, right there in the plaza. He hoped none remained behind the shroud of smoke as reinforcements.

Dozens of Perytons circled in the sky above the island. Their green feathers were black in the darkness, and when they passed across the face of the moon, their antlers seemed to claw the air. Had he been anyone else, they would have seen him already and attacked. But Smith was the Wayfarer—the Walker Between Worlds. He had eons of practice at being unseen.

But he had already known about the soldiers and sorcerers, the giants and Perytons. What troubled him the most were the other things—the beasts of the deep. A sea dragon rippled in the waves offshore, a thing of such length that he could only think of Jormungand, the Northmen's so-called world serpent. Three gigantic squidike creatures lay within the harbor, half in and half out of the water. It ought to have been impossible, but it seemed barely surprising in view of the sharks and eels that undulated through the night sky, swimming through the air as easily as they would underwater. Dozens, perhaps hundreds, of octopi hung like parachutes in the sky above the glass ships of Atlantis.

At some silent signal, the troops in the plaza began to move out, marching toward the harbor with giants and sorcerers at their side and Perytons flying above.

Smith swore in a language that had been old before the legends of this world had been born. But there was nothing he could do just now, not alone. This was not his world. Not his war. Atlantis could not be allowed to prevail because it might trap him in this one world forever, but his only power to stop them lay in his ability as a puppeteer. He might not have a role to play on the field of battle, but he saw the skeins of fate in every world, and knew when to pull those strings.

At least, he always had.

Straightening, keeping his grip on the spire, Smith reached out with the tip of his cane. He waved it once, twice, and a third time, then tapped downward. Though nothing but the night surrounded the spiral dome of the Great Library of Atlantis, the cane struck something solid.

Smith stepped away from the building and began to descend a staircase of sky. He did not need the cane to find each step, tapping ahead of him like a blind man. Instinct guided him, and power summoned the steps before the soles of his boots touched them. The Wayfarer followed the steps in a downward curve that led to a fifth-story window. He slipped between worlds for an instant and then out again on the other side of the window.

Inside the library.

His passage went unnoticed amongst the cases and shelves displaying thousands of scrolls from an age that Atlantis barely remembered—an age that even Wayland Smith could hardly recall. Glass and pearl architecture created a labyrinth of knowledge, but he navigated it easily. When he came upon guards, he paused. They did not see him, but beyond them, where scrolls had been laid out upon a table, a sorcerer—perhaps a member of the High Council—paused and glanced around, frowning deeply, sensing a disturbance in the air.

The Wayfarer withdrew.

He had seen all he needed, now. At the table, bent studiously over the scrolls the sorcerer had set out, there had been a young, olive-skinned boy with dark, serious eyes.

Prince Tzajin lived.

Damia Beck lay on her bedroll inside her tent. The wind whistled like distant ghosts passing by outside. Far off she could hear the snort and neigh of horses and the low mutter of voices from the soldiers on watch and those who were unable to sleep.

Her left shoulder burned where the Battle Swine had gored her, but a healing poultice had already done wonders. Still, her body ached. Sleep would have been a blessed gift, but it would not come easily, if at all.

A dog barked, off in the night, away from camp. She stiffened, wondering if it truly had been a dog, or the signal of some enemy. There were no dogs in camp. Likely it was some wild hound off in the woods or a house pet from one of the villages they had found abandoned on their march south. Three small villages had been evacuated, their residents taking shelter in the mountains or scattering to other towns where they might be safer. One had not been so fortunate. Most of the buildings had been burned to the ground. Old men had been cut down in the street. Women and children had been herded and then executed. Many of the corpses had been picked apart as though by vultures.

Every time Damia closed her eyes, she saw the bodies.

Yucatazcan soldiers had not done this. The Two Kingdoms had been at peace for a very long time. She had known and worked with southerners before. People were no different in other parts of the world, not fundamentally. They were all Lost Ones under the skin, all yearning for a home most had never known.

Whatever had happened in that village, she knew Atlantis must be at fault. Giants and Perytons must have broken away from the retreating Yucatazcan troops, the slaughter in the village a punishment of innocents, retribution for the humiliation they felt at being routed.

Smoke filled Damia's nostrils, even now. She had bathed in the river near the ruined village, but the stink would not leave her. Perhaps it never would. And perhaps it never should. King Hunyadi might have been waiting for her battalion to arrive, but Commander Beck had been unable to simply leave the dead for animals and carrion birds to gnaw upon. They had lost most of a day digging a mass grave for the villagers. While the infantry dug, she had sent the cavalry out riding in search of any signs that the Atlanteans might still be in the area, but they had found nothing. The oni in her Borderkind platoon, Gaka, was an excellent tracker. His third eye saw things no one else would, and the trail of the giants led directly southward.

From the devastated village of Ashford, Damia had marched her battalion onward. They had lost most of a day and she wanted to make up some of that time. The commander did not halt her troops until long after dark to make camp.

Now they rested, as best they could. Damia wondered how many of them were having nightmares, tonight. Perhaps that explained why she could not seem to get to sleep herself. Dreaming might take her right back to the half-eaten dead of Ashford, lying in the street amidst the charred remains of their homes.

"Heaven help us all," she whispered to the darkness of her tent, and the starry sky high above. She wished she could see the stars. Breathing the night air might help clear her mind. For a moment she considered leaving the tent.

Instead, she turned on her side and closed her eyes. Damia might be haunted, but she could not let her troops see. They had done the decent, honorable thing in Ashford, but for the sake of morale she had to appear confident and undaunted. They had to believe their commander had a hard edge to her soul.

Eyes closed, she saw the faces of the dead, and instead of drifting toward sleep, she felt more awake than ever. She listened to the wind outside, to the low garble of soldiers talking, and to the restless horses nearby. She caught herself waiting to hear the bark of that lost dog again, searching for its owners.

The night softened.

Instead of that distant bark, she heard a quick fluttering, as though of wings. A frown creased her half-conscious brow. The wind against the entry flaps of the tent—it must be. But the sound came again, and this time she knew it was not the wind at all.

Wings.

Then there came a gentle sound that might have been the entry flaps parting and a light step as someone entered the tent.

Perytons!

Her sword lay in its scabbard. Guns were faster. She lunged from the bedroll and snatched one of her guns from its holster, rolling as she moved, then came up onto her knees and took aim at the entrance to the tent. A dark figure stood there, silhouetted in the opening by starlight.

"I've been shot before and it hurt like hell," a voice said. "Could you point that somewhere else?"

A breeze blew into the tent and the feathers braided into his hair swayed.

Damia stared, letting the gun fall to her side. She strode over, grabbed Blue Jay by a fistful of his shirt, and pulled him into the tent even as she covered his lips with her own. His arms went around her, holding her gently, but Damia did not want tenderness. Not now. She pressed her body against him just as fiercely as she did her mouth. Idly she tossed her gun onto the bedroll and kissed him until they were both breathless.

Only when he broke the kiss and drew back from her, when she saw the powerfully hewn lines of his face in the slight illumination that came through the slit between entry flaps, did she see the concern in his eyes. Damia nearly asked him what was wrong, but then she felt the moist heat on her cheeks and tasted salt on her lips, and realized she had begun to cry.

Any other night, with any other person, she would have been mortified. But this was Blue Jay. Damia smiled and wiped away her tears.

"I missed you," she whispered. "Especially today."

She told him about Ashford, about the people who had been butchered there and the children whose bodies had been stripped of flesh by hungry Perytons.

"This war's about so much more than a broken truce," she said.

Blue Jay brushed his fingers through her long, wild hair. "For my kind, it always has been."

She nodded. "I thought I understood that before, but I didn't. Not really. Victory is the only possible outcome now, isn't it?"

His eyes darkened. "The alternative is unthinkable."

"How are you even here?" she asked, gazing at him as though she had just discovered some lost treasure. She could not take her eyes off of him.

The trickster took her face in his hands, studying her just as she had done with him, as though to make sure she was not some illusion, some beautiful mirage in the midst of ugly times.

"It's a long story," he said. "Best told on the road, I think. Truth be told, darlin', it's fortune that brings us together tonight. We got out of Palenque through the sandcastle and have been heading south to join Hunyadi, just like you. I've been scouting ahead from the air and saw your camp, came down to talk to the commander. I had the strangest feeling it would be you, here, but I brushed it off. I've never been a clairvoyant. Not one of my skills. But here you are. There's no magic to it, really. We're all on the road to war."

Damia felt her breath stolen from her again as his hands slid down over her body.

"You don't have enough trust in fate." A smile spread across her face. "There's magic in this, all right. All sorts of magic. But you said 'we.' Who else is with you?"

Blue Jay nodded, mischief returning to his eyes. Even in that near darkness, she could see its spark. "More than you'd think, and all camped just a few miles away. Li, Cheval, and Grin all came back from Palenque with me. But now we've got the gods on our side. Some of them, anyway. Ares and Mercury and half a dozen others or so from Perinthia. Fuck, there's a Titan, too. Cronus. Wait till the Atlanteans see him. Then we've got dozens of Harvest gods with us. The roots told them about the war, they said. Whatever it is, they know what's going on and they're helping."

Damia laughed in disbelief. "That's incredible. Almost gives me hope. The king will be very pleased. Did you round them all up yourself?"

He arched an eyebrow. "Me? No. It's all Kitsune's doing. Hers and Coyote's. They've had a hell of a time. The Sandman's out and about, hunting for her and for Oliver, apparently."

"But—"

"We thought he was dead? Yeah. We did. Looks like we were wrong. Maybe the Sandman can't be killed. I don't know. But, yeah, he's still alive. He took one of Coyote's eyes at the Atlantic Bridge and would have killed Kitsune had Coyote and Cronus not driven him off."

Damia shivered. "Do you think he'll come back?"

Blue Jay's eyes went cold. "No question. But we're on guard, now. For both Kitsune and Oliver."

She froze and stared at him. "You've got him? Oliver's with you?"

"And Julianna as well. Collette's off with Frost somewhere, but we'll catch up to them eventually. The important thing is that we're bringing Oliver to Hunyadi. A few months ago, they were hunting him. Now the king will put him up in front of the troops and tell them the Legend-Born has come. That ought to boost morale."

"We'll need it," Damia replied. "So, you really think the Bascombes are Legend-Born?"

Blue Jay stroked her arms. For a moment, his gaze seemed distant. Then he nodded. "They are. There's power in them like nothing I've ever seen. Magic I'm not even sure they understand yet."

Damia took that in, wondering what it would mean. If Oliver and Collette could really bring down the Veil, take the Lost Ones home, would she even go? She knew the answer.

Never. Her loyalty to Hunyadi might have been enough to keep her here, but now she had Blue Jay in her life. She would stay here with him, even if she was the last human in the legendary world.

Exhaustion caught up with her. Her whole body ached.

"You need to sleep," he said.

"Not yet," Damia said, as she began unbuttoning his jeans. The war could wait until morning.

CHAPTER 16

The fox trotted through the woods, hoping for a vole or mouse or insomniac squirrel, anything to capture her mind. It helped to have left her human form behind. The scents of the earth and growing things and the creatures of the wood filled her mind. The sounds of the nighttime erased the voices that haunted her from the day. Here she could find joy. Here, she was only a fox, and not expected to be anything but that.

The night offered the fox freedom from so many things.

A small something twitched in the underbrush and her stomach growled hungrily. The fox paused, inhaling the scent. A rabbit, up past its bedtime. Her lips stretched. Kitsune always forgot that as a fox she could not smile.

She lunged, paws clawing the dirt as she darted after the rabbit. It fled between two thick, tangled bushes, a hitch in its step that revealed some old injury. A swift flash of copper fur pursued the rabbit as it weaved around the base of a large tree and ducked underneath a fallen, rotting birch.

The fox leaped the dead tree and came down on the other side, paws digging into the ground, damp with rain from the previous morning.

Kitsune caught the rabbit easily and dragged it down, the two animals tumbling over one another. It tried to rise before she could, but its ruined leg failed it and the rabbit faltered. The fox pinned it under her forepaws, chest heaving with adrenaline and the thrill of the hunt.

Yet it had not been much of a chase, or a challenge. Though her stomach grumbled and she could practically taste fresh rabbit on her tongue, a twinge of regret touched her. What joy could be found in catching prey that could not possibly outrun her?

The fox stepped back.

Panting, the rabbit stared at her a moment, eyes gleaming pink in the moonlight. It rolled over slowly, twitchingly aware of her presence, keeping her in its peripheral vision. Quivering, it took a single hop, then waited to see if she would pursue. When she did not, the rabbit bolted, limping even as it ran deeper into the woods.

Sadness made its nest in Kitsune's heart. Yet this was not the ache of guilt and lost love that had plagued her before. This new pain came from acceptance. This pain would be with her for a very long time, and all she could do was hold it close. She had been face-to-face with Oliver, and nothing had changed. He did not hate her, but he did not love her. Whatever closeness the future might have held for them—as lovers or friends—she had ruined it by assaulting Julianna and abandoning them in Palenque.

Julianna.

The fox growled quietly, lay back her head to look at the moon, and wished she were a wolf so that she might howl gloriously in sorrow and fury.

Oliver's woman had been cold to her, but she had also been

right. Much as she hated it, Kitsune had to admire Julianna's self-control. Were their roles reversed, the fox-woman would have torn out her throat.

As a fox, and a trickster, there were many things about humanity that she had never understood or even experienced. A lesson had been learned, now, and she would never be able to unlearn it. Humanity meant pain. More than that, it meant living with pain every day, and still going on as if the world had not changed around you.

So Kitsune would go forward. She would march to war and she would fight for King Hunyadi—for her own kind and for the Lost Ones as well. But when the war ended, she thought she might retreat to the Oldwood where Frost and Oliver had first found her and simply be a fox for a while. Years, perhaps. Centuries. As long as it took to forget the lesson that living as a woman had taught her.

A quiet step came behind her.

She spun, forgetting the moon, and saw the coyote emerging from the trees. He had come to her downwind, so that she would not catch his scent.

His eyes had always laughed, even when he did not wish them to, dancing with the mad light of the jester, the trickster, of Coyote. But the Sandman had taken one, and the other had no laughter in it tonight, only tenderness. His coat gleamed sleekly, and he looked not at all the rangy mutt of a beast that he often seemed.

The fox cocked her head, studying him.

The coyote came nearer, but stopped several feet away. They began to move in a circle, but when the fox halted the coyote kept going around her once, twice, a third time. He lay back his head and howled. It had not the beauty of the wolf's cry, but the coyote's lament broke her heart anew. He had borne witness to her pain today, and suffered so much of his own. Now he had come seeking her, though she had made it plain she wished to be alone.

The fox did not try to send him away.

The coyote came nearer. He nudged her snout playfully with his nose, then darted away. Confused, she only looked at him. Again, he nudged her, then loped several yards and glanced back.

Only then did she understand. He wanted her to run with him. To play. To lighten her heart.

It amazed her to discover how wrong she had always been about Coyote. If not for him, she would still be wallowing in hatred and guilt in the cave at the back of his den.

The fox barked a little laugh and gave chase, wondering what she would do when at last the coyote allowed her to catch him.

The ferries didn't run in Boston Harbor in March, and wouldn't until the tourists started to show up in May. Sheriff Norris could have contacted the local authorities and gotten their cooperation—Sara had urged him to do just that—but he had balked, not wanting to have to come up with an explanation for their off-season visit.

Cops.

Sara had spent her entire life trying to figure out the mind of a policeman—her father—and still hadn't gotten very far. They were proud and stubborn and courageous and sometimes damned fools.

The sheriff had tracked down a local tour boat operator who was willing to take them out to George's Island for a fee. Now, on a startlingly brisk March morning, Sara turned up her collar and pulled her jacket tight across her throat. The similarity to her father's last known journey—on a rented boat out to a deserted island off the western coast of Scotland—was not lost on her. In truth, thinking of it made her feel a bit nauseated.

She stood inside the tour boat—its engine chugging, filling

their noses with a terrible oil smoke—and tried to imagine how cold it would be if she allowed that acrid odor to drive her out on the deck for fresh air. Finally, nearly choking, she stepped out on the prow of the boat and let the wind buffet her, whisking away the smell. Salt and sea filled her lungs now and she breathed it in gratefully. Her teeth chattered and she shivered, but she surrendered to the cold, letting it settle into her body. Somehow it made her feel more alive.

Jackson and Marc Friedle—*his name's Robiquet,* she thought, reminding herself for the hundredth time—remained inside for another minute or two, just talking. Every time Sara looked at him, she had difficulty seeing the human mask the goblin wore instead of the monstrous features that he had let them glimpse only twice. His true face would always be seared into her memory.

The seas were rough, even here in the harbor, and she stood with her legs wide so as not to lose her balance. The captain and mate moved the old boat easily through the water, laboring on a path between islands. Sara had been out here several times on tours when she was younger. Once her father had taken her out to George's Island for a picnic, and she remembered it well.

The island loomed ahead. The dock and visitor center were abandoned, left with the haunted quiet of the off season. Beyond them, the fort rose up in an imposing wall of stone, half overgrown. It had been built partially into the natural terrain, and the overall effect made it seem far older than it was. The thirty-acre island had been used as a training area for Union soldiers during the Civil War, and later the fort had become a prison for Confederate soldiers.

Must be a thousand ghosts here, she thought.

The idea had come to her mind unbidden, but she pushed it out of her thoughts. There were enough impossible things in the world without having to worry about ghosts.

As they approached the docks, the captain slowed the boat. The engine quieted to a dull roar and smoke billowed around them. The waves rocked them and the captain moved forward with caution. The first mate came onto the prow and threw bumpers over the side. The ferry dock was too high, so the captain chugged them slowly up beside the one built for private boats.

Sheriff Norris came out onto the deck with Robiquet behind him. The fussy-looking man made no move to assist, but Jackson took a rope from the mate's hands. When the mate had hopped up onto the dock, the sheriff tossed him the rope. They worked together to tie the old boat to the dock.

Sara didn't wait for a hand up. She leaped from the boat to the dock. Robiquet hesitated, but she didn't have the patience to wait for him. As she strode away, she heard Jackson talking to the captain, assuring him they'd be back to the boat in no more than an hour. Then the sheriff and Robiquet were hurrying after her. Apparently the goblin had gotten over his anxiety about leaving the boat.

When they reached the entrance to the fort, they found the gates padlocked.

Sheriff Norris turned to Robiquet. "There another way in?"

Sara started following the outer wall, turning to call back to the sheriff over her shoulder. "We'll walk around. At the back, you can walk up the hill—it's not too steep—and get right to the lookouts at the top of the fort."

She kept ahead of them. It wasn't just impatience that drove her on. If all of the things Robiquet told them were true—and she believed they were—then this spot was the closest she had come to the truth of her father's fate since he'd vanished in December. Sara felt breathless as she hiked the outer edge of the island, keeping the fort to her right. The terrain became difficult, but she did not slow down. That sense of nearness to her father propelled her forward, even as a terrible dread weighed upon her heart.

Robiquet didn't seem to have any trouble with the hills and pathways on the outside of the fort. Of course, he wasn't human. Sheriff Norris, on the other hand, labored to keep up. The man was in decent condition, but he wasn't exactly young, anymore.

Sara didn't slow down to wait for them until she had reached the rear of the island. There, she stood and stared up at the squat stone towers where the lookouts would have been posted. The frigid wind whipped up off of the water and it was icy on the back of her neck, but she barely felt the cold.

When Jackson and Robiquet caught up, the sheriff gave her a hard look, an admonishment for not having waited. Sara ignored it, and she paid no attention to the way he stood, catching his breath, obviously hoping for a rest.

She started up the hill.

At the lookout post, she moved around the tower and dropped down to the walkway behind it. She could not help wishing that she had brought her camera. Even at the worst of times, Sara saw the world through a photographer's eyes.

Again, she waited impatiently for the others to catch up with her. Robiquet kept pace with the sheriff, perhaps thinking that he would rather deal with Sara's impatience than Jackson's annoyance. When they reached the lookout, the sheriff sat on the edge of the wall and slid down to the walkway. Robiquet hopped down with the ease of a child.

Sara took the peculiar man's measure once again, still seeing in her mind the image of his true face.

"Lead the way," she said. "I hope you know what you're doing."

Robiquet turned to look at her, the human mask he wore furrowing its brow in displeasure. "You think I would have dragged you all the way out here if I wasn't sure?"

Sara shrugged. "I don't know what I think, especially when it comes to you."

Slowly, Robiquet nodded. "Fair enough, I suppose. Come along, then."

He led them to a set of darkened stairs that led down into

the tomblike stone passages of the old fort and prison. From above they could see that even during the day the stairwell descended into impenetrable darkness. Sara went to follow Robiquet, but Sheriff Norris put a hand on her shoulder and shook his head.

"I'll go next."

She understood immediately. There was no way to know what the goblin might try, down there in the dark, or what else they might encounter. If there was going to be trouble, Jackson wanted to be the first to come up against it. Sara bristled at the idea that she needed protecting, but she couldn't deny that a part of her was relieved.

The whole world—even familiar places—had become unknown territory to her and the sheriff since they'd met Robiquet. If there was some passage here on the island to the world of legends and monsters that he had told them about, then she was relieved not to be the first one to descend into the dark.

But she followed.

Her father had never asked her for anything except to come home and see him from time to time, but she had failed him in that. Ted Halliwell had his shortcomings, no question. But Sara had spent the last few months coming to terms with the truth, that he had not been the only one at fault.

She needed to tell him that.

Sara blinked as her eyes adjusted to the dark. The stairs led straight down and then turned right. Her fingers trailed along the granite walls as she took each step, just in case she stumbled. The presence of Sheriff Norris in the passage below her only made it darker, blocking out any light that might have come from below.

"It's this way," Robiquet said, his voice echoing back to her from somewhere ahead.

Then she reached the bottom step, turned left, and found that the three of them had entered a chamber that must once have been a part of the prison. The walls were featureless, win-dowless stone, save for one in which a doorway led out into the huge, grassy staging area inside the fort. Whatever door had once hung there had long since been removed, leaving only a crumbling frame.

"Why isn't there a door?" Sara asked.

"Maybe to keep people from getting trapped? The way they remove the doors from refrigerators at the dump," Sheriff Norris suggested.

Robiquet studied that doorless frame.

"Or maybe because they've got a bad history of closed doors around here," Sara suggested. The idea chilled her. Maybe who-ever was responsible for overseeing the island as a National Historic Site had grown a little afraid of the doors on George's Island over the years.

The sheriff looked at Robiquet. In the gray light that streamed in from outside, Sara saw the concern on Jackson's face.

"But this isn't the door we're looking for, right?"

Robiquet shook his head. "No. Your world isn't on the other side of the door we want. And there would be guards, remem-ber? It's this way."

The fastidious man wiped his hands together as though just being in the damp, dusty fort offended his sensibilities. He did not lead them out onto the grass of the fort's interior but across the chamber to another passage.

They followed him through what appeared to be a sequence of cells or bunk rooms, ending up in a large chamber whose en-tire inner wall was open to the vast courtyard at the heart of the fort. Wan daylight flooded the room, and Sara welcomed it.

"It's here," Robiquet said.

Surprised, Sara narrowed her eyes. At the back of the cham-ber, recessed into the granite, was a heavy iron door. The first door they had seen inside the fort.

Her heart skipped. A moment of uncertainty made her pause.

Sheriff Norris had no such hesitation. He strode over to the door as though confronting a troublemaker in a bar, every inch the cop that he'd been all of his adult life. The sheriff reached out and grabbed the door handle and gave it a pull.

Rust flaked and sifted to the floor, but the door did not budge.

"It's not going to open for you. What kind of secret would it be if any ordinary human could walk right through?"

Sara stared at the door, then stepped up beside Robiquet. In the half-light at the back of that chamber, she felt she could almost see the goblin face beneath his human guise.

"Open it," she said.

A flicker of fear crossed his face. Then he nodded and stepped up to the door. Sheriff Norris moved out of his way.

Robiquet grasped the handle and pulled. With a scrape of metal upon stone, it swung toward them.

Sara stared, a sick knot twisting in her stomach.

"What the fuck is this?" Sheriff Norris demanded. "What does this mean?"

Robiquet shook his head slowly, dumbfounded. "I have no idea."

On the other side, the door had been bricked up with stones and mortar. Wherever it had once led, it was a dead end now. A wall.

"Jackson?" Sara said.

The sheriff ran a hand over the stones. He dragged his fingers over the mortar. When he turned to look at her, his eyes were full of frustration and fear.

"This is recent. Someone built this thing just in the past few weeks. No more than that. Maybe less."

The three of them stood together for long moments, speechless, just staring at the wall. Sara was surprised that it was Robiquet who spoke first.

"I don't know what this means," he said. "It's been sealed from the other side. In all likelihood, it isn't just a wall. There are probably magical wards placed upon it as well. Whoever did this meant it to be permanent."

"So what now?" Sara asked.

Sheriff Norris ran his hand over the wall again. "Now we go home to Maine," he said, turning toward Robiquet. "If this Falconer got through, it wasn't here, right? I mean, there's got to be a door closer to Kitteridge—closer to the Bascombes' house. Where did you first come through?"

Robiquet nodded. "It's on Chadbourne Bridge."

Sara looked at him. "On the bridge?"

"You'll see."

"Then you'll come with us?"

He swallowed nervously and glanced away. When he looked up again, his gaze had turned hard.

"I loved Melisande. I don't mean I was in love with her, but I adored her. And her children were always good to me. He changed later in his life, after he lost her, but in the early days Max Bascombe had a wonderful vigor. Among ordinary men, he was extraordinary. Max had a keen intelligence that made him the smartest man in any room, but he could set anyone at ease. Melisande was seduced by his intellect and his charisma. She loved to dance and to laugh, and Max shared those passions. He made her believe there was magic in just being ordinary. Losing her destroyed him in many ways. He rarely laughed, and he never danced after she was gone. He became arrogant and grim. But I never forgot the man he had been, and how much he had loved her. I swore my loyalty to him because of that.

"But I ran away, Sara. I never should have done that. The only way to make it right is to go back, and hope that we can all find answers to our questions in the place where this all began."

In the dark, the soldiers of Atlantis prepared for war. From time to time, one of them would shudder and glance up into the star-scattered night sky, perhaps thinking how strange it was to encounter such a chill breeze so far to the south.

The winter man eddied and danced, nothing but ice and cold wind, a small storm of consciousness. Frost swirled in the darkness above the invasion force that Ty'Lis and the Atlantean High Council had mustered on the Isthmus of the Conquistadors. At least eight battalions of soldiers had come ashore—thousands of men and women in the armor of Atlantis, green-white faces turned upward to watch for the coming of dawn, when they would march north to engage King Hunyadi's troops. When their conquest would begin.

Frost studied the glass ships of Atlantis that sat just off the shore of the Isthmus. The soldiers spilled over the edge of the deck and walked underwater toward land, weapons at the ready. Air sharks knifed across the night sky. Octopuses floated close to the ground, tentacles drooping, dragging along the dirt. They kept near the water, touching the surf.

The first of the giants had come up out of the ocean not more than an hour before. Three more surfaced now, two females and a male, seawater spilling off of them in a salty froth. Their eyes were half-lidded and they walked sluggishly toward where the first arrival sat on the ground, a hundred yards from the nearest troop encampment. A tremor went through the ground as they all sat heavily. One closed her eyes and began to snore, though she remained sitting up, slumped over, practically in her own lap.

The little ice storm watched it all, deeply troubled. There were sorcerers down there, and Perytons as well. Many Perytons. For now they were at rest. They had sent scouts ahead, but for the moment the only creatures high in the sky were the air sharks, and they did not even notice the winter man's presence. Frost had no flesh for them to rend.

Still, he felt afraid. Not for himself, but for the future—for the outcome of the battle that the dawn would bring.

There were sorcerers as well. He felt sure one of them must

be Ty'Lis, but he dared not get close enough to them to find out. The rank-and-file soldiers would shiver with the chill of his presence when they felt that cold wind passing above and around them, but the High Council of Atlantis would not assign such an anomaly to odd weather. Ty'Lis, especially, would know the winter man was there, and Frost couldn't take that risk. King Hunyadi and the Euphrasian Borderkind had to know what sort of force they were facing.

To the north of the Atlantean invasion force were four or five ragtag battalions of Yucatazcan warriors. Their armor had been decorated with paint and feathers and the symbols of their Mayan, Aztec, and Incan ancestors. These were proud, noble, brutal warriors, yet their invasion had been driven back by Hunyadi's forces. Many had obviously been killed and now they were regrouping, promoting officers to replace those whose corpses had been left in Euphrasia.

Yet something had gone wrong. They seemed sluggish and grim. Frost thought he knew why, though, and Hunyadi would be very interested to hear it.

He took a final look at the glass ships anchored off of the isthmus. The temptation to destroy them, or see them destroyed, was great. But the army of Atlantis was so formidable he would advise Hunyadi to leave the glass ships alone. If fortune allowed Euphrasia to force the invaders to retreat, they had to have a way to flee. If the ships were destroyed they would have nowhere to run, and would be forced to stand and fight. Frost thought that might be a spectacularly bad turn of events.

You're getting ahead of yourself, he thought. First, Hunyadi's army had to stop the conquerors from invading Euphrasia.

In a gust of wind, Frost slipped across the sky, away from the troops and the glass ships. He traveled swiftly southwest. The indigo night glittered with a billion pinprick stars. It was warm, but not nearly so warm as it had been to the south. With the breeze blowing across the isthmus and the cool water, he felt good. Stronger.

He had left Collette in the shadow of a small, abandoned chapel on the outskirts of a small fishing village. The isthmus had little by way of farmland or fields for grazing. For those willing to settle on that unforgiving stretch of land, fishing seemed the only industry, and the only way to stay alive. Still, the chapel—dedicated to some local god or conscripted saint—stood crumbling and dark. Frost had seen such things many times before. Either the village had become prosperous enough to think they no longer needed to appease their god, or so withered that they no longer had faith that they could be saved.

The icy wind whipped across the roof tiles and through the gaps in stones. Just behind the chapel, where no one on the overgrown path could have seen him, Frost collected mist and ice and moisture from the air, pulling his substance together to sculpt his body anew. He glanced around, icicle hair chiming, and the ice of his face cracked as he frowned. He had expected to find Collette asleep, but did not see her.

Something shifted in the deeper darkness beneath a stand of trees perhaps fifty feet to the rear of the chapel. The petite figure resolved itself into Collette Bascombe. She had been in a stone grotto built by the architects of the chapel, with a shrine to whatever they had worshipped there. She emerged now, pale features illuminated in moonlight. With her reddish hair, mischievous eyes, and narrow face, she almost looked like a trickster.

"What is it?" she asked. "Why are you looking at me like that?"

Frost cocked his head, studying her. "You look different. It almost seems that with the truth of your heritage, the legendary part of your bloodline is coming to the fore."

Collette shook her head. "I don't feel any different."

"That's a lie, though whether to me or yourself, I don't know. You have magic in you. Your mother was Borderkind. As

Legend-Born, you're called to something greater than the ordinary life into which you were born."

"Bullshit." She smiled. "You sound like Oliver. I've been trying to tell him since he was a little kid that ordinary people choose to be ordinary. We all have magic in us, no matter who gave birth to us. Maybe the legendary have longer lives, and maybe they can do things that people can't, but it seems to me most of you are just as lost and wandering as the average guy or girl. It's what you do, not what you are."

Frost didn't challenge the assertion, but he did ask her why she had that grin on her face.

"Because I think my brother's finally come around to my way of thinking."

The winter man made no reply. Last he had seen Oliver, whatever friendship had once existed between them had turned to sour resentment. He understood and regretted this, but there was little he could do about it. He could not travel back through time, and even if he had that ability, Frost wasn't sure he would do things any differently. Collette and Oliver were still alive—thus far the schemes of Atlantis had been thwarted. How could he regret that?

"So, what's our move?" Collette asked, ignoring his silence.

"The invasion force gathers to the north. We leave now. When we reach their encampments, I will have to carry you over them to make absolutely certain they do not see us."

Collette frowned. "Over them? As in, through the air?"

The winter man smiled. "It would take us a very long time to dig a tunnel beneath them."

She shook her head. "Wait. Can't we just go around? Through the Veil? Head north and cross through again when we know we've gone far enough?"

Frost narrowed his eyes. "There are too many variables. Distance and time are different on the other side, as you well know. I am not certain where we would emerge in your world, now. We need to go directly to King Hunyadi, and as swiftly as we're able. My observations about the invasion force may be of great value to—"

"All right. I get it." Collette glanced around. "Which way?"

He pointed toward the path and they struck out from the chapel, headed due north.

"This should be loads of fun," she muttered.

The winter man smiled to himself in the moonlit night. He wondered if Collette had begun to trust him. And he wondered if he deserved her trust. While he did not want her to die, what truly mattered to him was that one of the Legend-Born survive to see the end of this war.

"Don't scream."

Collette shivered. She didn't like the sound of that. But there was precious little to like about anything tonight. They'd walked more than an hour before seeing the dark shape undulating across the night sky above, blotting out the stars as it passed. Frost had turned to her and with a gesture had lowered the temperature around them by fifty degrees. Ice crystals had formed on the air and her breath fogged.

The thing in the air had slid away from them. Her pulse steadied and she took a breath, then asked Frost what it had been. The answer had made her feel like throwing up. A shark? How could anyone be safe if there were sharks that swam through the air as easily as others swam through water? He believed that however the Atlantis-bred monster located its prey, it would have to do with heat or scent. His creating a little pocket of winter around her had hidden her from it.

In the midst of freaking out, she felt grateful for that much. Not that she wanted to be grateful to Frost, but she couldn't help it. She and the winter man had spent a good deal of time, now, keeping each other alive.

But what he'd just said made her forget any favors he'd ever done her.

"What do you mean, 'Don't scream'?"

Frost narrowed his eyes. Ice-blue mist swirled up from them. "Precisely what I said. You will want to scream. You will be afraid. But I swear to you that I will not drop you."

They had moved on from the air shark sighting perhaps another half mile. From the scrim of a stony ridge, they saw the troops mustered on the isthmus. Many were sleeping, but others were on patrol. Collette found herself strangely unafraid of encountering Atlantean soldiers, but if they were seen and a patrol raised the alarm, she feared what might answer that call.

She turned to Frost. "I won't scream."

The winter man nodded. If he doubted her, he did not put voice to those doubts.

He burst into a swirl of snow and ice. Frigid wind buffeted her. Collette shivered again and turned up her collar. Before her eyes the storm that was Frost grew, churning. The blizzard rose twenty feet in the air and spread a dozen in either direction.

She held her breath, staring in amazement at the power of the storm. The power of the winter man.

Then she gasped as the blizzard rushed at her. It whipped around her, circling a moment, and her teeth chattered. Her muscles clenched and she hugged herself against the icy grip of the storm. When the blizzard lifted her up off of the ground, blowing her up into the sky as though she had been catapulted, Collette nearly did scream.

Her mouth opened, but the freezing wind seared her throat and she clamped her lips. Her eyes went wide and she could not even curl in upon herself for warmth. The blizzard hurtled her through the air, buffeting her, carrying her on a slingshot wind, in a cocoon of driving snow. Her bones ached with the cold and she tried to breathe but found she could not. The wind lashed her face and she felt despair grip her heart. How could she survive this?

Barely aware of what she was seeing, she glimpsed enormous ships of glass in the distance, festooned with sails. She saw troops massing below as she spun across the sky in the grip of the blizzard.

Then the wind lessened. She found herself sliding downward, drifting. The blizzard buffeted her, blasted her, keeping her aloft. Her arms and legs pinwheeled as she descended.

The ground rushed up. At the last moment a final, powerful gust slowed her fall. Collette landed in a pile of fresh snow, tumbling through the white stuff and then onto rough, prickly grass and rocky earth.

The cold withdrew. The warmth of the southern night felt like a gift. Her flesh was seared. Her cheeks burned with the bite of the cold that had enveloped her. It was like nothing else she had ever felt and she wondered if she had frostbite.

The thought frightened her, but slowly, feeling and warmth returned to all but her hands and cheeks. Carefully, she sat up.

The snow was gone. Frost stood over her.

"We have to go. The hours before dawn are few, and we have no time to lose."

Collette stared at him. "Don't ever do that again."

His eyes narrowed. "What else—"

"Leave me behind, next time."

She wasn't sure if she meant it, and it seemed clear Frost was not sure either. Collette didn't care. She got up and marched north with him, bones still aching. It took a very long time for full feeling to return to her hands.

They'd gone only a few miles when they reached the end of the Isthmus. The Kingdom of Euphrasia spread out to the east and west. Already, Collette felt safer, and less inclined to be hostile toward Frost.

A Euphrasian cavalry patrol stopped them on the road. When they discovered that these strangers walking north were Frost of the Borderkind and Collette Bascombe, Legend-Born, a kind of euphoria seemed to come over them. One of the soldiers dismounted and gave Collette his horse. As she slid into the saddle, she felt a grim determination settle into her. They had arrived at last. Survived, at least this long. And now the war would truly begin.

Frost flowed through the air beside her as she rode, and one of Hunyadi's horsemen paced her on the other side. The familiar feel of the horse beneath her, the leather reins in her hand, filled her with new vigor.

They rode through the battle lines set up by Euphrasian troops, who were dug in and waiting for the attack they knew would come with the dawn. The cavalryman signaled to the soldiers on the ground and soon voices could be heard. Collette heard them calling her name. At first she didn't understand. How could any of these people know her name? Then she heard shouts of "Legend-Born," and she understood.

The human soldiers were all Lost Ones. She represented the hope of their parents and grandparents and ancestors. For those who had been born in her world and crossed over themselves, she would seem even more like a savior come to their rescue. The legend said she could get them home again. And for the others, she would seem like Moses, ready to bring them to the Promised Land.

If only they knew that the world they so wanted to return to was only a more ordinary reflection of this one, she wondered if they would still long to go there. But perhaps they would. This world wasn't home. Not really. They wanted to be reunited with their people. She could understand.

The thought made her wonder about Oliver. She had done her best not to think of him over the past few hours. But Collette felt sure he was all right. She had come to believe that if anything happened to him—if death came for her brother—she would know. Once, the idea would have seemed foolish to her. But now she knew it was not so far-fetched.

Hope went through the ranks as they passed. When she rode into the camp on the hill overlooking the battlefield, the word continued to spread. She could almost feel morale rising. Frost whipped along beside her, a blizzard sliding through the night air, but she could almost hear laughter coming from the storm he made.

The dour winter man was happy.

A small group of men and women in uniform—officers and advisors—were clustered outside a large tent at the apex of the hill. Twenty yards away, the cavalryman who'd accompanied them held up a hand to halt them. Collette pulled on the reins. She and the horseman both dismounted. The winter man coalesced out of the air and stood beside her. A young soldier—no more than a girl, really—ran over to take the reins of the two horses and led them away. Another, a boy of perhaps sixteen, came over and saluted the cavalryman.

"Run and tell the king that Frost has come with Collette Bascombe."

The boy's mouth opened in a kind of gasp, and then he grinned as he turned to bolt up the hill toward the tent of King Hunyadi. Collette's heart soared at the reaction her arrival had brought out in the troops, but a shadow lingered there as well. These people had no idea of the kind of horrors Atlantis had mustered. Hunyadi might, but the soldiers likely did not. She feared for them.

Moments later, the boy came back down the hill. Behind him walked a bearded man with a wide-brimmed hat and a cane with a brass head that glinted in the moonlight. When he passed the conversing officers, they fell silent and shifted slightly away from him. Power seemed to radiate from him. Yet from the officers' reaction she knew this could not be the king.

The man shooed the boy away and came down to meet them. He ignored Collette completely, turning to Frost.

"I'd not thought to see you alive again."

The winter man cocked his head. His fingers were like ice knives and from the way he stood, Collette wondered if Frost would attack the man or embrace him. He did neither.

"Are you disappointed?" the winter man asked.

"Quite the opposite," the tall, bearded man replied. He cast a quick glance at Collette and a smile touched his lips. "You've done well, Arcturus."

Frost bristled. He tossed his head back, hair clinking. "That's not my name."

The man waved away the complaint. Collette saw that the brass head of his cane was the head of a fox, and she remembered Oliver telling her about him. The enigmatic Wayland Smith.

"Atlantis attacks at dawn," Frost said. "I have details on their forces for the king."

Smith nodded. "Most of which I've already provided."

"I also observed the Yucatazcan warriors—those who retreated are now regrouping. But they don't seem to have the heart for it. I wonder if they haven't realized, by now, that they're being manipulated."

Wayland Smith frowned. "That may be, old friend, but they will still fight. They will fight and die because that is the command from Palenque. King Mahacuhta is dead, but Prince Tzajin lives. The only way the Yucatazcans will stop fighting is if the crown commands it, and that's not going to happen as long as Tzajin is a prisoner in Atlantis."

Frost swore under his breath. Cold mist plumed upward from the edges of his eyes again. "You're sure of that?"

"I saw him with my own eyes. Hunyadi needed a spy."

The winter man seemed surprised. "That's unlike you, taking so overt a role. You so love working in the shadows."

Smith gripped the head of his cane and glanced again at Collette, who'd watched the whole exchange.

"Time, I think, for you to speak to the king."

vid Tsing led his army along the Orient Road. Even above the stink of unwashed soldiers, he could smell the ocean on the breeze. The night was clear and warm and the starlight picked out each man and woman of the long march. At the back of the army, the Stonecoats trudged along at a steady pace.

The Jokao were tireless. They had also turned out to be an excellent source of information. Whenever the King's Volunteers—as they had begun to call themselves—stopped to rest, the leader of the Stonecoats would come and report what news the ground knew. As incredible as it seemed to Ovid that these stone soldiers could feel vibrations that traveled from stone to stone underground, he had no doubt of their value.

Atlantis had landed troops on the Isthmus of the Conquistadors. They massed there, now, preparing for war come dawn.

Ovid walked with one hand on his bow and the other on the

hilt of his sword. He often marched in the ranks, but now he had come out in front of the King's Volunteers. The Jokao estimated that they were barely a mile northeast of the Euphrasian army.

We're here, Mother, he thought. *It's time.*

Shaking off the ache of the long march, Ovid picked up his pace. Even as he did, he heard a familiar clacking sound and glanced to his left. The leader of the Jokao had come abreast of the front ranks of the King's Volunteers and now joined Ovid in the lead. Once upon a time, the Jokao had been slaves in Atlantis. They despised the Atlanteans—Truce-Breakers, the Jokao called them—more than anyone. Ovid wondered if the three marks on the Jokao's chest had been given to the Stonecoat while enslaved, but did not know how to ask without risking offense.

"We're close, now?" Ovid asked.

The Stonecoat nodded. "Quite close. A rider comes."

Ovid frowned and studied the road ahead. The moon and stars were bright enough that on the open road he could see quite clearly. As far as the horizon—a low hill—he could see nothing. But he did not argue. If the Jokao said a rider approached, then it had to be true.

Less than two minutes passed before a figure on horseback crested the hill.

The rider came on quickly. Ovid turned and called a halt to the King's Volunteers. The order went back through the ranks and quickly they came to a stop. When they had first set out, such cohesion had been difficult. Now, working together was second nature.

The horse's hooves kicked up dust from the road. The rider pulled the reins tight and came to a stop close enough that Ovid could have reached out and touched the animal. In the moonlight, the mounted soldier scanned the King's Volunteers and then looked down at him.

"Our outriders spotted you hours ago and sent back word,"

the soldier said, fine and neat in the uniform of the army of Euphrasia, emblazoned with the colors of King Hunyadi. His eyes narrowed. "Commander Damia Beck has sent me to discover your purpose. You're not soldiers, that's clear enough."

Hands still on his weapons, Ovid glared at him. "Is it? We've among us men and women—and Stonecoats as well—who've marched from a dozen towns and cities along the Orient Road from here to Twillig's Gorge. We've weapons and some of us training, and we've come to fight the invaders with our last breath. We're the King's Volunteers, boy. I doubt he'd have you send us away."

The horse snuffled and sidestepped a few feet, perhaps unnerved by the presence of the leader of the Jokao. The rider, also, studied the Stonecoat for a long moment.

"Come with me to see Commander Beck," the rider said. "Your troops remain here unless and until she or the king says otherwise. Is that clear?"

Ovid glanced at the Stonecoat, who nodded and withdrew back through the lines to join his kin. Then Ovid shouted for LeBeau, the swordsman who was one of his three lieutenants.

Without a word, LeBeau emerged from the troops and stood rigid, awaiting his instructions. They really were an army, now.

"It seems I must go and reassure this soldier's commander that we support the king and not the enemy. Until I return, the King's Volunteers are yours. And if I haven't returned by dawn, attack the Atlantean invaders and kill as many as you can."

LeBeau smiled thinly at that. "It'll be my pleasure."

The rider reached down for Ovid. "With me, sir."

Ovid stared at his hand.

"There isn't time for pride or propriety," the rider said. "You've brought the king a great many soldiers. If you want them to be of use, ride with me."

Ovid took his hand reluctantly and allowed himself to be

assisted onto the saddle behind the cavalryman. The soldier spurred his horse and then they were galloping up the hill. From the crest of the hill, Ovid could see the ocean. Below them, the Orient Road wound through the sprawled camp of the Euphrasian army, with various battalions of infantry and cavalry divided like neighborhoods. Indeed, the army seemed like an entire city from that vantage point. Legends and Borderkind were scattered amongst them, though many had gathered to the south, not far from where soldiers had dug in to guard against nighttime assault.

The rider galloped along the road, then cut away on a straighter path between two large encampments whose banners flew from posts in the ground, showing that they followed different commanders. Like most residents of Twillig's Gorge, Ovid had little experience on horseback, so he clung to the rider for dear life.

They passed a line of trees, beyond which lay a field of corpses shrouded in blankets and uniforms and ruined tents. Casualties of the Yucatazcan invasion. There must have been two or three hundred, at least, and there would have been others at the site of skirmishes all over southern Euphrasia.

"There will be far more blood spilled, come the dawn," the rider said. "Are your volunteers prepared for that?"

"We've come a long way," Ovid said coldly. "There has been plenty of time to think, and we've thought of nothing else. We'll live free, or we'll die. Atlantis cannot be allowed to prevail."

The rider only nodded. Ovid managed to get his name—Ufland—but nothing more. Then the young cavalryman slowed the horse to a trot and guided the beast in amongst a group of tents set closer together than others, as though this battalion were themselves bonded more tightly. Ovid spotted two Northlander ogres.

With a tug on the reins, Ufland halted his steed. Ovid slipped off of its back. The rider followed suit, handed the reins to another soldier, and started toward the tent at the center of the cluster.

Before they reached it, something moved swiftly at the edge of his vision and he turned to see a Naga slithering toward him and Ufland. Ovid blinked in surprise, then the serpentine archer had reached him. Most would be terrified by the look on the creature's face, but Ovid knew it as a grin. The Naga thrust out his hand and they shook.

"Welcome, Ovid Tsing," the Naga said. "Your bow will be very welcome."

"Thank you, Istarl," Ovid replied. "I'm honored."

This Naga had taught him how to use a bow when Ovid had been merely a boy. To see him now was strangely disconcerting, and yet comforting as well.

"Your mother is well?" Istarl asked.

Ovid gave a single shake of his head. "Returned to the eternal river," he explained, referencing the Nagas' beliefs about the afterlife.

The archer touched his forehead and then gestured to the horizon. "May her journey be gentle and sweet."

Emotion welled up in Ovid's throat. "Thank you, old friend."

He might have discussed his mother's murder, but the rider, Ufland, tapped his shoulder. Ovid turned to see a tall, regal woman emerging from the tent before them. Her skin was darker than night, and the moonlight shone upon her. She walked with one hand on the hilt of her sword, as if by habit rather than caution, and she strode toward them with a black cloak billowing behind her in the breeze.

A remarkable woman, that much was clear.

Ufland stood at attention and offered a short bow. "Commander, this is Ovid Tsing, leader of the militia on the Orient Road. They call themselves the King's Volunteers."

The rider could not quite keep the disdain from his voice.

Commander Beck silenced him with a hard look, and

Ufland gazed at his boots. Ovid liked her for that. The woman studied him a moment, then looked at Istarl.

"You know him?"

The Naga's serpentine lower half extended and he rose straight up so that he seemed also to be at attention. "I do, Commander Beck. Ovid learned the way of the bow from me and mine. He has courage and skill, though he is often far too serious."

Commander Beck arched an eyebrow and studied Ovid. "Too serious? From a Naga, that's saying something."

Ovid said nothing. The moment lasted several seconds, then the commander glanced up the road, the way Ufland and Ovid had ridden.

"How many are in your command, Mister Tsing? How many in the King's Volunteers?"

She gave them their name without a trace of irony.

"At last count, more than eleven hundred, Commander," Ovid replied. "And nearly fifty Jokao."

Commander Beck smiled, as though not quite sure whether she ought to believe him. "Stonecoats?"

Ovid nodded.

"Impressive, sir. More than a battalion, and Stonecoats besides." The woman seemed to mull this over for several moments, glancing at Ufland and Istarl, then she looked out over the ranks of the army toward the ocean. Toward the Isthmus of the Conquistadors.

"Only His Majesty, King Hunyadi, can give you a commission. But in times of war, adjustments must be made. King's Volunteers you call yourself, and King's Volunteers you will remain. We will consider you Commander Tsing from this point forward, as you have an entire battalion and more at your back."

Ovid blinked in surprise. But Ufland seemed aghast at the idea that volunteers would be given stature equal to trained professional soldiers.

"You have something to say?" Commander Beck demanded

of the cavalryman. "Some difficulty understanding the odds against us tomorrow, or the stakes involved?"

Ufland lowered his eyes. "No, Commander. None at all."

Beck nodded. She turned to Ovid. "Take his horse. Ride back to your volunteers. Break from the road and lead them to the ocean. Your battalion will move west at dawn and stop where the shore turns south and becomes the Isthmus. You'll guard the army's eastern flank, Commander Tsing, and watch for further Atlantean incursion from the water. If the invaders break through, you'll send the Jokao first. They'll likely kill a hundred Atlanteans for each Stonecoat that falls. If we're to die, Ovid, we're going to make the scheming bastards pay for every life lost."

Unsure if he ought to salute and not wanting to look a fool, Ovid only stood at attention as the others had done, chin high. "Understood, Commander Beck. The King's Volunteers will not let you down."

She studied him for one, final moment, then nodded.

Ovid started to turn, then paused. "One question, Commander."

Her only reply was another arch of her eyebrow.

"The Legend-Born. Are they here, with the army? Are they still alive?"

Damia Beck smiled. "Collette is here. She and her brother both escaped from the dungeon in Palenque. The Lost Ones may go home, someday, Commander Tsing. Would that please you?"

She said it as though she wasn't quite sure herself if it would be a good thing.

"I don't know," Ovid confessed, "but it would have given my mother great joy."

The commander nodded. "For your mother, then."

Ovid took Ufland's horse. Carefully, not wanting to look clumsy, he slid one foot in the stirrup and threw the other leg over, settling into the saddle.

"Thank you for that, Commander Beck."

The woman's expression darkened. "Thank me tomorrow, at dusk."

Unnerved, Ovid only nodded, turned the horse, and spurred it back toward the road and the King's Volunteers.

Ty'Lis stood on the eastern shore of the Isthmus and watched the waves roll in. The gentle hush of water over sand and stone soothed him. His robes undulated with their own ebb and flow, but he calmed himself. Nothing would happen tonight. The eastern sky had begun to lighten and it filled him with anticipation.

At dawn, it would begin.

The warm ocean breeze ruffled his yellow hair and his robes. Even at this distance he could hear the flap of the sails of the glass ships. The sound lifted his gaze and he studied the beauty of those vessels. Amongst them the Kraken swam, its body surfacing in ripples and links. The legendary beast had followed the fleet of glass ships out of instinct, but it would be no use to Atlantis in the war. The Kraken was a sea creature and could not walk on land or fly.

Still, its presence was powerful. Ty'Lis was pleased the monstrosity had made the journey.

The sorcerer glanced along the shore and saw at least a dozen octopuses dragging their tentacles in the rushing surf. They would linger that way until commanded otherwise. Some floated higher, above the troops already, swimming with the air sharks. But most of the nearly two hundred that had accompanied the invasion force were arrayed all along the coast of the Isthmus. At dawn, they would be ready.

A smile touched the sorcerer's lips. Ty'Lis had to fight the urge to look northward. Only a few miles distant, Hunyadi's forces waited with the Borderkind abominations whose extermination he had hoped would precede this war. Not that it mattered. Far more than half of the Borderkind in the Two Kingdoms and beyond had been slaughtered at his instruction. When the conquest of Euphrasia had been completed, he would finish the job.

Far more worrisome were the Legend-Born. They offered hope to the Lost Ones. And much worse, if their legend was true. Ty'Lis had hoped to execute them publicly, on the battlefield, to demoralize the Euphrasians and destroy any resistance.

Now he had been forced to conceive another plan.

A lovely plan.

Again his robe began to undulate. He ran his hands over the fabric.

"Shhh. Quiet, darlings. Quietly now."

A frisson of unease went through him and he realized what had disturbed him. Turning, Ty'Lis saw three sorcerers coming toward him, floating several inches above the ground, arms crossed in arrogance. The hems of their robes brushed the rocky earth that led down to the shore.

His nostrils flared. Ru'Lem could have come to speak to him alone. Instead, the leader of the High Council had brought two other councilors. They would speak down to him, of course. They always did, when more than one was present. Alone, none of them had the courage to treat him with disdain. Together, they were too proud to address him any other way.

The octopuses on either side of him drifted further along the shore, moving away, dragging snail trails in the wet sand with their tentacles. Ty'Lis clasped his hands in front of him, sleeves enveloping them, and waited for the councilors to arrive.

"You wander far, Ty'Lis," said the sorceress amongst them, an ugly crone called Nya'To, her skin and hair a tainted piss yellow.

Ru'Lem held up a hand and glanced at her, obviously displeased that she had spoken before him. The councilor on his right, a dark-bearded sycophant named Ha'Kar after his father, said nothing, watching the Council leader for any cue that he ought to speak or gesture or dance like the puppet that he was.

"Perhaps you ought to remain with us," Ru'Lem said. His silver hair had thinned with age to nothing but wisps, but his beard remained thick and knotted with iron rings. "When the battle begins, it will be swift."

Ty'Lis glanced at the sky. "We have a little time, yet."

How dare they? None of this would have been possible without his efforts. He had gathered the Myth Hunters. He had removed Prince Tzajin to Atlantis and corrupted the throne of Yucatazca. He had engineered the murder of King Mahacuhta. Now they swept in to claim the glory and presumed to instruct him? They might command the armies of Atlantis, but he was not some Lost soldier.

"All is proceeding as planned," Ru'Lem said, a warning in his voice as he knitted his brows. "We must all work together, now, to make certain there are no more mistakes. Your role has changed, Ty'Lis, but it is still vital to our success."

A horrid malignance wafted from him, both a stench and an aura of darkness that would have cowed anyone else. The other councilors seemed to absorb the hideous ambiance, exuding cruelty and predation. Ty'Lis only smiled, revealing jagged teeth. The arrogance on Ru'Lem's face wavered.

"We will not discuss the Bascombes' escape again. I have delivered to you precisely the circumstances the High Council desired. After centuries of your predecessors bowing to other kings and letting our world be further diluted by the influx of unwelcome intruders from across the Veil, I have given Atlantis the chance to do something about it. Now you have taken command of our future, Ru'Lem. I hope that your hands are strong enough to guide it."

The aged sorcerer sneered at him, lips peeling back. Thin even by the standards of Atlantis, his face had the flat, deadly aspect of a moray eel. It seemed as though he might issue a challenge at that very moment, but then Ru'Lem took a breath.

"It has been decided that you will command the Perytons

when the battle begins," Ru'Lem said at last. "They are unruly beasts, savage and useful, but loyal only to themselves."

Ty'Lis smiled thinly. "And to me. They are loyal to me."

"If we are to win the war, they must obey," the aged sorcerer said.

"Oh, victory is vital. But there are other factors to consider."

Before any of the councilors could reply, Ty'Lis raised a hand. He pursed his lips in a whistle that rippled the air. The octopuses up and down the shore made a terrible shrieking noise that made them flinch and cover their ears for a moment. Black smoke curled up from the palm of his upraised hand, pluming into the sky, and then it blossomed into a flower of deep purple light.

Ru'Lem raised both hands. The sound of the surf grew loud, but it did not come from the ocean. White froth and blue light steamed around the ancient one's fists. Nya'To and Ha'Kar reacted as well, drifting aside so that he could not attack all three of them at once.

Ty'Lis smiled and raised both hands, showing empty palms. "Do you think I am so foolish as to attack you, councilors?"

"Then what—" Ru'Lem began.

His answer came before the question could be finished. Powerful wings beat the air above them and they all looked up to see two Perytons gliding toward the ground. The moonlight cast twisted shadows from their antlers. Their green feathers looked black as tar in the night.

The Perytons alighted beside Ty'Lis, moving almost in a crouch, as though they might lunge. Their talons hung at their sides, but they were so swift that—this close—they could tear off a limb before any of the sorcerers crafted a spell.

"Why have you summoned us?" said one of the Perytons, its voice a low, rasping screech, almost birdlike.

Ty'Lis bowed to them. "Morning is not far off. This battle will decide the war. These councilors worry that you will not obey them."

As one, the two Perytons twisted their heads round to stare at Ru'Lem and the others with murderous eyes. "Obey?"

"Yes. I thought, perhaps, that I would let you explain to them that the Perytons are the allies of Atlantis, not our servants. I am certain you will be able to forge a relationship valuable to everyone."

Ru'Lem rose several inches from the ground. "The Perytons may be our allies, but you are a child of Atlantis, Ty'Lis. You will obey the High Council or be guilty of treason."

The Perytons spread their wings, feathers ruffling, instinctively reacting to the hostility between sorcerers. They hung their heads low, racks of antlers sharp and deadly.

Ty'Lis glanced at the eastern horizon, where the sky had lightened to an ocean blue. Dawn seemed to be hurrying this morning.

"Your cooperation will benefit all of Atlantis," he said to the Perytons. "Your people will not be forgotten. I will not allow it."

He turned to Ru'Lem. "The war is in your hands, now. But if it is to mean anything—if the High Council is to achieve its goals—then there are other chores to which I must attend."

The councilors began to move toward him, dark magic rising. Ru'Lem commanded him to stop.

Ty'Lis tugged his hood down over his face, pulled his cloak tightly around him, and vanished within it. He left behind a tiny swirl of air. A wave crashed on the shore, rolling in and erasing any trace that he had ever been there at all.

The Shediac River flowed through Wessex County, Maine, in a serpentine series of double-backs, trickle-pools, and rapids, so that its personality changed dramatically every half mile or so. In Kitteridge, where Robiquet had worked for decades as house manager for the Bascombe family, it flowed strong but silent, placid on the surface but with a deep, dangerous current. But upriver, in the town of Haskell, it passed under the

Chadbourne Bridge in a rocky cascade. The fishing off of the Chadbourne was fantastic, but nobody tried canoeing on that part of the Shediac. And Sara Halliwell had never heard of anyone committing suicide by jumping from that bridge. With the rough water and all of those jutting rocks, it looked like the kind of place to bust yourself up and survive to regret it.

As a little girl, Sara Halliwell had loved the Chadbourne Bridge. Fishing hadn't appealed to her, but several times her father had taken her along on an early Sunday morning to cast a line into the Shediac. It had always been springtime—a cold April morning, often damp and gray. He'd have coffee and she hot cocoa. Her dad hadn't spoken to her much during these ventures. Oh, he'd talked, but never really to Sara. There were no questions about school or what she might want for her birthday or how pretty she'd looked in her new Easter dress. Ted Halliwell had just talked about the weather and his philosophy of fishing and how much he loved the quiet out there on the bridge in the early morning.

Sara hadn't thought about those fishing trips in a very long time.

Now she'd returned to the Chadbourne Bridge on a drizzly gray morning—a little early in the year for her father's fishing trips, but the weather was much the same. She pulled her jacket tight around her and stared down into the tumbling rush of the Shediac River and she realized there were tears in her eyes.

Hastily, she wiped them away. Ted Halliwell's little girl didn't cry. No matter how angry and frustrated she'd been with him as she grew to adulthood, that was one lesson she couldn't seem to unlearn. Sara might shed a tear alone in bed or behind closed doors, but never where others could see her. More than one of her relationships had been doomed by this reticence.

She took a breath, wiped at her eyes until she was satisfied the evidence had been erased, and then turned toward Sheriff Norris and Robiquet. All of them knew the bridge well. But to Sara and the sheriff, it had always been just a bridge.

An interesting bridge, true. Spaced evenly along one side it had a pair of stone towers like castle turrets. Set into each tower was a metal gate. The bars looked to have been rusted and painted and rusted and painted dozens of times over the years. Sara had asked her father every time they crossed the bridge what the towers were for. He had a dozen different stories. One day he would say they were lookouts from the Second World War, from which soldiers watched for enemy ships coming up the Shediac to invade Maine. A week later he would insist that each of those towers had been used in the early 1900s to hold the worst criminals from the county jail, displaying them to the public as a warning.

There had been other explanations, but those were the two she remembered best. To this day, she had no idea what they were for. Sheriff Norris didn't know, either.

Even Robiquet could not say what the stated purpose of their original construction had been. But inside the tower on the east side of the river, he insisted that they would find what they had sought.

"Sara, are you coming?" Sheriff Norris called.

She turned to find that he and Robiquet had gotten the rust-flaked gate open. Lost in thought, she'd somehow missed the sound of grating metal she felt sure must have accompanied the act.

A truck rumbled by, an early morning delivery or a father off to work. Other than that, there was no traffic. Once upon a time, long before Sara had been born, the Chadbourne had been much traveled. These days, Route 7 was a faster way to get almost anywhere.

Sara cleared her throat. The dampness of the morning was getting to her. As she walked toward the tower, she saw Robiquet disappear into the shadows beyond that gate. Sheriff Norris went to his car—emblazoned with the Wessex County Sheriff's Department logo—and popped the trunk. He glanced around as guiltily as one of the many punks and thugs he'd no doubt tossed into lockup, then took out a tire-iron and slammed the trunk. He kept the tool down beside his leg, as inconspicuously as possible, and walked back to the tower on the bridge.

A light rain began to fall.

Feeling as though she were in a dream, Sara could only stand and watch as he walked by. He didn't even seem to notice her until he reached the open gate and paused to look back.

"You coming?"

Sara shook her head. "I don't think so."

Surprise registered on his face.

"I'll just . . . I'll wait here," she told him.

The sheriff gave her a thoughtful look and then went in without her. Perhaps he understood.

This time she heard the grating of metal. In the darkness inside that small tower, where soldiers or criminals or werewolves at full moon (for that was another of her father's tales of Chadbourne Bridge) had once resided, Robiquet and the sheriff pried open a door.

No. A Door. Capital D.

One that ought to have led to the other side of the Veil, where Ted Halliwell needed his little girl's voice to guide him home.

Only a minute or two after he'd gone in, Sheriff Norris stepped back out. He wore upon his face the apology of the surgeon who had failed to save a husband or a son, or a father.

He said her name.

Sara shook her head, then turned her back on him, grateful for the falling rain. Ted Halliwell's little girl didn't cry. At least not where anyone could see her.

Jackson said her name again. She heard him take a couple of steps toward her, then other footsteps, softer.

"I'm sorry, Miss Halliwell," Robiquet said, his words gentle as the rain. "There are other Doors, but I fear that whatever is happening on the other side of the Veil, they will all be blocked, now. If you need me, for anything, you'll find me at the

Bascombe house. I never should have left. I owed them more than that. There's a great deal of business to be dealt with at the house and with Max's law firm. I need to protect Oliver and Collette's interests for when they come home."

Sara frowned deeply. Cold rain ran down the back of her neck, under her collar. She could feel Jackson and Robiquet there behind her but decided not to worry about her tears. The rain would hide them.

"You really think they're coming home?" she asked, almost afraid of the answer. How could she lose faith if the fussy little goblin still believed?

She turned to find that, somehow, Robiquet was gone.

Sara and Sheriff Norris stared at the place where he'd been standing a moment before as rain spattered the bridge.

After a moment, Jackson led her back to the car. In silence, she climbed in beside him, wishing she had somewhere to go besides her father's house. Wishing she had someone to go home to.

It was time. Tonight, she would call her mother, and then the airport. She had left a life behind her in Atlanta, way back in December. She only hoped it was still there, waiting.

The first horn blew just as the burning corona of the sun peeked above the eastern horizon. Immediately it was joined by a chorus of others as the army of Euphrasia sent a signal through the ranks, from one battalion to the next, that the enemy approached.

King Hunyadi stepped from his tent, already clad in the leather armor that had been fashioned for his grandfather in times long forgotten. His father's sword hung at his hip. As a young warrior, he'd had another sword, a gift from the man who'd taught him combat, but he had given it over years ago as a symbol of his trust in a man named David Koenig, who in turn had eventually passed it to Oliver Bascombe.

The sword had been used to kill the king of Yucatazca. Whose hand grasped it now was a question Hunyadi did not wish to entertain.

His army rose up in a wave. Shouts carried up the hill. The thunder of hooves filled the air as the cavalry mounted their horses. In the strange light of sunrise, Hunyadi saw flaming arrows arcing high into the air above the front lines where Commander Alborg's third battalion was dug in.

The fiery arrows struck octopuses that floated over the trenches and the flames began to spread. An eerie, inhuman scream traveled all the way up the hill to where the king stood.

Thomas, a page who'd served him throughout this campaign, ran to him, eyes wide with fear.

"My mount, boy. Fetch the horse!" Hunyadi snapped.

All apologies, Thomas ran to do as he'd been bid.

Hunyadi saw a dark shape slinking across the sky and looked up. Alarmed, he drew his sword and ran downhill toward the place where an awning had been set up as a field hospital in preparation for wounded. The king shouted for them to take cover.

The air shark slid down as though it had been hunting for him. Which, of course, was precisely what the creature had been doing. The Atlanteans had sent the monster to kill him, and others would be coming as well.

Hunyadi barely noticed the little blue bird that darted across the morning sky until it changed. High overhead, the bird changed shape. With a flap of its wings it metamorphosed into a man, dancing and whirling in the air. Beneath Blue Jay's arms there remained the blur of mystical wings.

"Welcome back," the king whispered, even as Blue Jay spun, fifty feet off the ground, and cut the shark in half with a single slice of his razor-sharp wings.

The page, Thomas, ran toward the king, holding the bridle of his horse.

Blue Jay descended, turning and stepping on the air as

though in the midst of some kind of ritual, until he alighted upon the ground. His expression was grim but his eyes were bright with mischief.

The trickster bowed. "At your service, Majesty."

"Cutting it a little close, aren't you, my friend?" Hunyadi asked.

Blue Jay nodded. "Not by choice. The important thing is, we're here. I've got reinforcements for you, John. Gods and monsters and Borderkind as well. And Oliver Bascombe."

Hunyadi clapped him on the shoulder. "I knew you'd do it, Jay. Go, my friend, and bring them here. Right away. We've a war to fight."

The king turned to the page. "You, boy, run as fast as you're able. Bring Frost of the Borderkind here to me, and the Wayfarer as well." He paused and glanced at Blue Jay. "Send a runner to Commander Beck. I'll want her here. And summon the Legend-Born to me at once. Go, now!"

Grinning, the boy ran.

"Legend-Born?" Blue Jay asked. "Frost and Collette are here with you?"

Hunyadi nodded. "Oh, we've a hell of an army now, Jay. Atlantis has no idea what it's begun."

It didn't sound like any war Oliver could imagine. From time to time he heard the pop of a gunshot, but guns were so rare in the legendary world that those sounds were few and far between. The rest was thunder. Axes and swords and fists and the pounding of booted feet. Crackling noises and the rush of air blotted out other sounds from time to time, but those came from the spells of sorcerers, not cannons or rocket launchers.

All his life he'd wished for magic, but never for this.

With Julianna at his side, Oliver hurried up the hill amidst tents now abandoned by the soldiers who had camped there. Aides and runners and a handful of officers and advisors still rushed around, but the army had risen as one and gone to battle. Riders on horseback carried messages back and forth to the front lines. Legends flew overhead—some perhaps Borderkind, others surely not—but they drew no line between themselves and the Lost Ones of Euphrasia. The war involved them all.

Blue Jay climbed the hill ahead of them, effortlessly moving upward as though what he really wanted was to fly. The feathers in his hair danced as he moved.

"What about the others?" Julianna asked him. "The Harvest gods, and the ones who came with Kitsune?"

"Kit and Konigen are working that out. But none of us is going anywhere until we get orders from the king," the trickster said.

Oliver saw the irony. "I never thought of you as much for taking orders."

Blue Jay glanced over his shoulder, tall grass parting as he passed. "Another thing I owe the Atlanteans for. When it's all over, I'll make plenty of mischief. For now . . ."

The sounds of war carried to them up the hill, the area around the head of the Isthmus a natural theater. The acoustics sent a chill through Oliver. Their view of the ocean unnerved him. Normally the sight soothed him and it seemed somehow abominable to have a war on the shore. The ocean ought to have meant peace and tranquility.

"This is creeping me out," Julianna said.

"Hell, yeah," Oliver said, glancing at her as they labored up the hill. "Of course it is."

"I don't just mean the war. It's being up here, after they've all taken off. Like we've been left behind on purpose, cheese baiting the trap."

Oliver frowned. "This isn't—"

"I know." She waved his protest away. "But I'd feel safer down there with all the people who have weapons."

Even as she said it, they came around a tent and saw a larger one. Six riders sat atop their horses around the tent and a couple of dozen others were spread out at the top of the hill. Two massive ogres with twisted features and carrying war hammers stood on either side of the tent's entrance. In the air, robed in dark green, a trio of Mazikeen floated over the tent.

"The King's Guard," Julianna said.

Blue Jay glanced back at them. "Hurry, you two."

Oliver felt his pique rising. "We're only human."

The trickster said nothing. Julianna squeezed his hand.

"You're not," she said. "I'm having a hell of a time keeping up with you."

"You got me. My secret's yoga, in case you're wondering," Oliver said, but only because he couldn't think of any reply that wasn't a joke. How was he supposed to respond to that? He wasn't ready yet to start thinking about himself as being anything other than human, even though in his heart, he had always been a child of two worlds.

Julianna rolled her eyes.

He lifted her hand and kissed it.

Blue Jay stopped in front of the tent. Oliver and Julianna halted on either side of him. A severe young woman in the uniform of the King's Guard ran to meet them.

"Tell him Oliver's here," was all Blue Jay said.

The young woman—barely more than a girl—widened her eyes in surprise, nodded, and nearly fled into the tent.

"Damn, you're like Elvis now," Julianna whispered to him. "No last name needed."

The soldier emerged from the tent, pulled a flap aside, and nodded for them to enter. "His Majesty, King Hunyadi, will see you."

Blue Jay grumbled something about protocol in the middle of a war, but Oliver couldn't quite make out the entire sentiment. He held back so that Julianna could precede him into the tent, and went in last.

A table with maps of the battleground and troop deployment had been moved to one side and now stood forgotten. King Hunyadi still looked like the rough-hewn, bearded fisherman he had seemed when Oliver had first encountered him, despite the armor and the sword at his side. Damia Beck stood with him in the tent. Blue Jay strode over to the tall black woman and exchanged a quiet word with her, their fingers entwining. As they traveled together over the past few days, Blue Jay had spoken of Damia quite a bit—and Oliver remembered her from their brief encounters in Euphrasia—but he'd had a hard time picturing the beautiful, yet grimly serious soldier and the trickster in love. Seeing the way they looked at each other erased all of his preconceptions.

Frost stood in a far corner, deep in conversation with Wayland Smith. A hundred distrustful thoughts went through his mind when he saw them, but he spared them only a glance.

"Collette!" Julianna cried happily.

The two women ran to one another and embraced like long-lost sisters. Oliver stood by during their reunion, until Collette detached herself and turned to look at him with a mischievous grin.

"You've got a bit of a tan," Oliver said.

"I've been on a millionaire's boat in South America, sunning, enjoying life," Collette replied. "Of course, the boat was stolen and we were getting shot at, but beyond that, very luxurious. Hence the tan."

Oliver drew his sister into his arms and held her close.

"If he hadn't gotten you back here alive, I'd have killed him," Oliver whispered into her hair. "Damn it, Coll, I was afraid for you."

Collette ran her hands up and down his arms and stepped back. "Me, too, little brother. But at least you had Julianna to look after you."

"Oliver," Blue Jay said, sharply.

He turned to see King Hunyadi looking at him and Julianna expectantly.

"Your Majesty, I'm sorry," Julianna began.

"We're both sorry," Oliver said. "It's just that we were—"

Hunyadi held up a hand. His eyes spoke of hard-won wisdom, but also of a fondness that touched Oliver.

"I understand. And it's good to see you, my friends," said the king. "But the morning is fleeting and the time has come for all of us to share what we know. For the sake of Euphrasia, for the

Two Kingdoms, and two worlds, the Legend-Born must be pro-tected. Morale depends upon hope, and hope, right now, de-pends upon you two."

He nodded at Oliver and then Collette.

"Your presence means a lot to the human soldiers down there amidst the bloodshed and monsters. Still, it would be simpler if you were elsewhere."

Oliver opened his hands wide. "But we're here. And we can help, Your Majesty. All my life has been about pretending, whether in a court of law or on the stage. The time's come to do something real."

"You can't—" Julianna began.

"He's right," Collette interrupted. "We have—it's hard for me to say magic, but we have magic in us. We can help."

Frost flowed across the tent on a blast of frigid air. "No. Absolutely not."

Oliver turned on him, scowling. "You know, I've had just about enough of you pulling the strings. You've got some grand plan for us? Great. Hope that goes well for you. But we'll make our own decisions."

The winter man narrowed his eyes, blue-white mist rising from their edges. "I did what I had to do."

"Frost," Blue Jay warned.

Wayland Smith gazed at Oliver and Collette from beneath the brim of his hat. "The two of you must understand, the out-come of the war is vital, but there are even greater things at stake. We cannot risk your lives, no matter the cost."

Oliver pointed at him. "What makes you think I'm going to listen to anything you have to say? Last time I saw you, you murdered a man in that inn at Twillig's Gorge just because he figured out who I really was. You've been in this scheme with Frost from the beginning."

Smith raised an eyebrow. He glanced at King Hunyadi, then shifted his gaze back to Oliver. "If you must know, the scheme—as you call it—was primarily mine."

Oliver glared at him. "Well, then you're a fucking asshole."

King Hunyadi stepped into the middle of the tent, separating them.

"Enough."

They all looked at the king, but no one argued with him.

"I'm sorry," Oliver said. To Hunyadi, not to the others.

The king held up a hand again, brushing it away. He began to ask questions, and soon they were sharing their stories. Frost and Collette spoke of the Atlantean forces. Oliver and Julianna and Blue Jay talked about the chaos they had left in Palenque. Damia reassured them that the anarchy they had begun still raged in the capital city of Yucatazca and beyond.

"The rebels have nearly taken control of Palenque. They're demanding that Prince Tzajin return to Yucatazca and address the public himself. They will return control of the city to the prince, but only after hearing the words from his mouth."

King Hunyadi nodded. "Yes. According to Frost's report, mistrust of their purpose has caused the Yucatazcan warriors to lose heart. It may be that we can turn them to our cause or convince them to withdraw from the field of battle."

Oliver felt almost as though he were in a courtroom, and Hunyadi the judge. "If it pleases Your Majesty, I'd like to speak."

The king smiled thinly. "Now you ask permission?"

With a glance at Julianna, Oliver nodded. "Look, it seems pretty obvious to me that everyone's on the same page here. Maybe we'll win this war on the ground, but it's a hell of a gamble. Those ships Frost and Collette saw—who knows how many more of them there are? There could be another entire invasion force on the way. We need an ace in the hole, and Prince Tzajin is that ace. I've been thinking about this ever since we heard the kid was in Atlantis."

Oliver studied King Hunyadi.

"Your Majesty, I'm going to get him. I'll find the kid, get him out of Atlantis, and back here. It's pretty clear that Smith can travel in ways that the Borderkind can't—ways he doesn't seem interested in explaining to the rest of us, but that's fine. Let me choose a small group. I'll pick them myself. Smith drops us in the middle of Atlantis, as close as possible to the library where he saw Prince Tzajin. We'll bring him back."

At last, he allowed himself to glance at Julianna. Her nostrils flared with anger.

"Don't do this," she said.

Oliver didn't reply. He had to do it, and she knew that. After what Ty'Lis had done to them all—the murder of his father, the Sandman terrorizing Collette, the death of Ted Halliwell—how could he not do whatever was necessary to stop Atlantis?

"After what Ty'Lis did to you, Jules?" Collette said.

Julianna shot her a withering glance. "You can't agree with this."

"Agree?" Collette replied. "Hell, I'm going with him."

Silence fell. One by one, they all looked at King Hunyadi. The big man stroked his beard. At length, he glanced at Frost and Smith.

"Your Majesty, the risk," Smith warned.

Frost shook his head. The familiar sound of his icicle hair clinking made Oliver nostalgic for a time before resentment and deceit had come between them.

"You can't let them both go, Majesty," the winter man said.

"What a surprise," Oliver mused. "One of us is expendable."

Blue Jay glanced at Damia, who seemed to be growing impatient to join her troops. "They're right." He glanced at Oliver and Collette. "I'm sorry, my friends, but they're right. You can't both go. I'm not one of the Lost. It matters not to me if your people ever get home. But if you both die, that's a victory for Atlantis, and it could undermine all that Euphrasia is fighting for."

King Hunyadi raised both hands. "Agreed. And it is decided. Oliver, choose your allies. Smith, you'll take them in and bring them back, with the prince."

"I'm not supposed to interfere, John," the Wayfarer said grimly from beneath the brim of his hat. His eyes were shadows.

"You aren't. You'll ferry them, nothing more."

Smith didn't argue further.

Julianna had no such compunction. "So, what?" she said, staring at Oliver. "I'm just supposed to wait for you, again, wondering if you're dead or alive, trapped in this crazy place alone?"

Oliver glanced away. "You won't be alone."

"No," Collette agreed. "I'll be with you. They're not going to let me go."

Julianna glanced around the tent, fixing her eyes one by one on Frost, Smith, King Hunyadi, and Oliver.

"Fucking men." She turned and left the tent.

Collette stared at her brother for a moment. Then she went to him, hugged him close, and looked up at his face.

"I'll look out for her. You look out for yourself. Don't think I'm not pissed, though. I want you coming back alive so I can kick your ass."

Oliver kissed her forehead.

"Wouldn't miss that for the world."

Sara woke in the small hours of the night, the Maine wind howling outside the windows. A storm had blown up, but she couldn't hear the patter of rain. Just that wind, rattling the windows in their frames and whistling in the eaves. Her father's house was a relic of the past.

It surprised her to find that she'd fallen asleep. All day she had been on the phone, ordering the shutoff of the utilities, calling her friends in Atlanta and an editor she knew would give her work. Calling her mother, and crying again. Both of them weeping for a man they had never found a way to stop loving, even in the times when they had wanted to.

When she'd gone to bed, her mind had been bustling with activity, with plans and their repercussions, all the while trying to avoid the truth around which it all revolved. Her father's house would soon be empty, and it might be that way forever. She'd tossed and turned with these thoughts, wide awake, first too warm and tossing the covers away, then freezing cold and retrieving them, burrowing underneath.

Somehow, she'd managed to drift off.

Now she stretched, head muzzy with sleep, and listened to the creak of the old house and the cries of the wind, and wondered if that was what had woken her. The clock on the wall ticked. The seconds seemed to pass too slowly, lengthening, stretching out as though hesitant to move on. *Tick.* A breath. *Tick.* Its oddness drew her. Eyes closed, she listened intently, wondering if the battery was dying. And as she strained to make sense of the sluggish passage of time on that clock, she heard another sound.

A sifting.

A shiver ran up her back. Her skin prickled with gooseflesh. The sound seemed familiar, but she knew she had never heard anything precisely like it before. The sifting, scratching noise seemed to cascade toward her, and then abruptly ceased.

"What the hell?" she said, mostly to hear herself speak.

Sara turned, rising from the pillow, and her breath caught in her throat. The thing that stood by her bed could not have been a man. Not with those fingers like knives and its long, cruel face, and the terrible lemon eyes that shone in the dark.

She screamed, letting out a torrent of words and curses and pleadings to God as she scrambled off the bed. Her right ankle tangled in the sheet, she fell to the floor with a thump and then backed into a corner. As she went, those lemon eyes followed her, the hooded thing coming over the top of the bed at her as though weightless.

Perhaps it was because she had been sleeping in her father's house, or perhaps because all of her fear and grief were bound tightly to Ted Halliwell's vanishing. But in that moment, Sara called for her father like she had as a little girl, waking in the dark from a nightmare.

"Daddy!"

The cruel, hooded thing froze with its knife fingers stretched out toward her. Lemon eyes went dark.

Like a statue, it had frozen solid, halfway across her bed.

Within the consciousness of the Sandman, Ted Halliwell screamed his daughter's name. She'd called out to him. His powdered bones sifted with the sand and the dust, and he fought the horrid will of the monster. Holding him back was like stopping a bull from charging, yet he had done it. His soul felt as though the strain would tear it apart, but for the moment, the Sandman had been halted.

Grains of sand shifted. Skittered to the floor.

No, Halliwell thought. But he knew it was no use. His love for Sara had given him the strength to stop the Sandman, but he would not be able to hold the monster.

Pain clutched at the core of him, the part that would have been his heart if he still had flesh. The maelstrom that was the Sandman had slowed. It parted like curtains—like a veil—and he could feel the hatred searing him. Those terrible eyes looked inward, now, and they found Halliwell there, alone.

"I wanted my vengeance," the Sandman said. The voice echoed around inside the maelstrom, inside the consciousness that was all that remained of Ted Halliwell save those powdered bones, scattered amidst the grains of the monster. "The fox bitch, Kitsune, and the nothing, weakling man, Bascombe. They turned my brother against me and I wanted vengeance. You denied me that vengeance, little nothing man. You infest me like pestilence, like rot, like conscience, and I will not have it.

"You must be punished. The little girl's eyes will pop in

my teeth, and I will be certain that you can taste them on my tongue, as if it were your own."

The words/thoughts slithered inside Halliwell's mind, and whatever trace remained of him, soul or echo, shuddered—not with fear, but with rage. The man in him might have let death and this bizarre damnation corrupt his spirit, weaken him, but his daughter called his name and now this abomination mocked her love for him and her pain. The man might be afraid, but Ted Halliwell was more than a man. The soldier in him, the detective in him, the father in him was not afraid.

His grip on the Sandman tightened.

The monster roared fury. Halliwell felt aware of every bone shard, every particle of yellowed bone and marrow that mixed with the substance of the Sandman, and he reached out into the paralyzed limbs of the child-killer and he *took hold.*

Fucker, he said/thought. *That's my little girl.*

Awareness radiated out from Halliwell's consciousness. His senses searched the maelstrom, knowing already what he would find. There, hiding in the midst of the soul-storm created by the merger of their spirits, their essences, he found the third consciousness locked inside this body. Peering, spying, from the maelstrom, was the Dustman. Swiftly brutal, the Dustman might be the brother of the Sandman—another aspect of the same legend—but he was also a kind of mirror. The Dustman was an English legend, proper and grim. He was a creature of order, where his brother was chaos and anarchy.

Help me, damn you! The blood's on all of our hands, now. You can't just hide, or he'll erode you away to nothing!

Still the Dustman did not stir.

The Sandman remained paralyzed, but Halliwell's grip began to slip. Somewhere beyond the tiny universe that existed within the maelstrom, he heard his daughter's voice again. She muttered prayers to God. By now she'd be rising from that corner, trying to get past the monster to reach for the phone to call the police, or maybe she'd just run.

God, Halliwell hoped she would run.

"He's a coward," the voice of the Sandman sifted through the churning gloom around Halliwell. "He dared to stand against me, to betray his brother, and now he'll be nothing, no more than you."

Listen to me, Halliwell hissed at the Dustman. *All of those children you visited, the ones who couldn't sleep or didn't want to... you were gentle with them. You cast your dust in their eyes and they slept in peace and dreamed the way children should. I've felt your mind, I've seen it all in your thoughts. We're all part of each other, now. Is this what you want? To terrify those kids, to murder them in their beds, to mutilate their—*

"It's exactly what he wants," the Sandman said.

Halliwell's soul—whatever remained of it—froze at those words. Could that be true? Was that what the Dustman had always wanted? Was that why his brother was ascendant, now, because he didn't want to fight?

"You lie!" the Dustman roared.

He stepped from the maelstrom, closer to Halliwell now than he had been since the two of them were merged with the Sandman, spirits trapped within. In his greatcoat and bowler hat and with that mustache, he might have seemed almost absurd were it not for the hatred in his gleaming, golden eyes.

I thought I could do nothing, the Dustman said, but now the voice did not echo in the maelstrom. It was right beside Halliwell, in his own mind, thought to thought. *I'm only a facet of the legend. A shard. That's what you've become yourself, Detective. A facet.*

But that's all he is, Halliwell replied. *One facet.*

Yes.

Halliwell held out his hand for the Dustman to shake, to seal the deal.

The maelstrom calmed. Halliwell felt the Sandman try to break free of his grip and the form he had given himself in this nothing place, this spirit cage inside the prison of the Sandman, was thrown down.

"Go to hell," Halliwell snarled, and he stood, reaching out once again to shake the Dustman's hand. There was power in a vow. An oath. And that was what they were about to enter into.

Then the Sandman was there. Somehow he was their cage, but he was also there inside the mindscape with them. Those dreadful yellow eyes peered out from beneath his hood.

"I will not allow it," he said, almost a sigh, a skittering of words and sand.

Halliwell smiled. The bastard was too late. He and the Dustman clasped hands . . .

Sara ran around the bed, colliding with the closet door and pushing off. She lunged for the phone on the nightstand, snatched it off the cradle, and even as she did, she turned to look at the bizarre statue—rough like concrete—on the bed.

It said her name. The whispering voice did not sound cruel or mocking. Instead, it sounded familiar.

She froze.

No longer a statue, the thing began to shift and flow as though reality were ocean waves rolling in and reshaping it. The hood went away. The figure slid to the end of the bed, away from her, stood facing her. Its cloak had become a long coat, collar turned up high around its neck. A derby sat upon its head, made of the same material as the coat and the monster's hands, its flesh.

Sand.

It looked up at her and she caught her breath. Lemon eyes had turned golden. It had a thick drooping mustache, but all of the same shade, the same gray brown of sand.

But the face . . . she knew the face.

"Daddy?" she whispered.

The strength went out of her legs and she staggered back,

catching herself against the doorjamb, barely staying on her feet.

The thing looked unsure a moment, but then a smile spread across its face, lifting that mustache. Her father's smile. All of the things that Robiquet had told her—about the Veil and the creatures of legend, about the Borderkind—came back to her now.

"Dad?" she ventured.

"Yeah, Sara-love. It's me," he rasped.

His voice *sifted*, but it was his, like they were talking over a bad phone line and she could only hear him through static. Sara-love. He'd called her that all the time when she was little, almost unconsciously, just the way he'd done now.

A hitching breath came from her and she held a hand to her chest. Hope, she found, could be far more painful than grief.

"How can it be? What are . . . what was that?"

"A monster, sweetie. I was wrong, all those nights I told you they didn't exist. But we've got it under control, now. Locked it up in here and threw away the key."

All those nights, as a girl, when he'd come home late, Ted Halliwell had told his daughter he'd been catching bad guys. And when little Sara had asked if he had caught them, his answer had always been the same. Locked them up and threw away the key.

Sara took a step toward him, then hesitated, fear lancing through her. The image of that monster, of those lemon eyes and finger knives, lingered.

"What are you now, Dad?"

His face—sculpted from sand—contorted with sadness and loss. He reached out toward her, though she was still too far for him to touch her.

"I was away. Far away, Sara-love. All I wanted was to come back so I could tell you how sorry I am that I didn't understand when you needed me to. The life you have . . . I had dreamed it so differently for you. A wedding. A little girl of your own. It took me a long time to realize my dreams for you had to give way to yours. Hard for me. I figured it out, though, sweetie. Eventually, I got it. All that mattered was that you were happy. That you could be adored the way you deserved. But by then, I couldn't find the words to say it. If I'd seen you . . . but that never worked out. And then I was gone."

Sara stared at him. Her hand flew to her mouth and a small sound escaped her lips. Her eyes blurred with tears and she wiped them away.

"Maybe you don't remember, Sara, but that question . . . I asked you the same thing, once. The worst thing I ever did, asking you what you were. The stupidest, most heartless thing. And what did you tell me, do you remember?"

Sara did. "I'm me."

Her father, this odd figure in his hat and coat, this Sandman, took a step toward her. "I don't know what else I am, but I'm me. I'm what I had to be to get back to you, to be here to say I'm sorry, and that I love you."

Sara stared at him, her fear still fresh.

"Never was much good at saying any of the important things. But all I wanted was this chance to say it to you. I can . . . I don't want you to be afraid. I'll go now. But—"

"No!" Sara rushed to him, danger forgotten. The idea of losing him again made her cry out. She threw her arms around him. His coat—whatever he was—felt rough to the touch, but she held on tight, afraid he would slip through her fingers.

Whatever part of him this was, it had his voice and his heart. She could not lose those, now that she had them back.

"Please don't go."

Even if they had stayed that way for a year, it wouldn't have been enough for Sara. All of her hesitations and resentments were long forgotten. She had another chance with him, a chance for him to know her and know how she felt, and for him to understand.

In time, he stepped back.

Sara gaped. The silly mustache and hat were gone. The face

THE LOST ONES 315

belonged, now, only to her father. Even his eyes seemed more his own.

"Dad, you look—"

He reached up to trace his fingers along his features.

"How many of you are in there?" she asked.

He blinked and then looked at her in surprise.

"You're a pretty smart young woman, you know that?"

Sara smiled. "My father's a detective."

Ted lowered his gaze, then raised his eyes again. Sara knew that look. She had seen it hundreds, maybe thousands of times growing up. The words had not even begun to come from his mouth, but she could hear them. There was something he had to do. He couldn't be home with her right now, because there were some bad guys out there, and Detective Ted Halliwell was on the case. He had to stop them before they hurt somebody.

Her father saw her eyes, and he knew.

"I'll come back. I swear. I can do it, now. And I'll be here with you. But the Dustman and I have business to handle. Debts to pay."

"And you have to stop the bad guys," Sara said, her voice small.

As he nodded, the sand of his flesh and his clothing sifted again, and the hat and mustache returned. The Dustman. That's what he had called it; what he was, now.

"Yeah."

"Detective Ted Halliwell's on the case."

He smiled. "I promise I'll be back."

"You always promise."

"And haven't I always come back?"

Sara thought a moment, then reached out and touched his face in wonder. "Yeah. You have."

He kissed her forehead. His lips were rough as sandpaper.

"Close your eyes," he said.

She did. The sound came again, that scritching, skittering noise, along with a little breeze that made her shiver.

When she opened her eyes, he was gone.

But Sara found herself smiling.

Battle raged.

Ovid Tsing crouched, nocked an arrow into his bow, and fired. The arrow took an Atlantean soldier through the eye, the tip punching out through the back of his skull. The impact threw his head back but momentum carried him forward and he hit the ground, rolling, dead before he came to rest on the rocky shore where the Kingdom of Euphrasia met the Isthmus of the Conquistadors.

The eastern flank of Hunyadi's army had broken. The Atlantean attack was vicious, supplemented by Yucatazcan warriors. Air sharks darted across the morning sky, but they were far away, as were the giants, who fought Borderkind and northern legends at the center of the battle lines. Sorcerers of Atlantis hovered just over the heads of the troops—swords clanging, screams rising, blood soaking the earth—but a dozen Mazikeen hung in the air above the Euphrasian troops, fighting back. The magical combat seemed a war all its own, each side's sorcerers keeping the others from interfering in the ground war.

Still, the eastern flank had broken.

"To me!" Ovid screamed to his archers.

They knelt around him in a line.

Atlantean soldiers ran toward them, their armor gleaming, some of them in helmets that shone like the glass ships at anchor far off the coast. Their swords were raised high but they attacked in savage silence, unnerving Ovid, but only for a moment. He waited until they had reached the first soldier to break through, until they were trampling him under their boots.

"Fire!" he cried.

The archers let fly with their arrows. Men and women of

Atlantis went down. Even at a distance, Ovid could smell their blood. It stank like low tide.

He stood, shouldering his bow and drawing his sword.

Ovid Tsing raised his sword.

"Attack!" he thundered.

The Stonecoats marched around Ovid and his archers, the first wave to move in. The Atlanteans attacked them with sword and dagger, but blades broke upon the rock-skin of the Jokao. The Stonecoats marched right through them, crushing heads and breaking bones, and kept going.

Sorcerers and giants might be able to kill them, but not ordinary Atlanteans. And the Jokao held a seething hatred for the Atlanteans. The time had come for them to take vengeance upon the culture that had once held them as slaves.

"Ovid!" Trina shouted, running up beside him.

She pointed to the sky.

Dozens of octopuses were sweeping toward them, tentacles dangling. They floated like balloons, but even as he watched, an octopus snatched up a Stonecoat in its tentacles effortlessly, as if the Jokao were weightless. It could not kill the Stonecoat, so instead it hurled him out to sea.

"Archers!" Ovid cried. "Fire!"

His archers followed the command, taking aim at the floating creatures. Two were felled with that first attack. Ovid turned his attention back to the Atlanteans, many of whom were slipping past the Jokao. There simply weren't enough Stonecoats to kill them all.

"King's Volunteers!" he shouted. "Attack!"

He pointed his sword forward and the soldiers—men and women he had brought from Twillig's Gorge, or who had joined him along the way—rushed into war with their weapons at the ready.

For the first few moments, Ovid only stood amongst them as they rushed around him and watched. Blades and cudgels fell. Atlanteans and Euphrasians and Yucatazcans died, their blood mingling together on the shore. The ground drank it greedily, and equally. To Death, all blood was the same.

Ovid roared and charged, racing into battle. He caught a glimpse of LeBeau, but then he could focus only on the enemy. He slashed and stabbed and used his elbows and knees—whatever it took to stop them; whatever it took to kill them; whatever it took to stay alive.

The King's Volunteers tore into the forces of deceitful Atlantis with courage and determination and hope. Ovid's mother had understood that it was hope that they all needed the most. He had begun his militia for his own purposes, but now he fought for his mother, and for hope.

An axe swept toward his skull.

Ovid dodged, but not in time.

A sword stopped the axe's descent. A tall figure in armor stepped in, grabbed the axe-wielding Yucatazcan by the head, and snapped his neck, dropping the corpse to the ground.

Ovid stared. His rescuer stood a foot or more taller than he. She wore her dark hair in long braids and wielded an enormous, heavy sword. Her armor glistened with blood not her own. She gazed at him with lavender eyes, and Ovid knew that he stood face-to-face with a goddess.

She wore a wild grin, as though the war and bloodshed made her giddy, and then she rushed away from him, felling Atlanteans with crimson abandon.

Not far away, a massive wolf made of tangled vines and leaves lunged into the Atlantean ranks, tearing at them with its jaws, crunching a skull in its teeth.

Hope had arrived.

CHAPTER 19

n the shade of trees whose limbs were strung with moss, amidst the buzzing of insects driven into a frenzy by the blood and sweat of dying soldiers, Oliver gathered the small force he would take with him to Atlantis. They were on the other side of the ridge from the battlefield, out of sight of the slaughter, but even here, more than a mile away, the sounds of death echoed across the sky.

Oliver stood furthest from the crest of the ridge. Perhaps twenty feet away, Li sat cross-legged on the ground, the grass burning all around him, blackening the soil.

Not far from Li—it seemed this small group of Borderkind never strayed far from one another these days—Cheval Bayard lay on her side upon the grassy hill. The sun shone upon her diaphanous gown and silver hair, while Grin crouched nearby and watched the sky and the ridgeline for potential threats.

Furthest from Oliver, beneath another stand of trees at the

top of the ridge, stood the winter man. The ice that comprised Frost's body had become almost transparent. The colors of the landscape passed through him, bending and gleaming, casting a small rainbow from the prism of his torso.

Frost stood completely still, the icicles of his hair frozen in place. A light mist steamed off of him. Oliver thought he must be watching the battle, gauging the efforts of Hunyadi's army against the invading hordes. Maybe the winter man longed to join the battle, thinking he could be of more use to the soldiers than to the mission the king and Oliver had concocted.

Good thing I don't give a fuck what he thinks.

Oliver needed Frost with him. He'd witnessed firsthand how devastating the winter man could be in a fight. And as bitter as he felt toward Frost, they had been companions before. They'd fought side by side. Frost wasn't going to cut and run.

A shape streaked across the blue sky, high enough above the battlefield that they could see it, even on this side of the ridge. Oliver tensed at the sight of the green-feathered wings and the rack of antlers on the Peryton's head. He remembered Collette's tales of her captivity in the sandcastle and the eerie presence of the Perytons then.

He gripped his sword, prepared to unsheathe it.

Even as he did, a dark wind twisted into a funnel, reached up into the sky, and dragged the Peryton from the air. The Atlantean Hunter hurtled toward the ground, driven by the wind. It landed beyond their line of sight, but Oliver thought that the force of that wind and the impact must have broken every bone in the Peryton's body. A grim satisfaction gripped him.

He glanced around to discover that none of the others had moved, or even seemed to have noticed.

This is what I chose? Oliver thought. *The broken ones? That's my team, the scarred and haunted and mad. Way to go, Bascombe.*

But he'd chosen them each for a reason. He knew them—

understood them—and felt confident that not one of them had any illusions about the task that had been set before them. They could very easily be killed. Oliver did not think any of these Borderkind wanted to die, but he figured none of them was all that troubled by the idea. Not anymore.

Other than Oliver, only Blue Jay had a reason to come back.

As if summoned by the thought, the trickster crested the ridge at that moment.

"All right, here we go!" Oliver called to the others.

Cheval sat up and looked toward the top of the hill. Grin reached down to help her up, and together they watched Blue Jay join Frost under the trees for a moment. Then the trickster and the winter man started down the hill toward them, followed by five Nagas. The serpent-men slithered along the ground, bows and quivers slung across their backs, daggers held in sheaths strapped to their bodies.

"Well done, Jay. I thought Damia only had two Nagas left from her Borderkind platoon."

The trickster nodded. "She did. The others had come earlier and were fighting with a different battalion. When they heard it was for you, they all wanted to come. More as well. I had to turn some away."

Oliver clapped hands with Blue Jay. He had done the right thing. Even this number had begun to grow too large to sneak into Atlantis. They certainly didn't need an army. Still, the Nagas would be welcome and probably prove indispensable.

"Hello, brother," said the first of the serpent-men. "It lifts our hearts to see that you still live."

"Mine too." Oliver smiled. He thought he recognized this Naga from Twillig's Gorge, but couldn't be sure. If he'd spent more time with them, it might become easier to tell them apart.

But before he could say any more, he saw another figure trailing behind the Nagas, coming down the hill toward him. A frown creased his brow.

"Why'd you bring her?" he asked Blue Jay.

The trickster turned and studied Julianna. Her long hair flew around her face in the wind and she brushed it away. For a moment Oliver was taken back to that moment in their childhood—not the first time he had seen her, but the first time he had really noticed her in the way that boys notice girls. She had looked so regal, then. Imperious. Fearless.

Once again, the sight of her took his breath away.

But he could not let that cloud his judgment or weaken his resolve. He excused himself and strode up the hill to meet her. Just her presence did something to him. As he walked to her, without even touching her he felt the comfort of her strength. Oliver knew Julianna had been angry with him. Now she looked at him with those eyes—the way only lovers who'd had their whole lives to learn every facet of each other could share a look—and he knew she had put her anger aside.

"What is it, Jules?"

She gave him a sweet, sad smile. "You're leaving soon?"

"As soon as Smith is ready."

Julianna nodded. "I need a minute."

Oliver took a breath. He ran a hand over the beard that had become thick with the months he had spent beyond the Veil.

"I have to do this."

"I know. That's not what this is about."

"Okay. And not just a minute. You know I want to spend all my minutes with you."

"When destiny no longer decides for us," Julianna said.

Oliver wanted to laugh, to make a joke out of her words. Destiny. It sounded so foolish when spoken aloud like that. But Julianna was deadly serious, and he found that there was nothing funny about any of it.

He reached out and took her hands in his. The temptation to kiss her was powerful, but she'd come to say something, and he did not want to diminish that.

"What is it, Jules?"

"I want you to take Kitsune with you."

Of all the things she might have said, this must have been the most improbable. He stared at her.

"Why would you say that?"

"She's still here. She hasn't gone down to fight, yet. Neither has Coyote. The two of them are talking, not far from King Hunyadi's tent. Kitsune seems lost, to tell the truth. She talked gods up from their old temples and the Harvest spirits out of the fields, but she doesn't know what to do with herself, now. I think she did all of that to prove something to herself, Oliver. I think maybe she was trying to find a way to forgive herself."

He took a breath and glanced away. "All Kit ever wanted was to stop the Hunters from killing her kin, but she put all that aside to help keep *me* alive. I owe her for that, Jules. But I can't just forget what she did to us. What she did to you."

Oliver lifted his gaze, looking into the eyes that knew him so well. The eyes *he* knew so well. Julianna had always been the more logical of the two of them, the more reasonable.

"I want you to take her with you, Oliver."

He studied her. "Are you sure?"

"I can't blame her for loving you. How could I? And the more I've thought about it, the more I've seen her, I realize I can't blame you for being enchanted by her. She's magic, isn't she? That's what enchantment is all about."

Oliver pulled her closer. "I won't say she isn't fascinating. She is. But you're the only magic I've ever needed."

Julianna smiled. "Silly boy. Take her with you."

"If she'll go."

"She'll go," Julianna said. "She won't be right inside if she doesn't."

"Have you always been this smart?" Oliver asked.

"Pretty much, yeah."

The kiss happened, then, sweet and fine.

Afterward, Oliver could still feel it on his lips for a while. But the feeling did not linger forever, and when everything went to shit and his friends started dying, he wished he could remember how it felt.

In a spot almost hidden by the three tents pitched around it—including the tent of King Hunyadi—Kitsune stood absolutely still. The southern sun beat down upon her, but she had her hood raised nevertheless, lost in the shadows of her copper-red fur. For months she had practically hibernated, nursing her guilt and sadness, then she had emerged in search of purpose—and possibly forgiveness. But Oliver had made it clear that there'd be no redemption. He might forgive her, but he wouldn't help her alleviate her guilt. Kitsune had turned down a path from which she could not retrace her steps. No trail of bread crumbs would lead her back to the moment when she had let her inner fox get the better of her.

To hell with Oliver, then. She'd find a way to forgive herself. She'd make her own purpose.

"What the hell are you thinking?" Coyote demanded. Small and lithe, he paced the ground between tents, pausing from time to time to gesture with a red glass bottle of honey mead. The wound where his eye had been had begun to heal, white scar tissue replacing ragged, raw flesh. "You've done enough, Kit."

"Have I?" she asked, smiling slyly. "I'm not going to go down to that battlefield, cousin. A little slip of a fox would last mere seconds. But I mean to fight, to make the Atlanteans pay for all of our kin they murdered. I'll do what tricksters do. I'm going to get weapons—daggers and a sword, even if I have to pluck them from the fingers of the dead—and then I'm going to cross through the Veil. I'll do it just as we've done before, slip over to the ordinary world, get behind our enemies, then push back through to this world. In secret, I'll find the commanders of the invasion—the High Council of Atlantis, if they're here—and I'll kill them."

Coyote stared at her a moment, then took a long pull from the bottle of mead. He wiped his lips with the back of his hand like a common drunkard.

"So you're nothing but an assassin, now?"

Kitsune curled back her upper lip in a kind of sneer. "I'm whatever I need to be in order to make them suffer for what they've done."

After another swig of mead, he contemplated her a moment.

"Fair enough," Coyote said.

"I'm pleased you approve," Kitsune replied, making sure her sarcasm was evident.

"I don't."

She pulled her cloak more tightly around her, as though within that copper fur she could hide from him. "Why would you say that?"

Something flickered in his single eye then, but it wasn't the mischief of a trickster.

"I wish we could abandon both worlds," Coyote said, his voice low. Always snide, always mocking, always playing, that had been her experience of him for so long. Seeing the sincerity in him frightened her.

"I wish we could abandon these bodies," he went on. "Just be fox and coyote and run in the woods, like we did."

Kitsune held her breath a moment, then let it out slowly. "Maybe one day."

Coyote moved toward her. His skin glistened bronze in the sun. He held out the bottle of mead for her, and Kitsune took it.

"Where did you get this, anyway?"

He smiled. "Stole it from the king's tent."

With a laugh, she shook her head. "Trickster," she said.

"Oh, yes. Always."

Kitsune tipped the bottle back and took a sip. As she did, she saw the top of an enormous head on the other side of the king's tent. Cronus ducked down, trying to keep from being seen, but the lumbering Titan was not the most inconspicuous legend.

"We have a spy," she said.

Coyote frowned and, almost imperceptibly, moved into a defensive stance. Kitsune shook her head.

"No danger. Just an ancient god—a father of gods—simple and sweet."

She started around the tent, handing the bottle back to Coyote as he joined her. They emerged near the entrance to the tent and the giant Titan sat crouched there like a child caught at something naughty. A sad twinge touched her heart. Once, this creature had been one of the lords of the world, wise and clever and strong. Cronus still had his strength, but his other faculties had failed him.

"I thought you'd gone down to war with Salacia, Hesperos, and the others," she said.

Cronus rolled his massive shoulders in a shrug. His clothes and arms were spattered with the blood of enemies he had already killed this morning.

"I did," the Titan replied. "But I worried about you. When you fight, I'll fight. Must watch over you."

Kitsune smiled and glanced at Coyote.

But Coyote had no smile. He wasn't even looking at Cronus. Instead, he stared beyond the Titan. When Kitsune looked to discover what had drawn his attention, she saw Oliver striding toward them, one hand on the hilt of the sword that hung from his hip. With his longer hair and thickening beard, he did not look like someone who had only entered this world the first time months ago. At first glance, she would have assumed he had been here for years. Perhaps even since birth.

He was a warrior, now.

Cronus grunted angrily and turned to block Oliver's path.

"No," Kitsune said. The Titan turned to glance back at her. "It's all right."

Dubious, Cronus nevertheless stood back and let Oliver stride up to the spot where Kitsune and Coyote stood. He gave Coyote a brief glance, nodded once, and then focused on

Kitsune. Her face flushed under the intensity of his gaze and when he saw that, he glanced away for a moment.

"I'm sorry if I was rough on you before," Oliver said.

She stared in amazement. "You're apologizing to me?"

"Maybe I'm just trying to understand."

Kitsune glanced at Coyote, feeling awkward now that he and Cronus were the audience for this exchange. Still, things had to be said.

"That was all I ever wanted," she told him. "I never meant to—"

Oliver held up a hand. "I know. And I'm sorry to interrupt, and to rush you now, but we're out of time."

The warm breeze had been blowing the scents of distant flowers around them, but now the wind shifted and that smell was replaced by the stink of blood. Shouts of hatred and screams of pain filled the air, carried up from the field of battle.

"What do you need?" she asked.

"If Hunyadi doesn't win this war quickly, the army may not be able to hold out over time. There's no way to tell what kind of reinforcements might come from Atlantis."

"So you need to end it quickly," Coyote said.

Kitsune stared at Oliver. "You're still thinking about Prince Tzajin?"

Oliver nodded. "We're going to bring him back here, alive. Take Yucatazca out of the war or, even better, get them to switch sides."

Tentatively, she reached up and lowered her hood. The breeze felt good on her face. A lock of hair blew in front of her eyes.

"We?"

"Frost. Blue Jay and the others. Some Nagas. Me. And you, if you'll come."

Kitsune resisted the urge to smile. "Oh, I'll come."

Cronus tapped his chest with one gigantic finger. "And Cronus."

Oliver visibly winced. "I'm sorry, but we need to try to do this quickly and quietly. We'd like to slip in and slip out without attracting much attention."

Kitsune went to Cronus and reached up to put her tiny hand over his enormous one.

"I'm sorry, my friend. Go back to the gods—to your family. They need your help. As soon as we return from Atlantis, I will come and find you."

Cronus looked at her, sulking. "I have your promise?"

She smiled. "I promise."

With a dangerous glance at Oliver, the Titan ambled down the hill. When he had gone, only the three of them remained, and Kitsune looked at Coyote.

"And you? Say you'll come," she said.

Coyote took a long swig of honey mead, draining the last of the bottle, then tossed it toward the entrance to the king's tent. Calmly, he produced a cigarette from the palm of his hand, as though it had always been there, and lit it with a silver lighter that likewise seemed to appear from nowhere.

Little nothing sleights of hand, easy for a trickster.

"I wish you'd come," Kitsune said.

Coyote smiled, his single eye twinkling with mischief, but she thought it hid something else entirely. She studied him, trying to understand.

"I know what you're thinking," Coyote said, stepping toward her. "It isn't that I'm afraid. I'm going to smoke this cigarette and then I'm going down to war. I'll fight, Kit. With claw or sword, I'll fight. But I want to be with my kin, to fight side by side with the Borderkind. And it seems to me Bascombe's already got more than enough to take on his secret mission."

When the rangy little legend reached out a hand to touch the side of her face, then leaned in to kiss her, Kitsune could do nothing but kiss him back. And she found that she wanted to. He had comforted her when all she could do was howl her sorrow to the night sky. His presence would have soothed her. But she could not force him to go.

The kiss went on a few moments and then they parted. Kitsune glanced over to see surprise on Oliver's face. He shifted and looked awkwardly away. After a moment, he smiled slightly, and she knew he was happy for her.

"Go, Kit. I'll miss you."

"And you, mongrel."

Coyote laughed and waved to her, smoking his cigarette as he went off down the hill the way Cronus had gone. He seemed light of heart, mischievous as ever, but there was something quite final about his last words to her, as though he expected them to be a true and permanent good-bye.

Blue Jay smiled when he saw Oliver and Kitsune come over the top of the ridge.

"All right," he said, turning to the others. "Let's get this done."

Cheval rose up from the grass as though floating. She touched Grin's face tenderly, smiling, and then they joined Blue Jay and the Nagas, who had gathered there on the hillside. Distant cries carried over the hill, muffled and so far away. They could almost have pretended the war didn't exist, though it was just over the hill. They could have walked away. But the time for walking away had passed a long, long time ago.

Li rose from the burnt patch of grass where he'd been playing with a tiger cub he'd created from fire. With a gesture, he absorbed the fire-construct into the charred tips of his fingers and turned to walk over to Blue Jay as though there was nothing at all odd about this, as though he had not a care in the world. As though his heart was not shattered.

Li shot a grave look from those burning ember eyes at Wayland Smith. The Wayfarer stood away from them all, gazing into the sky to the north, back to the Borderkind, and the hill, and the war. He seemed almost to be waiting for a sign, or searching the clouds for angels to descend.

"Smith," Blue Jay said. "Are you ready?"

The trickster resisted the urge to call the Wayfarer "Uncle," as some of his kin did. Whatever Smith was, Blue Jay felt sure the tricksters had chosen him as a relation by sheer accident, or by Smith's own manipulation.

"Hmm?" He turned, eyes hidden in the shadow of his broad-brimmed hat. "Oh, yes. Ready whenever you are."

But there was something off about the Wayfarer. Blue Jay couldn't put his finger on precisely what troubled him. Perhaps it was the way he held his cane, as though he thought he might need it at any moment to fight off an attack, or if it was just the way he seemed so apart from the rest of them. Smith seemed so distant it was almost as if the conflict that unfolded here, the broken truce, the deceit of Atlantis, the murder of King Mahacuhta, concerned him not at all. It almost seemed Smith wasn't of this world.

"Oliver's here," Blue Jay said.

The Wayfarer blinked. He stroked his beard and glanced over at Oliver and Kitsune, who hurried now to join the gathered Borderkind.

"So he is," Smith replied. He nodded, raising his cane to draw their attention, even though his own attention seemed to wander. His eyes focused for the first time in minutes and he studied first Blue Jay, then Kitsune, and finally Oliver.

"Gather round, then," said Wayland Smith. "Like the campfire. Gather round."

The strangest look came over his face. Blue Jay saw Oliver's eyes narrow and knew he'd thought it odd as well.

As Kitsune greeted the others—though Grin was the only one to give her a warm welcome—Jay sidled over to Oliver. He slid his hands into the pockets of his blue jeans, the heels of his boots digging into soil made soft by a recent rain.

"Change of heart?" he asked.

"Julianna thought she should have a chance to fix things," Oliver replied.

Blue Jay raised an eyebrow. "Are things fixable?"

Oliver thought on that a moment. "My sister shattered an antique perfume bottle of my mother's one time. Pink glass. The stopper was a glass butterfly. My mother collected the things, but that one was her favorite. She glued it back together, but you could always see the cracks and there were a couple of chips from bits we never could find. Probably got vacuumed up. Most things can be put back together, but that doesn't mean they can be fixed."

Blue Jay watched him curiously for a moment. For the first time, he realized that this was not at all the same man he had first met in the Mazikeen's garden under the streets of Perinthia. In a way, Oliver was like his mother's perfume bottle. He'd been broken and put back together in a way that would never be quite the same. Yet in Oliver's case, it wasn't a matter of being fixed. The man he'd become was an improvement, cracks and missing chips and all.

"Saw you kiss Julianna good-bye," the trickster said.

Oliver smiled. "And Damia? Did you give her a good-bye kiss?"

An icy chill spider-walked down Blue Jay's spine. "She refused. Said good-bye was for people who weren't going to see each other at bedtime."

They were interrupted then by Smith, who called again for them to gather round. Gather round like a campfire. Oliver and Blue Jay joined Li, Grin, Cheval, Kitsune, and the Nagas in a circle around the Wayfarer. He leaned on his cane, fingers curled around the bronze fox-head, and one by one he looked at them.

"Those of you who are Borderkind have traveled between worlds before. What we are about to do is similar, but not precisely the same. We will not be stepping from one world to the next, but walking a Gray Corridor, a space between worlds.

This is why I am called the Wayfarer, the Traveler, and other names in other places. You'll form a line. Grip the shoulder or the arm or the hand of whoever is in front of you, and do not let go. If you do, you will likely be lost forever in the Gray Corridors. Borderkind or not. This is not the Veil. The magic that makes you Borderkind will have no effect.

"Li, if you intend to journey with us, you will have to withdraw the fire from your hands so that you will not burn whoever precedes you."

The Guardian of Fire nodded. It occurred to Blue Jay then that Li had not spoken in a very long time. He wondered if the burning man could still speak at all, or if the fire had seared his voice from his throat.

Li lifted his right hand. He stared at it a moment, brow knitting in consternation. After several moments, the flames retreated. What remained was blackened and cracked skin with pink raw flesh showing in between tiles of char.

Cheval looked kindly upon him and reached out. Gratefully, Li grasped her hand. Quickly, they formed a chain. Oliver drifted away from Smith, positioning himself amongst the Nagas, and Blue Jay was left to connect them to the Wayfarer himself.

"Don't let go," Smith said, eyes hard.

Blue Jay said nothing. After a moment, the Wayfarer nodded.

"The walk will take some little time. Minutes. Be patient, but also, be ready. When we arrive, it will be suddenly, and there is no way to know what will be waiting for us."

"Get on with it," Oliver said. "We've been spoiling for a fight for a long time."

Wayland Smith held his cane in one hand and Blue Jay's grip in the other. Smith took a single step forward. Jay felt his hand jerk slightly to the right, and then the world fell away around them.

"What the hell?" the trickster muttered.

"Don't let go!" he heard Kitsune cry.

THE LOST ONES   333

Smith paused and glanced back to be sure no one had been lost. Blue Jay felt his stomach twisting with the terrible sense of dislocation. He had not even taken a step himself. He'd lifted one scuffed cowboy boot and when it came down, he'd been here, wherever the hell here was. Gray mist drifted around them. The path was solid beneath his soles and his heels didn't sink in the way they had into the rain-sodden hillside.

"Follow," Smith said, and he started off.

Stunned into silence, perhaps afraid, no one spoke a word. Their strange parade followed along behind the Wayfarer without argument or hesitation. They passed hundreds of side paths, little ribbon trails that led off either side, into the mist. The first few times that Smith guided them into one of these turns, traveling paths that seemed barely there, Blue Jay tried to keep track, but soon he could not. Lefts and rights blurred together.

The place unnerved him with the weight of its possibilities. What would happen if he did let go? How far would they wander? Where did all of those other paths lead? Smith had said something about worlds, but there were only two—the ordinary and the legendary. So if Jay walked along one of the side paths, another ribbon, and tried to pass through the mist back to a tangible world, where would he emerge?

He decided he did not want to know.

Just when the claustrophobia of the place—odd, given there were no walls at all—had nearly driven him to scream, Smith slowed and glanced over his shoulder. The others might not have sensed it yet, or seen it in the Wayfarer's eyes, but then the graybeard spoke.

"We're—"

"—here," Smith said.

Oliver flinched, gripping the hands of the Nagas on either side of him, and began to look around, on guard.

Even as he did, the thick fog of the Gray Corridor simply vanished. Sunlight enveloped them all and Oliver had to throw up a hand to shield his eyes from the brightness. He staggered back a step.

A large hand clutched his arm in a painful, iron grip.

Oliver blinked the sun from his eyes and saw it was Grin who'd grabbed hold of him. He turned around to find himself standing on the very edge of a building over a hundred feet high. Below, the central plaza of the island city of Atlantis spread out. The ground had been tiled in a cascade of color so that it appeared to be a whirlpool in the midst of a red-and-blue ocean.

"Holy shit," he said, the words little more than an exhalation.

"Watch your step, mate," Grin said. "That's a long drop."

Oliver nodded. He glanced around to make sure everyone else had made it. Kitsune moved to the center of the roof, fur cloak tight around her, not at all pleased with their precipitous arrival. Blue Jay and Frost stood together. Li watched solemnly as the Nagas took up posts along the edges of the roof, bows at the ready, prepared to defend against an onslaught.

But it didn't look as though any attack was imminent.

Fish and eels slid through the air, but most were far closer to the ground and those who might be high enough to spot the intruders were far away, nearer the harbor and the outskirts of the city. There were weird, dangling jellyfish as well, but not a single octopus. They had all been brought to war, it seemed.

Very few people were out and about. Smith had reported seeing troops massing and sorcerers walking in the open, not to mention giants. No evidence of the war effort remained in the city center, but in the distance, at the harbor, he could see a single giant standing with his arms crossed, protecting Atlantis like some living Colossus of Rhodes.

"Quickly, all of you, this way," the Wayfarer barked, striding to one corner of the roof. From there, they could see an even taller building with a spiral dome, a breathtakingly beautiful thing that appeared, like the structure upon which they stood, to be made of a kind of obscure glass.

Sea glass, Oliver thought.

"The Great Library of Atlantis," Smith explained. "Where I found the prince upon my last visit. I'd wager he's there now. We'll cross—"

A gust of icy wind made Oliver shiver.

"And how will we cross?" Frost asked. The winter man drifted across the roof to stand beside Smith. "I could carry one or two, but not all."

Anger flashed in the Wayfarer's eyes. He reached his cane out over the edge of the building and swept it back and forth like a blind man. To Oliver's astonishment, it struck something solid. Wayland Smith looked down at the place where his cane had stopped, raised it, and tapped it down twice on clear air. His mouth formed words Oliver could not hear and from the side, it appeared for a moment that his gray eyes had turned oil-black.

The air became solid in a narrow bridge across empty space, from the roof upon which they stood to a huge, arched library window.

"Go," said the Wayfarer.

CHAPTER 20

o way was Oliver going first.

He had changed dramatically. He felt it in his bones and the way his hands seemed always ready to defend himself. The power of his touch, the destructive magic he could summon, resonated within him. These past few days had made Oliver believe that in his heart he could be a hero. But there was a vast difference between heroics and stupidity, and the idea of stepping off the roof of that building onto thin air seemed vastly idiotic.

"Hurry, you fools!" Smith barked.

Blue Jay stepped off the roof onto the solid air bridge. He could have transformed into a bird and flown across. Instead he walked quickly but carefully, barely looking down, even though Oliver found it difficult to see the edges of the bridge.

Li followed at a run, practically bounding across like one of his fire tigers. Seeing him, Oliver awoke at last to the reality of Smith's fears. They could be spotted at any moment, imperiling their mission. He swore under his breath and went to the edge. Cheval had already started across, grand and elegant as always, her dress gliding over the bridge like a ballroom floor. Grin paused three steps out. Terror lit his eyes and he gripped the edges of the nearly invisible bridge.

"Cross, stupid boggart," Smith snapped at him.

Grin sneered at him. "Sod off, you silly git."

Still, it got the boggart moving.

Oliver went next. He held his breath as he stepped off the roof. From above, the parameters of the bridge were obvious. That hardened air had a different texture and hue. It was simple enough to make out its edges, but that wouldn't stop a stiff breeze from knocking him off. Carefully, arms out as though on a tightrope, he went after the others.

Despite the heat, he felt a shiver go up his spine, and then a gentle gust of cold wind blew past him on the left, snow and ice swirling. Frost moved swiftly and then materialized on the window ledge, ice forming on the glass of the window.

As the Nagas slithered after him, arrows still strung at the ready in their bows, Oliver picked up his pace. At the end of the bridge, Blue Jay slid out of the way to let Li pass. The trickster winced at the heat that billowed from inside the charred ember flesh of the Guardian of Fire. Then Li reached the window and stood beside Frost.

Fire and ice.

Li put his palm against the window. Flames spread out across the glass and its frame, which seemed also to be some kind of glass or mineral. The heat blossomed outward, warping the air around it, and the window began to melt. The Guardian of Fire pushed inward and it collapsed in a dripping, wilting, burning mess on the floor inside the window.

Frost stepped through the window and with a gesture, snuffed the flames. A layer of ice formed on the melted remains of the window and frame, and then one by one they all entered the Great Library of Atlantis. Oliver knew he could have made the window simply fall apart—any of them could have broken it open—but working together, Li and Frost had made their entry nearly silent.

Wayland Smith was the last through the window. When he stepped down from the window ledge, the air shimmered behind him and Oliver saw that the bridge had disappeared.

"Always something new," Oliver said.

Smith hushed him. Oliver wanted to tell him to fuck off. The guy's arrogance could have driven a saint to violence.

They were in a roughly oval-shaped room with only one door. Cheval had gone to the door and opened it. She glanced out through the crack, then quietly closed it.

"Coast clear?" Blue Jay whispered.

Cheval nodded. They gathered by the door in nearly the same order they had crossed the bridge. The Nagas would watch their flank.

Eyes turned toward Oliver. For a moment he shifted uneasily at this attention, until he realized they were waiting for him to give the word. Frost had always been the one everyone turned to when he had traveled with the Borderkind before, and now Wayland Smith seemed to have taken control. But Smith had only been their transportation, their Traveler. Now that they were in the midst of things, they were all ready to defer to him. It had been his idea, after all.

"Smith," he said, "you're the only one who's been here before. Lead the way. Get us to the place where you saw the prince. Kitsune, stay with him. If there are scholars or teachers or sentries around, you'll catch their scent first. We're going to do our best to take them down quietly if anyone gets in the way. When it all goes to shit—and it will—then we pull out all the stops."

Oliver gestured toward the door. "Go."

To his surprise, Wayland Smith did not argue.

Cheval opened the door and Smith went out. Kitsune followed, disappearing into her cloak and diminishing into a fox, a low-slung blur of copper-red fur. She trotted after Smith.

Frost and Blue Jay followed. Oliver drew his sword—wishing for the familiar weight of Hunyadi's blade—and went next. Cheval and Grin hurried after him, then Li, and finally the Nagas, their serpentine bellies making a low hiss as they slid across the floor.

The library seemed like something made of ice, as if the winter man had built himself a palace. They emerged in a short hallway and followed Smith to what appeared to be some kind of central shaft. Stairwells rose up the inside of the shaft in great swoops of sea glass. Wood and stone were part of the design but the wood was like black ironwood and the stone smooth and contoured as though by centuries of ocean erosion. The architecture had latticework and arches that made Oliver think of beehive honeycombs and spiderwebs, its beauty both breathtaking and unnerving.

As Smith began to step into the atrium at the core of the library tower, Kitsune growled low and soft, a fox's warning.

Oliver snagged Smith's sleeve. The Wayfarer shot him a dark look but Oliver only returned it and gestured to the fox. Wayland Smith seemed troubled, but then the entire group took a step back into the shadows of the corridor as a small group of Atlanteans emerged on the same floor, across the open atrium, and started up the winding sea glass staircase. They were robed like sorcerers or teachers.

Smith's eyes narrowed. He glanced around the atrium, then back the way they'd come. Neither option seemed to please him.

At length, he beckoned for the Nagas to come forward.

As the serpentine bowmen moved past him, Oliver knew he ought to protest. The men and women on the stairs might be Atlantean, but as vicious and cunning as Atlantis had turned out to be, killing teachers in a library was not his idea of war. But even as these thoughts filled his mind, he considered the repercussions of failure and the benefits of their success.

The Nagas slithered up to the fluted balustrade, raised their bows, and let silent arrows fly with hideous accuracy. Whoever they were, scholars or sorcerers, they fell upon the stairs, some slumping on top of the others, twitching.

"Go," Oliver whispered.

He didn't want to have to look at those corpses longer than necessary.

They hurried past the Nagas and Smith led the way up the stairs. In a bustle of copper fur, Kitsune returned to her female form, hood hiding her features. Oliver wished she would turn so he could see her eyes. He wondered if she felt the same hesitations he did. Frost and Blue Jay looked grim as they went upward.

More quietly than he could have hoped, they moved through the Great Library of Atlantis, along latticework balustrades and up sea glass stairs and through honeycomb corridors. Sunlight streamed through the atrium from above, casting the entire place in the cascade of soft colors Oliver associated with the stained glass windows of a church.

Distant voices reached them several times and they had to pause, taking cover, or hurry on into a side corridor. Whispers and echoes seemed to travel through the place like some haunted cave. The first sentry they came upon died easily and without a sound. Kitsune slit his throat with her claws and his blood pooled thickly on the floor. Oliver's nose filled with the low-tide stink of an Atlantean's blood, and he tried from then on to breathe through his mouth.

Frost killed the second sentry, freezing him to death just inside a corridor archway. The pain must have been exquisite, for the expression on his face beneath the layer of ice that enveloped him was one of agony.

Time's running out, Oliver thought. *Any moment bodies will be found. Any second, they'll be on to us.*

He considered saying this aloud, but realized his companions did not need to be told. They knew. Minutes had passed and they seemed to be moving aimlessly through the library. They had come upon four different chambers that seemed to have been occupied by scholars at some point. Shelves and tables and glass cases showed scrolls and bound books upon display, many spread out as though abandoned in the midst of being examined, but they had found no sign of the prince.

The Wayfarer took them through the latest of these chambers and to a curving back stair that would bring them to the floor above. They could not be far from the spiral dome of the library, now.

A scream rose in the library, clear and resonant as a bell, echoing along corridors, rising to a terrible pitch before ceasing abruptly. Oliver exchanged worried glances with Blue Jay and Kitsune, and then shouts followed the scream.

"Bollocks," Grin muttered.

Wayland Smith had paused halfway up the curving stairs to the next level. Voices drifted down to them from the arch at the top. Oliver gripped his sword with both hands.

"Go," he whispered.

But Smith was already moving. The Wayfarer clutched his cane—which he almost never seemed to use to support himself—and took the stairs two at a time. They rushed the stairs, then, hurrying after Smith. Two Nagas positioned themselves at the bottom, bows at the ready, but the library was an enormous warren of chambers and corridors and as long as they were quiet, it would take time for the guards to find them.

As Oliver went through the arch at the top of the stairs, a new shout rang out.

"Who are you? Get out of here!" a man's voice thundered from the chamber they entered.

Scrolls and books filled the room, just as in the others they had entered. Shelves lined the walls and glass cases displayed ancient manuscripts. Pillows were piled in the corners and several spots around the huge chamber. Upon some of them were sprawled old men who had been interrupted in the midst of study. At the center of the room, a boy who could only have been Prince Tzajin sat at a marble table, around which several teachers were gathered. His olive skin marked him as Yucatazcan, particularly amongst the narrow, green-hued faces of the Atlantean scholars.

The teacher who had shouted stood just a few feet from the Wayfarer, but Wayland Smith only stepped back, leaning on his cane, and watched expectantly as events unfolded.

Blue Jay went for the prince.

The scholars produced daggers from their robes, ceremonial things with stone handles. They moved like fighters, not academics, and they shouted as they attacked the intruders.

A young, furious scholar tried to grab hold of the trickster, but Blue Jay spun in a quick circle, mystical wings blurring beneath his arms. The scholar lost his hands to their razor edge. Blood spurted and he screamed.

"So much for keeping silent," Cheval Bayard said as she rushed at the nearest Atlantean.

"Smith already screwed us on that," Oliver snapped.

The shouts from the chamber would echo through the library. They had seconds.

Grimly, Li stepped forward and took hold of the scholar who had challenged them upon arrival. The man tried to stab him, but the dagger only stuck in the embers of Li's flesh. Fire raced up the blade to him and the teacher began to burn, shrieking, and staggered away, crashing into a glass shelf and setting ancient scrolls on fire. Two of the other scholars ran toward him, but they had no concern for their burning, dying colleague. They snatched up the scrolls, trying to save them from the fire.

The Nagas slithered into the room. The archers moved swiftly, releasing their silent arrows once more. Of the scholars that had surrounded Prince Tzajin, only the two trying to rescue the burning scrolls—weaponless—were left alive.

Frost moved toward the prince. He knelt by the boy, whose eyes were wide with terror, and spoke to him. Oliver only heard phrases and words as the winter man tried to soothe Tzajin, told him they had come to take him back to Palenque, that all hell had broken loose and his people needed their prince. Tzajin said nothing. He could only shake his head, mouth open, as the corpses of his teachers bled and burned around him.

Cheval strode across the chamber and slapped Wayland Smith across the face. The Wayfarer's face darkened with fury.

"You may've killed us all," she said, rage making her more beautiful than ever.

"And you have no idea what you're talking about," Smith snarled. "I am not meant to interfere, to participate in any of this. I brought you here, and that is already more than I ought to have done. I could be made to suffer—"

The words were cut off by shouts from one end of the room. There were two entrances—the arch where they had come in, and double doors that led out toward the atrium and the winding stairs.

Atlantean soldiers appeared in the doorway. Kitsune growled and spun toward them. Oliver shouted to the Nagas. Arrows flew. Several found their mark, but others were stopped by Atlantean armor or knocked aside by the soldiers' swords. These were no scholars. They would not die as easily. Still, against Li and Frost and the rest, they had no hope of survival.

The winter man raised both hands and a storm erupted in the room, the air whipping snow and ice around, blowing scrolls off of tables and shattering glass display cases. The two surviving scholars finally drew their weapons, but Kitsune leaped at them, and Leicester Grindylow followed. They did not slay the teachers, disarming them instead. Grin tossed one into a bookshelf. Kitsune drove the other to the ground with pummeling fists and a hard kick to the head.

The first two guards through the door froze solid in the winter man's storm. One of the doors blew closed. The other guards retreated, but from the shouts out in the atrium, there were others on the way.

Oliver went to the boy, Prince Tzajin.

In the chaos, none of the others seemed to have noticed, but he still had the same slack expression of terror on his face, as though he had suddenly gone catatonic.

"Your Majesty?" Oliver said.

The boy's gaze shifted slightly.

Oliver turned just in time to see the sorcerers coming through the arch at the back of the chamber, where he and his comrades had first entered. He shouted, raised his sword, and rushed at them. The first sorcerer—a bald, scarred Atlantean man with sallow skin—sneered at him and raised a hand. A Naga arrow took him in the throat from the side.

Then Oliver was there. He bypassed the wounded, jaundiced sorcerer and drove his sword through the chest of the second to enter the chamber. The tall, spindly Atlantean fell to his knees, shock on his features. The others were still out in the corridor. Oliver reached out, grabbed the archway, and with his mind he reached into it and called up the entropy that gnawed at the ties of the world.

Kitsune grabbed hold of him from behind, hauling him backward as the entire archway collapsed, blocking the path of the sorcerers still out on the back stairs.

Li appeared beside them. On the ground, amidst the rubble, the bald, scarred sorcerer clutched at the arrow in his neck. The Guardian of Fire bent and placed both hands on the Atlantean, and his skin began to smoke, and then he caught fire.

"Get away from there!" Wayland Smith shouted.

The Wayfarer gripped Oliver's arm and hauled him back. A gust of blizzard wind snatched at Kitsune, shoving her aside.

The rubble of the collapsed archway blew inward, pieces of it colliding with Li. The Guardian of Fire crashed to the floor amidst the debris. Some of it began to burn, the flames out of his control. The fire began to spread.

Three sorcerers hurtled into the room at once.

At the doors to the atrium, the guards charged. Oliver didn't bother turning to see how many there were. The sounds of

THE LOST ONES 345

their pounding footfalls were enough to tell him what he needed to know.

The killing, the dying, had sickened him from the first blood shed. But there would be so much more.

Smith stepped into the breach between the sorcerers and Oliver and the Borderkind. *What the hell's he doing?* Oliver thought. *He said he's not supposed to interfere.*

The three sorcerers all turned toward Wayland Smith. Tendrils of magic reached out from one—just as they had from Ty'Lis in the dungeon of Palenque—and grabbed hold of him. The Wayfarer's feet went out from beneath him. The sorcerer reeled him in. One of the others opened his jaws and they stretched wider than ought to have been possible. Unhinged, showing rows of terrible teeth like the Manticore, things moving in the darkness of his gullet, the sorcerer bent to tear out Smith's throat. The third, a female, touched him with hands that dripped burning, steaming venom like acid.

"What the fuck are you doing?" Oliver screamed at Smith. "Fight!"

Smith managed to turn his head. "I see, boy. I see the weave of the world, and I cannot alter it by killing them. But I may be able to . . . erase them. I'll be back."

All three of the sorcerers had contact with Smith in that moment. They faded to ghosts and then vanished entirely, the Wayfarer with them. Wayland Smith had taken them into the Gray Corridors.

Oliver swore again, turned and grabbed the hand of the drooling Prince Tzajin. He slapped the kid in the face, but Tzajin did not respond.

"We've got to go, pal," he commanded. He tried to haul Tzajin out of his chair, but the prince did not budge.

Oliver used both hands and pulled on him, but could not move Prince Tzajin an inch from his seat. They'd come for Prince Tzajin, and Oliver wouldn't leave without him. But Smith had gone off somewhere, and as he glanced around, panicked, two more sorcerers entered the room, their eyes black as storm clouds.

Damia Beck screamed as she spurred her horse toward the giant. The ugly thing with its sickly pallor raised its war hammer and brought it down upon one of Damia's cavalry. Horse and rider—a woman named Tessa—were crushed into a stain on the battlefield.

If she could have taken a breath, Damia would have cried.

Her mind screamed, damning the giant. But only unintelligible roars came from her lips. So many of her people—cavalry and infantry—had been slaughtered. Her battalion fought on valiantly. Atlanteans by the dozens, perhaps hundreds, had fallen to their swords. But this would not be ended until nearly all were dead. The war, she had quickly learned, would be decided by attrition.

That meant the giant had to die.

A Mazikeen floated overhead, locked in magical combat with an Atlantean sorcerer. Their blood and magic fell like rain, spattering Damia's hair and her horse.

A skirmish crossed her path. Yucatazcan soldiers surrounded two of her infantry. They were so covered in blood and sweat and dirt—this man and woman—she could not see their faces as the Yucatazcan warriors slew them, hacking them apart as they fell to the ground. Bloodlust ruled the day. The screams of the dying were music to their murderers.

Even to Damia.

She rode down one of the Yucatazcans, but three others came at her. Yet she had not become commander based only on her leadership. Damia slashed down with her sword, taking off the forearm of one warrior. She plunged her blade into the face of the other, the point punching out the back of his head with a spray of blood.

Even as she did, the third dealt her a blow across the thigh.

Dark blood spattered the ground—Damia's own—and she clenched her thighs against the pain and guided the horse with her body, leaving her left hand free to draw one of her pistols. Damia shot the Yucatazcan warrior through the head.

The horse whinnied and reared.

A shadow fell across her.

Trying to stay alive, she'd forgotten how close she'd gotten to the giant. The monster lifted its hammer, staring down at her. Blood and strips of flesh and clothing hung from its teeth; it had been eating some of its kills. Flesh stuck to the bottom of the hammer. Fascinated and horrified, Damia froze a moment.

The hammer came down.

She tried to force the horse back with just her legs, but its reaction was too slow. The giant missed her, but the hammer crushed the horse's head. As the proud beast fell, she leaped clear. When she landed, the wound in her leg widened and she cried out in pain. Blood ran down the leg of her pants, filling her boot.

The giant reached for her. It meant to eat her.

Damia raised the gun and fired five times in quick succession, all five bullets tearing into the giant's face. The giant reared back, screaming and clawing at the ruined cavities where its eyes had been. Blinded, it reached out a hand, trying to scrabble for her, to destroy her in payment for its pain.

Staggering to her feet, ignoring the pain in her leg, Damia dropped the gun and took up her sword in both hands. She dodged the giant's searching hand, moved between its legs, and drove her sword up into its groin, thrusting so hard that the blade sank to the hilt up inside the monster's pelvis, in its soft innards. She twisted and carved and then backed away as a shower of shit and viscera gouted from the wound.

She fell, but managed to keep clear of the giant when it also collapsed, dead, on the battlefield. Beyond it she could see the war spread out across the Isthmus of the Conquistadors. The terrain had become little more than blood and corpses, but the armies still fought, climbing over mountains of the dead. The war had become a hideous, ugly, twisted thing.

Damia took off her black cloak. She tore long strips from it and bound her wounded leg.

Carefully, she climbed to her feet. The binding had stopped the bleeding, for the most part. She would live, but if she didn't get it sewn up, she wouldn't live for very long.

The nearest battle was a few hundred yards away but moving closer. One of the gods Kitsune had brought from Perinthia had been surrounded by legends of Yucatazca. They harried the tall, black-helmeted old god. No matter how powerful, the god was outnumbered.

Damia started in that direction, but then she saw one of the Atlantean octopuses drifting toward her as though on the wind. Its tentacles brushed the ground, caressing the dead, finishing off the dying.

She took out her remaining gun and raised her sword.

"Need a bit of help, love?" a familiar voice asked.

Red-cheeked Old Roger stood beside her. Once a Harvest god, the apple-man held a war-axe in each hand. Hatchets. The sort of thing that might have been used against his trees in the days before the Harvest had abandoned him.

But another figure appeared from her left, running toward the octopus—a huge figure with red skin and the head of an ox. Gaka, the oni who had been part of her Borderkind platoon with Old Roger, attacked the octopus with his bare hands. Tentacles wrapped around him, but the massive demon yanked the octopus from the air and swung it at the ground again and again until it was dead.

Damia smiled. No longer under her command, these Borderkind were still loyal.

"Orders, Commander?" Old Roger asked.

She saw that he looked not at her, but past her, and Damia turned to see that the remnants of her battalion had gathered on the field of battle. They had been scattered by the latest Atlantean push, but now they mustered behind her once more. The battle raged a hundred yards ahead, and it appeared Atlantis had gotten the upper hand.

Damia Beck raised her sword, a smile on her bloody face. "Attack!"

The wounded outnumbered the dead. Collette feared for her brother, but the pain and anguish around her would not allow her to wallow in her own concerns. The idea of being left behind did not suit her, but if she had to stay here in camp, then she wanted to be useful. Helping with the injured was the best way she could think of to do that. As a high school girl she had volunteered at a local hospital, which combined with far too many medical shows on TV to provide her with all she knew about medicine. Still, when she offered her help, a field surgeon put her to work immediately. She could clean and dress wounds and check on patients' pulses. Already she had held down a soldier while the doctor amputated his leg below the knee. He'd mentioned something about cauterizing wounds. She wasn't looking forward to that.

But she had to do something.

Someone shouted her name. She turned to see one of the healers—an ironic word on the battlefield—beckoning to her as two soldiers carried another on a blanket stretched between them.

Collette ran over as they set the blanket down. The healer slapped thick shears into her hand and Collette got to work immediately cutting away the heavy leather breastplate covering the soldier's chest. There came a cough and a spatter, and when she looked she saw blood bubbling from the soldier's lips. That crimson smear on her mouth made Collette realize the soldier was a woman. Not even a woman. Her eyes were ocean blue, her skin soft and alabaster white, save where the blood speckled it. Her cheeks still had a bit of baby fat. The girl could not have been more than seventeen.

The young soldier coughed again, breath ragged, and her eyes found Collette's. Blood dripped from her left nostril and ran down her cheek. The surgeon tore away her tunic. Collette had wondered where she had been cut or stabbed, but there was no open wound. Instead, the girl's entire right side had become a mottled mess of purple and black, blood welling under the bruised skin. Her small breasts rose and fell with her tortured breathing, but on the right side she was swollen. Between her breasts and lower, her skin had pulled taut over ridges underneath.

Broken bones.

The girl had been beaten by something inhuman or perhaps crushed underfoot. Collette studied her eyes again and saw the desperation there, the pleading for some kind of solace. She knew she ought to lie to the young soldier, tell her everything would be all right, that the surgeon would save her. But already the healer was drawing the torn scraps of her tunic up to cover her nakedness. There would be no surgeon for her.

Collette held the girl's hand and watched her eyes as she died, hoping she provided some peace in that moment but unsure if the soldier could even see her or feel her touch.

She tasted salt on her lips and realized she was crying.

The girl's hand was limp. Collette placed both of the soldier's arms over her chest. A shadow loomed over her and she looked up to find King Hunyadi blocking out the sun.

"Damn them," Hunyadi said.

Collette swallowed, coughed to clear her throat. "We're all damned today."

The king didn't argue. He had his helm and armor off and one of his shirtsleeves had been torn away. Blood and dirt smeared his bare arm and a long gash had been cut just below the shoulder.

The surgeon appeared behind him. "Collette, could you clean His Majesty's wound, please?"

She nodded. Wordlessly she went to fetch a bowl of fresh, warm water and a clean rag. First she washed out the wound as best she could, then applied a rough cream that she assumed was some holistic antibiotic ointment. By then the surgeon had reappeared and quickly stitched up the king's wound.

Hunyadi donned his armor and helm, tested his grip on the hilt of his sword, and thanked them both. The king took a look around at the wounded. Through the opening in the face of the helm, the anger and sadness in his eyes were plain. He turned and shouted a command and a page rushed over with a horse. Hunyadi mounted the sleek black beast and rode down to war once more.

Collette watched him diminish as he rode downhill. While she stood there, Julianna came up beside her, wiping blood from her hands.

"Are you sick of this yet?"

"Of blood? Oh, yeah. Never liked blood, even when it isn't my own," Collette replied.

Julianna shook her head. "Not just that. All of it. You're a legend, Coll. To these people, anyway. I mean, I understand why I'm here. Self-defense classes prepped me for dealing with an asshole in a bar or a perv trying to drag me into an alley, but not for war. I've done well managing to stay alive here for as long as I have. But you ... you've got this incredible destiny and you're just cooling your heels. I've seen what you can do."

Collette shook her head. "It's not like that. You think they left me behind because I'm the woman? This whole mission was Oliver's idea. He's the one who had to go. And if he was going, I had to stay behind. I still have no idea what, if anything, our destiny is, or what the magic we inherited from our mother is really going to mean. But finding out's going to have to wait until the war's over. Right now, these people just need something to believe in. Oliver and I can do the most damage against Atlantis by just acting as symbols.

"I'm here because . . ."

She saw the flicker of fear in Julianna's eyes, and Collette realized she could not complete the sentence. They both knew what the next words would be: *I'm here because Oliver could die.*

Oliver could die.

Collette knew what that would mean for the Lost Ones and the Two Kingdoms, and for herself as the last surviving Legend-Born. She didn't care. None of that mattered to her.

All she cared about was her brother coming back safely so that they could end all of this. So they could go home. Whatever home became when the war had come to an end.

Where the hell is Smith? Oliver thought.

"Somebody give me a hand!" he shouted, glancing around the library chamber as the Atlantean sorcerers began to force their way through the rubble of the fallen arch and soldiers came in through the other doors.

Kitsune appeared at his side, fur cloak rippling around her. She stared at him with jade eyes. "Bring the prince!"

Frustrated, Oliver glared at her. "I'm trying."

He let go of the boy's arms. The prince sat, eyes staring off into nothing as though he'd gone catatonic. Kitsune grabbed his arm and tried to pull. Oliver had found strength and quickness he'd never imagined he had since coming through the Veil and discovering he was half-legend himself, but neither he nor Kitsune could budge Prince Tzajin from his chair.

"We need Smith," the fox-woman said, glancing around in a frenzy. "He could move the boy."

"He's not here," Oliver said. "Just take him through the Veil. Go right through."

Kitsune nodded, eyes sparkling as though they were sea glass, like most of this structure. She held out her hands, reaching for the fabric of the Veil the way that only Borderkind could, and a look of horror spread across her face.

"What's wrong?" Blue Jay asked, dancing in toward them, the blood of Atlantean soldiers on his hands and streaked up his arms. The feathers in his hair were spotted with scarlet.

"I can't reach the Veil," Kitsune said.

Blue Jay paled. He reached his hands up just as Kitsune had, to no avail.

"It's got to be some kind of defensive magic. The sorcerers did something to the building," Oliver said.

Kitsune nodded, terror growing in her eyes.

"What if it's not just the library?" Jay asked. "What if it's the whole island?"

A Naga arrow whistled through the air past them. Grin began cussing out soldiers like he was at a London pub in the wee hours of the morning. Heat and frigid cold strobed through the room as Frost and Li concentrated on the rubble where the sorcerers were breaking through.

Oliver began to panic. He looked down, trying to figure out if the prince had somehow been chained to the chair or the floor. And he froze, staring under the table where Tzajin had been studying.

"Kit," he said, his voice a rasp.

The fox-woman followed his gaze and she froze as well. "How did that get here? Ty'Lis had it in Palenque."

Oliver nodded, still staring. The Sword of Hunyadi—the blade Ty'Lis had manipulated him into using to kill King Mahacuhta—lay under the table. Oliver crouched, fascinated, and reached out to snatch the sword up by its handle. The blade was scabbarded. It lay there as though waiting for him.

"What the hell is going on here?"

"There's only one way that sword could have gotten here," Jay said. "That's if Ty'Lis left it for you to find."

Oliver looked at him. "Oh, fuck," he whispered. "He knew we were coming."

Even as he said the words, Prince Tzajin began to gag. The boy retched, but nothing came out. His eyes were glazed, and then they began to bleed. Rivulets of scarlet ran like tears down his face. Blue Jay and Kitsune stepped back, but Oliver took a step nearer, bending toward him.

"What is it? What did he do to you?" Oliver shouted at the prince.

Tzajin's head lolled back, his mouth gaping open. Oliver saw something moving down there in his throat.

He staggered back, just as the first of the jellyfish flew out of the prince's throat. The kid kept gagging, choking as they forced their way out of him. His body convulsed. The jellyfish stung him with its gossamer tendrils, streaking Tzajin's face and neck with red lashes. Oliver drew Hunyadi's sword and hacked it in half.

But others followed. A second and third and then a vomitous flood of jellyfish erupted from the prince's throat. As he scrambled backward, Oliver heard the boy's jawbone crack from being forced open so wide.

Prince Tzajin had been left for them to find. Ty'Lis had used him as both bait and trap. The boy could not survive this.

"Go!" Oliver shouted at Blue Jay and Kitsune, but they were already moving. He turned to the others, gaze locking on the winter man, and suddenly all of their prior resentment seemed unimportant. "Frost, the prince isn't leaving this room. We go now, or we die with him!"

Li spun and burned half a dozen jellyfish in mid-flight. They popped and burst like blisters. But whatever Ty'Lis had done to Prince Tzajin, there seemed an endless supply of the creatures being born from his gullet.

"This way!" Frost shouted, and he started through the soldiers that crowded the doorway out to the atrium at the heart of the library. They were going inward, instead of toward any exit, but no way were they going to take on the sorcerers if they could avoid it.

Cheval went out the door right in front of Oliver, snapping a soldier's neck as she went.

On the landing, beautifully sculpted from Atlantean sea glass, they both stopped short. Beyond the balustrade they saw hundreds more of those jellyfish and at least a dozen octopuses floating in the atrium, just waiting for them.

"What now?" Cheval cried.

Soldiers stood at the top of a staircase to the left.

"We get the hell out of here," he said.

His other blade had been returned to its sheath. He fought, instead, with the Sword of Hunyadi. In his left hand, he held the scabbard, and he swung it as he ran at the soldiers, striking one in the head even as he used Hunyadi's blade to parry the attack of another.

The Borderkind joined him, bludgeoning and stabbing and burning the soldiers as they took the stairs. Blue Jay hurled two soldiers armed with curved, gleaming, ritual daggers over the banister and they screamed as they fell.

Oliver lost track of how many steps they'd descended. The octopuses and jellyfish and whatever other deadly things slid through the atrium could not really attack them while they were in the midst of the soldiers of Atlantis. He focused on just staying alive and moving downward, step by step.

Ty'Lis had left him the sword to send a message of mockery and triumph.

Oliver intended to use it to gut the son of a bitch.

CHAPTER 21

W hen I see the Wayfarer again, I shall kill him," Cheval Bayard said, her accent thickening with rage.

Leicester Grindylow muttered a curse in agreement. They had raced down corridors and broken down doors and, by sheer luck, discovered a twisting spiral staircase encased in glittering glass with views of Atlantis out of the window panes. The steps were narrow and steep and the glass walls smooth, but Grin and Cheval and their companions descended with reckless abandon. Every second put them in greater peril.

Cheval's silver hair flew behind her as she slid down the wild corkscrew of the staircase. They must have gone down several stories by now but had not come to a landing or a door, and Grin wondered if the spiral went all the way to the bottom.

How the hell had he come to this? His life had been so simple, once upon a time. A bit of mischief, a lot of beer, tending bar now and again...it had been a good life. But then the bloody Atlanteans had sent the Myth Hunters out after the Borderkind, and Grin had to make a decision—fight or hide. Sitting about drinking a pint, watching the world go by, was no longer an option.

He'd never been much for hiding.

Now here he was, watching out for Cheval, whose every glance broke his heart. Oh, he'd no romantic illusions. Lovely as she was, her fragility had been the thing that drew him to her. Damsels in distress. He'd always been a damned fool for them.

Grin kept his right hand on the wall and leaped down the stairs six or seven at a time, slipping and falling on his rear more than once, keeping his weight backward so he would not topple ass over teakettle. Several of the Nagas were ahead of them, and he had a feeling the others were lying dead back in that chamber where the boy who had once been Prince Tzajin had turned into a sorcerous trap. The Nagas slid down the stairs in pursuit of Frost, Oliver, and Kitsune. Blue Jay and Li followed Cheval and Grin.

A wave of heat swept down, prickling the skin at the back of Grin's neck, scorching him. Cheval cursed in French. Grin reached out and took her hand, then released it quickly. Tethered by their hands, they'd only end up falling.

He glanced over his shoulder and saw Li moving slowly, coming down the steps backward. He had both hands up and fire streamed from his fingers, liquid flame that roiled in the spiral staircase and melted the glass windows. Something popped and bubbled in those flames, and whatever chased them began to scream as it burned.

"Faster," Grin snapped.

"Any faster and I shall fall."

From below, around the spiral, Grin heard Oliver shout. He reached out and grabbed Cheval by the arm, not worrying about being gentle. She stumbled, but he hoisted her up a moment and then set her down, even as he kept going.

"Wait!"

She called after him but he did not slow. Cheval would be hesitant to alter her form on those glass stairs. The kelpy's body would be unwieldy in that spiral enclosure, and her hooves would slip too easily.

"Grin, what's going on?" Blue Jay shouted.

"Not a sodding clue!"

He didn't wait for Li or Blue Jay to catch up. Scrambling, sliding, leaping, he went round the spiral and discovered that the stairs did not go all the way to the ground floor of the library. Oliver, Frost, Kitsune, and the Nagas had spilled out into the largest chamber they'd encountered. High-ceilinged like a ballroom, its walls were covered with what might have been ancient Atlantean writing, sigils and words scrawled into every surface, including the floor and ceiling. Lights floated in the middle of the room like buoys bobbing in the sea.

The lights weren't alone.

Eels filled the chamber, long things with prehistoric faces and snapping jaws full of needle teeth. They darted and swam through the air. As Grin leaped the last few stairs and landed in a crouch on the ground, long arms ready to fight, he saw Frost make a pass of his hand and freeze two of the eels dead. They fell to the stone floor and shattered.

Kitsune growled and reached up to grab at an eel as it lunged for her face. The Sword of Hunyadi whispered through the air and Oliver slashed the eel in two, then spun to hack at another.

Grin saw immediately there were too many of them to fight in an enclosed space. Several others were slithering through the arched door on the far side of the chamber and beyond them a pair of figures—sorcerers, no doubt—stood silhouetted. Frost flowed through the room on a draft of frigid air. Ice formed on the walls. The eels slowed. Snow whipped in a churning whirlwind of blizzard and then froze right in front of the door, sealing the sorcerers—and any other eels—out for the moment.

Two of the eels darted down from the ceiling toward Grin,

blotting out the floating lights. He narrowed his eyes, waited for his moment, and reached out and snatched one of them by its middle. He had no time to stop the other. Instead, he fed it his left forearm, jamming flesh and bone into its jaws as hard as he could, trying to keep it from being able to bite down hard.

Dropping to the ground, he beat them both against the floor. Long sliver teeth tore into his left arm. But he swung the eel in his right hand down again and again and it split open, spilling wretched viscera. With his right hand free, he pried the teeth of the other eel off of his arm, then used both hands to rip its jaws open, tearing half its upper body in two.

He heard Cheval cry his name.

Spinning, he saw her jump to the bottom of the stairs. The light from outside the windows—the perfect sky above Atlantis—made her beauty even more ethereal. But the fear and fury on her face made her terrible as well. The others were still fighting the eels, but Cheval ran toward him.

"I told you to wait!" Grin snapped.

"I'm not going to let anyone else die to protect me. I cannot survive more grief," she replied. Her eyes locked on his a moment, then glanced past him.

Grin saw the eels reflected in her gaze. He turned as they swept in. Ice flowed across the room and brought one of them down, but there were just too damned many. As he reached up to bat one away, another swept in from the side and sank its jaws into his abdomen. He shouted in pain and began to pry it off, tearing its teeth away, puncturing its eyes with his fingers.

Even as he did, sensing his weakness, others swarmed him. Grin ducked his head, knowing it was futile. They were too fast and too savage. He would not get out of this chamber alive, would not leave Atlantis. The eels would strip the flesh from his bones.

Then Cheval was there. She moved so swiftly he caught his breath watching her as she tore two of the eels from the air and ripped them open. A third surged toward her throat. Cheval stopped it, but her left hand grasped its lower jaw and those needle teeth clamped down. It tossed its head up, wriggling as her fingers went down its gullet.

She cried out, more in rage than pain.

Grin ran toward her. Cheval glanced at him. She did not see the eel that knifed through the air toward her back, jaws gaping wide. Grin shouted her name, reaching for her, but his fingers scraped only air. The eel struck her lower spine with a splintering of bone and a rending of flesh. Her belly bulged and then it burst out of her stomach in a splash of blood that soaked the front of her dress, then tore the fabric, boring through her. Burrowing.

Cheval went down on her knees.

Grin heard more screams behind him, but they seemed to come from far away, muffled and inconsequential.

She could still live, he told himself. *If we get out of here. If we're gone.*

There was only one way out, now.

Grin grabbed her around the waist—the eel still in her— and ran toward the glass wall overlooking the plaza. The boggart gritted his teeth, dropped his shoulder, and hurled himself and Cheval at the window. It shattered with harsh music and then they were falling, tumbling over one another, twisting down through the air five stories. Grin pulled Cheval toward him, made sure he was underneath her when they hit the stones.

His back hit first. His head struck the plaza. Bones in his skull cracked like a lightning strike. Blackness swept in. As he began to lose consciousness, he felt the eel trapped between him and Cheval twisting, biting at his thick, tough skin. And he felt Cheval's blood soaking his clothes and the cold touch of her cheek against his own. Deathly cold.

The bright sunlight over the island of Atlantis seared his eyes for a moment, and then he slipped into soothing darkness and knew no more.

Jellyfish swarmed the chamber, coming down the spiral stair-case in a wave. Li had burned hundreds of them already, but with the eels now diving toward him, the Guardian of Fire could not destroy them all. A few moments were all the jellyfish needed.

Blue Jay danced in ancient rhythm, swung his arms, sum-moning his razor-sharp, mystic wings. He sliced an eel in two, then began beating away the jellyfish, cutting them to ribbons as they tried to attack him. Tendrils lashed his face, leaving burning streaks there. He hissed in pain but kept fighting.

A Naga arrow punctured a jellyfish only inches from his eyes and the thing sailed away, impaled. A heartbeat later, one of the Nagas fell hard upon the floor, writhing in agony as the jellyfish covered him, stinging, swarming, killing. The Naga twitched, then lay still save for the undulating jellyfish.

As he fought, Blue Jay glanced around and caught sight of another Naga down, being feasted upon by eels, their bodies waving in the air, as though underwater. A gout of liquid fire engulfed the Naga and those eels, charring them instantly. Then Li raced past Blue Jay, flames and heat flowing from his hands. But he seemed dim, somehow, and the fire weaker. Flickering. Finally burning out.

Cold wind swirled and eddied in the room.

Frost darted around that chamber, lashing out at the things that attacked them. Jellyfish fell to the ground and shattered, frozen solid.

Oliver swung Hunyadi's sword. His arms and face were streaked with red lashes from the jellyfish, but he'd managed to keep them off of him. Frost moved toward him, helping, keep-ing the Legend-Born safe as his first priority.

A large section of the glass wall had become a jagged hole, warm island wind and sunshine breezing in. Blue Jay's stomach clenched with dread, wondering if Grin and Cheval could sur-vive such a fall.

As the room filled with more jellyfish, more eels, he knew. "Frost!" he shouted.

The winter man and Oliver both turned to look at him.

"We're screwed. Get the hell out of here."

Even as the words left his mouth, they were punctuated by a scream unlike anything he had ever heard, mournful and full of surrender. He spun to see that in seconds, Kitsune had been overwhelmed by the jellyfish. They lashed themselves to her face and hair. Some wrapped around her arms. Still others moved beneath her cloak, stinging and struggling there.

Kitsune ran for the shattered window.

Oliver reached out for her as she passed him. Blue Jay saw the way their eyes met, the regret and terror in that glance. The trickster lunged after her as well, but he was too far away. Kitsune seemed almost to dance out through the broken window, for a single breath hanging in midair. Oliver planted a hand on the flat, unbroken glass above the shattered section of window, and it cracked, spiderweb fractures running through the glass as he reached out and grabbed hold of her cloak, that copper-red fur, glittering in the sunshine.

The jellyfish attached to Kitsune stung his hand, several of them in a single moment. Reflexively, he opened his fingers.

Kitsune caught Blue Jay's eyes as she fell. Her mouth worked silently, speaking words none of them would ever hear. She might have said *I'm sorry*, but he couldn't be sure.

"No!" Jay shouted.

Oliver stepped back from the gaping, jagged hole in the glass wall.

Blue Jay didn't slow down. He barreled past Oliver and out into the air above the plaza. The beauty of Atlantis, its muted colors and gentle spires and elegant curves spread out before him, with the green-blue harbor beyond. He caught his breath, wondering if this would be the last thing he ever saw.

The trickster bent, arms outstretched, and summoned his mystic wings once more. They blurred beneath his arms and he felt—as always—the pull of his other form, the bird whose soaring flight was such pleasure to him. But the blue bird could not save Kitsune. Only the trickster could help her now.

It felt like fire. The stings of the jellyfish burned her flesh and their venom raced through her blood. The stones below rushed up to meet her and Kitsune relished their approach, the escape from pain that impact would bring.

With her fingers, she traced the air, feeling it rushing between them.

A hand gripped hers. Her legs twisted and her free arm pinwheeled and she felt herself caught, her descent slowing. New stings pierced her and she wanted to let go, to fall, but the hand would not let go.

"Change!" Blue Jay shouted at her.

Her weight dragged on him. She tried to focus, realized he was moving and dancing on the air, the only way he could stay up without becoming a bird. Those blue wings that blurred, barely visible, under his arms, were not enough.

Reaching down to the center of herself where there was no pain, no fear—where there was only the fox—Kitsune changed. Her flesh rippled. Her fur clung to her, and as it did the jellyfish were shed from her body. She diminished into the fox—her spirit did not diminish with her flesh, however. The jellyfish on her head and forelegs were still there, too.

Blue Jay touched the ground. He reached down and stripped the last of the jellyfish from her, hurling them away, then set her on the stones of the great plaza. Her veins were on fire with venom, her skin lashed and scarred. Kitsune could not rise.

On her side, the fox saw Cheval and Grin locked in a rigid embrace. There were broken limbs, tangled together, where they lay on the ground twenty feet away. The fox turned her eyes upward and looked into the sky above the plaza—surrounded by the architecture of Atlantis—and saw the body of a Naga falling, serpentine body whipping in the wind, toward the ground. It struck hard and did not move.

The sky filled with horrors. Jellyfish and eels, yes, but also several huge air sharks and dozens of octopuses. They poured from the library, but most had already been there, waiting for them to emerge. Razor fish slid across the sky. Octopuses descended, tentacles dredging toward the stone plaza.

They were dead.

The fox wished she could cry, but her pain had taken even that from her.

A sudden eruption of snow and ice burst from the broken window on the fifth floor of the Great Library. A dark figure rode the storm. The blizzard swept toward the ground and she knew that, within the snow and wind, the winter man carried Oliver to safety.

Still alive, Kitsune thought. That was good. Of course, without Smith, they would all die.

She howled, as if to call out for him.

Perhaps Blue Jay understood, for he began to bellow at the sky, screaming the Wayfarer's name in fury. His voice echoed off of the polished surfaces of the buildings around them.

The side of the library—the place where they'd all gone out the window—became quickly engulfed in fire. The fox let her head loll back and saw Atlantean soldiers moving in from the edges of the plaza, blocking any hope of escape. Not that they had anywhere to go. They were on an island. Several sorcerers joined the soldiers.

Blue Jay swore. He'd always loved the curses of the ordinary world, of hard men and laughing women. It was part of his charm. Now he scowled as he leaped into the air. Only when the tentacles came down did Kitsune understand that the octopuses had reached him. His blue wings blurred the air again as he danced. He slashed the tentacles from the nearest one, but not all. Not all.

Two tentacles wrapped around his left arm. With his right, Blue Jay cut the octopus's head in two. It flopped to the ground, dead instantly, stinking, rotting innards spilling onto the stones. But those two tentacles dragged Blue Jay down with it.

He planted his boots and got up, struggling to free himself from that entanglement, pulling against the dead thing. The sound of its corpse sliding wetly over the stones sickened her. Kitsune felt as though she no longer lived in her body. The fox began to breathe quickly, raggedly. The fire on her skin, under her fur, had become all that she knew. Somewhere outside of her mind now—or perhaps withdrawn deeply inside—she could only lie there and watch.

Blue Jay tore himself loose from the dead octopus just as a second descended upon him from above. He didn't have time to turn, to dance, to slash, to even raise his fists in defense.

The octopus picked him up off the ground like a marionette. Its tentacles wrapped around Blue Jay's arms and legs, neck and middle. It lifted him up, and then it broke him. Legs and arms, neck and spine, all snapped like kindling.

Blue Jay changed, then, one last bit of magic. One last bit of mischief for the trickster. He became the blue bird again, and slid from the grasp of the octopus.

The bird fell to the ground, struck the stones, and did not move again. Three lone blue feathers spiraled down to land nearby.

The fox wept.

Collette felt wired, like she'd had several gallons of coffee. Adrenaline pumped through her, even though her arms and legs ached. Her clothes were covered with blood and the stink of it filled her nostrils. Twice she'd helped hold together the guts of a soldier so badly wounded that she had to vomit; both times she had returned immediately to the surgeon's side, doing her part. Doing her best. The smell of blood up inside her nose, the taste of it on her tongue, helped. It was far preferable to the shameful reminder of her vomit.

These men and women needed her.

They were dying down there on the battlefield. Her soul felt torn between the urge to run to their aid—to throw herself into the fight and do whatever she could to help with blade or club or bare hands—and the terror that threatened to drive her screaming over the hill, through the trees, and off into the unfamiliar lands of Euphrasia.

For half an hour, the urge to pee had been nearly overwhelming. Now it became painful. For the moment, the makeshift battlefield hospital—a dying place or a surviving place, but not really a healing place—had become quiet save for the moaning of the wounded. Another wave would arrive shortly, but her opportunity had come.

With a glance, she found Julianna. After all she had endured, some of the beauty seemed to have been eroded from her. Her hair was tied back with a strip of cloth and her clothes were also bloodied. Dirt smeared her face, hands, and arms. Dark crescents had appeared under her eyes. Yet she seemed more herself than ever before. All of the ephemeral qualities had been scoured away, and what remained was a woman Collette loved dearly, and felt proud to know. If they had to endure this, she knew they could survive it together.

Julianna waved. Collette smiled and dashed away toward King Hunyadi's tent. It seemed somehow disrespectful to piss that close to the king's tent, but there were precious few places she could go and be out of sight of the advisors and medics and aides, not to mention the wounded.

Once past the tent, away from prying eyes, she noticed the stand of trees at the top of the ridge behind the encampment. Twenty paces or less. Collette raced to the trees and went over the ridge just a few feet, dropped her pants, and crouched behind an old oak with a massive trunk. A sigh escaped her as she relieved herself, the sheer pleasure of reducing the pressure on her bladder enough to make her shiver.

"Not that much different from animals, really," said a voice.

Collette turned even as she rose, tugging up her pants and fumbling with the buttons. She staggered, nearly fell, her boot sliding in the soft, damp spot where she'd just pissed.

"What the hell is wrong with you?" she demanded.

Coyote stood leaning against a nearby tree smoking a cigarette he must have rolled himself. The pungent herbal odor made her nostrils flare.

"Ordinary folk, I mean," Coyote went on. "You people. Not much different from animals."

The lithe little man, that legend, glanced up at her from beneath narrowed brows and cast her a dangerous look. His arms were thin but corded with muscle. He stepped away from the tree, taking a long tug from his cigarette. Smoke plumed from his nostrils.

"I should've guessed you were the type for cheap thrills." Collette stood her ground. Then she frowned. Something was wrong. It took her a moment to figure it out, but then she stared at him.

"You're not Coyote."

He faltered a moment, then took another drag and gave a soft laugh, both self-deprecating and cynical.

"Coyote's missing an eye. I saw him earlier. If he could've grown one back, he would've done it already."

He sighed. "There's always someone cleverer than you are, girl. Hard lesson to learn."

A knot formed in Collette's chest. No mischief lingered in Coyote's black eyes, just a wrongness that made her stand a bit straighter, lean away from him.

And then he changed, but not from man to animal. The air rippled around him, his features blurred, and where Coyote had been there now stood a different man entirely. He had silver hair, and the tint of his skin marked him as Atlantean, but he wore dark pants and a blue cotton shirt that hung loosely on him. These were the clothes of a traveler, not the armor of a soldier or the robes of a sorcerer.

Collette took a step back, heart racing, ready to defend herself. "Who the hell are you?"

"One who's been in the dungeons himself, once or twice, just as you have; one who had to make a deal to get out. He offered my freedom in exchange for your life."

Collette couldn't breathe. She said one word. A name. An incantation. An accusation.

"Ty'Lis."

The Atlantean took a drag on his cigarette and exhaled white smoke. Then he shrugged. "I would've died of boredom in there, so I figured, why not? What good are the skills of an assassin if you've got no one to kill?"

The killer took two slow steps. He stood between her and the encampment. The only place for her to run was down the open slope behind her or along the top of the ridge, in and out of trees.

Collette shook her head. No running.

"You've made a mistake." She lifted her hands. "I have power you can't even begin to understand. I can *unmake* you, asshole. Dust to dust."

The assassin laughed. Then he lunged, too fast for her to stop him. He drove his fist into her face. Collette staggered back, nearly fell but caught herself, and scrambled away. He pursued her, reaching out with his left hand in an open-handed slap that she mostly dodged, only to see his right fist coming at her again.

Collette stepped into the punch. It glanced off the side of her skull, but by then she was in close. She hit him in the jaw with all her strength and it brought him up short, eyes going wide with surprise. Then she drove her forehead into his nose, felt it give way, and watched in satisfaction as he backpedaled, blood dripping from his nostrils.

He swore, then let slip a laugh. "Where'd you learn to fight like that, girl-creature?"

She could have told the assassin that she'd grown up a tomboy in Maine with rough winters and rougher boys, or that she'd lived in New York City for years and had to learn to protect herself, or that she'd had a husband who'd hit her exactly once before she'd taught him never to do it again.

Collette didn't say any of that. She just spat out some of the blood that gathered in her mouth from where his first punch had split her lip.

Then she smiled.

Not because she was some kind of tough chick, but because Julianna came over the top of the ridge at that very moment with an ogre's long-handled war-hammer in her hands. She swung it like a sledge.

The Atlantean heard her coming at the last moment and turned in time to avoid having his skull caved in. He caught the hammer blow in the shoulder. He was on the move when it struck him, but something still cracked in there. Collette heard it.

The swing took Julianna around in half a circle, and that was her undoing. The assassin reached for her hair, tangled his fingers in it, and yanked her backward. He snapped her right wrist and she cried out as she dropped the hammer. Her cry was cut off when he gripped her throat and produced a knife from a sheath at his back. He pressed its tip to her grimy skin, drawing blood.

The assassin started to turn her around, maybe to threaten Collette—Julianna's life for hers—but Collette didn't wait. She'd been in motion even as Julianna swung the war-hammer. As he tried to spin her around, Collette knocked the knife away and jumped on him, wrapping her arms around his throat and face, legs scissoring around his torso. Clutching him, she threw herself backward. Her weight dragged the assassin down, tripped him up, but he had a hold on Julianna, and she fell with them.

Collette Bascombe—unmaker, Legend-Born—tasted blood on her lips and knew that this time it was her own.

Time seemed to hesitate in the plaza at the center of Atlantis. Oliver felt off balance, as though the island had tilted a few degrees. Breath held, he stared at the blue bird as it tumbled from the sky, at the feathers that floated down after it. All sound seemed to cease in that moment as he watched the bird hit the stones and lie still. Unmoving.

Blue Jay is dead.

Kitsune the fox struggled to stand, then fell again, badly injured but still drawing breath. Where Grin and Cheval lay in a tangle of limbs, nothing moved.

Oliver looked up at Frost. The winter man stood perhaps twenty feet away, his fingers elongated into icicle spears, his body narrow from the heat, sculpted in knife edges. But when Frost lifted his gaze from the dead blue bird and met Oliver's eyes, he seemed closer to human than ever he'd been before.

They had been so foolish, these two. Oliver saw it, now, felt it, and knew that Frost did as well. They'd had a bond. The winter man ought to have honored it with honesty, but Oliver ought not to have been so stingy with his forgiveness, particularly when he knew that Frost's only real sin had been arrogance. Recognition passed between them now.

Whatever resentments had separated them were set aside.

Their friends were dying. They were each other's only hope.

"Can you reach it now?" Oliver asked.

"The Veil?" Frost said. His eyes narrowed and he reached out, fingers scraping the air, then nodded. "I can. Whatever magic blocked us from leaving the library doesn't extend to the rest of the city."

"Get us the hell out of here, then!"

"We can't leave."

Oliver spun, staring at him. "What are you talking about?"

"If we go through the Veil here, we'll emerge in your world thousands of miles from where we would need to cross back over to reach the battle lines, probably on an island with an ocean between us and the mainland. If you want to get back to Julianna and your sister, if we hope to bring word of Tzajin's death to Hunyadi, we've got to wait here as long as we can for Smith to return for us."

Oliver swore, knowing he was right. "What if Smith doesn't ever come back?"

The winter man felt the heat first. Oliver had become used to the constant change of temperature around him, the warmth of the island sun and the gusts of icy wind that Frost generated. But when Frost glanced up, already starting to back up, it took Oliver a moment before he felt the blast of heat coming from above them.

He glanced up and saw the Guardian of Fire falling toward them. No, not falling. Li had jumped. He plummeted toward the ground with fire and heat roiling off of him. Li landed on the stones and a tremor shook the plaza. A wave of heat swept off of him. It felt as though Oliver were standing next to a raging inferno, a forest fire.

Then the heat diminished. The fire in Li's flesh flickered and dimmed, and his skin looked more like charcoal-gray ash than the burning embers it had been before. Even in his eyes, the fire seemed to have abated.

Li looked up at Oliver, weary and full of anguish.

"Do something," he said.

Oliver began moving before he even became aware of his intentions. He strode toward the library, glancing up at the huge, burning hole they'd put in the side of the building. Li had melted the glass wall on the fifth floor. The fire had begun to spread. Jellyfish followed him down, floating and eddying on the wind as if they had all the time in the world. A few eels were among them, but most had apparently been roasted in the fire.

The jellyfish descended.

A blast of cold and ice erupted from behind Oliver, shooting skyward and freezing half of the jellyfish as they descended. Those covered in ice fell straight down and shattered on the stones, but the others kept on.

Oliver glanced over his shoulder.

Frost and Li kept their distance from one another. Ice and Fire, neither wanted to sap the magic and strength of the other. The octopuses and eels and jellyfish moved in to finish them off. Soldiers started to move in.

An air shark darted toward Li and he burned it in motion. The flames in the Guardian of Fire raged again, rising to inferno level. The shark fell, a black, burnt carcass, and split open when it slapped the ground. A curtain of fire swept across one side of the plaza. Soldiers had begun to advance, but the fire held them back. The first line of armored figures were set ablaze and fell to the ground, batting at the fire on them, or turned to flee, hair beginning to burn.

Li faltered, fell to one knee. Again the embers of his flesh flickered as though his fire might go out.

Frost attacked in the other direction, ice and snow and frigid wind killing some and halting others. But it would only be a matter of time. They could not stand against the forces of Atlantis—not with the sorcerers that were among them.

There would be no going home.

Oliver closed his eyes, just for a moment, and sent up a prayer that might have been to God, or to gods, or just a wish from his heart that he hoped Julianna would hear.

Keep my love with you always.

Collette would have to fulfill the prophecy of the Legend-Born. Her brother had other business.

He reached out and put his hands on the smooth outer wall of the library. His heart filled with sorrow and rage. His nostrils flared angrily and he closed his eyes again, then dug his fingers into the strange sea glass that made up the outside of the building. It flowed like liquid, like glass before it cooled.

The building shook.

Then it began to melt, collapsing in on itself. The wall bowed out above him. Oliver stood back, looked up in terror, and then ran.

"Frost! Li! It's coming down!"

The winter man burst into nothing but ice and snow, and that blizzard blew across the stones, sweeping up the dead blue bird as it went. Oliver ran to where Kitsune lay, still a fox—why had she not returned to her human form?—and bent to lift her in his arms. She was alarmingly light and she whimpered in pain, but her heart still beat. Her blood felt sticky on his hands, smeared on her fur.

Frost took form again beside the fallen Grin and Cheval.

Oliver ran toward them with the fox in his arms, but he saw the way the winter man stared past him and he paused, turned.

Li had not run. The Great Library of Atlantis melted and collapsed, entropy taking hold, all that held it together now undone by Oliver's hands. The Guardian of Fire stood his ground. A phalanx of soldiers rushed toward him, even as the last of the jellyfish erupted from the collapsing library. A sorcerer threw himself out of an upper floor, falling end over end toward his death. Two octopuses and several razor-fish aimed themselves at the lone figure still in the shadow of the library.

His hands came up. The fire in him erupted in one final, volcanic explosion. The heat seared Oliver's exposed skin and the blast blew him off his feet. He went down, cradling Kitsune in his arms, his elbows hitting the stones before he rolled, careful not to crush her.

When he knelt, his first sight was of Frost. Half of the winter man's face had melted off in the blast of heat. Snow and ice whirled around and tried to reconstruct it, but between the tropical sun and the heat from Li's fire, it would take time. Frost had been badly weakened. He staggered a little but managed to remain standing.

Oliver saw that Grin still lived. The boggart had a bloody, ragged, abdominal wound, but clapped one hand over it as he drew himself up to cradle the corpse of Cheval Bayard in his other arm.

The Nagas had never gotten out of the library.

That left only Li.

He had incinerated dozens of soldiers and perhaps hundreds of the ocean monsters that patrolled the skies above Atlantis, but one look at Li told Oliver that the Guardian of Fire was through. He still stood, hands raised, pointed toward the remains of those he'd just burned, where the stones were blackened and cracked.

Yet all that remained of Li was ash, standing in the shape of a man. As Oliver looked, the last of the fire flickered out. A pile of gray ash, looking like a statue, stood there in the plaza. The wind kicked up and began to pull the figure apart. Cinders blew away, Li quickly eroding, every ashen particle coming apart as though Oliver had unmade him as well. But he hadn't done this. The Guardian of Fire had burned out at last.

The upper part of the library toppled down onto the spot where Li had stood, and then he was only a memory.

Oliver swore under his breath.

"Good-bye, my friend," Frost said, and Oliver couldn't be sure if he spoke to the ashes of Li that blew on the wind or to the dead blue bird he now held in his frozen grasp.

The fox shifted in Oliver's arms. Grin hissed in pain, tears running down his face.

The killers of Atlantis—soldier and sorcerer and monster—surrounded them and began to close the circle.

Oliver and Frost exchanged another look. The winter man nodded.

Shifting Kitsune into the crook of his left arm, Oliver knelt on one knee and reached down with his right hand. He splayed his fingers on the stones of the central plaza. The treachery had to stop. The conquerors had to be prevented from fulfilling their dark dreams.

Steadying his breathing, Oliver let himself feel the stones, and the soil beneath them, and the bedrock of the island. His muscles stiffened painfully and he strained, throwing his head back. At his touch, all cohesion began to unravel.

The ground began to quake. Fissures opened in the plaza, cracks running jagged across the stones. Frost called out his name, urging him on. Wayland Smith had marooned them on this island, had left them to die, but Oliver wouldn't abandon the cause that had brought them here. They could not save the life of Prince Tzajin, could not bring about the end of the war that way. So he would end the war another way.

He would unmake Atlantis.

Buildings cracked. Glass shattered and fell. The plaza buckled and the stones they stood upon sank several feet, surged up slightly, then sank another seven or eight feet. All around them, the structures started to fail, collapsing in upon themselves.

Soldiers broke ranks, fleeing. Sorcerers tried to use their magic to keep buildings from falling, to no avail. Then the water began to flow, rushing in from the harbor and surging up from the foundations of buildings, quickly starting to flood the plaza.

Oliver stood. The damage was done. It had all begun to fall apart.

Atlantis had begun to sink.

he Sandman appeared on the battlefield in a whirling cloud of dust. As it settled, blowing away, and he was revealed, soldiers on both sides shouted in fear and moved away from him, their war for the moment forgotten. Halliwell shuddered, hating that he wore the hood of the Sandman rather than the Dustman's coat, but his arrival garnered the response he had hoped for.

He strode through the battle. With regret, he moved between fallen men and women, unable to pause to help them. Others would reach them. Not that they would have accepted help from him in his current guise. Even those with the worst injuries, with open wounds and missing limbs, tried to drag themselves away from him.

Like a ghost, he haunted the field of battle, drifting, the sand rising around him. There were Yucatazcan warriors amongst the bloodied, screaming soldiers, but most were Euphrasian or

Atlantean. His mind had touched the Dustman's. They were still two spirits, but now had full access to the thoughts of the other. Halliwell had become the Dustman. The Dustman had become Detective Ted Halliwell. It was strangely calming.

Giants walked amongst the combatants, but only a handful. There were Stonecoats and tall warriors who could only be what the Dustman thought of as gods. A massive stag—perhaps fifteen feet tall or more—kicked its hooves at Atlantean soldiers and thrashed a Peryton from the air with its antlers. The stag was made entirely of plants, tree branches, wheat and cornstalks. It smelled wonderfully of fruit.

The Sandman smiled. Halliwell smiled. The Dustman smiled.

An octopus drifted above the soldiers. A dead woman, half-naked and missing one leg, dangled broken from its tentacles. It unfurled other tentacles and snatched up a Euphrasian soldier wearing the colors of King Hunyadi. The soldier screamed as his bones shattered. A god in black armor, red eyes burning from within his helm, charged up from a pile of corpses he had created and swung his sword toward the octopus, but the cowardly thing moved away. It would only hunt the easy prey.

Halliwell wanted to kill it. But not now.

A moment later, a Peryton took his choices away. Broad wings threw their shadow down upon him, blotting out the sun. He glanced up with the lemon eyes of the Sandman, glaring at the Atlantean Hunter. It dove down at him, talons hooked and antlers lowered, intent upon tearing him apart.

Halliwell let it come. The Peryton's talons sank into his cloak and dug into the shifting sand and dust and ground bone of his body, harmless. He reached up and grabbed the antlers of the Peryton in one hand and twisted, snapping its neck. His free hand darted at its face and before he realized what he was doing, his knifelike fingers pried one of the Hunter's glazed eyes from its socket and raised it to his lips. His tongue reached, yearning, for the dripping, bloody eye.

The Sandman began to shudder.

The Dustman crushed the eyeball in his hand, felt it pop.

Halliwell let the corpse of the Peryton fall to the battlefield and wiped the viscous remains of its eye on his cloak. Disgust coiled serpentine through his heart, his shared soul.

With Sara, back in the ordinary world, he could be himself more easily. Sand, yes, and a legend. A monster. But still Ted Halliwell. Here, in this place, he had to hold the reins more tightly to make sure the little voice of the Sandman down deep inside of him did not rise again. The Dustman helped. Together they could stifle the Sandman forever, perhaps destroy him. But vigilance would be necessary.

We must help Hunyadi's army.

You know what must be done, the Dustman replied.

Is it difficult?

Not at all. It is part of our magic. What we are.

Halliwell went down on one knee, thrusting the long, narrow fingers of both hands into the blood-soaked dirt. For a moment, he wondered what would happen, and then he knew. All he needed to do was visualize. In his mind's eye—in the Dustman's mind—they could see the constructs.

The earth churned nearby. From deeper, where there was dry, rough soil, a hand thrust up from underground. Quickly, the warrior dug itself out. It rose, clad in armor of its own, and drew its sword. But the warrior was only dirt and sand and stone, as were its armor and sword. A construct.

The construct turned, opened its mouth in a silent battle cry—for it had no voice, no life or mind—and it ran into battle. A Euphrasian cavalryman had been toppled from his horse. The animal was dying, bleeding. A warrior of Atlantis stood over the fallen man, more than eight feet tall and splashed with the blood of others. A deadly enemy.

The sand creature brought its sword around—a blade whose edge was as sharp as diamond—and cleaved the

Atlantean in half at the torso. Both halves of his body hit the ground together.

Halliwell and the Dustman willed it, and more constructs began to rise. Six. Eleven. Nineteen. At twenty-seven, he could do no more. To extend himself any further could have led to a loss of control, and Halliwell could not risk it. In his mind, the Dustman began to manipulate the constructs, controlling them from afar, a puppeteer.

But Halliwell didn't mind. What he did next would be for him, and the Dustman did not need to be involved.

The sand of his body shifted and resculpted itself, and now he wore the bowler hat and mustache and greatcoat of the Dustman again. He went to the fallen soldier and held out a hand to help him up.

The horseman stared at him, eyes wide with terror.

"Get up, pal," Halliwell said, aware of the incongruity of his voice, his words, coming from the mouth of a legend. A monster.

The horseman shook his head once, slowly.

"Suit yourself," Halliwell said, dropping his hand. In the chaos of war, with shouts of fury and screams of agony and the clashing of weapons, somehow his own voice and the breathing of the downed horseman were louder than anything.

"Julianna Whitney. Bascombe's fiancée. Is she here?"

Suspicion clouded the soldier's eyes. A sadness came over Halliwell as he realized that, once again, he would need to use fear to achieve his ends. Fear was always swiftest.

The sand ran like mercury, shaping itself again, and now the cloak returned and his vision became jaundice-yellow. He saw the soldier through the Sandman's lemon eyes.

Finger-knives reached down for the terrified horseman, snatched his arm and dragged him up to his feet . . . off his feet. Halliwell dangled him off the ground.

"Is Julianna here?"

The horseman nodded. He pointed up the slope toward the tents at the top of the hill in the distance. The king's encampment.

"Helping the wounded," the soldier said, his eyes and voice desperate.

"Of course she is." Halliwell smiled. With the Sandman's face, the expression was enough to make the soldier begin to cry.

Halliwell dropped him and started away from the battle, up the hill, leaving his constructs to aid Hunyadi's defense against the invaders. He would see to Julianna's safety through the end of this battle. He owed her that. And then he would go home, where Sara waited for him, and he would be her dad again. Whatever else he had become, he was still that.

Sunlight glared upon Ovid Tsing's face, but his eyes were closed. Half-conscious, he stared at the inside of his closed eyelids, at the bright red glow of the sun. His lids fluttered. He wanted to wake. But he winced at the glare and pressed them closed again, let his head loll to one side. Beads of sweat dripped and ran across his scalp and along his neck before falling. His clothes were damp and sticky, but he felt sure sweat did not get so heavy.

Blood, then.

He shifted, trying to move onto his side. Pain lanced the left side of his abdomen and a trickle of something traced his skin. Might have been sweat, but he doubted that. Blood ought to have been warmer, but as hot as it was outside, perhaps his skin had become hotter than blood.

His blood felt cold on his skin.

Ovid wished for a breeze. The wind had not died. He heard a tent flapping nearby. His body strained as though he could catch the wind if only he were more attentive. It took some time before he realized that the tent itself was acting as a windbreak, keeping any breeze from reaching him.

Darkness claimed his thoughts. When again he became aware of the heat on his face, the glare on his eyes, his side felt tight. Gingerly, he managed to reach down and touch the place where the Yucatazcan spear had punctured his flesh, and he found a bandage there. A sigh of relief escaped him. They'd taken the time to bandage him—probably to stitch him up as well. Ovid interpreted that to mean the field surgeon didn't think he was going to die today.

Carefully, he tried to sit up. Pain surged through him again and he faltered. The darkness threatened, but did not overcome him. He lay back with his eyes pressed closed, hissing air through his teeth, waiting to feel the trickle of a freshly reopened wound on his side, but no blood flowed.

From far off, he heard the echoes of combat, the shouts of men and women, gods and monsters, the clang of weapons. He wondered how the King's Volunteers were faring without him, and imagined they were probably doing just fine. His lieutenants were well trained, and they had heart. They had come here with only victory in their minds. Nothing else would do, save death. Ovid only hoped it would not come to that.

Good son.

Ovid frowned, eyes still closed. Had he heard a voice in the cacophony of battle or in the flap of the nearby tent? Perhaps someone inside of the tent.

In his mind's eye, horrid memory played out against the red-flare curtain of his eyelids. He saw again the broken corpse of his mother in the grasp of the Sandman, the gore-encrusted holes where her eyes had been. He saw, all too clearly, the face of the monster—the face of Ted Halliwell, the man who'd come to Twillig's Gorge searching for Oliver Bascombe.

What Halliwell had to do with the Sandman, he didn't know. But whatever face it wore, it was a monster, and it had his mother's blood on its hands.

Moisture ran down his cheeks again, but it wasn't sweat this time. Ovid let a few tears fall before regaining his composure.

He opened his eyes and let the sun sear them a moment as though it might burn his grief away as it dried the tears. Once again he let his head loll to the side...

And the Sandman passed by. Wearing Halliwell's face, it weaved amongst the wounded where they had been stretched out on the open ground and strode toward the enormous tent upon which flew the flag of Euphrasia and the colors of King Hunyadi.

He blinked, certain that somehow his subconscious had summoned only a mirage of his mother's murderer. The heat, the loss of blood. But no matter how many times or how firmly he squeezed his eyes closed, when he opened them, the Sandman remained. Halliwell, the monster, remained.

Its presence created a fresher wound than even those he had sustained on the field of battle.

Ovid gritted his teeth. Slowly, warily, he rolled onto his side and then onto his chest. Breathing evenly, preparing himself, he pushed up onto his knees. Black dots swam at the edges of his vision, but he kept breathing and they faded. Teeth still gritted against pain—which inexplicably spread to his shoulders and legs—he staggered to his feet. Something tugged in his wound, perhaps a single stitch breaking free, and a single track of blood spilled like a teardrop down his belly and thigh.

He began to limp after the Sandman. When he passed a wounded soldier—a woman who'd once been beautiful—he bent carefully and borrowed her dagger, nearly passing out in the process. But he remained conscious. The woman seemed near death. Fluid rattled in her throat when she breathed. She would not miss the dagger.

Ovid had come here to fight a war for the king, for his country, for himself, and for his mother. For all of the Lost Ones, and the things that they believed in.

Fate seemed to have other ideas.

Atop a small mountain peak fashioned entirely of ice, Oliver Bascombe stood with his sword raised—cradling the wounded, shuddering, unconscious fox in his left arm—and waited for the air shark to make its move. Octopuses had tried, but Frost had destroyed them utterly. Now, though, the winter man was otherwise occupied.

The craggy ice structure upon which they stood, back-to-back, had become an island in the great plaza at the center of Atlantis. The ground still shook, aftershocks of Oliver's power. He had unraveled the very foundations upon which Atlantis stood. To the south, on the far side of the island, red and black lava spewed from a volcanic fissure underwater.

From what Oliver could see, much of the island was under-water now. Buildings still jutted from the rushing flood that poured in from all sides. Hills and trees emerged from the water. In the distance, another island loomed but seemed untouched.

Only Atlantis had been affected.

Atlantis was sinking, crumbling into the ocean. Undone. Unmade. But Oliver and the winter man were sinking with it. They had quickly discovered that the sorcerers here—the ones who had not gone off to war—cared less about murdering them than about saving their city. Magic spread out across the island, bands of energy that seemed to be trying to raise it up, to somehow keep matters from getting worse.

Another building fell, entire stories cascading down upon one another and crashing into the water.

Oliver had a feeling that soon the sorcerers would realize that their efforts were useless, and then their minds would turn to vengeance.

The air shark turned lazily in the air, as though it hadn't a care in the world. Everything else alive in Atlantis seemed fran-tic, but the shark moved almost languidly. All that mattered was its prey.

Out where the harbor had once been, massive sea-serpent

coils undulated in the water. Ocean waves rolled in through the city. The Kraken—if that truly was the Kraken out there—would soon find the water deep enough to come into the plaza. The ice mountain that Frost had created eroded by the moment as the warm seawater washed over it, and would not survive an attack from the sea monster.

Oliver set Kitsune down at his feet and risked a quick glance over his shoulder.

Frost had thinned to slivers. Mist rose from his jagged body and much of the blue had gone from his eyes, leaving only white—and not even white, but a clear ice. At his feet, Leicester Grindylow sat bleeding, wincing from broken bones, and cradled the corpse of Cheval Bayard close to him. Boggart and kelpy would remain with them, no matter what, as would the dead little blue bird who had once been the most loyal friend to them all.

"Where the hell is he?" Oliver screamed, giving in at last to the frenzy of panic that churned inside of him, spilling over. "Where's Smith?"

The winter man pointed.

Oliver turned just as the air shark made its move. He raised the Sword of Hunyadi. The shark darted at him, its dead black eyes more terrifying than the fury of any demon. There would be no dodging it, now. Swift as legend, Oliver raised the sword up in both hands and brought it down with all his strength. The blade slit the shark's head, punched through into the lower jaw and out through the bottom. He forced it down and the thing began to whip its huge, powerful body in the air. In seconds, it would knock Oliver into the water, where other things waited.

Putting all his weight on the hilt of Hunyadi's blade—its tip now lodged in ice—he drew the other sword, which he'd carried to Atlantis, twisted it and plunged it through the shark's right eye.

It thrashed again. Oliver lost his footing and slid, beginning to fall, nearly knocking the fox off of the ice mountain with him. He tugged Hunyadi's sword out of the shark's snout and the beast fell, twitching and slipping down the ice mountain and into the rushing water, the other sword still stuck through its eye socket.

Heart pounding, muscles torn and aching, Oliver clawed his way back to the top of the ice mountain and stood, wearily holding the Sword of Hunyadi out before him again. The fox looked up at him and he thought, perhaps, she smiled a bit.

"Well done," Frost said, and his voice had become little more than a chilly whisper on the wind. "I wonder, though . . . if Prince Tzajin was left here for us, a trap, then where is Ty'Lis? Why is he not here to see our deaths? And if he's not here killing us, then who *is* he killing while we fight for our lives?"

Oliver slammed the heel of his hand against his head. He looked down at the rising water, felt the ground tremble underneath the ice. He had wanted to punish them, yes, and to stay alive. But he had never wanted to destroy the whole city. King Hunyadi would cheer—his whole army, and the rest of Euphrasia would want to give Oliver a medal—but how many had he killed?

And where *was* Ty'Lis?

"Where else would he be?" Oliver snarled at him, lips pulled back, almost feral. "He's in Euphrasia."

Oliver felt the truth of it. There were no choices left for them, no way to prevent whatever it was Ty'Lis really had planned. Only one way out of this situation presented itself.

He shook his head, threw up his hands, shaking the Sword of Hunyadi. "Shit! Shit, shit, shit! We've got to cross the Veil, right now, no matter where we end up in my world. Smith's not coming. We'll worry about getting back to the front lines when we're out of this mess!"

He sheathed the Sword of Hunyadi and bent to heft Kitsune into the cradle of his arms again.

"Oliver," Frost said, that voice barely a suggestion, now. "You'll have to help me. Help me open the way."

Grin had risen painfully to his feet. The boggart had to be in agony and he swayed there, atop the ice mountain Frost had made, but he picked the corpse of Cheval Bayard up in his arms.

"Do it, Ollie," Grin said. "Open the soddin' path for us. We've got to find the sorcerer yet, the bloke what started it all. I'll have his guts for garters."

Frost held the dead blue bird in one hand—*Blue Jay's dead, oh, shit, how do I tell Damia?*—and looked expectantly at him. Oliver nodded his head. The winter man raised a hand. Oliver shifted the fox's weight onto his left arm and followed suit.

The air rippled. Oliver felt it. For the first time, he touched the fabric of the Veil. Frost had given him something to grasp— he wasn't sure if he could have done it himself—but now it felt to him like some great curtain in the sky, and he knew it would part just that easily. Reality would not tear, it would simply open.

Before they could move, a figure stepped through the Veil from the other side. He hovered in the air above the flood waters and the drowning city of Atlantis.

"No need for that," the Wayfarer said.

Oliver stared at Smith. The Traveler had lost his hat and cane somewhere along the way. He seemed thinner, almost skeletal, and a long scar ran across his forehead and slashed down over one eye, leaving a gaping hole. Somehow, the wound was old, yet Wayland Smith wore no patch.

A dozen questions occurred to Oliver, but only one made it to his lips.

"Where the hell have you been?" he demanded.

Smith flinched, eyes narrowing. He shot Oliver a dangerous look. "You're mistaken, sir."

Before Oliver could ask him to elaborate, other figures began to appear in the air around the melting ice mountain, one rotund and blind, another ancient and bent, one dark-eyed and wreathed in shadow, another scarred and cruel, and still another bearded and glorious like some ancient storm-god. Among them was one female, thin and lovely, though gray streaked her red hair and wisdom crinkled the corners of her eyes. Of them all, only one did not hover in the air, and this last was a giant, thirty feet tall if an inch.

They had not come through the Veil. Nor were they sorcerers of Atlantis. They had, all of them, simply stepped in from the Gray Corridor where only the Wayfarer could walk.

For they were him, each and every one.

They were *all* Wayland Smith.

King Hunyadi could no longer feel his arms, save for the dull weight of them and a throbbing in his hands where they were closed tightly around the grip of his sword. He bled from a dozen nicks and cuts and several more grievous wounds. But his heart pounded in his chest and in the back of his throat he felt a new battle cry rising. He opened his mouth and set it free, raising his sword, urging his army to press on. Their ranks had been thinned, but they fought on—soldiers and volunteers, legends and gods alike. They fought on.

His royal guard stood with him, now, and they cut through Atlantean soldiers with ease. Armor cracked like the carapace of some crustacean and dark green blood flowed. It had been some long minutes since he had seen a Yucatazcan warrior, and he wondered if they were all dead or had fled. To the far western battle lines he saw two giants, but no sign of any others. Monsters still darted across the sky above his head, but many had been pulled out of the air or caught in the crossfire of magic as the Atlantean sorcerers and the Mazikeen tore at one another's souls. Dark light streaked above, whirlwinds of power ripped at green-feathered Perytons.

But the war had begun to wind down. Too much blood had been spilled. Soon, the deciding moment would come, but Hunyadi could not yet guess the outcome.

He stepped over the cadaver of a fallen horse, sword at the ready. His personal guard shouted to one another as they fought on, sword and axe and spear clashing with the weapons of their enemies. The stink of blood mixed with the acrid odor of smoke and burning flesh. Fires flickered here and there on the battlefield.

A figure in ragged, bloody clothing appeared beside him. His face was streaked with gore and one of his eyes had been torn out. The king's guard moved to attack, but Hunyadi saw that the man did not carry a weapon and raised a hand to wave them back, though he did not lower his own sword.

"Hell of a day, Your Majesty," said the one-eyed man, and his grin revealed sharp, blood-stained teeth.

Only then did Hunyadi recognize Coyote. The king knew the scruffy trickster's reputation well enough and was surprised to see him on the field of battle.

"Hell is the word for it," Hunyadi said, "but we have the advantage now."

"Then let's finish the fuckers."

The king knew he ought to make Coyote swear an oath of fealty, but the blood on his teeth and the wounds he'd already sustained were proof enough of his loyalty in this war.

"Well met, trickster," Hunyadi said. "We'll make an end of it together."

A fresh phalanx of Atlantean soldiers filled the breach Hunyadi's men and women had just made. Haughty and unmarred by combat, they marched over their fallen brethren.

Raging with adrenaline, half-mad with war, the king laughed and lifted his sword. "Come on, then, traitorous bastards. We shall make the ending swift!"

An Atlantean officer shouted for them to attack.

Coyote transformed from man to beast, dropping to all fours and racing toward the Atlanteans, teeth gnashing.

Hunyadi's guard did not need an order. They roared and hurled themselves into battle, weapons swinging. Blood flew, spattered Hunyadi's face and eyes. He wiped it away, ducked the sword thrust of an enemy, and then moved in close to the Atlantean. He grabbed the soldier's wrist, snapped it, then hacked down at the back of the man's legs, slashing tendons and muscles.

He left the soldier alive, but crippled. Finishing him would be merciful, but he had no time for mercy.

An arrow took Hunyadi in the shoulder from behind, spinning him around. He had barely begun to stagger toward the archer when two of his royal guard fell upon the man, hacking at him like slaughterhouse butchers.

A voice cried his name. King Hunyadi turned to see one of his royal guard picked up off his feet in the single, massive hand of a Battle Swine. The huge, boarlike creatures moved in—a dozen of them at least. Bones shattered. The royal guard began to fall.

Then the Stonecoats were there as well. One of the Battle Swine charged, head down, at a Jokao. Massive, gore-encrusted tusks shattered on the Stonecoat's chest, then the Jokao plunged a hand into the Swine's chest and tore out its black, cold heart. Another Swine roared in fear and pain and went down, Coyote on top of him, jaws ripping at his throat.

Hunyadi let loose another battle cry, his voice almost gone. He rushed at one of the Battle Swine, drove his blade into the softness of its throat, and the beast fell. Atlantean soldiers moved on him and the king rose, battling them off. The rest of his royal guard surrounded him, and soon the Atlanteans had begun to withdraw.

"Push them back into the ocean!" Hunyadi called, hoarse.

The soldier beside him—Aghi Koh—fell to her knees and clutched at her throat, which bulged with purple bruises. Her eyes began to bleed, and then oily black fluid jetted from her mouth. She bent, vomiting tarry stuff onto the ground. What followed was water—only water—but it stank of the sea.

Two other members of his royal guard—loyal soldiers, loyal

friends—fell and began to vomit as well. Things squirmed in the water they threw up. Aghi fell dead, her wide eyes turning black. Crimson blood seeped from her ears, streaked with black. The others who surrounded Hunyadi suffered the same fate.

Grieving and enraged, the king spun around, searching for his enemy. He spotted the sorcerer, twenty feet away, standing amidst the soldiers of Atlantis. His skin had the chalky greenish hue of his people, but he was an ancient thing with gossamer silver hair; his beard was thick and had several heavy iron rings tied into its length.

King Hunyadi recognized him as Ru'Lem, one of the High Councilors of Atlantis.

"Now, little monarch," the sorcerer sneered, "this war is over."

His spindly fingers scratched at the air, casting his spell anew, and Hunyadi fell to his knees, just as his royal guard had done. He hunched over, losing sight of the sorcerer.

Ru'Lem strode toward him, perhaps craving the satisfaction of watching, up close, as the king died.

"You are hardier than your—" he began.

Hunyadi sprang upward, driving his sword into the robes of the ancient sorcerer. Anything but a heart-strike would not do, but he felt the blade slide against bone, felt the resistance of thick muscle and gristle, and knew that his aim had struck true.

Ru'Lem's eyes widened and a hiss of air escaped his lips with a burble of greenish-black blood. A question. Hunyadi knew it could only be one question.

"Old fool," he rasped. "Did you think I wouldn't prepare for you and your kind, that I wouldn't have had the Mazikeen place a dozen protective wards around me? Had you struck me down with a blade or had a Swine break my bones, you might've killed me. But magic is a coward's weapon. When a warrior kills..."

King Hunyadi stared into Ru'Lem's eyes, gripped the sword in both hands, and gave it a powerful twist, destroying the sorcerer's heart.

"... he does it in close."

The High Councilor dropped to the ground, corpse sliding from the king's sword. Hunyadi spun as a Battle Swine rushed at him, but a Harvest god struck it from the side, a massive stag, trampling it underfoot. A shadow fell over them and he glanced up to see the Titan, Cronus—whom Kitsune had brought from Perinthia—arriving as well.

Then Coyote and his own soldiers charged past him, sweeping into combat against Atlanteans and Battle Swine. The Jokao were joined by Harvest gods and Borderkind and legends. An ogre wielding a war-hammer clapped the king on the back with a booming laugh, then rushed into the fight.

The ground began to tremble and up from the blood-soaked battlefield came creatures of dirt and rock and clay, first one and then several more in quick succession. Their eyes gleamed a dreadful yellow, even with the sunlight upon them. King Hunyadi stepped back and raised his sword, staring in horror at these monstrous things, thinking that the sorcerers of Atlantis had unleashed some new abomination upon them.

But the creatures began to attack the Atlanteans instead. Swords plunged through them. Arrows lodged in them but did not slow them at all. They flowed over their victims and brought the enemy soldiers down, smothering them, breaking them, in some cases scouring all flesh from the bone. It was a hideous way to die, and he gave a prayer of thanks to whatever gods might be listening—thanks that these monsters were on his side.

"The tide is turning," a voice said beside him.

Hunyadi turned and looked into the dark eyes of Damia Beck. She seemed almost unscathed, save that her clothes were coated with dirt and blood and had torn in several places. The sight of her lifted his spirits. If he'd had a crisis of faith, even for a moment, during the battle, Damia restored it. She carried herself like a queen or a legend unto herself.

"What are they, Damia?"

Her dark eyes narrowed. "I don't know, really. The closest I've ever seen were things at the Sandman's castle, things he created. But the Sandman's dead, and if he weren't, he certainly wouldn't be our friend. But they're deadly, and magic doesn't seem to faze them. The Sandmen have tipped the scales."

"All right. Watch them carefully," the king said. "Report."

"Yes, sir. The Yucatazcans withdrew nearly an hour ago," she said. "We have a prisoner who claims that unrest in Palenque and doubts about their Atlantean allies have caused them to retreat. Those few Yucatazcan Borderkind who were fighting against us have defected to our cause. And the Atlanteans..."

"Yes, Commander Beck?" he said, his ragged voice a growl.

"We've got Atlantis on the run, Your Majesty."

CHAPTER 23

T he world blurred around Julianna. Sounds seemed to run together. She whipped around, catching sight of trees and the sun-baked rocks. Collette rushed up and planted a hand between her shoulder blades, and Julianna stumbled. Her legs caught up to her momentum and she ran uphill, toward the top of the ridge with Collette at her side, propelling her along. Both of them were staggering, mouths drawn back in pain as they ignored the wounds the Atlantean assassin had given them.

Run or die. Julianna knew that no third choice existed.

"You won't get far!" the assassin shouted after them.

Julianna could feel him in pursuit. She did not dare turn to look. Sound washed over her, but in its midst she felt sure she heard his boots pounding the hill, closing in. Collette seemed almost to be falling uphill.

A numbness came over Julianna. Cold certainty that she would not be alive when and if Oliver returned.

Somehow that woke her. Her pulse thundered in her ears and her throat closed with dust and heat and fear. Collette faltered, nearly fell, but Julianna grabbed her hand and hauled her up and onward. She slid a hand behind Collette's back and practically dragged her over the top of the ridge.

She had a glimpse of the Euphrasian encampment, of the colors flying over King Hunyadi's tent, and of the battlefield far below. Then she turned her ankle, struggled to catch herself, but fell, and she and Collette were crashing to the ground again together, tumbling. Sharp, dry grass prickled her skin and jabbed the wounds on her face and throat. White lights exploded at the corners of her vision and for a moment the world blurred again and she thought she would pass out.

Then the assassin fell upon her. Julianna wished she still had the ogre's hammer, and room to swing it. But the assassin sneered at her and grabbed a fistful of her hair, dragging her upward. She cried out and struggled to stand, so that her scalp would not tear.

"Ty'Lis said nothing about killing you," the Atlantean said. "But you hurt me, and I pay what's due."

Collette started to rise, moving toward him. Julianna saw her out of the corner of her eye. The assassin seemed not to notice, or care.

Shouts went up from the encampment. They were fifty yards from the wounded soldiers, and those not so badly injured began to rise, painfully, intent upon stopping the inevitable. There simply wasn't time.

Julianna screamed.

As the echo carried across the camp, something else moved at the edge of her vision, too close and too swift to be Collette. With a fistful of her hair, the assassin clasped the other hand around her throat and began to choke her.

The shadow became solid.

A hand thrust past Julianna, gripped the assassin by the neck, and hoisted him off the ground. He let go of her hair as he twisted and fought, kicking at the tall figure in its dark hood and cloak. His fingers pulled away the hood and Julianna knew what she would see—the hideous, lemon eyes of the Sandman.

How it could be, she did not know. Kitsune had warned them, but she had seen the Sandman and his brother, the Dustman, die with Ted Halliwell.

The Sandman pulled the struggling assassin to him and put the other hand over his face, smothering him. His palm sealed the assassin's mouth—he clawed at the hand suffocating him, to no avail. Sand spilled from the assassin's nostrils. His eyes were wide and frantic, but in seconds his struggles slowed and then ceased completely.

The monster let the assassin's corpse fall to the ground. Then the Sandman bent, grabbed his head in both hands, and twisted it, breaking his neck with the snap of dry kindling.

"Julianna, run!" Collette shouted.

But she could not. At best, she had time to stagger back a few steps before the monster murdered her as well. Yet when the Sandman turned toward her, he made no move to attack.

The sand of his features re-formed itself, flowing and sifting. His cloak became a jacket. Julianna shook her head in disbelief. The Sandman and Dustman had destroyed one another, the substance of their bodies merged forever on that eastern mountain plateau with the bones of Ted Halliwell.

But she stared, now, into Halliwell's face. Sculpted of sand, yes, and with the bowler hat and thick mustache of the Dustman, but she would know the detective anywhere. They had spent weeks together, searching for Oliver, searching for answers, trying to find a way home. Sometimes they had been friends, and sometimes strangers. But she knew him.

The eyes were his.

"Ted?"

This Halliwell—the creature of dust and sand—nodded.

"Julianna?" Collette ventured, coming closer, moving around

to stand almost beside her, staring. When she inhaled sharply, Julianna knew she had recognized him as well.

"How?" Julianna asked.

The Dustman shrugged. "Some things are impossible. Doesn't mean they aren't real. We learned that one, didn't we?"

A hand fluttered to her mouth. A kind of giddy relief went through her, despite all the horror that continued there in that place of war. Ted Halliwell had died before her eyes, but somehow he lived.

He lifted his gaze to her and one side of his mouth lifted in an odd grin, twitching his mustache. "I made it home. I saw her. I can go to Sara any time I want, now."

Bittersweet tears threatened at the corners of her eyes. She felt so happy for him, but a sour knot twisted in her gut. Ted had died, but somehow it had freed him of this place. Julianna could never leave. And if dying was the price, she didn't think she could pay.

"That's wonderful," she said.

But his eyes narrowed. He saw her pain, and understood.

"I wanted to come back, though. Had to make sure you were all right. That Hunyadi didn't lose his throne."

Collette glanced down at the assassin's corpse. "That's what you came back for? Justice?"

"Once a cop..." the Dustman replied, with Ted Halliwell's voice.

Footsteps came from behind them. Julianna and Collette turned to see a wounded man come around the side of King Hunyadi's tent. He had a hand over his stomach, blood soaking his bandages. In the other hand he carried a long dagger.

"Justice?" the man said, the word barely more than a grunt. "What does a monster know of justice?"

Collette grabbed Julianna's arm, tried to pull her back. "Who the hell is this?"

Julianna blinked. The grim man's face was familiar, but it took her a moment to place him. It seemed like a lifetime ago that she and Halliwell had sat on the patio at the café in Twillig's Gorge, where they'd met Ovid Tsing for the first time.

"Mister Tsing—"

Ovid stalked toward Halliwell. He pointed with the dagger. "You murdered my mother, detective."

Halliwell flinched. "The Sandman—"

"No!" Ovid snapped. "I saw your face. I remembered you. You plucked out her eyes, and you ate them, and you smiled at me!"

Julianna froze.

The Dustman shook his head, and the sand sifted again, and now he was just Ted Halliwell. Still made of sand, but no bowler, no mustache, no coat. Just that cantankerous, aging cop who loved his daughter with his whole being.

Ovid lunged.

Halliwell did not move. He let the dagger come.

"No!" Julianna screamed, putting herself between them.

She felt Collette grab at her arm, trying to stop her, but the dagger plunged into her abdomen. All the breath rushed from her in a hiss of air and her body went rigid. Her eyes widened and she stared into Ovid Tsing's face in surprise, then fell to her knees.

A flash of regret was the only sign that Ovid even noticed he had stabbed her.

Collette screamed her name and went to her, lifting up her head and talking to her. Julianna could barely hear the words. Collette pressed a hand against the knife wound, trying to stanch the bleeding, and then she began tearing at Julianna's shirt.

But Julianna only stared at Ovid, the man who'd done it to her, and who advanced on the Dustman yet again.

Halliwell let him come.

"I'm sorry," Ted said with sorrowful eyes. "I couldn't stop him. I was . . . the Sandman kept me trapped inside and I couldn't get out. I'm so sorry."

He kept apologizing even as Ovid plunged the dagger into him again and again, stabbing his chest and neck and even his face. The blade slid in and out of the sand with a dry shushing. Ovid screamed and stabbed harder, gripping the dagger in both hands.

Halliwell had become the Dustman again, but still had those grieving eyes.

Ovid fell to the ground, the wound in his abdomen leaking blood badly now. Julianna saw that he had stabbed her in almost the precise spot where he himself had been injured.

He wept in frustration and helplessness.

Julianna looked up at Halliwell. He started toward her. His lips formed words of concern. Her head lolled to one side, and she looked up at Collette and smiled.

A single voice cut through the cloud of shock that had enveloped her.

"If you'd stayed in the dungeon, you'd have saved us all a great deal of trouble."

The shadows cleared from her vision for just a moment and she shifted her gaze to see the pale face of Ty'Lis only a few feet away, hateful features framed by that yellow hair. His robes moved as though in some breeze that Julianna could not feel. The sorcerer had come for them. For Collette. For the Legend-Born.

Oliver, Julianna thought, wishing for him, as though upon a star.

Then she slipped away, into the darkness.

With the warmth of Kitsune's body in his arms and her blood soaking into his shirt, Oliver stared at the figures floating in the air around the ice mountain Frost had made. Atlantis trembled, the water surged upward, now only ten or eleven feet below him. The winter man stood on a higher peak, the dead blue bird in his hands, and Leicester Grindylow beside him carrying the body of Cheval Bayard.

"They're all Smith," Oliver said.

He stared around at them—the giant and the female, the fearsome warrior, the scarred monstrosity, the thin wizard—and knew it had to be true. Each one of those figures, somehow, was the Wayfarer.

"Do you know what's going on?" he asked Frost.

The winter man had become a jagged skeleton of ice. He shook his head, mystified.

Oliver turned his focus to the aged, withered Smith whose left eye socket was a scarred pit. At first, he'd thought this the Wayland Smith he knew, but then the others had come.

"What the hell is this?"

Another building crumbled. The ground shook and Oliver nearly fell, then. He clutched the bleeding fox against his chest. If it came to that, he would fall into the churning floodwaters before he would let her go to her death alone.

A strange calm settled upon him. The soldiers of Atlantis had been washed away, save for those who had sought higher ground on roofs and domes and could only wait to die. Some leaped off, diving into the water, taking their chances with the ocean, perhaps in hopes that they might find a boat or something to float on. Or perhaps they could breathe in the water. The people of Atlantis were not human, at least not by Oliver's reckoning.

The sorcerers were gone as well. He imagined they were not drowned, but instead had fled the destruction of their kingdom.

Some of the creatures—the monstrous sea-beasts that the sorcerers had commanded—still darted through the air above the sinking island, but they paid no more attention to Oliver and the Borderkind, or to these new intruders. Whatever malign intelligence had commanded the octopuses and air sharks, or whatever training they'd received, the chaos had them confused and panicked.

Oliver stared at the one-eyed Smith and waited for an answer.

"Damn you, where is he?" Frost said, his voice a kind of hiss. "Where is the Wayfarer?"

The question seemed foolish. The look on the one-eyed Smith's face told Oliver precisely how foolish it was. The female actually laughed, softly. The giant Smith cursed and spat.

"The Wayland you knew has . . ." the one-eyed Smith began, then faltered. He shook his head, as though deciding not to share whatever he had been about to say. "He has done something that we Wayfarers have all agreed never to do. We are Travelers, Oliver Bascombe. Walkers between worlds. We are not meant to interfere with those worlds we visit, for they are not our own. Yet our brother—your Wayland—has shown us that there are times when it is not possible to stand aside, when we must become involved.

"Every world has a Wayfarer. This dimension's Wayland was weakened by the creation of the Veil—"

The others began to shout him down. Chagrined, the one-eyed Smith held up a hand and nodded, and his siblings fell silent.

"We need him back," Oliver said. Nothing else mattered, now. Confusion threatened to distract him, but he had to keep his focus. "He brought us here through the Gray Corridor, and we have to return to the battlefield. Ty'Lis—the murderous, twisted son of a bitch responsible for all of this—he's there, and I think he means to kill my sister, and King Hunyadi."

But the one-eyed Smith only shook his head. "He cannot return. His power has failed at last. The Veil holds him back, trapped in the Gray."

The winter man seemed somehow stronger. Some of the ice in the mountain blew up into snow and accumulated around him.

"Then you must take us!" Frost demanded. "If his interference stranded us here, you must balance the scales."

The one-eyed Smith glanced around at the others. They all began to nod, slowly, and as the old, withered Wayfarer turned to look at Oliver again, one by one they began to fade to gray, to wisps of nothing.

Oliver's heart sank and he buried his face in Kitsune's copper fur.

Only then did he notice that all had gone silent.

He raised his eyes and saw Frost and Grin there in the mists of the Gray Corridor beside him, bearing their dead. Oliver felt the fox's weak heartbeat pulsing against him as he looked around.

"Which way?"

Then he saw the figure, there in the mist, ahead of them on the path. A figure with a broad-brimmed hat and a cane with a brass head. The figure said nothing, but started along the path.

In the mists on either side, other figures moved.

Other Wayfarers.

It seemed the wind was at his back, and the mist rushed past as though they were flying, hurtling along the Gray Corridor.

The Wayfarers vanished.

Oliver paused, looking around, panic seizing him. Frost and Grin began to call for Smith.

The gray mist faded.

"This way," Oliver said.

"How do you know?" Grin asked.

"I just . . . I feel it."

In three steps, they emerged from the Gray Corridor and found themselves on the hill above the battlefield, within sight of the wounded being doctored and the dead where they lay stacked like cordwood, and the tents of the King and his officers.

And Oliver heard his sister scream.

Ty'Lis opened his cloak.

Collette stared a moment and then a hand flew to her mouth as she retched. She wished she could look away, but knew it might cost her life. Beneath the cloak, the sorcerer wore nothing save a wrap that covered his genitals. Even so, only small strips of his greenish-white flesh were revealed. The rest of his bony body pulsed with living things, bulbous, translucent creatures with masses of long tendrils. They might have been jellyfish, but Collette had never seen jellyfish like this before. They were suctioned to the sorcerer's flesh, and she felt sure the traces of green that seemed to swirl inside of their bodies were the blood of Ty'Lis.

In her arms, Julianna had fallen unconscious. A coldness came over Collette's heart, and she felt as though some hard shell covered her.

"Beautiful, aren't they?" Ty'Lis asked, and from his thin smile, she knew he meant those words.

Ovid Tsing remained on his knees, clutching his wound with one hand and his dagger in the other. Collette snapped at him, said his name, and the man looked up with eyes so lost she doubted he would ever find his way again. Right then, she didn't care. She needed him.

"Watch over her," Collette said, pointing to Julianna. "You owe her that."

Ovid began to crawl toward Julianna.

Collette glanced at the Dustman—at the legend Ted Halliwell had become—and saw that his eyes glowed with a golden light. She wondered if that was a good thing, or if the monster had emerged from within him again.

The Dustman said her name, raising a finger and pointing past her.

The jellyfish had begun to detach themselves from Ty'Lis's body. One by one they pulled away with an obscene sucking noise, leaving behind small, throbbing holes in the sorcerer's flesh.

They darted through the air, trailing tendrils. Ty'Lis wore a cadaverous grin and he flicked his fingers outward as though orchestrating their every move.

Weaponless, and with only the power in her hands, she

knew she had to get in close. Collette lunged at him. One of the jellyfish lashed at her arm with its tendrils, a dozen searing lines upon her flesh. It attached to her skin and she felt something puncture her arm, felt something wriggling into the hole it had made.

She screamed in revulsion and panic, but she reached for the sorcerer just the same.

Powerful hands gripped her shoulders from behind, and then her feet lifted off the ground. The Dustman hurled her away to tumble across the rough hillside, coming to rest only inches from the dead assassin.

Collette scrabbled to her feet, chest heaving. Her arm burned where the jellyfish was wrapped around her. Retching again, she forced herself to get control and tried to scrape the thing off against the dirt and grass. Its tendrils tore free, leaving stinging red welts behind, but whatever proboscis it had thrust into her arm could not be so easily dislodged. She grabbed it with her free hand and pulled it loose, screaming again as it tore skin and tugged on muscle. Then it was out, and she was bleeding. She tested her arm and hand. Everything still worked.

Enraged, she rose and saw the Dustman moving toward Ty'Lis in a cloud. Sand and grit swirled in the air, dragging jellyfish down and smearing them on the ground. Others flew right at the Dustman, trying to latch onto his sifting, shifting form, only to be scoured away. Petite as she was, still it unsettled her to have been cast off like some discarded toy. But Collette figured the Dustman had earned her forgiveness.

Then Ovid cried out, and she saw that the Sandman had not gotten them all. Jellyfish had descended upon him and Julianna. Tendrils rose and fell in the air, whipping their exposed flesh. One of the things had attached itself to the back of Ovid's neck. The young warrior did nothing to try to remove it. Instead, he spread himself out over Julianna, trying to save the life of the woman he'd stabbed only moments before. Most of the creatures were attacking him.

"I freed you!" Ty'Lis screamed. "How dare you interfere?"

The Dustman had gone away. Ted Halliwell had gone away. The thing that attacked Ty'Lis now appeared to be the Sandman, through and through. The gray hooded thing with those finger knives seemed almost to glide along the ground, reaching for the sorcerer.

Not the Sandman, Collette thought. *It's Ted, still, somehow. In there, it's Halliwell, or he wouldn't be helping.*

Adrenaline surged through her, but she thought something else moved through her veins as well. Her body trembled with the urge to act, with the power to do something. But Halliwell would destroy the sorcerer, certainly.

Even as the thought entered her mind, Ty'Lis raised his hands. From the holes where the jellyfish had been feeding upon his blood, streams of liquid shadow erupted, blackness that seemed to eclipse the sunlight around them. Like the tendrils of the jellyfish, they whipped through the air and wrapped around the Sandman, but these were not physical things like the jellyfish. They were forged of the dark magic of Ty'Lis.

The Sandman staggered, struggled. His form changed, shifted, sifting to the Dustman and then to Halliwell. The sand began to slip through those tendrils of darkness, flowing toward the sorcerer, scouring Ty'Lis's face, tearing the flesh.

The air seemed to compress between them and then it burst in a brilliant scarlet light, an eruption of magic that blew Halliwell off of his feet. The sand creature struck the ground and shattered, sand and dust and grit spraying all over the hill.

Ty'Lis did not so much as look away.

The Sandman began to draw himself together. The sorcerer had expected it. Those black tendrils tore at the remains of the monster, of Halliwell, pulling him apart as he tried to repair himself. Ty'Lis threw back his head, jaws opening impossibly wide, unhinging, and something began to push itself up from within, wet and spiny, a gleaming carapace, a creature from the depths of the sea.

It stripped off the flesh of Ty'Lis as easily as removing a coat.

Collette could not breathe. Altanteans could not all be these creatures. So what the hell was it? A parasite? Or was this simply what the sorcerers of Atlantis became, within?

As Halliwell fought against the magic of that ocean sorcerer, the creature turned to look at her, and those piss-yellow eyes were the same. This was no parasite. She stared into the true face of Ty'Lis.

And he stared back at her.

Collette's hands flexed emptily.

Turning, stumbling on her injured leg and with the pain in her arm screaming in her brain, she stagger-ran to the top of the ridge, practically threw herself between a pair of trees, and went sprawling on her hands and knees, headfirst down the other side.

When she picked up her head, she saw the war-hammer Julianna had hit the assassin with. She scrambled over to it and picked it up in both hands. Collette had never been especially strong. All her life she'd been teased—sometimes lightheartedly and sometimes cruelly—for her size. When she met children, sometimes as young as twelve, who were taller than she was, invariably she would blush, feeling awkward.

The war-hammer seemed no heavier than a baseball bat in her hands.

Collette started back over the ridge.

Oliver and the winter man ran side by side. The temperature here was perhaps fifteen degrees cooler than on Atlantis, but the air hung thick with humidity, and Frost had almost instantly accumulated that moisture to repair himself. His icy figure remained sharp and thin, but no longer the skeletal shape he had become.

They weaved through the wounded, Oliver leaping a man who howled for the doctor, raising the stump of a ruined arm.

Frost disintegrated into the air, becoming the churning blizzard Oliver had first encountered a lifetime ago in his mother's parlor on that stormy December night.

Grin had been left to look after Kitsune—still in her fox shape—and the cooling corpses of Cheval and Blue Jay. Oliver and Frost were the only ones left to fight Ty'Lis, and somehow, despite the mistrust and resentment that had come between them, that seemed right.

They reached the tents of King Hunyadi and his entourage. Oliver kept his focus on the flag flying the king's banner. He dodged around a tent and then emerged at the rear of the camp, a stone's throw from the top of the ridge. The Sword of Hunyadi felt right and comfortable in his hand.

When he saw the monsters fighting, his first thought was that two of the legends involved in the war had somehow carried their conflict far from the field of battle. The thing still on its feet had a hard ridged shell like some kind of crustacean, black and wetly gleaming. Ribbons of oily shadow extruded from small holes all over its body, and Oliver had seen dark tendrils like that before. Atlantean sorcery.

But there was no sign of Collette, and that was a good sign.

The ocean creature attacked something else that struggled to rise from the ground, those oily ribbons whipping and tearing, but as Oliver ran—the blizzard of the winter man rushing along beside him—he realized what he saw was the Sandman. The monster's substance thrashed against those black ribbons, which somehow had power over the shifting sand.

"Magic," he grunted, breath coming raggedly as he ran. "Ty'Lis can't be far."

"*That is Ty'Lis,*" whispered a cold breeze at his ear. "*Dark sorcery, Oliver. He's transformed himself into a Curlesh, a legend from ancient Atlantis.*"

"Why the hell would he—"

"*Harder to kill,*" the icy breeze replied.

But Oliver had stopped listening. As they neared the stretch of rough ground where Ty'Lis and the Sandman fought, he saw two human figures on the grass, covered in the same sickening jellyfish they had barely escaped in Atlantis. A man lay atop a woman, and the disgusting things covered nearly all of the man's body and lashed at the exposed flesh of the woman he shielded.

Oliver would have known her in a darkened room, or across a crowd of thousands. He knew her now. Julianna's hair. Her hands. The slope of her jaw, where only a tiny bit of her face was visible. He knew her better than he did himself.

"What have you done?" he screamed.

The Curlesh turned at his voice. The Sandman partially slipped his bonds and a long arm sculpted of sand lashed up, driving finger knives at the eyes of the sorcerer Ty'Lis. The Curlesh dodged its head and its shadow tendrils tore the Sandman's arm apart, but by then, Oliver and Frost were nearly upon them. He didn't know where his sister was, but as long as Collette was elsewhere, she would be safe.

Those piss-yellow eyes turned toward Oliver again. Ty'Lis raised his monstrous hand.

"You should be dead!" the sorcerer shouted.

A rush of turquoise light burst from his fingers and shot toward Oliver, who had no defense against magic. In that very instant, the winter man took form in front of him, ice and snow carved into the body of Frost. Ty'Lis's spell struck him and Frost melted on contact, turning to a cascade of water that splashed to the rough grass with the stink of the ocean at low tide.

"Son of a bitch!" Oliver roared, raising the sword and charging right across the puddle that Frost had become. "*I* should be dead? You should be dead!"

He brought Hunyadi's blade around in an arc with a speed and a strength he knew were inhuman. The sword struck the Curlesh's carapace at the neck with a metallic clang and glanced off, sending up sparks. Ty'Lis reached for him with a huge hand. Oliver spun inside his reach and knocked the arm away with another blow from his sword.

"Kill him, Bascombe!" shouted a voice.

Oliver caught a single glimpse past Ty'Lis at the Sandman. As the creature struggled against those ribbons of darkness, its murderous features changed and Oliver saw the face of Ted Halliwell. Kitsune had told them the Sandman had survived, but now he knew it was far more than that. Somehow, Halliwell had survived as well, as a monster.

In that heartbeat of distraction, Ty'Lis struck him across the face, the hard shell of the Curlesh gashing his flesh. Oliver staggered back and fell. His fingers managed to hold onto the sword, but as he began to rise, several of those ribbons of darkness—stinking of ocean magic—darted toward him and trapped his arms to his sides even as they bound his legs.

The Sandman, Halliwell, whatever it was, rose up behind Ty'Lis, but the sorcerer's putrid tentacles ripped him apart again.

"It ends now, Bascombe," the sorcerer said, his voice low and distant, as though coming up from inside the cavernous chest of the Curlesh.

"What're you, a complete idiot? You blind as well as stupid?" Oliver raged at him, struggling against the black ribbons. "There's revolution in Yucatazca, and I only got a quick look at the battlefield, dumbass, but that was enough for me to figure out you're losing this war!"

The face of the Curlesh had no expression, but its eyes twitched and the hinged mouth opened in what might have been a mocking smile. "It matters little. Every Door leading to the ordinary world is gone. I've had them sealed. Only a handful of Borderkind still live, and those will be eradicated. All that remains is for me to kill you and your sister, and the Two Kingdoms will be mine. Atlantis will rule. There are more soldiers to be had, other armies to manipulate. This battle will not decide the war."

The confirmation that Collette was alive filled Oliver with strength.

He sneered. "I hate to break it to you, asshole, but Atlantis isn't sending any more troops. All you've got left is whoever's on the ships floating off the coast. Atlantis is gone."

Those black ribbons continued to tear at the Sandman, off to the sorcerer's left. But Oliver had his attention now.

"You lie."

Oliver grinned.

Oily tentacles slammed him to the ground.

An icy breeze ruffled Oliver's hair. Tiny bits of sleet stung his right cheek. He heard the voice of the winter man in his ear. *"Tell him."*

At the very same moment, Oliver saw motion on the ridge behind Ty'Lis. Astonished, he watched Collette slip between two large trees and start swiftly, quietly, down the slope toward the monstrous sorcerer, carrying an enormous war-hammer in both hands.

"*Now,*" the winter man's voice urged.

So many had died in Atlantis. Oliver felt sickened by what he had caused there. He could not have known the extent of destruction his touch would bring, but he would regret it for the rest of his life.

After today.

"No lie. I'm Legend-Born, remember?" Oliver said hurriedly, not daring another glance at Collette for fear of giving her away as she crept toward Ty'Lis. "You saw what I did to the side of the palace in Palenque. I unmade it. You thought we were only symbols, but the power inside of us is terrifying, even to me. You put your twisted magic inside that little boy, the prince, and left him as a trap for us. You left me no choice. I put all of my power down into the island, into Atlantis. I unmade it, you bastard. It's gone. Swallowed by the ocean. Lost under the waves, just like the old stories."

Ty'Lis shook. The Curlesh opened its mouth and bellowed. "You lie!"

But the sorcerer knew the truth. Oliver could see it in those horrid eyes as Ty'Lis spread the fingers of his right hand and began to speak the words of an incantation in the arcane tongue of ancient Atlantis. Streaks of mist swam like tiny eels around his fingers, a cloud of vague forms that began to lengthen as they slithered away from the sorcerer's hand, moving toward Oliver.

The storm blew past Oliver.

Ice and snow churned around him, blotting out the sun for several seconds. He heard the bellow of the Curlesh again, furious at the winter man's attack. The transformed sorcerer raised both hands as though to defend himself. Nearly all those oil-black ribbons of shadow struck out at Frost, but the winter man had no form. He was only storm, now, and far too swift for Ty'Lis.

The carapace of the Curlesh froze solid, rimed with ice. The tendrils of shadow faltered, some dissipating into black smoke. Even with his body frozen, fresh tentacles began to extrude from those same holes in the sorcerer's hard shell.

But for the moment, Oliver was free.

He leaped to his feet and raced at Ty'Lis. He held the point of his sword straight in front of him, hoping to crack the carapace.

Ty'Lis began to move. The moisture on the black shell of the Curlesh had frozen, but now the ice showered down, cracking and shedding.

A tall figure sculpted itself out of sand just to the sorcerer's left. Not the Sandman, however. Detective Ted Halliwell wore the high-collared greatcoat of the Dustman, but otherwise was himself. Then he exploded in a storm of sand, a scouring flurry of dirt and grit and dust. The sand blew around the ancient monster Ty'Lis had become and began plugging the holes that the jellyfish had left behind. The ground erupted around the legs of the Curlesh and hardened around them, trapping it in that position.

The ribbons of black smoke were cut off, the holes filled with sand.

Frost took form at last, just a few feet from where Julianna lay—too still, too damned still—beneath the twitching man, the jellyfish savaging him. The winter man froze the creatures with a flick of his wrists and a gust of wind that turned them to ice.

"Collette!" Oliver shouted. "Now!"

His sister had made it within a few feet of Ty'Lis. Had she not been slightly uphill, the pixyish Collette wouldn't have had the height for it, but she swung the war-hammer with inhuman strength—legendary strength—and it struck the sorcerer in the side of the head. The carapace of the Curlesh cracked.

"Monsters! Destroyers!" Ty'Lis roared. "I'll kill you all."

Oliver might have laughed at the irony. Instead, he felt sick, and determined to finish the job.

"It's not enough!" he called to his sister. "Use your hands!"

Collette didn't have to ask what he meant. She dropped the war-hammer and grabbed hold of the Curlesh's torso from behind. Ty'Lis tried to wrest himself free, but the ground held his legs tightly. Magic began to swirl around his hands again, the air shimmering like heat haze. Grotesque, guttural sounds came from his throat in a terrible incantation.

Sand blew down his throat, gagging him.

And Collette's touch began to do its work. The black carapace of the Curlesh faded to a brittle gray.

Oliver drove the Sword of Hunyadi through the center of the sorcerer's chest. The shell cracked easily, giving way, and the blade plunged through meat and bone and punched out through the Curlesh's back.

Collette called out in protest. He'd nearly skewered her as well.

When he pulled the sword free, Ty'Lis fell to the grass,

twitched once and then was still. A small dust storm blew up and then sifted itself into the body of Ted Halliwell, wearing that long coat with its high collar. Ted Halliwell, the new Dustman.

Collette picked up the war-hammer and brought it down on the skull of the Curlesh over and over, pounding the shell and bone and flesh of Ty'Lis's head to pulp and powder.

Oliver spun and ran to where Frost stood over Julianna and the bald man whose flesh had been ravaged by the jellyfish. He knelt and pulled the man off of her. Frozen jellyfish shattered to shards of ice as he rolled the man over and felt for a pulse.

Whoever he'd been, he was dead.

Julianna's eyelids fluttered, but did not open. Her breathing was labored and blood soaked through a bunch of ragged strips of her shirt that had been pressed over some kind of wound in her belly, but she was still alive.

A sound came from Oliver's throat. Perhaps a prayer of thanks, perhaps a profession of love. He took her hand, letting his pulse and his breathing slow down.

"Ovid Tsing," the winter man said.

"You knew him?"

"From Twillig's Gorge. He was a good man."

Oliver nodded. "He tried to protect her."

Collette's shadow fell over Julianna. Oliver looked up at his sister's sorrowful eyes.

"He's the one who stabbed her," Collette said. "By accident. He wanted to kill Halliwell. Julianna got in the way."

A sad smile touched Oliver's lips.

The Dustman came to stand beside Frost. "Bascombe... Oliver... she'll die without real medical attention. She needs a real surgeon. A hospital."

Ted Halliwell had been a cop for decades. From what Julianna had said, he'd been in the military as well. He'd seen his share of wounds. He knew what he was talking about.

Oliver slid his arms under Julianna and lifted her off the ground, rising to his feet.

"Then I'll take her there."

Halliwell shook his head. The sun glinted off of bits of quartz mixed with the sand and dust that comprised his face. "She's one of the Lost Ones. Julianna can't go back."

Oliver glanced at his sister. Collette nodded.

"Yeah," Oliver said. "We'll see about that."

Collette stood next to him. Without exchanging a word, they reached out together, searching for the Veil. They were Legend-Born. They were made for this. Wayland Smith had introduced their parents just to bring about the birth of children who were half-human and half-Borderkind. What that truly meant, Oliver didn't know, but it had to count for something. They had magic on their side. Power and prophecy.

"I . . I can't," Collette said.

"This isn't right." Oliver could feel the Veil. He could sense its presence there, just beyond the reach of his mind and the power inside of him. He knew the Borderkind must find it that way, but they could open a passage, they could travel through.

"I felt it in Atlantis," he said, turning to Frost, Julianna heavy in his arms. Her breathing seemed more ragged. "I helped you open it."

The winter man nodded. "You helped widen it, but I opened the way."

"Then open it now!" Collette said.

Frost hesitated. Oliver could see it in his eyes. He hated all that Ty'Lis had done, but he had stood against Atlantis at the beginning because they had sent the Myth Hunters out after the Borderkind. He had saved Oliver's life not because he wished the prophecy of the Legend-Born to come true, but because it meant defying the Myth Hunters and their master.

The winter man feared the unknown. He was afraid of what would happen to his world if the prophecy came true. Oliver saw it all in his eyes, and he understood. But this was Julianna's life.

"If we were ever friends . . ." he began, but could say no more.

Frost glanced from Halliwell to Collette and back to Oliver. In the end, he reached out a hand and touched Julianna's hair, and he nodded.

With a gesture, the winter man opened a passage. The air trembled and a kind of archway appeared, mist swirling on the other side. Through the mist, Oliver could hear the honk of car horns and the roar of engines. Somewhere children laughed, and a mother shouted at her child to stop running.

Oliver glanced at Collette as his sister reached out. She grasped the edges of that passage, invisible to the eye, but he could feel her take hold and knew that he could do the same. Perhaps they could use their power to unmake the Veil, and perhaps not.

Now wasn't the time to find out.

"See you soon," Oliver said.

Collette nodded.

He hefted Julianna, bent to kiss her forehead, and then stepped forward. As he moved through that tear in the Veil, trying to cross the border between worlds, he felt resistance. Julianna was one of the Lost Ones. The Veil's magic had been woven to keep her from traveling back to the land of the ordinary. But Oliver was not Borderkind. Nor was he merely ordinary. Nor was he a Walker Between Worlds. He'd been a lawyer and an actor, a son and a lover, a brother and a friend. Though they weren't yet married, he understood that he'd become a husband, and nothing meant more to him than the woman who would be his wife.

He was both a legend and a man.

He stepped through the Veil, forcing aside whatever magic conspired to keep Julianna from coming home with him. Oliver Bascombe did the impossible. He tore the membrane of the Veil.

And the magic began to unravel.

EPILOGUE

n late October, with the trees afire with the red and orange of autumn foliage, Damia Beck sat atop a gentle grassy hill with her legs drawn up to her chest, chin resting on top of her knees. She gazed out across the valley below. Fishermen who had been up before the sun stood on the shore of the lake, casting their lines with an easy grace. A shepherd guided his flock in a silent parade up a distant hill. Morning light silhouetted the battlements of the Castle of Otranto on the horizon.

Damia loved it here. Her world had been integrated into the ordinary, little fragments of legend and wonder scattered all over the human realm, missing pieces of history returned to their rightful places. None of the roads she had known her entire life led to familiar places anymore. Euphrasia had been broken up, pieces of it merged into the human world in North America, Europe, and Asia. The capital city of Perinthia no longer existed. King Hunyadi's palace still stood, but in a forbidding old mining town in the north of England.

Hunyadi had always loved Otranto more. She and the king had that in common. Its appearance in the mountains not far from Innsbruck, in Austria, had been met with fascination by the locals—a far better reception than the legendary had received in some places.

She did not blame the Bascombes. Oliver had not brought the destruction of the Veil with any purpose, no matter what so many of the Lost Ones wished to think. He had unraveled its magic for the sake of love. No matter her misgivings, no matter how difficult this new world had proved, Damia understood that. She wished him well.

But she hated him a little, too.

Damia took a long breath and squeezed her legs more tightly to her chest. The irony cut deeply. The Lost Ones—both those who'd crossed over themselves and those whose ancestors had first gone through the Veil—had yearned to return to the ordinary world...to go "home." But no matter what the legendary had called them across the Veil, Damia had never felt lost there, amongst the magical creatures and mystical places. Here, amongst ordinary people, she truly felt lost for the first time. More than anything, she wished she could go home.

But there would be no returning, now. Home, as she'd known it, no longer existed.

"I wish you were with me," she said softly. Only the rustle of the leaves in the trees responded. "I might have learned to see this world through your eyes. At your side, it could have been a grand adventure."

A pair of tiny birds darted from the nearest tree. Several golden leaves fell, drifting to the ground like feathers.

Damia smiled as she watched them wing their way across the sky, turning toward the lake and then the castle in the distance. Reluctantly, she glanced at the small mound of earth to her left, beneath the tree. A stone marker had been planted at the head of the mound to identify the tiny grave where the blue bird had been buried. She had briefly considered having his name engraved upon the stone, along with some declaration of her love. Awful enough that she had buried Blue Jay here, instead of in the land where his legend had originated, but she needed him close by her.

The stone had been etched with a single word. Four letters that comprised her wish for his spirit, for the wings of his soul, as well as a constant reminder to live by his example.

Soar.

Damia stood, shook fallen leaves from her cloak, and looked out at the lake and the castle once more. A soft smile touched her lips. She glanced at the small grave.

"I know what you'd say. Time to make my own adventures."

She stared again at the four letters etched into the marker and nodded. Then she turned and started away.

On the other side of the hill, a complement of twenty members of the King's Guard awaited her on horseback. Hunyadi himself spurred away from the others. He held the reins of her horse—its saddle as black as her own battle dress—and he brought the beast to her. Damia recognized the honor. That the king should keep hold of her horse while she spent a few minutes on farewells, instead of delegating the job to some page, was a gesture of extraordinary respect and fondness.

"I'm grateful, Your Majesty."

"As am I, Commander, for so many things," the king replied. "We must ride, now, though. The journey to Vienna is long."

Damia gripped the pommel, put one foot in the stirrup and threw her other leg over. In the saddle, holding the reins, she felt her mind clearing. There was work to be done. The United Nations was holding a special session in Vienna to meet with representatives from Euphrasia, just as they had already met with the new king of Yucatazca—some cousin of Mahacuhta's—in Rio de Janeiro. Hunyadi had made Commander Beck the Euphrasian ambassador to the UN. It meant everything to her.

Many of her people were attempting to return to the nations of their births, or of their ancestors' origins. But Damia would always be Euphrasian.

"Let's be off, then," she said.

Damia snapped the reins and the horse began to trot. His Majesty rode at her side and the King's Guard fell in behind them.

As she rode, she caught sight of a pair of birds—perhaps the two she had seen moments ago—taking flight from the Castle of Otranto. They darted across the surface of the lake, flying low, chasing one another, moving as though dancing together on the air.

She watched until they soared up and over a distant hill, out of sight.

On a blustery afternoon in mid-November, the trees mostly stripped of leaves and scraping skeletal branches at the low-slung gray sky, Sara Halliwell drove along a winding road to the north of Kitteridge, Maine. The Old Post Road seemed to go nowhere, the sort of route that would make those unfamiliar with it wonder with alarming frequency whether or not they had taken a wrong turn and gotten lost. In truth, the Old Post Road did lead somewhere, but the towns to the northwest existed in a locale that could only be considered the middle of nowhere.

Sara had spent the late spring and early summer in Maine with her father, helping him to adjust to what he'd become, and the way the world had changed for all of them. There had been so many questions, government inquiries, and requests for help from friends and allies who were having an even more difficult time coming to terms with this new world.

Many still thought of her father as a monster. To their eyes, he had discovered the soulless killer who had murdered so many children, and had become that very thing. Several newspaper editorials had suggested that he stand trial for the sins and crimes of the Sandman. But that was only talk. Even if they could find a jury willing to convict him, the law would not be able to hold him.

Eventually, those voices found other things to rage about.

During those long months, Sara and her father found a new peace. The relationship would never be perfect, but Sara felt sure that things like that, like the perfect father-daughter relationship, were the real myths. She loved him, and he loved her. Whatever Ted Halliwell had endured, he had awoken to a new life in which the choices his daughter made in her life troubled him not at all. Her happiness was all that mattered to him. Sometimes they bickered, but there was a tenderness even in that.

Sara had spent the late summer and early fall in Atlanta, packing up her studio and meeting with former clients, hoping to get leads on new business in the northeast. Her new photography studio in Boston wouldn't open until January or February, but already she had work lined up.

Yet the idea of photographing fashion models and advertising layouts again left her cold. She kept it to herself, but there were so many new beauties, so many bits of breathtaking magic in the world now, that those were the things she wanted to capture with her camera.

Still, a girl had to eat.

The road ahead curved to the right and she followed it, the car buffeted by the November wind. The weatherman had predicted rain, but so far she had not seen a drop. She glanced at her odometer, trying to figure out how far she'd gone since getting onto the Old Post Road. If the directions her father had given her were accurate, she ought to be almost there by now.

Almost as the thought occurred to her, she caught sight of the house looming up on the right. Beyond the pine trees and bare oaks, situated at the peak of a distant hill, stood a massive, sprawling Victorian. On that grim day, the lights in its many windows were warm and inviting. Smoke rose from two separate chimneys.

Sara caught her breath and put her foot on the brake, slowing to turn into the dirt path that led up through the trees. She drove carefully up the hill until she arrived at the front of the house, where she parked and climbed out of the car.

Her keys dangled from her hand as she stared up at the house.

It had been built entirely out of sand.

The front door opened and her father stepped out, wearing that long coat that he so favored but thankfully without the silly bowler hat.

"Hello, sweetheart," said the Dustman.

Sara ran to him and threw her arms around him. She kissed his rough cheek. The sand was warm.

"Did you bring your camera?" he asked.

"Oh, right." She went back to the car and popped the trunk, pulling out her camera bag and slinging it over her shoulder. When she returned to him, he stepped aside to let her into the house.

"What's the big mystery, Dad?" Sara asked.

Her father smiled. "Come in."

She went through the door. He followed and closed it behind her. Sara gazed around, mouth open in wonder. The house was vast inside. A long corridor led away on either side of the grand staircase in the midst of the foyer. The stairs split, both sides leading up to a balcony on the second floor, overlooking the entryway. The place felt a bit chilly, but she could smell the woodsmoke from the fireplaces, and the oil lamps that seemed to be everywhere gave the house the feeling of an age long gone by.

"Follow me," he said, starting for the stairs.

"Dad?"

Ted Halliwell turned and smiled at his daughter. "Sara, follow me."

She did, up the stairs to the second-floor balcony. The wide corridor there led deeper into the house. Both sides of the hall were lined with doors, and the corridor seemed impossibly long, as though it might go on forever.

"Magic," she said. It wasn't a question.

Sara turned to her father. Adjusting the strap of her camera bag over her shoulder, she stared into his eyes. "What is this? Where does it go?"

"Not 'it.' They. Every one of these doors opens into a different part of the world, some ordinary and some legendary. We can go anywhere in the merged world, see everything with our own eyes, or through the lens of that camera."

She stared at him, shaking her head, speechless.

The Dustman shrugged. "You've got no plans for the next couple of months, until you open your new studio. You said so yourself."

He reached out for his daughter's hand. "So, where do you want to go first?"

Sara laughed, stared down that long corridor at all of those doors, fighting disbelief. But there was no room in the world now for disbelief.

She took his hand.

"Surprise me."

On a cold, crisp night during the first week of December, Oliver Bascombe sat in the familiar chair in his mother's parlor and stared into the fireplace. The logs roared and crackled with flames. He'd built himself up quite a blaze and sat, now, reading Jack London's *The Sea Wolf*. The book brought him comfort. Since childhood, he'd read it many times, always in this room, in this chair. In his imagination, he had sailed aboard *The Ghost* with Wolf Larsen, traveling into danger and adventure.

Oliver slipped a finger into the book and reached up to rub at his eyes. The fire flickered ghostly orange on the walls. He might be getting tired, but he thought, perhaps, something else troubled him beyond the heat of the fire getting to his eyes.

The Sea Wolf had lost some of its magic. Danger and adventure no longer had the allure for him that they had when he'd been a boy.

A gentle knock came at the door, and then it swung open. Unbidden, Friedle entered the room carrying a small tray, upon which sat a steaming mug of the thick cocoa the man had been making for him ever since his mother had died. Oliver knew memory could play tricks, but it seemed to him that Friedle always got the cocoa exactly right. Nobody else had ever been able to duplicate it.

"Good evening, Oliver," said the fussy little man.

Oliver smiled. "Friedle, your timing is incredible. You have no idea how much I needed this right now."

But of course he did. Friedle had been watching out for Oliver and Collette for years, keeping them out of too much trouble. He seemed always to know what they needed, and to be there when it mattered most.

"Thank you," Oliver said, taking the tray from him and setting it on the coffee table.

"You're very welcome."

Oliver took a sip from his cup. A smile creased his lips. Perhaps Jack London's stories were no longer enough to transport him back to his childhood, but here in this room—which he would forever think of as his mother's parlor—with the fire burning and the taste of that cocoa on his lips, he remembered what magic felt like.

Not the magic in his hands, or that which had returned to the world... the magic that only existed on the inside.

Friedle started to withdraw. Oliver glanced at him. They

knew, now, that Friedle had never been his real name. The goblin who had served the legendary Melisande—his mother—was called Robiquet. But from the moment they had returned to the house on that high, craggy bluff overlooking the ocean, Oliver and Collette had persisted in calling him Friedle. For his part, the fussy man seemed to prefer it. Friedle behaved as if nothing had changed, save for the absence of his former employer, Max Bascombe.

"I miss him," Oliver said.

"Pardon?"

"My father. It's strange, don't you think? I spent so many years wishing for the courage to get out from under his shadow, and now that he's gone, I want him back."

Friedle nodded. "We all miss them, when they're gone. He wasn't a bad man, your father. He was just afraid for you."

Oliver took another sip. "I never thought of him as afraid of anything."

"For himself, of course not. The only thing that frightened Max Bascombe was the idea of something happening to one of his children."

The cocoa tasted sweet as ever, thick on his tongue. In his entire life, he had never invited his father to join him in the parlor on one of those long nights when he would retreat here. The old man would have declined, he was sure. Still, Oliver wondered.

"Thank you, Friedle."

"I'm quite looking forward to tomorrow," the old goblin said. "Good night, Oliver."

"Night."

After Friedle had gone, he sat with his finger still holding the page in *The Sea Wolf* and sipped his cocoa until only traces were left at the bottom of the cup. Only then did he consider the book again, but after a moment he put it aside, not bothering to mark his place.

"Hello, little brother."

Startled, he looked up. Collette stood in the doorway in blue flannel pajamas covered with monkeys. She looked adorable as hell, but he wouldn't mention it, knowing she would hit him.

"I thought you'd gone to bed."

As he spoke, Julianna appeared in the hallway behind Collette in a burgundy terry cloth robe that usually hung on the back of Oliver's bedroom door but was rarely worn.

"We couldn't sleep," Julianna said.

Mischief sparkled in her eyes and her smile lightened his heart.

"Excited about tomorrow, or nervous?" he asked.

Collette came in and sat on the sofa beside his chair. "What about you, Ollie? You're not nervous?" She picked up his cup and peeked inside, disappointed to find it empty, though Oliver felt sure that Friedle had brought the two women their own cocoa tray before retiring for the night.

Oliver held out his hand to Julianna. "Not at all."

She wrapped her fingers around his and he pulled her onto his lap on the chair. A stranger would not have seen the tiny wince at the corners of her eyes, but Oliver felt what she felt. The scar on her abdomen ought to have been the only re-minder of the dagger Ovid Tsing had stabbed her with. But, all these months later, it still pained her sometimes when the weather was damp and cold. He suspected it always would.

"Are you sure?" Julianna asked, touching the smoothness of his face. The scraggly beard he'd grown during their time across the Veil had been gone since June.

He kissed her, pressed his forehead against hers, and watched the reflection of the firelight glowing in her eyes. "Completely."

"It's going to be a pretty extraordinary day," Collette said.

Oliver and Julianna broke their trance and looked at her, content in one another, but never to the point of excluding her. They were a family now, the three of them. Always.

"A year late, but here we are," Oliver replied. He ran his hand across Julianna's back, thinking about their guest list. There would be many of the same guests who had been supposed to attend last December, but others had been added. Sheriff Norris. Ted and Sara Halliwell. The legendary and the ordinary alike had been invited. King Hunyadi himself had promised to attend.

"I wonder if Frost will come," Julianna said.

Oliver smiled. "We'll know by dawn, I think."

Collette looked at him oddly, then cocked her head. "I've been wondering if we'll see Smith."

"I doubt it."

His sister gave a small shrug. "Maybe not. But I don't think we've seen the last of him. Not forever."

Julianna lay her head against Oliver's chest. "Everything has changed. The whole world."

Oliver stroked her hair and bent to kiss her again. "Not everything. The important things haven't changed at all. The things that matter."

Collette jumped up. "Speaking of which, it's almost midnight and you two crazy kids are getting married tomorrow. You know it's bad luck for the groom to see the bride on her wedding day before the ceremony."

Julianna rolled her eyes. Oliver did not want to let her go. The memory of her lying there on the ground with blood soaking her clothes remained fresh in his mind. He saw her that way many nights when he closed his eyes, and sometimes he dreamed of that moment, just as he dreamed of the sinking of Atlantis, of the people hurling themselves from buildings, of the power that had been in his hands.

He could never change the past. He would never allow himself to forget. The outcome had been a triumph over savagery and tyranny, but the cost meant he would never celebrate.

Somehow, he and Collette and Julianna had all survived.

"Oliver," Julianna whispered in his ear.

He let her pull away. She gave him a wistful look, her gaze lingering on his eyes, and then she kissed him again, slow and sensuous. When she stood and started for the door, Oliver took a deep breath and let it out, casting away the shadow that often hung over him. It was a time for joy. And whenever Julianna was around, he could surrender to it, and to the whims of fortune.

To magic, for better or for worse.

Collette kissed him on the head. "Get some sleep."

She followed Julianna out of the room, and Oliver was alone again.

The fire had begun to die down. After a few minutes, he rose and picked up the cocoa tray. There would be enough chaos tomorrow without anyone having to worry about cleaning up after him.

A gust of wind rattled the window. Oliver glanced that way and knitted his brows. Curious, he walked over and touched his fingers to the glass, tracing lines in the icy condensation on the inside of the window.

Outside, it had begun to snow. The first snowfall of winter. It seemed that Frost would attend the wedding after all.

Oliver turned, and the fox was there.

Kitsune sat warming herself in front of the fireplace, her tail swishing happily. Her copper fur glinted in the flickering light of the dying blaze. Strips of opalescent scar tissue lined her body and head and snout, places where the fur would never grow again. The scars had a hideous gleam in the firelight.

The fox turned her jade eyes toward Oliver. Myriad emotions swirled in her gaze—gratitude and love and regret and something akin to happiness. Or perhaps those were merely the things he hoped or expected to see.

Oliver dropped to his knees and she came to him, nuzzling against him. He stroked her fur without a word. Frost had told him that Kitsune's wounds were so grievous, that her flesh had been so badly damaged, that she could never change shape again. She would be a fox forever.

"I'm sorry," he said. "For so many things."

Kitsune lifted a paw and placed it against his chest. Oliver bent and kissed the soft red fur atop her head.

The fox turned from him, trotted toward the window, then paused to give him a final glance. A gust of wind came down the chimney and the fire flickered. He shifted his gaze only for a moment, but when he looked back she was gone, as though she had never been there at all.

A melancholy smile touched his lips. Oliver hesitated only a moment and then carried the tray toward the door. His mother's parlor had always been an escape for him, a place to which he retreated whenever he began to worry that his father might be right, that his journeys into his own imagination were foolish.

He stepped out into the corridor and pulled the door closed behind him, but it swung open just a few inches.

The door to his mother's parlor did not close properly anymore.

Oliver suspected that it never would.

ABOUT THE AUTHOR

CHRISTOPHER GOLDEN is the award-winning, bestselling author of such novels as *The Myth Hunters, Wildwood Road, The Boys are Back in Town, The Ferryman, Strangewood, Of Saints and Shadows,* and the *Body of Evidence* series of teen thrillers. Working with actress/writer/director Amber Benson, he cocreated and cowrote *Ghosts of Albion,* an animated supernatural drama for BBC online, from which they created the book series of the same name (www .ghostsofalbion.net).

With Thomas E. Sniegoski, he is the coauthor of the dark fantasy series *The Menagerie* as well as the young-readers' fantasy series *Outcast* and the comic book miniseries *Talent,* both of which were recently acquired by Universal Pictures.

Golden was born and raised in Massachusetts, where he still lives with his family. He graduated from Tufts University.

He has recently completed a lavishly illustrated gothic novel entitled *Baltimore, Or, The Steadfast Tin Soldier and the Vampire,* a collaboration with Hellboy creator Mike Mignola. There are more than eight million copies of his books in print. Please visit him at www.christophergolden.com.